AWESTRUCK AT DUSK

ALEJANDRA ANDRADE

FIRST EDITION

Book Cover and Interior Design by David Provolo
Cover Art by Sulamit Elizondo

ISBN (hardcover): 978-607-29-3150-3
ISBN (paperback): 978-607-29-3149-7
ISBN (ebook): 978-607-29-3151-0

www.alejandra-andrade.com

Follow the author on Instagram: @alejandra__andrade to learn more about the upcoming books in the Moonstruck Series.

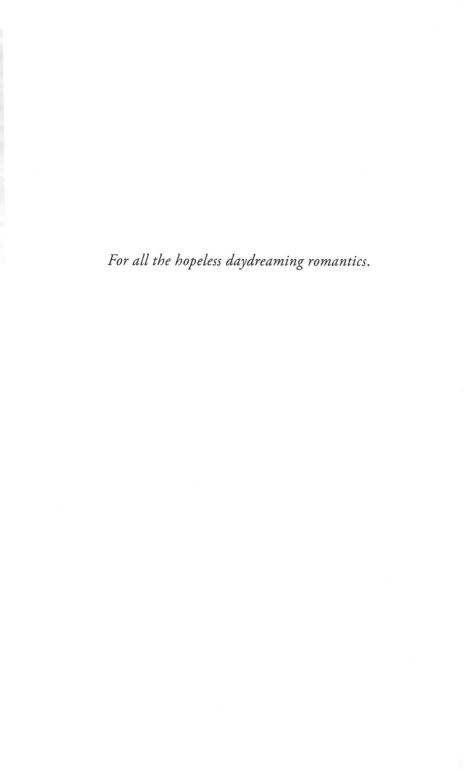

For all the hopeless daydreaming romantics.

TABLE OF CONTENTS

CHAPTER 1

Nightmares

March 19, 2010

I WOKE TO THE SOUND of my screams in a bed I didn't recognize, in a place I didn't recognize. The lights were out, and all I could see was the thin line of light coming in from the door. No windows, only four walls around me. My hand was still in a cast up to my mid-forearm.

Joel ran inside the dark room I was in with wide, panic-filled eyes, leaving the door open. I held my hand up, looking for shelter, and shut my eyes for a second, allowing them to adjust to the sudden luminescence that dazzled me.

I sat up and felt Joel's weight on the bed as he sat beside me. *I'm still in the hospital.*

It took me a few seconds to realize I was in a small guest room inside William's hospital room. But the last thing I remember was sleeping beside him in his bed, so I was clueless how I woke up here instead.

William shouted from afar, asking Joel if I was okay. Joel placed his arms around me and replied in Swedish with a calm voice that seemed to set William at ease for the moment.

"You okay?" Joel asked. I was still panting with terror.

It was the first time I woke up screaming, but the warmth

building up in my gut told me it wasn't going to be the last.

"Yeah, it was just a bad dream," I replied, holding on tightly to him, letting out a long breath, fully charged with relief.

William was fine.

He was out there recovering in his bed. In my dream, he … it was best not to dwell on the might have beens. But Caleb was still gone. The void inside my chest reminded me of that fact.

Shit.

Gently, I released myself from Joel's embrace and took my hands to my face; the pain alone bent me over. The tears burned my throat as I swallowed them back. I couldn't allow myself to break. Not now.

"How did I get here?" I asked Joel in barely a whisper. He stared at me as if I were a ticking bomb running on its last seconds before exploding.

"I carried you here. It seemed like you needed to rest, and well, Nathan called asking for you," Joel whispered back. "He's outside in the waiting room and wanting to see you. I thought it would be best if—"

Nathan's arrived …

"Thanks," I replied almost immediately. Joel didn't need to finish that sentence. The thought of Nathan walking into William's room and seeing me sleeping in his bed made me want to bump my head against the wall. Now that I was sobered up from that moment, I couldn't help but think how stupid I was to even do that in the first place. Thank God I woke up here instead. "I fell asleep I—that's not what—"

"Hey, it's okay." Joel nodded once. Fast and sharp. He then offered me a tight-lipped smile. "It's been a rough twelve hours for you. For everyone. I hope you're feeling better."

"I'm—yeah. Thanks." I didn't know if I was better. I simply existed. But seeing Nathan was something I needed so badly.

Something I knew would help make everything feel better. "What time is it?"

"It's um"—he looked at his watch—"twelve-o-five."

"What!" That meant Nathan had been waiting a while for me to wake up. I needed to see him. Now.

"Guille!" William called. God, he shouldn't have been exerting himself like that. He needed peace and quiet. I got up reactively and almost tumbled down on the floor.

"Easy." Joel caught me before I could fall. "You might still be under the effect of the medication you took earlier."

"Thanks, I—I'm fine now. I just got up too fast." Not really. I was so dizzy that if I didn't have things to do and people to talk to, I would've gladly collapsed on that bed again.

At a slower pace, I walked out of the guest room, which consisted of a small bed and a nightstand, and stood next to William's bed.

"Hi." I forced myself to smile.

"Hey." William's face looked tense, his jaw popped, and no, that wasn't what I wanted to see. "What happened in there? Are you okay?"

I didn't want him to worry about me when I was the one worried sick about *him*. He still needed to recover from surgery, and I wasn't planning on relaxing until he checked out of the hospital.

I could deal with the guilt and the machinations of my subconscious in the privacy of my own head.

"Um, yeah." I made myself smile again, trying to reassure him. "It was just a nightmare." I waved a limp hand in a careless motion, trying not to give it any importance. "How are you feeling?"

"I'm doing okay," he answered, his features relaxing.

"Did you get any sleep? You should be resting right now."

"Well, my mother just left. Tobias and Eric stepped in for a while too, so I snoozed here and there in between visits."

Oh. Shit. *Did they see me sleeping in William's bed?*

"Oh, um, did they—"

"No," he replied with a subtle frown. "Joel was the first to come in after you fell asleep. He moved you before anyone else stepped in. Don't worry about it." He licked his lower lip and looked away.

"No, I—I'm not worried. I just wanted to know." Lame answer.

William countered with a snort and a couple of slow head shakes. He was most probably annoyed about my concern with being seen sleeping beside him, but the situation was complicated enough as it was.

That's when the memories of a few hours ago crashed on me. The things he said, the things I said back. And how I still meant and felt every single word, including those that remained unspoken.

A tingling warmth that I couldn't seem to catalog occupied my gut, and my head still felt heavy from the medication. But I can't say I didn't welcome the feeling. It was better than having my brain's functions reestablished. I didn't want to think about Caleb. About him being gone. I refused to accept my reality.

"One of your agents dropped this for you earlier," Joel said, cutting in. And I thanked him for changing the subject. He handed over a small bag to me.

"Oh, thanks." I placed it on top of a chair and opened it to find a single black hoodie inside.

At least the color was suitable. But now I had to change out of the green Hammarby hoodie William gave me, and there was no way he wouldn't notice because I couldn't step out of his room wearing it. Nathan was somewhere outside waiting for me.

Nathan.

There was no easy way to do it.

William's brows bunched up. He kept looking at me funny with narrowed eyes, scanning through the mess that leaked out of my brain, like he could sense my awkwardness. I didn't know where I stood with him. All I knew was that the way he kept looking at me still provoked the same things it always did … but somehow, it was worse now. How had things changed so much in the last twenty-four hours?

Dealing with the guilt was the toughest part. I still couldn't brush off the feeling that he was lying in that hospital bed because of me. It was getting harder for me to look at him.

"I'll be right back," I said, finally finding my voice, walking toward the small bedroom where I'd woken up a few minutes ago to change out of the hoodie. But a loud knock on the door startled me before I could reach the guest room's door.

The muffled sound of voices arguing on the other side of the door became audible, and the door flew open.

"Murph."

I dropped the bag on the floor, and Nathan flew across the room. He held my face in between his hands and placed a soft, quick kiss on my lips. He embraced me gently and kissed my hair.

"I'm sorry. I was going insane out there. They wouldn't let me in, and Joel just texted me to let me know you had just woken up," he explained. He was talking so fast that I could feel the anxiety dripping off of every word. "Oh God, I'm so glad you're okay." He kissed my hair again as I hugged him tight around his waist with one arm.

He didn't even notice what I was wearing or what I smelled like. Good.

Nathan backed away from me and walked over to William's

bedside. "How are you holding up, mate?" Nathan offered his hand to him, and William took it, smiling back at him with a tight mouth and a simple nod. "I wanted to thank you," Nathan said, his voice almost breaking. "Thank you for being there when I wasn't. I have no words for what you did."

"Don't, it's—" William trailed off and looked at me for a split second. "I'm glad I was there, too."

Nathan nodded at William and walked back to me. I was paralyzed. And it seemed to me like Joel was too. "Let me take you home, love."

Home.

I didn't want to set foot in my apartment. I didn't even know if it was possible to go back.

"Just a second," I said to Nathan, squeezing his hand for a couple of seconds before I let go. I walked over to William's bed. "I'll come back. I just—I need to—"

"Sure," he said with a smile, but his eyes sang a different tune—one I could easily recognize.

And I didn't want to go! How dare I leave him in that bed while I got to walk out of the hospital like nothing? It wasn't fair, and I couldn't play dumb anymore.

No.

Caleb was right. He was always right. And as I reminded myself of my last conversation with him, a sinkhole broke its way through my chest.

My feelings for William were strong, and now there was *no way* for me to deny them. There was no place for me to hide. The thought of losing him ignited a riot inside me that demanded answers and resolutions.

And the only problem was I didn't know what the hell I was going to do.

CHAPTER 2

Let's Talk

NATHAN GRABBED MY BAG, held my hand, and led me out of William's room. When we stepped out, I saw David looking fresh and polished in his usual black suit standing next to agent Robbins.

My eyes locked with David's, and my first instinct was to run toward him and hug him. Tears automatically streamed down my cheeks. It was impossible to keep the tears in check. David kept clearing his throat, in an attempt, I assumed, to keep himself from joining me. Caleb and David were not only a team but good friends too.

"He's gone, David," I whispered. "I-I don't even—"

He let out a sharp breath. "I'm so sorry, Miss Murphy." His words were filled with both gentleness and profound sadness.

"I'm sorry too," I told him. I knew he was probably having a hard time processing Caleb's death. Just like me. I wondered where Aaron was. I really wanted to see him. He was surely devastated. Caleb and Aaron were like brothers. And he's the one who brought Caleb in for the job. Aaron recommended him when my father wanted to hire someone else after my mother died. I'm sure he must feel responsible, but he wasn't the one to blame for any of this.

I offered David a sad smile afterward and went back to Nathan, who immediately placed his arms around me. "We should get you home, love. Let me take care of you," he said softly, placing a kiss on my cheek. Nathan grounded me and immediately set me at ease.

I decided to make a quick stop to see Mimi before we left. It was comforting to see that her daughter April was there to keep her company. I had only met April once before today. It was hard to see her without feeling awful about what happened to her mother because of me.

They both insisted on how it wasn't my fault after I apologized more than a few times. Everyone kept saying that, but unfortunately, I couldn't agree with them.

Thankfully, Mimi was doing okay. She seemed well, just kind of sleepy. They were going to keep her in the hospital for the rest of the day just to make sure.

Nathan walked up to me and said, "We should go, Murph. Your father's waiting for us. He wants to talk to you."

We left after saying goodbye to Mimi and April.

Once inside the car, I immediately rested my head on Nathan's shoulder. He lowered his face closer to me and sniffed twice. "Why do you smell like a lad?" he asked with a laugh.

Shit.

I thought he hadn't noticed, but the scent was strong and obvious.

And delicious.

"This is William's hoodie," I told him bluntly, unable to discourage a frown.

I tried to avoid Nathan seeing me wearing it, but when he did, he probably thought it was the one he gave to me. And I wasn't going to lie, not that I had the energy or willingness to do so. Besides, our relationship had always been based on trust and transparency.

Nathan looked down at me, tilting his head, finding my eyes. His brows met as he offered a hint of a smile.

I continued explaining with a somewhat plain tone, not wanting to sound like anything but informative. "William gave me his hoodie back in December and splashed it with his cologne. I'd never used it before, of course. It's been inside the box it came in until today."

I was going to keep explaining, but Nathan jumped in with a question. "And why are you wearing it?" He didn't seem angry, but I could tell he was confused and very curious to know the answer to his question.

I whispered back my reply, "David asked Agent Johnson to bring me the Hammarby hoodie *you* gave me because I love it, and I guess everyone can tell by how often I wear it."

I tried laughing to release some tension. But I looked away and kept going when I saw Nathan didn't laugh at all with me.

"Anyway, my hoodie wasn't in the closet. Mimi was going to wash it, and Agent Johnson somehow found the box with *this* hoodie and brought it to me." I sighed. "I'm sorry."

"Why hadn't you mentioned any of this before?" Nathan asked. I couldn't tell if he was hurt or annoyed by the fact. But I didn't blame him. I'd be a mix of both if I were in his position.

"I didn't want to cause any more trouble," I said as I let out a breath. "William gave it to me a few days after the Opera thing happened. I just put the box away in my closet without any intention of wearing it."

"Okay." Nathan tucked a strand of hair behind my ear and wet his lips. I could see he wasn't thrilled with the hoodie story but seemed like he was trying to let it go.

My hand cupped his cheek, and my thumb grazed his neatly kept stubble. Somehow his eyes looked greener, and I couldn't help but stare at them as my mind drifted away into thought, just thinking how glad I was to get to see them again.

Nathan observed me with a tad of concern as I swallowed back the lump in my throat and offered me a tight-lipped smile that only lasted a fraction of a second and said, "I think I need to talk to William once he gets out of the hospital, though. I'd really like for all of us to get along, especially after what happened last night."

The SUV stopped, but we weren't in my apartment. We were at my father's place in the Upper East Side. Agent Robbins and David stepped out of the car and stood outside our door, waiting for us to be done talking.

Nathan grabbed my left hand and squeezed it. "I'd like to know what William's real intentions with you are. It's best to get that out of the way sooner rather than later." He took the back of my hand to his lips and kissed it. "For some reason, I feel like he's just playing around with all that nonsense. And apparently, he's going to be your neighbor for a while. Well, at least not for the next month."

Nathan was making me anxious. I didn't want him talking to William about any of that. Because no, William wasn't *playing around*. That had been made clear yesterday. And again, I didn't even know how *I* would deal with my feelings or what William would reply to any of Nathan's questions, but his last remark caught my attention the most.

"What do you mean? Why aren't we at my place?" Not that I wanted to go there. I didn't think I was ready to go back after what happened, but was I moving in with my father?

"You're moving in with your father."

Fuck.

"What?" I grimaced. "Why?" My father kept making decisions for me, and I was the last to find out, as always.

"Security is going to be reinforced in both the building and in your apartment. And until the modifications are completed, you'll be living here. At least that's what your father told me when he called me earlier."

"Okay, but *a month*?"

"Why don't we go up and talk to him?" He kissed my cheek as if I were a fragile antique piece at a museum and knocked on the window twice. Agent Robbins opened the door for us.

We stepped inside the building, and the smell of the place brought back memories of my childhood. Memories that had been buried a long time ago. And that's the main reason why I'd been avoiding coming back here altogether. My father and I always met in my apartment.

I didn't know what was harder: to be reminded of how my mother was clearly missing in my childhood home or going back to my apartment to deal with the demons that awaited there with long, sharp, hungry teeth.

"Kiddo!" My father exclaimed when he opened the door for us. He hugged me and greeted Nathan afterward with a firm handshake and a warm pat on the back.

I ambled inside, taking in the space. I didn't have the clearest memory of the apartment, but I had this feeling that everything was *exactly* as it was before we left for Rome almost seventeen years ago. The framed photographs everywhere, the smell of leather furniture, the big pieces of artwork hung around the place.

"Why don't we take a seat in the living room," my father suggested. "Robbins, David, will you join us, please?"

As I walked to the living room, I spotted two flower arrangements sitting on the coffee table.

"Oh, these are yours," my father said to me. "They were sent to your apartment, but I had them brought up here with your things."

"Who are they from?"

"Those are from Christopher and Nina, and the big one is from the Sjöbergs."

David must've told CJ what happened. I hadn't even checked my texts, and I wasn't in the mood to see anyone. But I took the card that came with each flower arrangement to remind myself to thank them and sat on the edge of the sofa where I immediately searched for Nathan's hand.

After everyone was seated, my father took the floor. "A few things are happening right now, and I think it's fair for you to be informed," he said to me. His cell phone rang, but he silenced it right away.

Wow. He always took his calls, even if we were in the middle of dinner.

"I want you to move in with me for a few weeks," my father continued, "and I'll explain to you why I think that's important."

"Yes, Nathan told me," I said dryly.

"Most of your things have been moved to your old bedroom. If there's anything else you need that wasn't brought here, let me know, and we'll have someone fetch that for you."

"Thank you."

"David, would you mind explaining to Billie what happened yesterday and why Thomas was allowed inside the building?" my father said with a stern voice. He didn't look happy.

"Yes, Mr. Murphy," David replied with a nod. His usual bubblier self was gone. We were all still processing Caleb's death. It was strange to see David taking the lead instead of Aaron or Caleb. Not that David wasn't capable of it. I just wished I knew him more.

"Thomas bribed one of the new door guards"—David continued with the briefing—"who, in return for that money, allowed Thomas to go up to Miss Murphy's apartment with the excuse of giving her a surprise.

"He's been fired, of course. Thomas wasn't on the list of people allowed into your apartment, and he should've had knowledge of that fact. But he claims Thomas said you were back together and showed him keys to your apartment, which made him doubt, and well … he clearly wanted to take the money."

Nathan squeezed my hand and rubbed my back a few times, showing me his support. And I needed it. I couldn't stop thinking about how there had to be something I could've done to prevent Thomas from going this far. Maybe if I'd taken his calls and really explain my feelings, he would've eventually made peace with it and Caleb would still be here.

"The door guard in question orchestrated everything to clear the way for Thomas. He waited for Senad, who worked the shift with him, to go on a bathroom break. That's when Thomas slipped in."

"That being said," my father cut in with one of his scary faces. The one he shows when he feels like things aren't going his way. I've seen it only a few times, but it's his way of showing people around him that he means business. David and Agent Robbins seemed to pick up on that because they both straightened in their seats as my father continued talking.

"I've convened a meeting with the building's administration and the rest of the owners to talk about how we can increase security in the building. The Sjöbergs," he said, "who basically own half the building, agreed immediately. We just need to talk about what changes can be implemented and when. And until all of that's settled, I'd like for you to stay here, kiddo." My father nodded once at David, prompting him to continue with the briefing.

David cleared his throat and said, "Nicholas and Senator Hill have been apprehended in D.C. Nicholas drove to his parents' house as we expected he would. At first, he was aggressive and unwilling to cooperate. When he heard about Thomas's death, he went into panic mode. We couldn't get him to calm down."

Nicholas and Thomas were close. I'm sure the news of his death must've been very hard for him to reconcile, especially when he was the one who constantly egged him on and aided him with his plans. I wondered if things could've ended differently for Thomas if he would've gotten the professional help he needed to deal with his family issues, including the death of his brother, and didn't have Nicholas around him all the time. That friendship, in my opinion, led to Thomas's downward spiral.

"A doctor had to be brought in to assess him since he wouldn't calm down," David continued. "But he did, eventually. And finally, after a tough round of negotiations, he agreed to share a great deal of information for a shorter sentence once he completes a drug rehabilitation program."

"Nicholas was using?" I asked, not completely surprised by that fact.

"Cocaine and marijuana," David replied quickly. "Not only was he using, but he was selling. And Thomas was his business partner."

What? I squeezed Nathan's arm and sat closer to him. My head shook from side to side as I bit on my lower lip. I lifted my gaze from the floor and David nodded a few times, allowing me to process the information.

"But was he selling while dating me?" I asked them. "And how is it that this never came up in the background check?"

"That's my fault," my father said, his lips going into a tight line. He seemed beyond disappointed now, embarrassed almost. "When Thomas came into the picture, I was careless about it. I ordered a quick background check because I already knew his father. Thomas was studying at Princeton. He had good grades. He rowed crew. There wasn't anything there to make me believe we needed to be any more thorough with him."

"I see," I replied, fidgeting in my seat. "What else did Nicholas say? Was Thomas dealing while dating me?" I asked again. I needed to know this. How could I've missed something like that?

"Thomas wanted to stop selling when he met you," David said. "Nicholas wasn't happy about it. He didn't want things to change. He kept promising Thomas he'd be able to get out soon. But the thing is, they used Thomas's apartment to hide some of the product, so Nicholas *needed* him for the operation to keep going as usual."

That's what Nicholas had on Thomas.

And now I understood many other things like why Thomas always carried a lot of cash with him, the errands he ran at random hours, him not wanting me to go to his apartment, and how he allowed Nicholas to be the obnoxious shit he was all the time.

I was in shock and furious beyond measure. At him, of course, but mostly at myself for not being able to see Thomas for who he really was. It was also scary to have someone standing in front of you and not fully know them when you think you do … that's insane. What had I gotten myself into?

Caleb had sniffed out Thomas as a bad apple since day one. He had the most accurate internal radar, and I chose to ignore it, and with that I lost him. It only took one second for Thomas to pull that trigger and take him away from me. To take *his* life away from him. I would never forgive myself for that. Never.

Nathan coddled me, and I allowed him to do so. It'd all been too much to process. I was still trying to avoid my mind from wandering too much about Caleb. I knew that once I went there, it would be very difficult to come back out.

"Anything else?" I muttered with a sigh. It was best if they laid it all out to me once and for all.

"Well, there's the matter of Senator Hill. Thomas and his mother had been previously in contact with a detective behind Senator Hill's back," David continued. "We found that information in the folder he brought with him last night to your apartment.

"We contacted Detective Gomes, who had been putting together a case against Senator Hill. That made things easier in regard to having him apprehended in a timely fashion. There was a surveillance tape that Thomas had promised Detective Gomes to get a hold of, and he finally did. We assume that's what he wanted to tell you."

Thomas kept saying how he had proof now, and at the time, I didn't understand what he meant by that. He wanted to tell me everything. To show me the evidence.

"And? What will happen to him?" I asked. I hoped he would go to jail for a long time. Not only did he murder his son, but he ruined both Thomas's and his poor mother's lives. And now Thomas was dead too, in part, because of his father and the trauma he inflicted on his family.

"We were informed that Senator Hill's attorneys are trying to find a way to get him out of it, of course. We'll just have to wait and see what happens," David explained.

"Thank you, David," my father replied in a dry tone. He didn't even make an effort to smile like he always did when he addressed the guys. "I believe that covers it all for now."

David and Agent Robbins excused themselves, and my father escorted them out of the apartment. He came back and retook a seat right in front of us. He leaned back and crossed a leg on top of the other in the usual elegant way he did and said, "Okay, kiddo. Now let's talk about Caleb."

CHAPTER 3

Kriah

"I'VE SPOKEN WITH Caleb's family," my father said, looking away for a second to clear his throat. He was very fond of him. Caleb's death must've been brutal for my father, but he rarely showed any emotion. He had different ways of coping with the pain, like burying himself with work.

"They are requesting assistance in moving his body back to Tel Aviv as soon as possible. They want to handle the burial service in the Jewish tradition, which requires for us to get him back there as quickly as possible since embalming and cremation are forbidden in their custom."

I wished he would just stop talking. Burial service? Embalming? Cremation?

All I could ever think of asking was, "Can I go?"

"To—Tel Aviv?" my father asked with a raised brow. I knew what that meant—a negative. But I *had* to ask. *What if he said yes?*

I nodded with wide, hopeful eyes.

"I'm afraid not, kiddo. I'm not comfortable with you—"

"I *need* to see him," I cut him off, my voice battling against the territorial lump in my throat.

"That's what I was getting at," he replied. "You'll be able to see him today"—he looked at his watch—"in an hour, that is. I suggest you take a shower and get ready so we can leave."

"Can you stay?" I asked Nathan. "Or do you have to go to the office at some point during the day?" I knew he had a hectic work schedule, but I didn't want to be alone. I needed him.

"Of course," Nathan replied smoothly. "I took the day off from work today. I already let them know I won't be available until Monday." He kissed my temple. "I'm all yours."

"Aaron's been guarding Caleb's body ever since he got the news. You'll meet with him at the funeral home. He'll fly back to Tel Aviv to make sure the transport goes well. He'll also be staying there a few days for the burial."

"When does Aaron leave?" I queried.

"As soon as you're done."

"Okay," I said with a sigh. I would take whatever I could get, even if it meant only a few minutes with Caleb.

"I'll be in my study making some calls just to make sure everything's good to go, kiddo," my father said with a tight smile, squeezing my shoulder with a shaky hand as he walked past me. He then walked back and kissed the top of my head. "Nathan, please make yourself at home." He excused himself and left for his study.

"I'll go take a quick shower," I said to Nathan, standing up.

Nathan stood up too and embraced me. "Everything is going to be okay, love. I'll make sure of it."

"I know." I didn't know. Nothing felt okay, and it seemed like it would be like that for a while. But I sure hoped for things to get better.

One day.

☾

We arrived at Gutterman's in Brooklyn, where Aaron had been guarding Caleb's body. A man who introduced himself as Mr. Waldman led the way after explaining how an exception had been made, since no viewing or visitation is customarily allowed in a Jewish funeral.

He was adamant when communicating the haste with which I should complete the visitation. Caleb's family grew restless, so the sooner Aaron left for Tel Aviv, the better.

I wished I could go too.

Mr. Waldman knocked on a door, which Aaron quickly opened and gestured for me to step inside the small, dimly lit room. Nathan and my father waited outside.

"Aaron!" I threw myself into his embrace as we both burst into sobs.

We held each other for a minute in silence. There were no words that could describe our grief. They weren't needed at all.

I gently broke away from Aaron's arms. He wore black slacks and a black sweater that had been torn on the right side of his chest. I could see the black fabric of the shirt he wore underneath his torn sweater.

"Right this way, Miss Murphy," Aaron said, leading the way to a simple wooden casket. It was closed. "Do you want to see him? Are you sure it—"

"Yes. *Yes*, I have to," I replied, brushing the endless tears away. When my mother died, I wasn't allowed to see her. It was a closed casket funeral, and I carried the pain of not being able to see her one last time for too long. I never could say goodbye to her.

"Okay," he said, standing next to the coffin. He opened it just enough for me to see his upper body and invited me to come forward.

I took a deep breath and three steps forward.

There he was—my Caleb.

Aaron moved to the side, but I reached out for his arm and whispered, "Stay. Please." He nodded and stood beside me as I linked my arm with his.

I looked away and closed my eyes for a few seconds as my throat closed in on me, unable and unwilling to accept Caleb's fate. He didn't deserve this at all. He should've been alive, always by my side ... he promised. I needed to concentrate on taking slow and deep breaths or risk losing it on the spot. The thought of letting myself go, to feel the feelings wanting to come up to the surface was terrifying. I was afraid I wouldn't be able to pull myself together if I allowed myself to go there.

Caleb's peaceful expression resembled that of a sleeping child. I'd do anything, give up *anything*, to have him wake up right now.

Please ...

"Here," Aaron said, handing me Caleb's Statue of Liberty keychain I gave him for his birthday yesterday. "He was carrying this with him. I'm sure you'd want to have this."

"No," I said in between subtle pants. "It's Caleb's." I grabbed the keychain and placed it inside the casket, underneath the flap of his jacket. "He said he'd keep it forever."

"They won't bury him with it," Aaron said. "You should take it. I know he would want you to have it." He offered me this broken look that almost paralyzed me. To see Aaron like this so affected, wasn't something easy to witness.

I nodded once, took the keychain, and placed it in my pocket. Something about this felt right. It was a good idea to keep it. I smiled a nearly cracked smile because I could listen to Caleb complaining inside my head about almost leaving it behind.

But that smile *did* crack in the end when a sudden searing

blaze of anger overcame me. I wanted to scream, to throw a fit, to break something. It wasn't fair. *Why him?* He was so young, bright, and had such a strong and powerful body. Again … Why?

But I knew the answer, and it stung as that little voice inside my head kept reminding me: *Because of you, that's why.*

There was a knock on the door. Aaron opened it just a tad and asked Mr. Waldman to give us a couple of minutes.

My hands moved to my face as I crouched on the floor. I had to leave soon, and once I did, Aaron would take Caleb away from me.

Forever.

I had mere seconds before I'd be asked to leave, so I stood up and sat in a chair beside the casket.

Waiting.

Aaron walked toward me and grabbed a pair of scissors from the small side table to my right. "It's customary in the Jewish tradition to rip one's clothes to express grief when losing a loved one," Aaron explained. "We call it Kriah, which means tearing." He pointed at his chest to his torn-out sweater and offered me the saddest smile in the world.

The thought of Aaron ripping his sweater out of pure grief contracted my heart.

"I think you should do it," he said. "It's um—it helps."

I nodded. It sounded like something I definitely wanted to do—*needed* to do. The anger and grief had whipped up a powerful electrical current inside me that begged for an outlet. And I didn't even know how to start handling that kind of energy on my own.

"I'll cut a small piece of your sweater, enough for you to rip it open. It's usually on the right side for relatives other than parents or close family members, but one can choose to rip the left side when experiencing deep feelings of grief," he kept explaining.

"Left," I muttered under my breath. *Left.*

Aaron took a step forward and said, "We stand up to show strength." I did, instantly. "Are you wearing something underneath your sweater?"

"I am."

He pulled my sweater gently and cut it approximately an inch. He placed the scissors on the table again and said, "I'll recite a blessing while you do it."

"Okay." I inserted my fingers in the incision and gripped each side firmly. With eyes closed, I pulled at my sweater while tears flowed from them like two open faucets. My healing wrist hurt like hell when pulling on the fabric, but I didn't care.

Aaron began reciting the blessing as I kept pulling on the small tear, slashing it open, feeling how every thread and fiber popped under my fingers. My jaw locked, and my teeth ground against each other.

I pulled so hard at one point that I ripped the sweater open almost completely. I directed my gaze toward Aaron and hugged him again, my wrist protesting with pain. But that ache was nothing compared to the grief that ravaged me.

"Thank you."

Aaron took a step back and walked toward Caleb's coffin.

"It's time to go," he said.

I followed him and helped him close the casket just after taking one last look at Caleb. I placed my hand on it and closed my eyes for a second.

"I love you, Caleb," I whispered to him. "I promise, okay?"

I promised to be true to my heart, just as he always had been—like he always had encouraged me to be. I vowed to trust my gut and stop ignoring my feelings.

Aaron led the way out after I was done saying goodbye and opened the door for me.

"Caleb, he"—Aaron pulled an envelope out of his pants pocket—"wanted you to have this." I took the envelope and pressed it in between my palms.

"He gave this to me back in September when you two—ended things," he explained. "He said if something ever happened to him, he wanted you to have this." Aaron laughed the softest laugh ever and handed the letter over to me. "I don't think he thought I'd ever give this to you." He paused for a second with shuttered eyelids and pressed his lips as if wanting to seal them shut. He finally took a deep breath and said, "I didn't either."

"Thank you. And—take care of him for me," I pleaded, placing the letter in the back pocket of my black skinny jeans. I'd left my bag in the car.

"You can count on it." He nodded and hugged me one last time before I shut the door behind me.

Nathan waited for me just outside the door. He took my hand as Mr. Waldman led the way out. My father was outside talking on his phone. Nathan and I thanked Mr. Waldman and waited for my father to be done with his call before leaving.

"Are you okay?" Nathan asked, glimpsing down at my torn sweater.

"I ah—yes," I said, looking away. "It's a Jewish custom to deal with grief."

I'd been standing on the edge of a cliff all day, falling over and over. And every time I did, I would stand up and climb back to the top, looking down at the abyss again—ready to launch myself once more—an endless loop.

But how to break the cycle?

"Would you steal me away and take me to Tel Aviv?" I asked Nathan, looking over my shoulder. I wouldn't want my father to overhear our conversation. "I want to meet Caleb's family and tell them how sorry I am about everything. I need to be there during his funeral."

I didn't care about the consequences. I could deal with my father later. And if he locked me up in my apartment for life afterward, then it would've been worth it.

I'd rather beg for forgiveness than beg for permission.

"I know, love. I wish you could meet Caleb's family too," he replied with a melodic voice. He didn't think I was serious.

"I mean it, Nathan," I said, taking a few safe steps away from where my father stood. "We could fly out tomorrow morning and stay there for a couple of days and come back. It's spring break, so it's perfect. That way I won't skip any classes. We can be back on Tuesday. I'm sure you can take two days off and work remotely. Aaron will be there, too."

Nathan stared at me with a poker face while I explained my plan to him.

"Please?"

"Bloody hell, you're *actually* asking me to take you to Tel Aviv?" he replied with a panicked expression on his face. "I-I can't, love. Your father … he'll kill me if I take you. He'll never trust me again."

I shook my head and looked down at my feet, feeling completely defeated. Helpless. A cold slap in the face to remind me that I'm being held back against my will with rose gold chains. Nathan cared too much about my father's opinion, and he would never do *a thing* to fall from his good graces.

As I realized that, I panicked. I needed Nathan to be willing to take chances for me. To be my partner in crime and rebel with me. If only a little. Although, I knew what I had asked of him was a lot.

But no.

He was very much like my father and shared a similar point of view regarding my safety. I could tell right away he disapproved.

"Besides, you still need to give your statement to the police," Nathan added. "We can't just leave. Your father's been stalling and giving you space for you to be ready to talk to them."

"Of course. Yes. You're right," I replied, summoning an empty smile to offer him some kind of agreeable gesture in return—anything to cover up my complete disappointment.

CHAPTER 4

Sister-in-Law

April 2, 2010

"HEY!" I SAID, walking into William's hospital room. "Today's the big day."

William was finally getting discharged, and I wanted to be there when he did. I'd been visiting him almost every day for a little while. I felt responsible for what happened to him, and the least I could do was show my support.

My visits were very friendly. We were never alone. There was always someone else there too, which was for the best. I wouldn't want to be alone with William. Not yet, at least. I could tell by the way he kept looking at me that he probably had something to say.

But my life was a mess.

I had trouble concentrating at school. As much as I tried, I couldn't stop thinking about Caleb—missing him. And the night terrors wouldn't cease. I would wake up to the sound of my own screams every other day.

My nightmare was always a variant of the following scenario: Thomas shooting William. Thomas shooting Caleb. Sometimes both. But I always woke up before seeing what Thomas's next move would be after shooting them.

Thankfully, my father never heard me scream as our rooms were on opposite ends of the apartment, and he's always been a heavy sleeper. Not that he slept much, but when he did, he fell deeply into sleep.

Nathan wasn't too enthusiastic about my visits to the hospital, but he understood where I was coming from. He was still playing around with the idea of us all being friendly, and I was doing just that. Not that William would reciprocate our peace offering. He'd already told me several times how he wasn't interested in a friendship with either Nathan or me. But that was food for another day's thought.

One day at a freaking time.

Not living in my apartment made it harder for Nathan and me to have the privacy we wished we could have. The privacy we *needed*.

We sneaked around to his apartment to have sex only a few times, but it all felt too rushed since my father imposed a 10:00 p.m. curfew on weekdays. And although I wanted to be with Nathan, a part of me was too sad all the time to genuinely enjoy that intimate time with him.

Complying with the curfew and juggling Nathan's work schedule with mine complicated things for us. And my father kept close tabs on my every move during these past few days. He also assigned Agent Johnson as Caleb's replacement. I finally found out her name was Amena. I liked her.

He mentioned a few times how great it was to have a female agent on the roster. That way, she could follow me inside the bathroom at school or other public places where Aaron and David couldn't follow.

Excessive.

Not that I was going out much anyway. But at least I was allowed to visit William.

This time, it was only William's assistant Alice and me in his room. Nathalie, his mother, was usually around, and that made my visit even more formal—less relaxed.

I liked Nathalie, and I usually ended up chatting more with her. I honestly didn't mind. What I wanted was to convey my support for William's recovery.

To be present.

Alice sat cross-legged on a sofa chair near William's bed with her laptop resting over her legs. She seemed busy as she made a few calls.

William sat on the edge of his bed, looking almost good as new. I hadn't seen him in the last couple of days, but his face was now the color it should be, and his eyes were sparkling brightly.

"I'm so fucking ready to leave," he said with a laugh, stretching his arms and his neck.

I believed him.

It'd been two weeks since his surgery. I'd be banging my head against the wall if I were in his position.

Alice pulled her cell phone away from her ear and said, "Hi, Billie!" She shot a quick smile my way and swapped her face back to work mode as she turned to William. "The media's found out somehow that you're leaving today. There's a bunch of photographers from different media outlets and cars outside. They all want to get a shot of you when you leave the hospital"— she placed the phone back on her ear—"Warren, calm down. Give me a minute."

William raised his brow and looked away.

"It's not like he's walking out the front door," Alice continued her conversation on the phone. "Yes, there's a private parking lot. The problem is that the photographers spotted Cooper coming in because they're *that* crazy. They even know what William's driver looks like." Alice laughed an angry laugh. "No, Warren.

What the hell? William's *not* going to fire Cooper. *Calm down.* I'll think of something." She ended the call and tossed her phone to the side. "Jesus."

"Thank God I have you to deal with Warren," William said, pinching the bridge of his nose with his eyes closed. Warren was William's publicist.

"Thank God you have *me*. Period," Alice returned with a chuckle.

"Why don't I give you a ride back home?" I suggested. "Just let me know where you need the guys to park the car, and we'll drive you back. Cooper can stay here to create a diversion."

"You're fired, Alice. I've found your replacement," William joked.

"Ha-ha," she said in a dull tone without looking up from her laptop's screen as she typed like a deranged hamster. "But that might actually work." She met my gaze. "Thanks, Billie."

William tried standing up. "Ow." He winced with pain and placed his hand over the left side of his stomach, where he took the bullet. For me.

"Are you okay?" Alice and I said at the same time. Alice dropped the laptop on the sofa chair and stood up reactively.

"Why are you even standing up?" Alice complained. William turned his gaze toward the duffel bag on the floor next to the bathroom door. "The nurse said someone would come over and help you change into your clothes, so don't even think about it."

"I'm leaving today, and there'll be no nurses back home. I think I'm capable of changing into my own clothes. Thank you, Alice," William replied in a dry tone, taking slow steps toward his bag.

"Oh, like I'm not going to be your nurse, right?" Alice quipped. "I'm going to need a raise because convalescent William is a major pain in the ass."

William parted his lips, probably to argue with Alice when she spoke again, "Don't you *dare* deny it. Remember when you did that stupid stunt while filming, and you got your hamstring effed up for a week?" She then turned to me. "I had to fly over to freaking Morocco to babysit him because he couldn't walk two steps without complaining."

William laughed. "You had a great time in Morocco that week with what's her name? Fatima? Don't forget that."

"Shh!" Alice took her index finger to her lips. "Don't *ever* mention Fatima whenever Luna's around." She looked at me for a second—a silent threat of sorts. But I would never say a word about her personal affairs to anyone. "It's a touchy subject for us."

"Relax. Luna's not here. And I already know that," William said, patting Alice's back as he took slow but steady steps toward the bathroom.

Alice rolled her eyes at him, and I turned around and carried his bag with my left hand. My right was going to be in a cast for a while. I still couldn't deal with the constant itchiness.

"Do you want to change in the bathroom or the guest room?" I asked William. "I don't think it's a good idea for you to be carrying any sort of weight just yet."

William stopped and turned to look at me. "Thanks," he said, brushing a golden strand away from his face. "The bathroom's fine."

Alice sat back on the sofa chair when she saw I had things under control.

William hated wearing his hospital gown. He'd told me every single day I went to visit. And I'm sure he hated even more that we all had to see him wearing it and to depend on someone else to get basic things done. I know I would.

He wanted to carry his own bag and prove his manhood but come on, he didn't need to prove shit.

I turned on my heel and placed his things on the elegant marble countertop of the bathroom's vanity. "Do you need help with anything else?" I offered.

He stood next to me, and Alice shouted from afar, "William! Your ass is showing! Geez! Cover yourself up, or I'll have to give Luna a call and let her know I'm not gay anymore!"

Alice! A snort escaped my nose when I couldn't prevent myself from laughing.

My gaze disobeyed my mental command of looking away and took a quick peek because it's like when someone tells you not to look and you just *have* to. And yes, William's gown was open wide on his back. His perfectly toned ass was on display for everyone to watch. For *me* to watch. Alice's focus was back on her computer's screen. She'd already stated how uninterested she was about William's bum.

Shit. I turned around and covered my eyes like the pathetic person I am.

"You're such a *perv*!" Alice kept objecting, her typing still audible. "And now you've scared Billie off with your embarrassing exhibitionism kink."

I had to disagree with her. William's behind was the exact opposite of disgusting *or* scary. But she sang to a different tune.

The bathroom door shut behind me, and I turned around with a gasp.

"Saw anything you like?" William asked, his fingers lazily tying his gown behind him.

Yeah, he was good as new and already back to making me feel uncomfortable with every opportunity he had.

"I uh—didn't see anything, really. I—"

"Such prudes, you Americans," William said, taking his stuff out of the duffel bag and placing it on the countertop. "I guess we're more comfortable with nudity in Sweden. Besides, it's only a matter of time before you get to see me naked."

"William!" I widened my eyes at him, grabbed one of those mini soaps from the counter, and threw it at him. He laughed.

"Great, so you agree then? Because I didn't hear you denying it."

"I agree with Alice," I lied, walking toward the door.

But he grabbed my arm as I passed by him and whispered in my ear, "No, you don't, älskling." His tone changed from playful to low and husky in a second. "And—thank you."

"What for?" I asked, looking up to meet his gaze, swallowing a new lump in my throat.

"You know, for being here for me," he kept muttering. "I appreciate you coming here almost every day to check in on me." He said it with such warm sincerity that I could feel myself thaw on the bathroom floor.

"Yeah, well … you being here in the first place is on me, so it's the least I could do."

"Everything okay in there?" Alice said over the door. "Billie, knock twice if you're alive!"

"Go! *Away*!" William shouted with the sharpest edge of annoyance in his voice.

"Your phone won't stop vibrating! It's Zara!" Alice replied.

Zara. Nathan's sister. I'd forgotten about her existence.

"Jesus, Alice! Tell her I'll call her back in five!" William ran a hand through his hair, seemingly irritated at being interrupted. It was the first time we had time to talk privately in the last two weeks. And now I couldn't stop thinking about the nature of his relationship with Zara.

"We need to get you to stop thinking like that," William said to me. *Clearly*. "None of this is your fault. And I'd do it again if I had to."

I bit the inside of my bottom lip as I tried squashing the

butterflies wanting to take flight in my stomach. And with that, I took a step back.

"Don't," he said. "You keep backing away from me. That needs to stop too."

Alice knocked again. "Zara says it's urgent."

As much as my internal voice opposed what I was about to say, I said it, "Why don't you take that call, and I'll go talk to the guys about how we're sneaking you out of the hospital."

I reached for the doorknob, but William placed his hand on top of mine. "We're not done with this conversation, Guille." He released my hand and allowed me to open the bathroom door. "I guess it'll be easier to talk now that I'll be back home."

About that …

"Um, I'm not currently living in my apartment right now," I said, turning around to meet his gaze. "I'm staying with my father for now."

Alice handed the phone over to William, but he kept staring at me, his mouth slightly parted. He then stared at his phone's screen and muted the call. "Indefinitely, or …?"

"No," I said quickly. "No, of course not. It was initially for a month while they made a few security changes in the building and my place. But they're almost done, or so I've been informed."

And I planned to move out as soon as I could. My father offered to let me stay as long as I wanted. But I wouldn't be able to move in with my father forever, although I'm sure that would've made him happy.

What I needed was to go back to my apartment. To have my space back.

To be left the fuck alone.

"I'll go talk to the guys. I'm sure you can't wait to pull that gown off your shoulders."

"Can't wait," he said, his gaze suddenly becoming hungry.

He looked down at my lips for a second, and it almost killed me. "But I might need help with that."

"Shut up and get dressed," I said with a laugh, trying to distract myself from William's recurrent innuendos. "I'm sure Alice would love to help."

"No, I wouldn't!" she yelled from her seat. "But I'll text you so you can tell me when your guys are ready to scurry us out of here."

"I'd rather have bossy Guille helping me out," he whispered. "That's my favorite Guille."

Damn it. My face warmed up, and that was my cue to leave.

William let out a breath with a laugh.

"Love that peachy color on your cheeks, by the way," William said. "But no reason to get nervous. I'm sure you'll want to wait to break the news to Nathan about how you're ending things with him before we get into any of *that*. Which we will, I promise."

"William, stop," I said in a serious tone. I knew his style consisted of laying it all out to me in a funny-joke-kind-of-way, but I knew he wasn't kidding. And this was where I drew the line.

If he was saying that, it meant he *really* wanted me to end things with Nathan.

At first, my heart leaned more toward Nathan, but now it was pulling a *two roads diverged in a yellow wood*,[1] and I didn't know what to do with that overpowering feeling.

After William got hurt, something shifted inside of me, like a switch that turned on, and as much as I fought it, I couldn't seem to find a way to turn it off.

The thought of him getting hurt again, or worse, losing him,

---

1 Frost, Robert. "The Road Not Taken." Mountain Interval, Henry Holt and Company, 1916.

changed me. It made me feel this *need* to have him around—to see him, just to put my mind at ease. To let me know he was okay.

And I wasn't trying to complicate things or hurt anyone, but I couldn't help it.

It was … chemical.

"You can't play dumb forever," he called me out.

I knew that too, but I hadn't even grieved Caleb properly. How was I to peer inside my heart and ask the dreaded questions I *knew* I had to?

Someone was going to get hurt—by me. I understood that. And I would too, in consequence. I wasn't sure if I could take any more pain. So I kept stalling, looking away from my feelings.

Playing *dumb*. It's so easy to play dumb.

"Please, stop." It was the only thing I could do right now. Ask him to stop and allow me to have more time to process life, death, and all the in-betweens. For now, all I could offer him was my friendship, even though I knew he would never reciprocate it.

"I won't stop anymore," William replied, his gravelly voice on full display. "I tried, and I'd made my peace with it knowing that I'm not strong enough to do so. And something tells me you're not that strong enough either."

I peeked over my shoulder, and Alice's attention was embedded to her computer screen, completely unaware of our conversation.

Good.

Besides, this Zara situation was starting to give me an itch. And I'd never experienced jealousy as I had with William. I was absurdly territorial about him. But again, it wasn't my place to ask, and the gnawing curiosity was uncomfortable and exhausting. And I'm sure he could see right through me.

"My sister-in-law has been waiting a while for you to take

that call," I said, pointing out the fact that there was a girl on the line eagerly waiting to talk to him. And that girl was my boyfriend's sister.

"Shhhit." William pulled up his phone and unmuted it. "Zara?"

I shook my head and walked away as he continued his conversation with her in Swedish. I needed to enroll in Swedish lessons, if only for peace of mind.

"Guille!" he yelled before I stepped out of his room. "We're not even close to being done with this conversation."

I knew that too.

CHAPTER 5

1984

April 7, 2010

TODAY WAS AN OFF DAY—one of those heart-wrenching, nauseating days.

I was moving back to my apartment. I'd been looking forward to it, or so I thought, right until the moment I packed my bags and headed back there.

My feet had a mind of their own. They fidgeted and shook uncontrollably as Aaron and Amena drove me there because I was going into this alone. Do I even have to explain why my father couldn't offer to come with me? No. I thought Nathan would though, but he'd already missed a few days from work here and there to be with me when I needed him. It felt selfish of me to ask for another half day's worth of his time to walk me back to my place. I mean, Aaron was with me. He would have to be enough.

Living in my father's place right after Caleb's death granted me a temporary escape since everything about my home inevitably reminded me of him.

I'd been skyping with my therapist from Norway. She held my hand through the process of grieving my mother's death. She knew me, knew my past. It was easier to keep talking to her than finding a different therapist in New York and going back to square one. I didn't have time for that. I needed to figure out all my feelings—the quicker, the better.

She suggested I start a journal and scribble about my thoughts in a random way. No dates. Just write on the first blank page without any order. And I'd been doing just that. I bought a Moleskine notebook and carried it with me all the time.

I took the small notepad out of my bag and grabbed a pen that I could barely hold in between my fingers. The freaking cast was in the way. My writing was almost illegible, which turned out to be very convenient.

Who's going to walk me up to my apartment every day?
Talk to me about the hard things?
Ask about my real feelings or confront me about them?
Who's going to console me without saying a word?
And make me feel safe just thinking his name?
Who's going to put me first ALWAYS, no matter what?
Care as much as he did?

I let out a sharp breath through my mouth and shut my notebook. I tucked it back in my bag and looked out the car's window.

I knew I had Nathan. Even if I was still trying to figure out the meaning and extent of what having him meant. But Caleb's unconditional presence filled a space that I'd crafted just for him, and the emptiness threatened to devour my soul completely. And I was in no shape to decipher the hidden desires of my heart, which began manifesting against me in the past few weeks.

However, I was still hanging on to Caleb's letter and avoiding reading it altogether because I didn't know what awaited me once I read it or how it would make me feel.

Maybe if I stalled for an undetermined amount of time to feel stronger about not having him would be enough to give me the courage to read it because, in a way, it would be like talking to him.

My *last* conversation with Caleb.

And as long as I kept his letter unread, I would still have an opportunity to listen to him one last time. And yes, I could read it several times, but the first time you read a letter carries a weight—a certain magic. That feeling of not knowing what word comes next, what thought, what emotion will surface. It's too special.

So not yet.

I was clinging to my last chance until I felt not only stronger but deserving too. I'd been burying the feelings of guilt deep into a dark little corner of my soul. And it was slowly consuming me without my knowledge.

At least I'd have a place to hide from the world on my birthday—which was only four days away. It was easier to cave myself in my apartment than in my father's place. Although he was never around, anyway.

But there's no place like home. And mine was 485 Park—a wiped-out crime scene that was very much imprinted in my mind.

Aaron parked on the curbside. I took a deep breath and stepped out of the car when Amena opened the door for me.

Nathan promised to stop by after work. And as I walked into the lobby and was greeted by Senad, Bruce, and a new door guard with big smiles, I hoped he would. Soon. Because the memories of the incident were stampeding in my direction with my brain as their aim. And as much as I hated to admit, I wasn't strong enough to deal with all of this on my own.

The elevator required a keycard now to gain access, and I spotted at least four new surveillance cameras in the lobby.

Aaron and Amena helped carry my things, which consisted of a couple of suitcases with my clothes and a backpack.

"This is your new set of keys," Aaron said, handing them over as the elevator went up to the ninth floor. "All the locks have been changed, including the one on the service door. I'll hang on to a copy of these, just in case."

"Thank you," I said with a tight smile, looking at Caleb's Statue of Liberty keychain in my hands. It had found a new home, right beside the Eiffel tower keychain he gave me.

The elevator doors opened before us, and we walked toward my door. There was a surveillance camera with a bird's-eye view of my doorstep.

Shit.

I looked up and asked, "Who's monitoring these cameras?" Apparently, I've become a living and breathing character in Orwell's *1984*. "Are there any cameras inside my apartment?"

It was best if I asked beforehand. I don't think I would be able to take it if I found a camera stepping in. I couldn't promise I wouldn't knock it down either.

Aaron looked up at the camera with a frown. "Your father insisted—no one's watching, per se. The intention is to have the opportunity to review if needed," he explained. "There will be an agent assigned to this specific camera. But he won't be watching every second of the day. The camera sends alerts when triggered by unusual movement and other parameters that have been integrated into the system. If the agent deems it worthy of reporting, the first flag goes out to me."

I shot Aaron a side-glance.

"And no, there are no cameras inside your apartment. But three more panic buttons were installed. I'll show you where they are right now if you want."

"Is there audio recording in this camera?"

"No, there isn't. Just video."

Thank God.

The three of us stepped inside my apartment, and everything was pristine. They'd done an excellent job cleaning, physically speaking. But I'm sure the ghosts were out there hiding, ready to haunt me at night.

Aaron showed me the three new panic button locations: One in the kitchen, one in my bathroom, and one in the guest bedroom. With that, all areas had a panic button now.

"Thanks, Aaron. Nathan's heading over in a bit. Can we get him one of those keycards for quicker access? Or are you going to have to bring him up every time?" This was getting super annoying.

"Your father doesn't want anyone coming up unannounced, so one of us will have to give Nathan access from now on," Aaron replied. "Perhaps you could talk to your father about this in a few weeks. I'm sure he'll feel more at ease once he sees you're safely settled here."

Right.

I thanked Aaron and Amena and shut the door.

Welcome to house arrest.

☾

William was home, and something told me he had company. I hadn't seen him since I helped him sneak out of the hospital a few days ago. And we hadn't had that *pending* conversation yet. Alice rode back with us, so thankfully, the conversation had been all fun and games.

I could hear a guitar and his piano simultaneously playing, accompanied by a muffled laugh here and there.

The doorbell rang, startling me as usual and skyrocketing

my anxiety. It was a mixture of expecting it to be Nathan but scared about it not being him. Maybe Aaron wanted to tell me something. Or maybe my father decided to show up at the last minute. But I wanted it to be Nathan. I'd been stress-unpacking for the last hour just to kept me distracted.

It was so uncomfortable and scary being alone in my apartment. I knew the threat was gone, but the heavy and traumatizing feeling about what happened wasn't.

I peeked through the peephole and sighed with relief when I opened the door.

"Hi, love," Nathan said, walking in. Aaron nodded at me and turned around to leave. Nathan shut the door behind him and kissed my cheek. "I see there's a new surveillance camera outside your door."

"I know. It sucks. At least it doesn't record any audio." I shrugged, grabbing Nathan's hand and pulling him toward my bedroom. I wanted to finish unpacking. "But I wouldn't be surprised if my place was bugged."

He laughed. "I'm sure it's not, love. And if it is, we'll keep an agent entertained," he said, closing my bedroom door and pinning me against it. "I miss you."

"I miss you too," I said, a bit startled. I didn't mind Nathan's usual playful roughness, but my mind was playing tricks on me, reminding me of how Thomas physically maltreated me that day.

I swallowed down the feelings. The last thing I needed was for any of that to affect my relationship with Nathan.

And we *did* have audio surveillance—William. He'd already admitted to being able to listen to us having sex. And I didn't know how to talk to Nathan about how that bothered me without giving him a wrong idea or creating unnecessary drama.

Besides, I wouldn't want *anyone* to listen to us having sex, but the fact that it was William made it even more mortifying.

Nathan kissed my neck and pulled the hem of my light sweater slightly upward, sliding his hand against my skin. "You're so soft," he whispered in my ear. He pulled my face closer to him and brought his lips to mine, kissing me with a claiming hunger.

My arms hung beside me, my left hand in a tight fist.

Both of his hands traveled to the small of my back as he took a few steps back, pulling me with him, his mouth still unwilling to detach from mine.

Relax.

"I feel like we haven't had proper sex in forever," he said, pulling my sweater over my head in a swift movement. He tossed it on the floor, smiling at me, and took his jacket off next. That smile gave me the comfort I needed to loosen up. It was Nathan. I was safe with him.

I uselessly tried to unbutton his shirt, but my cast made it difficult for me to do so.

"I've got it," he said, unbuttoning his shirt. "Let me take care of everything, okay?"

Nathan's hand then moved to my jeans. He slowly pulled them down, and all I could hear inside my head were the ticking seconds of my mental timer. Once I ran out of seconds, I would have to say something to Nathan about my discomfort regarding the thinness of the wall dividing apartments 9A and 9B.

"I couldn't stand rushing with you. I want to take my time making love to you," Nathan said, drawing a line of kisses down my stomach.

The past few weeks had been a challenge for us. We had to make up an excuse to go to Nathan's apartment and keep things quick before my ridiculous 10:00 p.m. curfew. And his job was more demanding every day. He was working his way into becoming a partner at Chapman & Payne, which came with more responsibilities and longer working hours.

But Nathan's never been one to hurry with me, and I reminded myself of how much I loved that.

He lifted me from the floor and dropped me on the bed on my back. He grabbed my left wrist and took it above my head as he kissed my neck, and that just did it for me.

"No!" I yelled quickly, sliding to the side, away from him.

Nathan immediately recoiled and sat on the bed, his palms slightly up. "What happened?" he asked, disconcerted. "Did I hurt you?"

"N-no, of course not, I'm—I'm sorry," I said, panting. I crawled on the bed to reach him and placed my arms around him. "I'm sorry, I don't know what—"

"Hey, it's okay," he said in a mellow voice, running a hand through my hair. "I got too carried away. I didn't mean to make you uncomfortable."

"You did *nothing* wrong," I insisted. He hadn't. "It's just ... this room. And the way you grabbed my hand and pulled my arm up just—" I trailed off and closed my eyes, taking a slow breath in.

I hadn't given Nathan any explicit details on how things went down with Thomas. It was hard for me to talk about it. Feeling helpless underneath his strength had been overwhelming. Not being able to move without knowing what the person holding you down wants to do to you is a terrifying feeling.

"Thomas pinned me down on my bed, and grabbed my wrists, and—h-he even at some point kissed me," I revealed as I shook my head a few times. Fast. "I had to make him think I wanted to hear him out, to make him think I—" My voice was low, almost a tremble.

"Oh, God, Murph. Why wouldn't you tell me about this?" Nathan asked with a tense jaw. He seemed furious about the situation. "I'm so sorry, love." He carefully placed his arms around me.

"I don't know. It's been a lot. And a part of me felt ashamed of—I-I don't know—of being so vulnerable. I couldn't *move*. I didn't know how far he was willing to take things," I said with a shudder.

Nathan's breathing was deep but steady. I could see how hard it was for him to keep it together. But what was he to do? Thomas was dead. It was over. The only thing left was the trauma I carried.

"And I haven't told you this either, but I freed myself using the Krav Maga techniques you taught me," I said with a sad chuckle.

"What?" He reciprocated a lazy laugh. "Oh, Murph, you're brilliant." He kissed my hair. "So, you flipped him like we practiced?"

I nodded with a small smile.

"What else?" he asked, looking proud.

"I ah—punched him in the groin after flipping him. But he wouldn't let go of my right wrist," I explained, showing my cast. "I poked his eyes with the claw thing you taught me, and that got him to free me, but my wrist was broken by then."

"Shit, Murph."

"I tried escaping, but he caught me, and that's when William came in. But um—I'd rather not talk about that part if that's okay."

"Of course," he replied softly. "I completely understand."

I kissed his cheek. "I wished I'd told you about this before. But I just—I couldn't."

"I get it, okay? I can wait for you to feel ready again. We don't have to—"

I placed my hand on Nathan's cheek and took my lips to his. I kissed him slowly, tenderly, and he kissed me back. "I don't want to wait," I whispered.

It was nice and comforting even to remember what having Nathan so close to me in this way felt like. It's as if I hadn't been allowing myself to do so in the past few weeks. But I felt safe and loved and I didn't want all those feelings to go to waste. I wanted to feel them even if they threatened not to last long because they were only given this small, allotted time to exist within the chaos.

We could hear music coming from William's apartment across the wall as we kissed. I didn't think William was within hearing range. That meant I had one less thing to worry about.

For today.

I laid on my back and pulled Nathan with me.

"I can be gentle," he said in between kisses.

"I know you can."

CHAPTER 6

Come Rain or Shine

April 8, 2010

THOMAS HAS ME PINNED *on my bed. His hands tightly fastened around my aching wrists that throb with pain. William darts into my bedroom, and without a second thought, Thomas brings his gun up and shoots him twice.*

Boom. Heart.

Boom. Head.

William falls limp on the floor, and Thomas takes the gun to his head next. I close my eyes, and an intense bang is heard, waking me up.

I sat up in my bed, panting, sweating. And I quickly realized that the intense sound came from the wall dividing William's room with mine because he knocked again, startling me.

My mind was still lingering in that void in between dreams and total awareness. But the doorbell rang a few seconds later, followed by a few desperate knocks, and that sure woke me up.

I rushed to the door, knowing perfectly well that it was William. He must've heard me scream. I didn't want him to worry. This was my cross to bear. Not his.

After unlocking the multiple fancy new locks on my door

with my left hand, I finally managed to open it. William dashed inside without a second thought and placed his arms around me.

"You were screaming," he said, resting his chin on the top of my head. "Was it a nightmare again? Like in the hospital?"

Feeling his arms around me had me relaxing once again. The warmth and gentleness with which he did was so comforting.

Since it was early, he didn't smell like his cologne but rather like a fresh summer breeze. Clean. Soapy. Crisp.

"Yes, but I'm fine," I said. "It's fine."

You're fine. Thank God.

He grabbed my face in between both of his hands and met my gaze. My lips trembled, and I could feel myself swallowing back the tears. "I'm sorry," I said, feeling a rogue tear rolling down my cheek.

"What would you be sorry for?" he asked, wiping the tear away with his thumb.

"Nothing. I'm just—I didn't mean to startle you," I muttered. "I don't know how to make the nightmares stop."

"You don't have to make anything stop," he reassured me. His arms embraced me once again, and I allowed myself to rest my face in the refuge of his chest. "What you went through wasn't just—anything. You need to allow yourself to heal from it all."

"*We*," I corrected and reminded him. "What *we* went through. And it was even worse for you. Y-you took a bullet. For me! And I shouldn't—"

"Stop. I'm here for you," he said. "Right beside you. Whenever you need me"—he cupped my chin with his fingers and met my gaze—"okay?"

I nodded, slowly breaking away from his arms, and spotted William's watch on his wrist. I grabbed it to see the time.

8:43 a.m.

"Shhhit," I said, turning around, heading for my bedroom.

"What's wrong?" he asked, following me.

Don't follow me here!

"Nothing's wrong. I'm just late. I need to be at the Ballet in Lincoln Center at 9:00 a.m. We're photographing a few dancers for my Core Studio," I replied, grabbing something to wear. I paused and looked over my shoulder. He was leaning against my closet's door frame. "I—kinda need you to leave now."

"I know," he said with a laugh. "I was waiting for you to throw me out. You never know. I was hoping you'd start getting undressed since you're in such a hurry."

I took one of my socks off and threw it at him. "There you go."

He caught the sock in mid-air and laughed harder this time.

He shot the sock back at me and said with a grin, "See you around, 9A. I'm glad you're back."

9A. It's been months since he last called me that. It reminded me of the day we met.

He walked away, and I yelled, "You owe me a paella, 9B."

Easter was last Sunday, and when we bought the Paella from a Spanish restaurant to celebrate at home, I couldn't help but remember how William promised to cook one for me this Easter. And I didn't expect him to cook it. He'd just been discharged from the hospital. But I thought it was fun to remind him of the promise he made.

Come rain or shine, he'd told me. Only this time it really poured.

William turned around and said, "Shit, you're right." He ran a hand through his thick, golden hair down his neck.

"I'm just messing with you," I said, shutting a drawer. "We ordered one. Easter was saved." I walked out of the closet and headed toward the bathroom.

"Was it any good?" he asked as I washed my face.

"It was … meh," I replied, rinsing my face with water. I was shocked at how comfortable and natural it felt to have him standing there watching me get ready for school. "I've had better." I patted my face with a hand towel and looked for my brush.

"I'll be your best," he said with that signature smirk of his. But it wasn't as annoying as it used to be. "I'll make sure of it."

"Your paella is that great, huh?" I countered, brushing my short hair, still not fully accustomed to the change, and held it with a hair tie.

"That too." He smirked again. I snorted and shook my head with a nervous smile.

"You *really* have to go." I needed to change, and he was still standing there entertaining me. I was already going to be late and having William distracting me wasn't helpful.

"I'll throw the paella into your birthday gift bundle." He stepped into my bathroom and pulled the hair tie off my hair. He threw it on the vanity counter with a wink. And with that, he left.

I couldn't help but smile.

But please … no gifts. I didn't want to think about celebrating my birthday at all. Lily insisted on how turning twenty-one was such a big deal—that I should celebrate. *You owe it to yourself,* she said.

But I didn't owe myself shit. It didn't feel right to celebrate when Caleb had died a few weeks ago. I deserved to be locked up in my apartment, and that's it. Being old enough to buy my own wine did sound like something to look forward to, though.

I changed into my clothes, grabbed my things, and rushed down to the lobby. David sat behind the wheel.

"I'm sorry. I'm a bit late," I said, taking a seat inside the car. Amena shut my door and climbed into the passenger seat next to David. "We're going to Lincoln Center, please. And I wouldn't mind if you want to drive like a maniac."

"I can do that, Miss Murphy." David laughed and sped off.

We arrived at 9:06 a.m. David didn't disappoint; he was a skilled driver. Amena opened the door for me and followed close behind as I raced to the Ballet. Luckily, my group hadn't gone inside yet. They were waiting a few minutes for everyone to arrive.

"Hey," I said to Nolan, standing next to him. "I made it."

"You okay?" he asked with a frown but attempting to smile.

"Yes, perfect. Just slept in."

"You look more like the kind of person who didn't sleep at all rather than one who overslept."

"Oh, thanks for the flattery," I joked. "Do I look like shit then?" I didn't have time to apply any makeup. And my eyes could've used a bit of concealer.

"No, Bee, come on. That's not what I meant," he said, looking embarrassed, his dark waves flying across his forehead. "I'm just—worried about you, okay? That's all."

"I'm fine. I swear," I insisted. He grabbed my arm and pulled me away from the group. "You know you can talk to me. I know you tend to keep things to yourself. That you're … reserved. But sometimes just talking about *things* helps a lot."

I let out a breath of defeat. "I know. It's just—it's all been too overwhelming."

"Are you still having nightmares?" he asked.

I nodded with my lips pressed into a line. I'd told him about my first nightmare at the hospital, and that got him worried.

"I just want to make sure you don't have like—PTSD or something. That shit doesn't go away by itself, Bee."

Nolan's dad was a war veteran. He knew what PTSD looked like. I would never compare his father's experiences at war to what happened to me that night with Thomas. I was confident about being able to deal with it. Besides, I was talking to my therapist twice a week.

"Thank you. I swear I'm fine," I kept lying. I'd already put everyone around me through a lot. I didn't want to burden Nolan with my issues.

"Why don't we get some coffee later today and talk?"

"Um, sure." I smiled. "Why not." *Yes, to coffee. Always.*

We joined our classmates, and Bryce, a girl from my class, approached us. It's the only class I had with her, and I hadn't seen her since before Spring break. She didn't attend the week before.

"Hi, Billie!" she said, beaming.

"Hey, Bryce." Our instructor led the way inside, and Bryce walked next to us as we followed the group, lagging in the back.

"You're dating William Sjöberg, aren't you?" she asked, her big, dark-brown eyes staring at me with intense curiosity.

What?

"Um, no. No, I'm not. Why would you think that?" I asked as a warm feeling boiled up in my stomach. Nerves. Nolan stared at me with a *what the fuck* face.

"Oh girl, come on. You can tell me," she said, placing her hand on my shoulder. "I saw the pictures of the premiere. I didn't know you were friends with the Sjöbergs. That is *so* cool."

"Exactly, we're just friends," I replied, looking forward. The last thing I needed now was to have people spreading rumors about that. I knew the pictures were out in the world. And I still hadn't talked to Nathan about it. I didn't even know if he saw them or not.

"I saw you on a blog post in Haute Magazine's website too," she whispered as Miss Burgess, our instructor, explained a few things about what we were expected to do once inside. And I wanted to listen to that explanation. But Bryce wouldn't shut up.

"Haute? I'm sure you confused me with someone else," I

replied, trying to listen to Miss Burgess speak.

"The pink Enzio de Luca suit with the moon? The short red hair? It was definitely you," she kept saying, tucking her brown hair behind her ear. "You looked great, by the way. And with William looking at you like that … ugh. *Please* tell me you're secretly dating, and I swear I won't bother you again for the rest of the day. He's *so* hot."

Bryce pulled her phone out and took a selfie of us together.

"Bryce, what the hell?" Nolan whispered to her.

"I'm sorry, miss, I'm going to need you to step back," Amena said out of nowhere with a commanding voice.

Shhhhit.

A few of our classmates turned around to see what was happening, but luckily Miss Burgess was now stepping into the theater, unaware of our interactions.

Bryce looked confused. My security detail used to keep a certain distance before, and they would never engage with the students. But my father's neurosis pushed them to keep closer tabs on me now. To be neurotic like him.

I had to take a deep breath and force a smile. "Amena, it's okay," I said to her.

"Miss, I'm going to have to ask you to delete that photograph from your phone," she said to a puppy-eyed Bryce, completely ignoring me. *Damn, she's tough.* I felt so bad for Bryce.

Bryce's implications were annoying, and the selfie was a bit too much, but I didn't want her to feel like crap about it either. It wasn't such a big deal, and she didn't mean any harm. She was just curious. I think.

"Um, sure. I—I'm sorry, Billie," she said, tapping her phone's screen. Nolan rolled his eyes and shook his head. Amena had scared the shit out of her.

"Bryce, it's okay. You don't have to delete it, okay?" I whispered.

"Just don't post it anywhere because Nolan says I don't look my best today." I laughed, trying to soften the mood.

"I didn't—" Nolan started to say, but I nudged his arm with mine and widened my eyes at him. *Just play along.*

"Miss Murphy, if I may suggest—"

"Amena, it's fine, really," I insisted. She nodded and took a few steps back.

End of drama.

I had enough shit going on to be bothered by a selfie, and all I wanted was to photograph the three beautiful ballerinas that were waiting for us on stage.

CHAPTER 7

La Pièce de la Résistance

April 9, 2010

"OH, MY GOD! You're William Sjöberg's girlfriend?"

Nolan and I looked at each other after the barista at the coffee shop almost screamed the question at me. She covered her mouth, looking shocked as she waited for my reply, which consisted of me denying it and looking away.

Nolan and I then sat at the table where Emily, his girlfriend, was waiting for us. I couldn't help but think of Bryce when Nolan told Emily what had happened with the barista. She thought the whole thing was funny and suggested not to worry about it.

Those damned photographs.

It was weird to be recognized like that by a random person who saw the premiere photos. It made me want to crawl under my seat. The truth is I hadn't gone out much in the past few weeks. I just hoped getting asked that didn't become a recurrent theme on my every outing.

This reminded me of William's celebrity status, which was something I used to constantly forget. I couldn't, for the life of me, comprehend how they could live their lives in the spotlight like that—being followed, recognized, approached.

I'd only witnessed a glimpse of their fame, and it was madness.

I was convinced I wouldn't be able to stomach it if I were in their shoes. But that was yet another confusing thought that was ready to be shoved under the rug.

We gave Nolan a ride to his job on my way back home. Nathan promised to head out of the office earlier today, since it was Friday. We planned to order something for dinner and just stay in for the rest of the night, just the two of us.

Lily was out of town, and I hadn't seen her or Joel in days, but she promised to be back for my birthday.

I took my time showering, enjoying the hot water on my back, feeling myself relax, and the doorbell rang.

Nathan.

I jumped out of the shower and wrapped a towel around me as I rushed to open the door, leaving a trail of water behind me.

"Hey!" I said, opening the door just a tad, my smile melting on my face. *Hell no.* I shut the door in William's face and rested my forehead on it for a couple of seconds as I heard William's laughter.

"Open up, Guille!"

"No!" I shouted back. "Go away!" I wouldn't step out to chat when I was dripping wet wearing nothing but a towel—besides, that freaking surveillance camera. I didn't know *who* was watching, but I didn't want to put on a show for some random agent.

"Get dressed!" he shouted. "I have a surprise for you!"

William and his impromptu shit, as always.

"What kind of surprise?" I shouted back. Damn, I was curious.

"Get dressed!"

Ugh. I did as I was told and walked back a few minutes later shouting, "It better be good, William! You made me cut my shower shor—"

I trailed off when I opened the door, my jaw dislocating.

"Dave, this is my neighbor Billie. Billie, this is my friend, Dave."

I offered him my hand, speechless, gaping.

This was Dave *freaking* Matthews standing in front of me.

(

"Oh, my God!" I squealed as the elevator doors shut behind Dave when he left. My hands shook with excitement. "He's so nice—wow. I can't believe I just met him!" I couldn't stop beaming. We only talked for a couple of minutes since he was on his way out.

William leaned against my door frame, smiling, shaking his head with his arms crossed at his chest. "That's the kind of reaction I expected when I first met you," he admitted. "I guess I should've been a rock star instead."

"It's never too late to find your true passion," I joked. But that made William frown, for some reason. "You—okay?"

"What? Yeah." He smiled again. "Anyway, I can't say I wasn't frustrated by the fact that you didn't recognize me. It'd never happened to me before that a girl around your age didn't know who I was. I didn't know how to act at first. It was—I don't know, strange but also liberating. Like for once, I had a real chance of testing out if being *me* was good … enough."

"William," I said, tilting my head. *Of course, you are.*

"And shit, I guess I didn't make such a good first impression, did I?" he said with a laugh, dragging a hand over his lips. "But Joel kept messing with my head. He was like, *there's no way she doesn't know who you are*, and it fucked me up.

"I *needed* to know if you were genuinely unaware or if it was just something you were trying on me. But after that weekend at the cottage, Joel finally believed you."

I snorted. "Lily mentioned that about Joel a few months ago. How he couldn't believe it at first. But yeah ... I'm just *that* stupid." I chuckled.

"No, you're *not* Guille," he said with a slight grimace and a frown. "You're one of the smartest, most cultured, and interesting people I know. And even if you would've been faking it, I wouldn't have fucking cared because it was working like a charm. I couldn't stop thinking about it—about you." William stood up straight and took a step forward, crossing the threshold. "I wanted to decipher you. To know *everything* about you. I wanted so bad to peek inside your head."

Waiting for the violent cascade of emotions to settle was useless. I swallowed hard and looked away for a second, but they never ceased. William needed to take a step back, or maybe I had to, but I knew I couldn't. And apparently, neither did he.

I looked up into William's light sapphire-blue eyes instead, listening to my lungs say, *fuck you, I quit*, hoping he would say something to break the breathless stillness. But I was helpless against William's raw honesty and his powerful presence. Always. Every single time.

"But then I realized it wasn't so hard to do," he continued, and I took a slow breath in, realizing my lungs were *just kidding*. "That's one of the things that endeared me the most about you. That you don't have to say a word for me to know what you're thinking."

That was a recurrent theme. How transparent I am. Caleb used to say something similar, how he could read my every gesture.

God ... I miss him.

I parted my lips to speak, to say whatever nonsense my brain had whipped up for me at the last minute, but a *ping* in the distance released me from the William-induced-trance I was under as Nathan stepped out of the elevator and headed our way. No … *marched* our way.

"Hey, you!" I said to Nathan, looking over William's shoulder with an unnaturally wide smile—cortisol flowing through my veins, stress tackling my nervous system.

Nathan quickly closed the distance between us, the heels of his dress shoes clicking hard on the floor with each step he took.

He leaned in and gave me a quick peck on the lips. "How's everything, mate?" he said with a blank face, offering his hand to William, who instantly shook it.

"Great, thanks," William said, his upper lip tight with the usual indifference. "I was wondering if we could talk."

What? Please say no!

"That's a great idea, actually," Nathan replied. He looked away as if thinking how convenient that was. "Do you mind, love?"

"Of course not. I'll be inside." *Pulling my hair out.*

William shot me one of his fake studied smiles that I hated so much and walked out to talk to Nathan in the hall. *What the hell are they going to talk about?* I had an idea of what Nathan had in mind, but William?

I shut the door, walked to the kitchen, and opened a bottle of wine after fighting with the corkscrew. Heck, it was my birthday weekend. And this is what I envisioned as a perfect celebration—a good glass of wine with dinner at home. Maybe more.

No one was going to make me feel guilty for drinking alone while I waited for Nathan to be done with the most nerve-wracking conversation ever about *God knows what.* And by no one, I meant *me.*

There was still this part of me that kept pressuring my mind into feeling guilty about Caleb's death. That I didn't deserve to move on with my life.

Torturing myself with those thoughts just made me want to keep drinking, so I kept myself busy with that to fool my mind into forgetting and decided to think about what to order instead.

I was thinking Italian, so I called the restaurant since I knew what Nathan liked, and he'd already told me it was my turn to choose tonight.

A stark silence filled the living room when I ended the call. There was no sound coming from the other side of the door. Good. That meant they were modulating their voices. But I couldn't hear a damn thing! Although I was convinced they were most probably speaking in Swedish.

That's when I googled Swedish courses on my phone as I poured my second glass of wine. I never could pick up a single word whenever I heard any of them speaking Swedish. It was so frustrating. I couldn't live like that.

Nathan and William had been out there for a while, and I grew restless, which only accelerated my sip rate, making me down that second glass of wine like it was nothing.

I could already feel *the presence* flowing through my veins.

Naturally, I poured myself a third. I was in a *don't let me see the bottom of my glass* kind of mood, and luckily, I was the one pouring the merlot.

Nathan waltzed right in when I took the first sip of my freshly poured glass of wine and shut the door behind him.

"Saucing up?" Nathan asked with a laugh. I took another sip with lifted brows and nodded. "Can I join in?" He took a seat beside me on the living room couch.

"Sure, but you've got some serious catching up to do," I replied.

Nathan leaned in and poured himself a glass. He then placed a soft kiss on my lips.

"I know. I can tell by that cheeky smile of yours that I'm

already behind schedule," Nathan returned, bringing his lips to his wineglass, his gaze refusing to release mine. *God, he's sexy*.

And yes, I was already *sauced up* in the most relaxing way ever. "But don't worry, I'll catch up with you in a bit," he added, taking another, longer swig.

I'm sure he would. Nathan would drink, and I could never tell how drunk he was. He had this abnormally high tolerance for alcohol. His face never gave him away.

But not me.

I was the opposite of that. One drink, and the corners of my lips moved up involuntarily.

That got me thinking about how much he must've drunk that day at the Super Bowl. A shit ton, that's how much. Luckily, Joel was there to handle it.

Ugh! The curiosity was eating at me. I wanted to ask what he talked about with William. I mean, they were out there for a while. But I had to be subtle about it. Maybe let him tell me about it.

"I ordered dinner for us," I said instead, dropping my wineglass on the coffee table and placing my arm around his neck. I was operating with one hand and a few fingers. There were things I could do but holding a wineglass with a cast wasn't one of them. "I ordered the usual for you from Alessandro's."

"Scrummy," he whispered, kissing me gently. Once. Twice. His lips lingering longer each time. "Your mouth tastes *delicious*."

"Like wine," I breathed back.

"My point exactly."

He dropped one of his slow, heated kisses on me, and I could feel my face flushing from the warmth of both the kiss and the wine waking me up inside.

"I met—Dave Matthews—just before—you arrived," I said in between kisses.

"You did, huh? Wow, that's amazing." He pulled away from me just a little to meet my eyes. "William didn't mention that," he said mostly to himself.

Why would William mention it?

William did whatever the hell he wanted and said whatever the hell he wanted *when* he wanted. And I didn't think Nathan was on the top of his briefing list.

"Well, I did," I said, bringing my lips closer to his. "It was so exciting."

But Nathan backed up again slightly, not at all harshly but somewhat, making it seem like he had something picking on his mind.

"I couldn't talk to William about the things I wanted to," he stated, placing his wineglass on the coffee table beside mine. Now *I* needed my wine back because what did they talk about then? "He wanted to talk about Zara. And that pretty much monopolized our entire conversation."

A couple of involuntary coughs escaped my throat.

"You okay, love?"

"Yes," I said quickly, grabbing my wineglass and taking a sip. "Something got stuck in my throat." There I was, choking on my own saliva. I could feel my hands shaking because I *craved* to know what William had to say about Zara. *Please keep going.*

"Zara's flying in tomorrow morning, and she'll be staying with William since 'he's got a spare room.'"

No *fucking* way.

"He explained how he helped Zara get into Juilliard. I mean, he talked to a few people, and they really liked her audition materials. Apparently, they've both been plotting this for a while," Nathan said, rubbing his face. "So he's taking her to Juilliard to make sure everything's ready for her to start the fall term."

What the hell is happening? Zara's staying with him?

I already disliked Nathan's "baby sister" too much; who's my age, by the way. And I've only seen her in pictures. I was sure Zara was great because Nathan wouldn't stop telling me that. And I guess that's what annoyed me, that William probably agreed with Nathan.

No … he most definitely *agreed*.

And we couldn't have been any more different. Long, brown waves with caramel highlights framed her oval-shaped face. Her eyes were of the palest blue shade. Her big, white smile was the center of attention in every picture Nathan showed me of her. And *tall*, Nathan said when I asked about her height.

Five-*freaking*-ten.

She wanted to be an actress, and she certainly looked like one. Like someone that would look great standing beside William.

Maybe she *was* an excellent match for him since they would be doing the same thing for a living. Zara could understand the world he lived in better than I ever could. It was hard to realize that.

Nathan's my boyfriend. Yes. But I'd already begun to acknowledge my feelings for William, even if it was something I didn't want to do, even if it was the scariest thing ever. And the feelings were very real—alive, almost, and stared back at me a lot.

Nathan took an angry sip of his wine and set it down again.

"So that's why I had you waiting too long. I spent most of the conversation reminding him how he better not lay a bloody finger on her. You know, in the *friendliest* way possible."

That's my man.

"And to be honest, after listening to all of this—to how close they really are, I don't think it's even relevant to question him about his feelings for you. My question now is, what does he want with Zara?"

That makes two of us.

"I was so fucking annoyed at seeing William hovering around you all the time. But I know now that he's been messing with me, probably distracting me of the fact that he's trying to make something work with my sister."

No.

I didn't want to believe that. And it hurt me to see Nathan having these thoughts when I had all this extra information that I withheld from him about things that William had said to me. About his feelings. But then I doubted myself again because what if Nathan was right?

William had been friendlier to me, more aware, and caring. Involved. Maybe he'd decided to be my friend after all now that he had something going on with Zara. It could be that I got it all twisted. But he kept flirting, hinting. And in the hospital, when I first saw him after surgery, the things he said ... they felt real.

And just now, before Nathan arrived, he was opening up himself to me even more.

Zara *had* to be just a good friend. I refused to believe otherwise.

I know I'd previously asked William if *we* could be friends. Damn it! But that was before when I'd just started dating Nathan. Before I thought I'd lost him. Before my feelings for him grew and expanded inside my chest.

We said we'd be friends in another life, not this one—never.

Perhaps there was something else I was missing to make sense of this—a missing puzzle piece. *La pièce de la résistance.*

But what?

"He even paid for everything, can you believe that?" Nathan added, looking away. Defeated. "I don't even know how much going to Juilliard costs, but it's not cheap."

Wow. I knew William had a lot of money, but paying for Juilliard? Helping her get in? William must've genuinely cared about Zara. You just don't do that for anyone.

"I'm just fucking jealous, you know? *I'm* her brother, and I know I don't have the kind of money to pay for that right now or a big enough place for her to stay with me. And I know I'll get there eventually. It's just—"

"Why doesn't she stay with me?"

It was the least I could do for my sister-in-law.

CHAPTER 8

Perfect Stillness

"YOU WOULD DO THAT?" Nathan asked, his eyes gleaming with gratitude.

"Anything for you." I kissed his cheek. He seemed relieved like I took a weight off his shoulders and tossed it out the window. I knew that's what he probably preferred, for her sister to stay with me instead.

But I knew Nathan too well to know he would never ask unless I'd offered it myself. And I didn't know if having Zara stay with me was the best idea. I would most likely freak her out with my nightmares. Nathan didn't know how bad or how frequent they'd been. I didn't want him to worry.

I'd rather deal with the embarrassment than sleep a wall away from William, knowing Zara's there too, *supposedly* sleeping in his guest bedroom, while a million scenarios developed in the deep wells of my imagination.

"I was planning on talking to Joel about this. I mean, she could stay with them too."

"It's fine, really. I want to meet Zara and get to know her better."

"It'll only be for a few days, maybe a week, I promise," he said, his voice low, placing a gentle kiss on the corner of my mouth. "I'll talk to her tomorrow and see what she's really up to. She'll have plenty of time to find her own place before the fall term begins. There's absolutely *no way* I'll be fine with them being flatmates."

Good thinking.

"She can stay as long as she needs, no problem."

"I'm so cross, though," he added. "I don't get why she shuts me out like that. And I have to find out through William of all people? For Christ's sake." Nathan shook his head, seemingly exasperated. "William said she was *afraid* of telling me. That I would disapprove."

He did disapprove. Before, Nathan told me how he thought it was ridiculous for Zara to want to be an actress. And that's why I guess Zara wasn't keeping Nathan in the loop. She knew he wasn't supportive of her dream.

This was all too complicated—the entanglement of it all. And not knowing if William and Zara were just friends destroyed me. I needed to see them interact, and all I wanted was to go to bed and let it be tomorrow.

"And where do your parents stand in all of this?" I asked. I was curious to know why Nathan assumed somewhat of a father-figure role with her.

"My family isn't the most—functional family out there," he began.

Whose is? There must be some perfectly oiled families out there, but I could relate to Nathan on this one.

"Evie's got her family now and is devoted to Ollie and her husband George. She's never had the time or energy to deal with Zara.

"Charlotte, as you know, is getting her medical degree, so she's up to her neck with school. She still has a few years left to go, and her focus is entirely on that. And my parents, well—

they've got their own problems to deal with. I've never told you this, but we grew up listening to them fight almost every night.

"They tried so hard during the day to act like everything was perfect. They never fought in front of us or said a foul word to each other when we were around. Never. But I remember *dreading* that moment at night where we all went to bed, and the fighting started. The screaming and shouting."

I grabbed Nathan's hand and squeezed it. I tried to find his gaze, but he withdrew himself. I'm sure he wanted to let it all out before he allowed me to coddle him.

"My mom did a better job at hiding the pain. But my father—he would have a narky attitude all day after having a big fight. We could easily tell things were bad. And I guess that's why I developed this—temper. I always found an excuse to get into fights at school, trying to vent. The martial arts helped me with that later on. Joel was helpful too. He would listen when I had no one to talk to. I always felt like I had to be strong for my sisters. That's why I would never talk to them about it."

He finally turned his head slightly my way, meeting my gaze from the corner of his eye, his teeth nibbling on his lower lip.

"Zara was just a poppet, and she would come find me at night, scared shitless by the racket coming from my mum and dad's bedroom. Zara would crawl into my bed, and I would do my best to get her back to sleep. We've always been close. It's not that anything bad happened, but the age difference just pulled us apart a bit. And then one day, she woke up and decided to make William her *bestie*," he said with a certain edge that reeked of resentment.

"And William jumped right into it, of course. In *his* eyes, I was taking Joel away from him, so now he'd take Zara away from me just to even the score.

"And now that I've talked to William, I'm convinced this

whole thing with you hasn't been anything but a continuation of this—ongoing, passive-aggressive battle between us that's been perpetuated through the years. It's childish as fuck if you ask me, and I have played my part too, as much as it hurts to admit."

Nathan unknowingly nuked my heart. Listening to the determination with which he said those things—it hurt. I knew he was speaking from experience, assuming things that had probably checked out in the past. But again, he didn't know William's true feelings for me, and now … neither did I.

I knew nothing.

"It's so strange. We're almost thirty, and my dynamic with William turns me into this angry, unstable adolescent chap again," he continued, draining his wineglass. I mirrored his move and set mine on the coffee table again.

"William has a special talent to pull that out of me, to connect with that. And we haven't been able to disengage. But my fear now is that Zara might get hurt. I know how she is. She *dives* into things. All in. Wholeheartedly. And I'm afraid she might get hurt in the process because I don't really know what the *bleeding hell* is going on between them."

"I'm sure it's nothing," I said, wanting to believe the words myself. "Once you talk to her tomorrow, you'll feel more at ease."

The doorbell rang, and Nathan shot up from his seat and opened the door. Our food had arrived. He greeted David, paid the delivery guy, and came back inside, pushing the door shut with his foot.

We sat down to eat and uncorked another bottle of wine. Well, Nathan did. I kept the wine flowing on both of our glasses as the self-designated bartender that I set myself to be for the night.

The mood lightened up dramatically during our meal. We both needed to change the subject. So I talked to Nathan about my photo shoot at the Ballet, and the three beautiful ballerinas we met. The photographs turned out amazing. I promised to show them to him some other day.

As soon as we were done with dinner, something stirred deep inside me, as if someone would've gone inside my head and turned the lights out.

A profound and nostalgic sadness invaded me, and the unregistered amount of wine I drank only amplified the downhearted feeling.

Before Nathan could notice the shift in my energy, I stood up and cleared the table. He excused himself to the bathroom as I took the dirty dishes to the kitchen, where I decided to wash them to empty my mind.

I didn't even know the exact reason for my sadness. I sure had a lot from where to pick and choose, but what I mean is that I didn't have something particular in mind that was making me feel this way, rather than an overall numbness that weighed on my mind.

Buried deep in my thoughts as I washed the dishes, I felt two arms surrounding my body. I let out a short but loud shriek, followed by the sound of a broken plate.

"Shit. I-I'm sorry," I said, kneeling on the floor, picking up the pieces. Nathan talked to me, apologized, asked me to stand up, but I ignored him. Not intentionally; his voice was far away. I could only focus on picking up the shards of ceramic.

"Murph."

I had a pile of the bigger pieces set to the side and stood up to fetch a bag to discard them and a broom to sweep the smaller remains.

"Murph, let me help you."

My cast was getting in the way, and I couldn't hold the broom correctly. Nathan seized my arm gently and made me stop. He grabbed both of my arms to get my attention and directed his gaze at me, studying my face. "*I'll* do it." He enunciated those three words slowly as if realizing I was far away, and he had to demand my attention back somehow.

It worked.

My face scrunched up. I looked down, and a sob escaped my throat, followed by heavy tears that fell from my eyes to the floor without touching my face.

Nathan cupped my chin up with two delicate fingers and placed his arms around me. We stood like that for a while until he led me to my room.

Neither of us spoke a word.

He knew I was having trouble dealing with everything that had happened a few weeks ago. And my conversation with him about Zara and the things he revealed to me about his family had hit me hard too. It left me punch-drunk.

Nathan helped me out of my clothes and placed one of his t-shirts he kept in my place over my head. He walked up to my bed and undid it. He then offered his hand to pull me in, and I took it.

I crawled into my bed and rested my head on my cool puffy pillows, watching him strip off his clothes until he wore nothing but his boxer briefs. He then walked around the bed and spooned me.

He kissed my hair a few times, and without saying a word, I shut my eyes and allowed myself to grieve with him by my side—to feel it all pouring down and soaking off into the floor of my mind. He seemed like he needed this too. The stillness. The warmth.

How could I ever let him go?

CHAPTER 9

Quiet

April 10, 2010

I OPENED MY EYES, panting, my head pounding from the imminent headache surfacing from the comfort of my lazy neurotransmitters—fully charged, ready to strike. My face was humid with the tiniest drops of sweat, but the sensation of it was cold. Not warm or sticky. Just ice cold.

"Murph?" Nathan whispered, brushing his unruly brown waves off his forehead. His eyes were big, trained on my face. Worried.

Did I scream?

A knock on my wall confirmed to me that I probably did because William wanted to know if I was okay.

Shit.

"Ah, hi," I said, rolling on my side to face him, ignoring the wall. Ignoring William.

My eyelids fluttered a few times, quickly, as I adjusted to the faint bluish light coming in through the sides of the window shades. It was early in the morning.

"What was that?" he asked.

"What was what?" I asked back. I didn't know if he meant the knock on the wall or my screaming or both. But just then,

William knocked again.

I closed my eyes for a second, exhaling slowly through my nose.

"That." Nathan jerked his chin at the wall behind me.

"Did I—scream?" I asked, double-checking. He nodded, so I dragged myself out of bed, knocked back twice, and threw myself back next to Nathan.

Ouch.

I grimaced, feeling like my body would break down and my head would detach from it any second now if I didn't maintain myself in a horizontal position for a little longer.

"That was William," I replied to the obvious question. "He's just probably wondering if I'm okay."

Nathan clicked his tongue, seemingly unhappy about my too-familiar interaction with William. I was about to reply when my cell phone vibrated on my nightstand. I picked it up and saw William's initials on my screen.

As I stared at the screen, Nathan said, "Aren't you getting that?" He sat up, and I bit the inside of my cheek, wondering if he wanted me to take it or not, but I didn't have the energy to get into an abstract and figurative mood, so I took the call, just as he suggested.

"Hey … No, I'm fine … No, I'm not. Nathan's here … Yes … Um, what? … Did I? … I-I'm sorry I didn't mean to … No … Okay … I know … Okay … Thanks, bye."

"I'm sorry," I said to Nathan, lowering my brows and dropping my phone on my nightstand.

William had just informed me he heard me screaming *his* name.

The last time I did that, I was in big trouble, so yeah, it

wasn't something he could hear without reacting. This is why I didn't mind that Nathan hadn't stayed over until now. I was trying to avoid this from happening. To freak him out as my brain processed trauma during my sleep.

William wanted to come over and check on me; that's why I told him Nathan was here. But that just made his voice go low and dusky. I was sure once Zara arrived in a few hours, his mood would brighten up again.

"I keep having these nightmares, and I don't know how—"

"It's okay," he replied, kissing my cheek. "Do you want to talk about it?"

"No," I said quickly. "No, I—no."

Nathan couldn't help but snort with a smile. "Okay, *no.* But how about I make you forget about it?" He leaned in and kissed me, his hands wandering up my thighs, making me gasp.

Saying no to Nathan wasn't just something I was strong enough to do. But it was so still and quiet outside that I swear I could even hear birds singing. Or maybe I was just going insane.

But I *knew* William was most likely still in bed, resting on the other side of our ridiculously flimsy four-inch drywall.

I know I shouldn't have cared. But I did! I'd throw myself out the window if I heard anything of the sort coming out from his bedroom. I wouldn't be able to stomach it. No.

Never.

It'd been merely three weeks and a few days since he admitted to listening to Nathan and me having sex, admitted to going crazy because of it. So how was I to ignore William and deliberately hurt him like that?

Another proud and immature part of me taunted me with the idea of Zara arriving today. *What if she wants to stay with him and not you? What if she shares his bed? What if he cares about the both of you, just like you care about both of them?*

I was running out of time. The ticking seconds laughed at me as they sauntered away, reminding me how I couldn't live like this. It's as if I were stuck in between night and day—eternal dusk. Not fully able to drown in the darkness or wallow in the light.

I pulled away from Nathan in a tender way and said, "Could you bring me some water?" He seemed displeased. I assumed he would rather go back to what his fingers had started to do, but my mouth was parched, and I needed a minute to think about how to handle the wall situation.

He needed to know that I felt uncomfortable knowing William could hear us.

Nathan stood up and flew to the kitchen. He didn't seem like planning on taking too long to return, so I rushed to the bathroom, half-stumbling my way there, but he appeared when I was brushing my teeth.

"That's not fair." He laughed. "Now I have to brush my teeth too."

"You don't have to," I said after rinsing my mouth.

"Oh, I do. Out you go," he said, handing the glass of water to me. I smiled and walked back to my bed, taking a long drink as I sat on the edge. I took a deep breath and settled the glass on my nightstand.

Nathan stepped out of the bathroom wearing a grin, running a hand through his hair and down the back of his neck. He stepped in front of me and kissed me, slowly laying me back on the bed. His fresh, minty tongue wasn't playing games. No more teasing. Claiming.

"You won't hold back," he said, almost an order. It's as if he could tell that was exactly what I was planning to do. And a part of me wanted to obey that order—to give in.

But how?

I wished I could be like those people who don't give a shit about anything. People who just live, and feel, and do. But I couldn't be like that. And I couldn't figure out if it was wrong for me to care too much—about William.

And there I was, stuck again in the last second of nightfall.

I needed to break free.

"Wait," I finally dared to say. Nathan stretched his arms up and pulled away. Fast. The gray of his eyes more prominent than the green, trained on me, waiting for an explanation. "I need to talk to you."

He allowed his weight to fall to the side, right next to me. I could *see* why he was so annoyed about making him stop. And I really didn't want to have to do this. I never had.

Say it quickly, don't hesitate.

"William can hear us having sex, and I'm not comfortable with it."

"We—would have to be having sex in the first place for him to be able to listen, love," he said, his voice a tad bitter. Grouchy. *I get it.*

"What I *mean* is he's heard us before. And that's beyond my comfort zone," I explained. "I can't loosen up, knowing he's right beside us. I hold back, involuntarily."

Nathan snorted and sat up straight, and I did too because I wanted to level up with his angry, fiery gaze.

"When did he mention this to you?"

"On the night of the premiere."

"Bollocks."

"Nathan, I'm telling you the truth."

"Then why did you hold back on me when I came back from the Super Bowl if not because of him? I remember thinking you were still angry at me about the order of protection we made you sign, but no."

"Nathan, I swear I didn't know. At the time, I only assumed he did, but I didn't know for sure." I said, trying to keep my voice down. "I can hear him playing the piano all the time, shutting doors, laughing. So I thought if *I* could hear him, then he could hear … us."

"And why would he bring it up in the first place? Why does he care? I mean, you're having sex with your boyfriend, so what? It's not like you haven't heard anything coming out of *his* room. I'm sure you have by now. Knowing how he is."

"I haven't."

"So he's celibate now?" He scoffed. "He can't go a couple of days without getting laid, believe me. We grew up together."

All the curses I ever knew or heard of were plastered on my frontal lobe as I shouted them inside my mind. So I bit my lower lip to hold in the cocktail of emotions—trying to prevent my features' translucency from giving any of that away.

I knew William had a past. One I knew *nothing* about, but I could only imagine. And I *didn't* want to keep feeding my imagination, but I was afraid Nathan would start hitting me with William's stats about his bedroom's extracurricular activities any second now.

What Nathan said could be true, but I hadn't seen a single girl coming in or out of his apartment other than Alice and Luna. Whatever Nathan claimed William liked doing and the frequency of it wasn't happening in his apartment.

And I knew Nathan was sick and tired of listening to how everything lately had something to do with William. It must've been annoying for him, especially after learning what he told me last night about their weird *relationship*—if it could be cataloged as such.

"We would be having this same conversation if it were Tobias living next door," I added. That statement seemed to put Nathan at ease. But it was the truth. Somewhat.

That the depth of the discomfort might've been different, yes. That I'd rather have anyone else living beside me instead of William … absolutely. Was there anything I could do about it? No.

"The only thing I can do is tell you how I feel," I told him. "Would you rather have me make some stupid excuse instead? I wanted you to know the truth."

Nathan laid on his back and threw his hands behind his neck. "I'm sorry," he said, looking at the ceiling. "I'm just nervous about Zara arriving today." He pulled a hand from behind his neck and rubbed his face.

"There's nothing to be sorry about. I'm sorry too. I get it."

I do.

I moved closer beside him and kissed the corner of his mouth. "Me trying to be more—*quiet* doesn't mean I'm not enjoying myself, okay?"

"Why don't you show me," he said with a cheeky smile.

"What?" I said with a nervous laugh.

He moved on top of me and said, "How you make your best effort in keeping yourself quiet."

CHAPTER 10

Dresses

NATHAN LEFT AT around 10:00 a.m. They needed him at the office for a quick conference call with a client. He promised to be back at noon. I hoped he did. I needed him to be here when Zara arrived. I'd offered to go pick her up at the airport, but Nathan told me with a somewhat sharp tone that William had that taken care of. Cooper, William's driver, would be picking her up.

I took a shower and changed into black jeans and a long-sleeved, emerald dressy blouse.

The doorbell rang, and I rushed to see who it was. It was still early, so it couldn't be Nathan or Zara.

"Halò," Mimi said with a warm smile, putting a couple of grocery bags on the floor and opening her arms as she invited me to a hug. I threw myself into her embrace.

"Hi! I didn't know you were coming today," I said, surprised.

"Oh, yer father didn't want me coming back until Mundae. But I'm bored awready. And I missed ye, dear."

"Oh, I missed you too, Mimi," I said, breaking away from her arms. My father gave Mimi some well-deserved vacation after what happened. He was so worried about her. He offered her indefinite time off at first, but she refused. "Come in, come in. Don't you have keys anymore?"

"I do, but I didn't want to startle ye. I thought it was best to announce myself," she said. I grabbed the grocery bags with one hand and took them to the kitchen.

Having Mimi around always made things feel better. She immediately offered to cook something for me, and I accepted. I was starving and hadn't eaten a thing.

The doorbell rang again. It was Aaron standing outside my door with a rack of clothes beside him.

"Hey," I said, offering him a sad smile. Looking at Aaron was hard. He reminded me of Caleb. And by the look on his face, I think I reminded him of Caleb too. The wounds were still too fresh. Raw.

"This arrived for you, Miss," he said, raising a brow and looking at the rack of clothes. "It came with this envelope."

Aaron rolled the rack inside and handed over the envelope. I thanked him, and he excused himself and left.

The envelope was black with the Enzio de Luca logo in a hot-stamped silver foil. I opened it and read the note:

Miss Guillermina Murphy,

We are excited to announce that the Enzio Privé Spring 2010 Couture collection look you wore to the premiere a few weeks ago sold out after being requested by many of our regular and new clients. We want to show our appreciation and congratulate you on your birthday by gifting you these four exclusive pieces from the Fall 2010 Ready-to-Wear Collection.

We hope you can celebrate in style.
The Team at Enzio de Luca

Oh. My. God. I was in shock. How did this happen? I put the note inside the envelope it came in and left it on the foyer table. The four dresses they sent me were *gorgeous*. Each had a tag: 49, 50, 51, and 52. I assumed they were the looks' numbers as they rolled out on the runway.

Two of the dresses came in a lighter watermelon color with various beaded prints. One had an orange beaded tiger with blue, white, and black touches of color with floral accents all around. The other one had a beaded floral pattern in shades of pale blue and orange.

These dresses' silhouette was similar: short, fitted bodice, straight neckline with inch and a half wide straps, with a slightly asymmetrical hem, and subtle triangular cut-outs mid ribcage.

The other two dresses were short too and of a bright watermelon color. They both had an asymmetrical one-shoulder design, but the prints and textures of them were slightly different. They were all beautiful.

Too bad I didn't have any plans to celebrate my birthday.

☾

Mimi's food was delicious, as always. I sat to eat as she drank a cup of coffee with me. The caffeine was doing wonders for my hangover. She asked me a lot of difficult questions about everything that happened. She mostly wanted to know how I was fairing after Caleb's death. She knew how close we were. But talking to her was always easy.

I was glad to see she was okay.

We cleared the table, and the doorbell rang once again. Since it was almost noon, I thought it might be Nathan.

"Hey!" Lily shouted. "I'm back!" She hugged me tightly, and I hugged her back. It was great to see her. "What is *this*!"

Lily gaped as she walked toward the rack with the dresses. She browsed slowly through them with wide eyes.

"Who sent these?" she asked. "Was it …?" Lily jerked her

head to the left toward William's apartment.

"Oh! No, no, he didn't send these." I grabbed the envelope and showed it to Lily. "Go ahead," I said with a nod. She opened it and read the note.

"This is *insane*!" She placed the note back inside the envelope and gave it back to me.

"I know, right? It's—weird. I wasn't expecting this at all," I said. Lily went back to looking at the dresses. "Do you want one?"

"What? No! Of course not. They're all yours."

"I know, but you've given me a few bags and—"

"Billie, these are yours, okay? Now we have to figure out when to use them."

"But these two are so similar. Please, take one. Besides, it was thanks to you that Enzio de Luca agreed to dress me up for the premiere in the first place."

"Well … it wasn't *all* because of me," she confessed.

"What do you mean?"

"Billy, he"—Lily snorted and continued—"he's the one who requested it, and you know how it is. They never say no to him. Are you mad? I'm sorry."

"No, of course not," I replied. I don't know why I didn't think of that before. It had William written all over it. And him casually being there for the fitting … not an accident either.

I walked over to the rack and grabbed the two bright watermelon-colored dresses. "Choose one right now, or we can't be friends anymore." I laughed.

"I'm not going to put our friendship at risk." Lily laughed too. "Ah—this one." She grabbed one of the dresses and hugged me. "It's beautiful, thank you. You really didn't have to." She hung it back on the rack. "Now, which one are *you* going to wear for your birthday celebration? Tomorrow's the big day! We need to decide where we're going and make a reservation."

"Um—I don't want to go out. I think it's best if I just stayed home for this one."

"Billie, not again with this. You're turning *twenty-one*," she grumbled. "We could go to a bar or a club. I'm sure Joel can help us find a place with one of those private areas where we can celebrate."

I stared at her, thinking how to get out of it. She was the sweetest. I knew she cared about me and wanted to celebrate my birthday, but I wasn't in the mood at all.

"Come on! I'll take care of everything. You just need to choose a dress," she insisted.

"I'm sorry, Lily," I said with a frown. "Why don't you and Joel come over tonight? We'll open a bottle of wine, and we'll plan something casual for tomorrow, maybe dinner somewhere. Just the four of us."

"Sounds good. Whatever you want, okay?" She smiled a heartwarming smile that let me know that all she wanted to do was make me feel better. And I was thankful for it. For her. But I just couldn't pretend that I was in the right headspace to go out and party. "You miss him, don't you?"

Always.

I sighed. "Yeah, all the time."

"Is that why you don't want to celebrate?" she asked. Lily always knew how to pull the truth out of me. But I looked away, refusing to answer her question, afraid I would start crying. "You know Caleb would want you to be happy, right? You don't have to punish yourself like that. None of it was your fault."

Then why does it feel like it is?

"I know, Lily. But it's not even been a month since Caleb died. And I'll be out partying? It doesn't feel right."

"Look, I totally get it. And I respect your decision. But it's not fair for you to beat yourself up like that. We all love you and want to celebrate your birthday because we could've lost you too that day. And thank goodness we didn't."

"It does make me happy to know you want to make me feel special on my birthday. But it's too soon."

"Okay," she said with a smile. "Why don't we—try these on?" She grabbed one of the dresses and placed it against her body, moving her eyebrows up and down.

"Sure," I replied. It sounded like fun.

The doorbell rang when Lily and I started pushing the rack to my bedroom. It was a bit past noon already. "Coming!"

I opened the door, and it was *not* Nathan.

CHAPTER 11

Zara

"SURPRISE!" ZARA SQUEALED with excitement and threw her arms around mine. "I'm so happy to finally meet you, Billie." She pulled away, grabbing my shoulders. "I'm *obsessed* with your hair." She reached out and touched one of my short, auburn strands. Aaron was standing behind her with her luggage.

Zara looked *drop-dead gorgeous*. She was even taller than Lily, and her long brown waves danced around her beautiful face. And her broad, luminous smile was almost blinding. Just by looking at her, you could tell she was different—special.

Smile back.

"Zara?" Lily rushed over to greet her with a big smile on her face. I thanked Aaron and rolled Zara's suitcase inside my apartment as they hugged each other.

"Nathan told me I should knock at your door since Will's at some *bloody* meeting. It's rather convenient that you guys live next to each other," she said with a chuckle. "But I'll get out of your way as soon as he arrives, no worries. I hope you don't mind me waiting here, Billie."

Will. Zara had to have her own little nickname for him. And she didn't know she was staying with me. Yet. I guess Nathan *forgot* to mention that part.

And speaking of Nathan …

"Zara!" he yelled as he stepped out of the elevator. His face lit up as he marched our way. Zara closed the distance between them, and they met halfway with a warm hug.

"Aw, Nate, I've missed you!" Zara seemed like the untroubled, happy-go-lucky kind of girl. Her personality shone from a mile away.

"I see you met Billie," he said, looking at me, beaming. He seemed thrilled to see her.

"I certainly did," she replied with a grin, nudging Nathan's arm with her elbow. "I already told her I'd leave once Will arrives."

"About that," Nathan said, closing the door behind him. "I thought it might be best for you to stay here with Billie. She's got a spare room, and that way, you could get to know each other better."

I glanced at Lily, and her eyes went wide for a second. I wished I could communicate with her telepathically. Well, we sort of did. I knew what she was thinking, but I didn't know if she knew what *I* was thinking. She probably did.

"Oh, nonsense," she replied with her crisp British accent, waving a relaxed hand at him. "I wouldn't want to impose. I'll be fine with Will."

She rummaged through her bag, took out a brand-new pack of cigarettes, and tapped it on the palm of her hand a few times.

Ooh, cigarettes.

"Ciggie?" Zara waved the box around. "Anyone?" She shrugged at the silence.

"I'll have one," I said, swallowing down my pride. A part of me didn't want to cave into Zara's charm; to like her. What if I grew fond of her? And what if seeing her with William was painful? That's why I needed a smoke.

"Why don't we go to the rooftop?" I suggested. "We can't smoke in here."

"Let's go, sis," she said, placing an arm around my shoulders. Zara calling me *sis* hit me like a clean jab to the gut. For several reasons. "You guys coming?"

"Yes," Nathan said with a sour face. Dealing with Zara wasn't going to be easy. It took me three ridiculous minutes to realize how strong-willed of a woman she was. She wasn't one to take orders from anyone. I'm sure Nathan knew that too, and probably the reason why the exasperation began to draw on his face.

"I've got some things to do right now," Lily said. "But I'll call you later."

She grabbed the dress I gifted her after I reminded her to take it. Then, we all walked together toward the elevator and stepped in when it arrived.

"I won't let you go to sleep until the clock hits midnight, okay?" Lily approached me for a hug when the elevator stopped at her floor. "I want to be the first one to wish you a happy birthday, even if Nathan objects."

"I'd like to see you beat me to it," he played along, holding the door.

"It was nice seeing you, Zara," Lily said to her. "I'll see you around."

"Likewise."

Lily walked away after a quick wave of her hand, and the elevator shot up to the fourteenth floor.

"So, tomorrow's your birthday?" Zara asked with a raised brow. I nodded with a tight smile. "Twenty-one?"

"Mhm. You're twenty-one, too, right?"

"I am. My birthday is in February," she replied.

We moved out of the elevator, and she lit up a cigarette as we climbed the flight of stairs to the rooftop. Smoking wasn't allowed inside the building, but again, she wasn't one to follow the rules.

Nathan pushed the heavy door and held it for us as we stepped on the rooftop. Zara gave me a cigarette and lit it up for me.

Oh, yes.

"I'll have one too, please," Nathan joined in. Zara smiled and tossed him the box. Nathan took a cigarette out, and Zara helped him with the lighter.

I walked toward the far end of the rooftop, and they both followed me. It'd been months since I last came up here. Memories flooded my mind. So many things had happened in this place. And then I realized it was the first time I'd come up here with Nathan.

"And do you have any plans for today or tomorrow? I'd love to celebrate with you," Zara said, taking a slow puff.

"About that," Nathan intervened. "I didn't know how to tell you, love, but Mr. Chapman wants me to attend an important dinner with a big client tonight since he won't be able to make it. It's a rather fancy event, and since you've mentioned a few times how you don't want to celebrate your birthday, I was wondering if you want to come with me."

"You're *mad*!" Zara said to him. "Will and I can take her out someplace fun while you go to your corporate zombie event." Zara lifted her brows a few times. "You can catch up with us once you're done. I'm sure Lily, Joel, and Tobias would love to come along. Does Eric have a fake ID? I guess we can find a way to sneak him in."

Zara needed to be sat down for a briefing. It worried me how oblivious she was to everything. Didn't Zara know about Nathan and William's conflicted relationship?

Nathan took a long, steady whiff of his cigarette as he stared at Zara.

"I don't think that's a good idea," I said to her as a chilly spring breeze swirled around us. "I—I'm not in the mood for a big party, but thank you. Really."

"Oh, that's okay, Billie. I get it." Zara licked her lower lip with a frown and took another puff.

"So, would you like to come with me?" Nathan asked again.

"Yes, of course," I replied. I kissed Nathan's cold cheek and rested my face on the warmth of his chest for a second.

Zara's phone rang, and she took the call in Swedish, but I heard the name *Will* a few times. *That nickname is going to drive me nuts.* She tucked her phone back into her jeans pocket and took another smoke out of the box, lighting it up with the last burn of her current cigarette.

She offered me another, but I still had around half of mine left.

Nathan dropped his cigarette stub on the floor and grabbed another.

"Zara, I want you to stay with Billie," Nathan said after she lit him up. He took the first puff and leaned back on the rooftop's railing, releasing the smoke to the side, crossing his arms at his chest.

"I don't mind staying with Billie, but I want to spend more time with William," she said with a *don't fuck with me* kind of face. And for some reason, it stung more to hear *William* coming out of her mouth with that edge. Like she owned the name. "There's a ton of things we need to do and talk about, and I don't want to use Billie's apartment like a hotel. I'd rather stay with him."

Nathan shook his head and bit his lower lip with an irritated smile.

"You'll stay with Billie," he said with a glacial tone, pointing at her with his cigarette.

Zara snorted, and a shameless smirk etched itself on her face.

"The last thing I need is *another* father, Nate," she snapped back. "Besides, don't you want privacy? I will only be in your way."

Zara glanced at me. Was she expecting me to participate in this conversation? I would rather eat my cigarette. Besides, I don't think she would agree with my opinions. It was best to keep them to myself.

"It's a two-bedroom apartment. We have all the privacy we need," Nathan retorted.

Well, about that ...

"I'm staying with *him*," she said matter-of-factly, looking Nathan straight in the eye.

Jesus. I guess that settled things. She would make a good lawyer, just like Nathan. She could use that determination for acting too.

The rooftop's door shut with a loud thud, startling me. Zara and Nathan couldn't have been any less bothered by it. They were busy glaring at each other, but Zara's gaze had gone round and sad while Nathan's was still feeding on fire.

"Zara!" William shouted from afar with a thousand-kilowatt smile. Zara turned around, flicked her cigarette to the side, and dashed up to William, whose long stride had almost reached us.

"Will!" He took her in his arms, hugging her with the same enthusiasm with which she embraced him. He kissed her hair, and they walked in our direction, chatting in Swedish.

What the fuck. These guys were practically engaged.

"Hey," I replied curtly. I took one last puff of my cigarette. It had almost hit the filter, but I wanted to annoy William by doing so. I turned to the side, blew out the smoke, and flicked it away. He pressed his lips together and glanced at Zara.

"*Har du rökt?*" William addressed Zara with his special deep timbre that only came up when he spoke Swedish, his brows lowering.

"*Ja.*"

"*Jag tycker inte om det,*" he replied to her, glancing at me for a quick second. *What?*

"I don't like you smoking either," Nathan said to her. Oh. I knew Nathan wasn't a fan of seeing me smoke, but he knew I hadn't picked up the habit. It was a little something I reserved for special occasions such as these. That's why he never said a thing to me about it. Besides, it'd been months since I last had a smoke.

On the other hand, I could ruin William's week just by holding a cigarette. I knew that much.

"You can't tell me *not* to smoke when you're holding one in between your fingers," she said to Nathan with a snort. "And *you* need to fucking relax." She poked William playfully in the chest, and I wished I had enrolled in that Stress Management Meditation course Nina offered a few months ago because all it took was one of Zara's fingers touching William to destabilize me.

"Can I have another?" I asked Zara. Unfortunately, these were the tools I had to cope with the situation.

"Sure, sis," she chirped, pulling another cigarette out.

William laughed softly as Zara lit up my cigarette. "I'm so glad you too are getting along so well," he said with a smug face.

My blood boiled at his cynicism.

"I need to talk to Zara in private," Nathan said abruptly. "Would you mind, love?"

"No, of course not. Not at all."

"Let's go," he said to her, jerking his head. She put her cigarette out and nodded with a sigh as in, *let's do this thing.*

"I'll meet you guys later," I told Nathan, lifting my cigarette. I wasn't planning on putting a good cigarette out. "Mimi's home. Just knock."

"I'll keep her company," William said, the corners of his

mouth slightly lifting, his hands moving inside his pockets.

Nathan snorted. "Whatever," he said, kissing my cheek. "I'll see you in a bit."

They both walked away, and the door shut behind them with a bang.

"So that's Zara," William said. "Your *sis*." He laughed again. He plucked the cigarette out of my fingers and tossed it away.

"Hey! I'd just lit that up!"

"I *hate it* when you smoke that garbage," he said, taking a sharp breath in through his nose. "You're just like Zara. Stubborn, unruly. You'll get along perfectly well."

"I don't think I'm rebellious."

William snorted. "Oh, you *are* älskling. You're just being restrained. But that itch you feel inside you, urging you to be set free, will only grow stronger with time. Fast. I've told you before. You won't live like that forever. You can't. You'll explode one day if you do."

I'd forget how well William knew me. The things I'd shared with him in the last year were enough for him to understand the hidden desires of my heart.

Freedom.

"Yeah, well, it seems to me like I'm far away from breaking free from my father's grip," I said in a bitter tone. "After what happened"—I shook my head a few times—"he'll never back down."

"You're just scared," he said, taking a step forward.

"I'm—I'm not."

"You are."

I hated how William taking a simple step in my direction could alter my body's chemical composition. I *hated* it.

"Let's go for a pre-birthday ride. I'll get the Porsche," he said. "We'll sneak out." He was dead serious.

"You're *insane*." The kind of insane that called my attention. "And should you be driving? You're still recovering from surgery." I turned around and leaned against the railing, looking down at how hundreds of cars drove around the city.

"Your guys will catch up with us, of course, eventually," he added, standing beside me. "And Dr. Lindström didn't mention anything about driving, although he did ask me to refrain from other ... bedroom activities. For a while." He smiled, and I focused my attention on counting cars.

He *was* insane. For a number of reasons. And him not being allowed to have sex by medical instruction was music to my ears. I hoped he would communicate that to my *sis* as soon as possible.

"But what about Zara? Won't she get jealous?" I taunted him. Trying to measure the situation. "And Nathan ... I don't think you want to mess with him right now."

William stood behind me and grabbed my shoulders. My body tensed up, my lungs resigned, and the smell of him that close to me was going to be the end of me. He leaned in and whispered in my ear, "The only person who's jealous ... is you. And you don't have to be jealous of your *sis*. We're just friends. Trust me."

He released me, and I took a deep, ragged breath. I heard him chuckle behind me.

Trust—my personalized brand of kryptonite.

I'd learned from experience that I *could* trust him, but he kept throwing these challenging situations at me. Things that made it very hard for me *not* to react—to doubt. And the fact that I couldn't just ask directly about it was even more exasperating.

Besides, he spoke for himself, but I didn't know a thing about Zara's heart. What if she was madly in love with him? In secret. Or maybe it wasn't a secret, and he knew already.

I turned around to face him, and he pulled his cell phone

out of the back pocket of his jeans. He clicked on his phone and lifted it to his ear, looking at me.

"Cooper ... Hi, could you bring over my car, please ... Great ... I'll meet you downstairs in ten ... Thanks, man."

He ended the call and placed his phone back into his pocket.

"Last chance. Are you coming?" he asked. I wished I could allow myself to do so. "It'll be the most fun you ever had in your life. I promise you that."

I believed him. And he was right. A part of me was dying to break loose. To jump in that car and have William drive me as far away as possible just to feel the thrill of it. It was a matter of time before my mind started begging me to do something like that.

"If it were a '65 Mustang Convertible. I'd say yes," I challenged him.

"In what color do you see this car?" he asked, amused, smiling ... *beautiful*.

"Red, of course."

"I'll let you know when I get my hands on one." He winked at me, turned around, and walked away. "I can't promise to take long enough for you to sort that stubborn mind of yours! So hurry up with that!"

"I was kidding!" I yelled to his back with a laugh.

He grabbed the door handle and turned around with a smirk to shout, "No, you were not!"

Yeah, I wasn't.

CHAPTER 12

Single Child

I LINGERED A WHILE longer on the rooftop, alone, enjoying the stillness of it. No Zara and Nathan arguing, no William tempting me to escape my security with him … no drama. Just me and my thoughts. As if they weren't like a turbulent storm at sea. But I was used to it—the structured chaos inside my head.

My phone buzzed in my pocket as I picked up the multiple cigarette stubs we left on the floor and disposed of them on the rooftop's trash bin. I took my phone out to see who it was.

Lily: Joel talked to Nathan. He told me about that boring dinner you guys have tonight. Could we at least see each other tomorrow? I'll bring cake and some of those almond croissants you love. Just a cozy celebration at your place.
Me: I know, sorry! His boss asked him to go, so it's kind of a big deal. I like your plan for tomorrow. I'll text you in the morning, ok?
Lily: Sounds good! Have fun tonight.

A loud *vroom* flooded the air from below. I leaned against the railing and looked down.

Black Porsche.

A smile appeared on my face. I welcomed it.

William sped off with a screech of his tires, and I thanked

Odin I hadn't participated in William's crazy plan. I'm sure I'd be screaming by now. Probably laughing too, wanting to cry a little as I begged him to slow down, but enjoying the thrill. He'd be ignoring me, as always, and doing whatever the hell he wanted to do. And I'd be secretly enjoying it.

I couldn't help but laugh as I imagined a bunch of made-up scenarios in my mind.

William's a wild soul, and I guess that's why I was so drawn to him, because I *craved* that for myself. To hell with safe. Give me an untamed and unadulterated path.

But he vanished from my view in seconds. And with him, the cloud of dreams and the adrenaline that rushed through my veins out of pure speculation. Speculation about what that ride with him would've looked like. Where he'd planned on taking me, how long it would have taken for my security to realize I was gone—to catch up with us.

A cold gust of wind slapped me in the face.

Wake up.

Suddenly, the day got too chilly, so I sauntered to my apartment, dragging my thoughts back with me and a mild headache that kept throbbing on my temples from the wine I drank last night.

Taking ibuprofen in the morning would've been a great idea, but no. That's how I rolled. Always thinking I was strong enough to deal with shit on my own. Sometimes you just need to take the damn pill.

I took my time with every stride, giving Zara and Nathan as much time as I could give them. I knew they needed to sort a few things out, and I'd rather not be present when they did. It was too uncomfortable to witness. And there wasn't much I could do to help.

C

Nathan and Zara sat on the living room couch when I unlocked the apartment and walked in. They were still talking. Nathan lifted his hand and waved it in a quick move. They seemed chill so I approached them.

"Hey, you," I said, taking a seat next to Nathan. "Are you guys done, or do you need a few more minutes? I could go to my bedroom if—"

"We're done, love," Nathan muttered, placing his hand on my thigh, kneading it a few times. Zara glanced at me and smiled. It was a different kind of smile. Sympathetic? I wondered what Nathan and Zara had talked about. But whatever it was, they both seemed exhausted by it.

Zara's luggage was still sitting in the foyer, staring at me. I didn't know what that meant. Was she taking it inside my guest bedroom? Was she waiting for William to come back? Should I ask?

No need.

"Zara will be staying with William." Nathan cleared things up for me in a neutral tone. I guess he'd exhausted all the fire when talking things through with Zara—or yielding to her, from what I could tell. "I'll go home, take a shower, and meet you here in about a couple of hours or so. Does that work for you, love?"

"Ah … yes. Yes, of course," I replied. I was so buried in my thoughts that for a second there I lost Nathan. I couldn't stop thinking about how Zara was staying over with William.

As much as he implied nothing was going on between them, I couldn't stand the thought of them together every night, waking up and having coffee in their pajamas, or William making her breakfast because let's be real, he *was* going to cook for her at some point. Shit. I couldn't deal with that.

I didn't care if they were *just friends*. It hurt to watch when *I* couldn't even be his friend. I was nothing. A neighbor. And she was reaping off all the benefits.

My temporary solution consisted of smiling at Zara and Nathan. I could slosh in a pool of my bitterness in the comfort of my bedroom. Behind closed doors. Because I couldn't allow myself to show any emotion regarding Zara's decision—*obstination*—to stay with William during her visit.

Nathan got up, kissed the top of my head, and left after saying goodbye to Zara and me.

"Ugh!" Zara blurted out with exasperation, throwing herself flat on the couch as soon as Nathan walked out.

"What's wrong?" I coaxed myself to ask. We needed to be able to talk to each other.

"Is Nathan as controlling with you as he is with me?" she asked, glancing at me from the horizontal angle at which she found herself.

"He's—not, actually. He's great," I said. Something shrunk inside my gut. A reminder of what a great guy Nathan was. He loved me, cared for me, made me feel safe. And here I was all messed up in the head because of William. *But he's great too.*

Zara took a deep breath and let it out with a sigh. "You should get ready for that boring event Nathan's making you go. What are you planning to wear?" She sat up straight and shot up from her seat. "What about those pretty dresses?"

Zara walked over to the rack and scanned them. She grabbed one and held it flush against her body, looking down at herself. "These are pretty. I bet they love you at Enzio de Luca after helping them sell a ton of those blush pink pantsuits," she said. "And everything William touches … it turns into gold. But don't get me wrong, you looked great." She glanced at me with a lifted brow.

"How do you—"

"Oh, I"—she laughed as she returned the dress to the rack—"read the note." She tilted her head toward the foyer table where I'd left the envelope. "And I saw the pictures of the event, too. I wish I could've been there with you guys. Too bad Nathan couldn't be there either, but you seemed to be having a lot of fun."

There you go. Just friends, my ass.

Zara just admitted to seeing the photographs of William and me at the premiere. I still didn't know if Nathan had seen them, but I wasn't going to ask him. If he hadn't mentioned anything about them, then I guess he hadn't.

I wondered if Zara was jealous. I couldn't tell if she was trying to be chatty or polite or if there was any underlying intention in her conversation with me. Figuring that out would be my next mission if I chose to accept it. *Don't.*

"You should wear this tonight," she said, grabbing the dress with the beaded tiger. "Nathan's gonna *drool.*"

I stood up and walked up to her. "Do you think something like this is appropriate for tonight?"

"This is Enzio de Luca. It's appropriate for anything you want. For Nathan's boring dinner or a picnic at the park." She laughed. "Besides, it's your birthday at midnight, and you get to do whatever the fuck you want. Huh. That kinda rhymed."

It did.

I wasn't sure if I was getting tricked, but I took her word for it.

"I'm going to take a shower. Do you need anything? Something to eat or drink?" I offered. "Please make yourself at home."

"Actually, I'm a bit hungry. Is it okay if I just grab something from your kitchen? I could order something too."

"Of course. Mimi's here. She'll be glad to cook something for you. I'll go talk to her."

"Thanks, Billie." She smiled.

I found Mimi in the kitchen and brought her over to meet Zara. Mimi smiled at me and guided Zara to the kitchen where I knew she'd take good care of her. Then, I grabbed the tiger dress and brought it with me to my bedroom.

It was my second shower of the day, but this felt like a necessary one. I wanted to take the smell of smoke off me and William's stupid cologne out of my nostrils.

Styling my short hair was more complicated than my long, boring hair. I missed it. I liked the short hair too, but I had cut it on an impulse. However, the freeing sensation I experienced when Frankie cut it had been amazing.

I decided to blow-dry it, attempting to make it slightly wavy and parted in the middle. I dabbed a bit of peachy blush on my cheeks and cherry lipstick on my lips.

Wearing a coat would be necessary because I was destined to freeze my ass off on the way there if I didn't. I could always take it off once I arrived. This wasn't the kind of dress that was made to hide behind a coat.

I walked out of my bedroom wearing my cozy, knee-length robe because I wanted to change until the last minute when I knew Nathan would be almost here. Zara sat in the dining room, her plate empty, her hands on her phone, her attention on the screen.

"Wow! Looking great, sis," Zara said, looking up at me. I was back to being her *sis*. Surely the food agreed with her. I swear I sensed an edge to her words before when she mentioned the premiere photographs.

While I showered, I thought about two options. She was either jealous of the misleading shots of William and me or being protective of Nathan. I didn't blame her for either of those two possibilities. There was a third scenario that was basically an entanglement of the previous two.

But I was sure something bothered her.

The doorbell rang, and Zara fired up from her seat. I walked toward the door, but she flew past me and said, "It's Will. I got it—*coming*!"

Zara opened the door, and William stared at me with a lifted brow. My hands moved to the flaps of my robe just to make sure everything was where it had to be.

"Glad to see you're back in one piece," I said to him. Maybe getting him to talk would stop him from staring at me like that. "I heard your engine roaring all the way to the rooftop."

It worked. He laughed.

"The engine feels great when you're sitting inside the car," he replied, brushing a golden strand off his forehead. Zara pushed her suitcase with a frown, rolling it abruptly toward William. He stopped it with a foot and lifted the handle. "Easy, tiger."

Zara rolled her eyes at him. "Let me grab my backpack," she said, heading toward the living room. "What took you so long? I need to take a shower and get dressed if we want to be on time," she complained.

"Any—fun plans for tonight?" I asked, already bothered by the obvious fact.

"Ah, yes." William looked away, his golden-brownish brows moving up and down, seeming uncomfortable. As if he would rather not answer my question. He pointed at Zara and said, "I need to tire her out."

"Funny," she said, unamused. "Let's go. See you around, Billie. Have fun tonight." Zara approached me for a hug that I wasn't expecting and left. It was clear that she was in a hurry to leave.

William nodded, held the doorknob, and pulled it to close the door, but he stopped a second before shutting it.

He parted his mouth to speak, looking at the floor. He smiled and looked up at me, meeting my gaze, no, trespassing it.

"Aren't you gonna *hike up* that robe?"

I shook my head with a smile. How to forget?

"Never," I said with a laugh.

"Never say never." He dropped the suitcase's handle for a second, brushed his lip, and rushed out to roll my *sis's* luggage after Zara shouted his name, leaving me to wonder how *the fuck* would I sleep at night for the next week that she'd be around. Not that I was getting much sleep anyway.

I didn't understand how to handle this sister dynamic. I thrived as a single child.

$$\mathsf{C}$$

Nathan texted me to let me know he was running late, so I grabbed a book and took it to my bedroom. But I couldn't read a single word because all I heard was Zara laughing through the wall. And the sound wasn't as far away as I would've liked it to be. She was inside William's bedroom for sure.

A thousand minutes later of me staring at the same page of my book, I heard a few doors shutting and then ... silence.

They left. Together. *To tire her out,* William said. I'm sure they were going to some fancy party or some shit like that. And I only dreaded the moment when the night would eventually come, and they returned to William's apartment. Again, together.

Maybe I could sleep in the guest bedroom this week—anything to avoid listening to their interactions a wall away.

Out of the blue, I was reminded of Caleb's letter. It was right there beside me inside my nightstand drawer. Pulsing. Waiting for me to read it. My hand moved involuntarily to open the drawer as I contemplated reading it.

Another text from Nathan popped up on my screen, making me shut the drawer. It wasn't the time to read it. I'd need an entire weekend alone to do so, and Nathan was on his way. I stood up from the bed and wished I could stay here instead as I took my robe off.

The dress was beautiful, and it fitted me perfectly. It was heavy from all the beading but not as much to make it uncomfortable. Just enough to remind you that you're wearing a piece of art as clothing.

I put my shoes on and sprayed perfume behind my ears, neck, and on my wrists. The doorbell rang, and I grabbed my purse, quickly filling it with my stuff.

Mimi greeted Nathan when I walked toward the foyer. They both turned to look at me.

"Oh my—wow," Nathan said. "You look absolutely stunning." He approached me with a grin and ran his hand around my waist, kissing my cheek next.

"I agree," Mimi said with a chuckle. She excused herself after telling us to have a good time.

Nathan wore a black suit with a deep burgundy tie. He looked so handsome and smelled delicious.

"Do you think this dress is okay for the occasion? Zara said it was, but I didn't ask you about—"

"It's *perfect*."

"You don't think it's too short?"

"I do, and I love it." He laughed, and I shoved his shoulder playfully. "I'm kidding. I already said it's perfect." He ran his hand up my thigh. "See? Perfect."

"Let's go," I begged. I didn't need much convincing to skip this event. "We're already running late."

"To be continued," he said with a genuinely cheeky smile, taking my hand. I grabbed my coat on our way out, and as I was locking the door, he pushed my hair to the side and kissed my neck; once, twice, he wasn't stopping.

"Hey," I said, turning around. "Remember we've got HAL9000 looking at us." I jerked my chin at the surveillance camera.

Nathan laughed. "It's Saturday night," he said, his lips a breath away from mine. "Let the poor guy watching have some entertainment. He must be bored to death watching your door all day."

"It only gets triggered when there's unusual movement, and I fear this might classify as such." I gave him a quick peck on the lips to cheer him up. "Or if you want to jump ship, I'll be glad to stay here with you all night."

"I'd love that too, but unfortunately, we have to go. I'm all in for an afterparty later tonight, though," he replied, kissing my lips back. He glanced at his watch and said, "Shit. We *are* running late. Let's go."

Aaron, David, and Amena were already waiting for us downstairs and had the engine going. Looking at Amena always made my stomach churn. She was Caleb's replacement and a daily reminder that he was gone. Fuck, I missed him.

I had to remind myself to breathe at a steady pace to avoid drifting into that dark place in my mind that usually sucked me in at the most unexpected of moments. And it's not like it asked for my permission to do so.

"You okay, love?" Nathan said as we stepped inside the car.

"Yeah, it's just—" I trailed off intentionally. It was the only way to prevent myself from crying.

"Caleb?" he whispered. I nodded. "You miss him."

"I—do. But ... Why don't you tell me more about this dinner we're going to? Is it going to be super boring?" I asked, trying to get into a different headspace.

"You have no idea."

Perfect. Just what I needed.

☾

We drove all the way down to the Financial District and parked a few feet away from Battery Park right outside Cipriani. I'd never been to this place.

"Okay, we're here," Nathan said, unwilling to release my hand. There was a lot of security at the place. More than a few guys in suits stood outside, guarding the entrance—not an unusual sight for me. It reminded me of Paris.

"What's Big Mike doing here?" I wondered.

"Oh, I forgot to tell you. Your father is invited to this dinner. That means he's arrived."

Oh.

Amena and David followed close behind while Aaron stopped to talk to Big Mike. One of the guys posted at the entrance opened the door for us, and we walked right in. The place was pitch-dark and creepy as hell.

"Where is everybody?" I asked, looking up at the dimly lit, triple-height, vaulted ceilings. But the faint glow showering the architectural masterpiece above us didn't do much to light our way moving forward. I was afraid I would stumble.

And before Nathan could reply, the whole place came to life at once, and what felt like a thousand people screamed, "Surprise!" I covered my mouth with shock. I didn't even know that many people.

I turned to Nathan and whispered, "You said it was going to be super boring."

"No. I said you had no idea."

Damn, I was an easy target.

CHAPTER 13

Another Surprise Party

NATHAN WRAPPED HIS ARMS around me and said, "Come on, love. Everyone's waiting for you." He took my hand and pulled me toward the party. I took a deep breath because I didn't know how I felt about this. A part of me was upset because I clearly said I *didn't* want to celebrate. And I had a specific reason for that.

Caleb.

It didn't sit right with me to celebrate, and on such a grand scale, when he was gone because of me. His family was still mourning back in Israel. *I* was still dealing with the pain.

Yet another part of me understood all Nathan tried to do was cheer me up, that there wasn't any ill intention of planning the party. And I knew that, but it didn't make it any less uncomfortable for me to deal with the polarized feelings inside me.

It was all too much to take in.

The place was beautifully decorated. Modern lounge furniture with golden throw pillows on each side of the space created a wide corridor in the middle where golden cocktail tables and stools with black leather seats were arranged in a diamond-shaped pattern.

At the far end, a low, wide, black wooden dais was filled with every instrument you could think of. They all rested on their respective stands. There were a couple of microphones too.

To the left of the stage, a DJ played house music from his illuminated booth.

A massive bar with more than a handful of servers coming and going was set up against the wall to the right. And a few rectangular tables with black tablecloths were placed against the left wall. Nathan told me that's where the food would be served.

I was about to ask about the food, but Nathan said I'd have to wait and see.

God. This could've easily been a wedding if a bride and groom were to walk in.

Almost everyone I knew was here. Familiar faces popped up everywhere. I spotted the entire Sjöberg family scattered around the place, including their parents, Sivert and Nathalie, who were on opposite sides of each other.

I couldn't find William, though. He had to be around because Zara was here too, chatting with Sivert and Tobias. But I hadn't seen him yet.

At least I was glad to know that *this* was the place William had brought Zara to "tire her out." However, I wasn't too sure if I wanted to witness how that happened.

Nolan, Emily, Ben, Heather, and other friends from Parsons chatted over drinks in the lounge area. Even Bryce was here. She was going to flip with the Sjöbergs, or maybe she'd already flipped. Her eyes looked big and round, so yeah, she'd probably seen them.

CJ, Nina, and Ren sat together at one of the cocktail tables and waved hello when I spotted them. On the table next to them, Alice and Luna sat with their drinks while they chatted.

Everyone looked so elegant, and there were many people I didn't recognize too, probably invited to fill out the place because it was *huge*. But before I was done scanning the guests, my father approached me.

"Kiddo!" He held me tight around his arms. "I know you didn't want to celebrate, but it's your twenty-first birthday. We *had* to do something about it."

We? I wasn't sure yet about who'd been in charge of planning the surprise party.

"It's okay, Dad. Thank you for all of this," I said, hugging him back. "But next year, I won't be surprised anymore if you do this again. You've lost the surprise factor." We both laughed.

Our relationship had been bumpy in the past few months, but I was glad to see him.

"I know. I promise we'll do whatever you want on your birthday next year, yes?"

I nodded. "So, who planned the party?"

"Well, it was Nathan's idea," he said, jerking his chin at him. I mouthed "thank you" to Nathan and squeezed his hand. "But then we all wanted to participate when he told us about it. I called in a favor to rent this space on such short notice. Lily jumped in to help Nathan organize everything. William's in charge of the food, wine, and music." *What!* "Alice, his assistant, helped out a lot too. She's a nice girl."

Wow.

A server approached us holding a camera when I was about to ask a follow-up question. She requested Nathan and me to hand in our phones and gave us a laminated number in return after we did.

"You'll be able to claim your phones on your way out with this number. Just hand it in to any of the servers," she explained. "And this is your camera, miss. We have an extra battery in the back for you if you run out of power." I thanked her, and Nathan offered to hold the camera for me.

"It's a phoneless party," Nathan explained.

"*You* handed in your phone?" I asked my father with skepticism. He laughed and said, "I did. It was Lily's idea."

"But she didn't want you to miss out on taking photographs," Nathan added. "So I stole this camera from you yesterday when I went down to your apartment to talk to Zara. We also rented out some Polaroid cameras so that the guests can take photographs. The servers will go around at some point with a small basket collecting any photographs that people want you to have."

That was the cutest idea *ever*!

"Wow. Thank you. I love it."

Yes, it all sounded great, but I still had doubts about it all being excessive. I wanted to be happy and excited, but I was having the hardest time doing so.

"And ... David's back with your birthday present, kiddo," my father said, looking over my shoulder with a smile. Sophie and Cecile had just walked inside the venue.

"What!" I shouted. Nathan told me he'd see me in a bit, and I dashed their way as fast as my shoes allowed me to and greeted them with the tightest hug. "Hey!"

Shit, I obviously started crying. For a thousand reasons.

When they visited in October, I was feeling down too, and seeing them had been very helpful, but that was *nothing* compared to how crushed I'd been the past few weeks. To how much I needed them this time. I was barely holding myself together.

Nathan had been a great support system, but he was busy all the time. His schedule went from hectic to insane. He wanted to get the big promotion to partner, and he kept promising how once he did, he wouldn't have to travel as much or work so late, but I had my doubts. I never complained about it, though. I knew he had to do whatever he had to do. He loved what he did, and I was happy for him.

"I'm so sorry, Billie," Cecile said. "I wished we could've come before when Caleb—"

"I know. It's okay." I patted my face carefully to remove the tears, trying not to mess with my makeup, but when I saw my fingers, they were stained with my smudged-up mascara. "Damn it."

Cecile walked away to get me a napkin.

"When did you guys arrive? And for how long are you staying?" I asked Sophie.

"Last night. We leave on Monday, and I know it sucks," she said. "We slept at a hotel yesterday, but we wondered if you wanted us to stay with—"

"Yes!" I said, almost desperately. "Stay with me."

Sophie laughed. I had to take advantage of Sophie and Cecile's express stay in New York. And I never thought I'd be thankful that Zara wasn't staying in my guest room.

"Yay!" Sophie squealed and clapped twice excitedly. Cecile came back with a napkin and helped me wipe the mascara off my lower lids.

"I think you're good now," Cecile said. "And no more crying, okay? We'll cry all day tomorrow if you want. But let's have some fun tonight. You deserve it. There's *nothing* wrong with celebrating your birthday, okay? Caleb would've wanted this."

As much as I hated to admit it, she was right. If I could somehow speak to Caleb right now, I knew he'd be pissed about seeing me moping around for him. He'd hate that and would definitely want me to have fun tonight. I *had* to get out of my head and enjoy the night.

The only way I could do that was by forcing myself to forget. And at the time, I didn't realize how wrong I was, but I was trying to cover up the pain with wine. And that's precisely what I had in mind for tonight.

"Okay, let's go." I linked my arms with theirs, and the three of us walked to meet my guests. "Ren's waiting for you," I whispered to Sophie.

"I know! We spent the entire day together. I miss him so much all the time. I don't want to leave!"

"I don't want you to leave either."

Ren and Sophie were trying the long-distance relationship thing. It was going as well as it could be expected. At least they made the most of it when they saw each other, which wasn't as often as they liked.

Cecile was still single. After breaking things off with Paul, she tried to deal with the heartbreak by partying hard and having a bunch of one-night stands. That's what Sophie told me once in confidence. She was a bit worried about her, but Cecile always liked to pretend like she was okay.

I could relate to that last pretending part.

And I didn't want to mention it, but Tobias was here. It was going to be hard for her to see him because it would remind her how she messed things up with Paul. But something told me Cecile liked Tobias. She was just too proud to admit it.

I could relate to that too.

Nathan chatted with Lily and Joel, and I wanted to say hi to them, so I told Sophie and Cecile that I'd be right back.

"Lily!" I sang with a laugh. She glanced at me, and I shook my head playfully. She wore the Enzio de Luca dress I gave her. "Are you considering a career in acting? You'd be a *terrific* actress."

She laughed as I hugged her. "I'm so sorry! Nathan was the one who gave me a script. He didn't want you to suspect at all. Was it worth it?"

"It was. I wasn't expecting any of this. But I'll be waiting for the almond croissants you promised to bring over tomorrow." I joked. "The dress looks great on you, by the way." *Obviously.*

"Thank you! I love the color. And yes ... You'll have the croissants tomorrow, I swear!"

I hugged Joel next. "Thank you for this," I told them. "You really didn't have to."

"Oh, we had to," Lily replied. "I wouldn't in a million years allow you to skip celebrating your twenty-first freaking birthday."

A server approached us with wine, and my eyes twinkled. *Yes, please.* That right there was the solution to my problems.

Lily and I grabbed a glass, but Nathan and Joel declined the wine and ordered "drinks for men," which was basically whiskey on the rocks.

Someone tapped my shoulder, and I turned around to see Tobias. "Billie!" He wrapped his arms around my waist and lifted me.

"Would you mind putting my girl down?" Nathan said with a laugh behind me. Tobias obeyed Nathan and replied something in Swedish. They laughed and shook hands with a loud clap and pulled themselves in for a few pats on the back. "Glad you could make it, mate."

"I thought you were still on the road promoting your new film," I told Tobias. I'd grown so fond of him lately. And I was so proud of him. His film was doing great at the box office. He was like the big brother I never had.

"I still am. We're almost done, though," Tobias said, sipping on his beer. "But I'll have to fly to L.A. first thing tomorrow morning. I'll probably have someone drag me straight to the airport because I ain't leaving until someone throws me out of here. And I *won't* let you sneak out either. Jordan! Hey, man!" Tobias shouted at some guy.

I turned around to see who Jordan was. "Is that—" I said in a whisper.

"Yes, it is," Tobias replied before I finished the question.

"Nathan's been doing a good job of getting you up to speed with your pop culture." He grinned. "I'll be right back, Billie."

I shook my head with a snort.

Jordan Schreiber starred in a movie with Joel. A movie Nathan and I watched a few months ago. He was good friends with the Sjöbergs. The guy had short, dark brown hair, light brown eyes, a tattoo sleeve on his left arm showing off from his black, short-sleeved, button up shirt.

He looked big and brawny, but not scary. I'd confirmed this fact after watching the film. His classically handsome face softened up the bad-boy look—a little.

Jordan was one of those guys that stood out in a crowd for sure. Bryce stared at him as she took a swig of her drink. Her eyes were about to pop out of her face. Nina and Cecile couldn't stop looking at him either as he strutted past them to reach Tobias.

I sipped on my wine and couldn't help but laugh a little. It was *delicious*, by the way. I had to ask William about it since apparently, he'd been the one in charge of that department.

Where the hell is he? I was surprised Nathan and William agreed to collaborate. I guess Nathan could use all the help he could get, being as busy as he usually was.

Nathan talked to Joel, so I hung out with my friends from school for a while. I entrusted Nolan with my camera and asked him if he could take a few shots whenever he felt like it. He was happy to do so.

Then I stopped by to say hi to CJ, Nina, and Ren, who were already chatting with Sophie and Cecile.

"Oh em gee! That dress is—*wow*, Billie." CJ scanned me from head to toe and stood up to twirl me. Nina agreed with CJ while Sophie giggled at CJ's theatrics. CJ grabbed the Polaroid camera on the table and took a selfie of Nina and me with him.

Nina wore a little black dress with a halter neckline, her

hair was longer now, and she wore it straight and parted in the middle. She had minimal makeup on and golden earrings. She looked *stunning*. I think it's the best I've seen her look. And I told her so immediately.

After we were done with the back-and-forth compliments, Nina said, "Everyone's saying there'll be a jazz band playing later tonight. I'm excited." That explained the varied instruments on the stage.

"Really?" I chuckled with a furrowed brow. "I have absolutely *no* idea of what's happening tonight."

"Hey, sis!" Zara said from behind me.

"Hey—sis!" I replied, turning around to see her—another stunner.

Damn.

Zara wore a tight, waist-high, midi pencil skirt in nude color and a short-sleeved cropped top with a boat-neck neckline in the same nude shade. A couple of diamond studs decorated her ears, and a thin golden chain with the letter *S* hung around her neck. Her long, brown waves flowed around her perfectly done face.

S for Saunders? Hopefully not Sjöberg. Probably both. Ugh.

She hugged me and said, "Aren't you going to introduce me to your friends."

"Oh, of course!" I broke away from her embrace. "Guys, this is Zara, Nathan's sister. Zara, this is Sophie and Cecile. They're my friends from Paris. They arrived yesterday."

"I've heard so much about you, Cecile," Zara said with a smirk.

"Nice to meet you, Zara," Cecile replied with a raised brow. My *sis* had a way of saying things to make it sound innocent when it always had an underlying meaning.

I saw Zara talking to Tobias before, so I guessed that he'd probably told her about Cecile. About what *happened* back in October.

"This is Ren and CJ," I said, gesturing at them with a hand-wave. "And this is Nina. They were the first friends I made when I came back to New York." CJ pulled me by the waist and laid a kiss on my cheek.

"Nice to meet you." Zara shook CJ and Nina's hand with a smile and said, "I'll see you guys around." And with that, she left. Probably looking for William.

CJ drained his martini and placed it back on the table. "She likes you," he said, raising his hand to catch the attention of one of the servers.

"Zara likes *who*?" I asked. *Not me.*

"She likes Nina."

"Oh, shut up!" Nina said with a laugh.

"Um—hi," CJ said to the server with a flirty smile. "Can I get another fifty-fifty, please, and … do you guys want anything else?"

"I'm good, thanks." Nina lifted her half-full glass of whiskey soda to make a point.

"Another glass of wine for me, please," I replied. I asked the server if he could bring me the bottle to see the label since William was nowhere to be found. Sophie and Cecile ordered more wine too. Ren was still working around his beer.

"Okay, so Zara likes *Nina*?" I asked CJ incredulously. CJ was misinformed. He loved the idea of everyone being a little gay, which always made me laugh. But he was so wrong about Zara. He didn't know the things I knew. Or seen the way she looked at him. Her attention was all focused on William, in my opinion. But his theories were always entertaining.

"Yeah, I'm never wrong about these things," CJ said, leaning back on his chair and crossing a leg over his knee. "And the platinum-blond baby Sjöberg? I've seen him looking at me funny. Like he wants to take a closer look, but he's afraid he'll like what he sees, you know what I mean?"

"*Eric?*" I asked with a grimace, turning around to find him. He was chatting with a couple of guys in the distance. Eric was getting taller. He was at that age where they change every six months. Still somewhat growing out of that awkward teenage phase. "I remember he had a crush on me when we first met. He was the cutest."

"Not everything's black or white, Billie," CJ replied. "Especially here in New York. I feel like most of us are fluid. That would be my advice for Nina this evening." He winked at her, and Nina rolled her eyes but glanced right to where Zara was as she took a sip of her drink, possibly wondering if the things CJ said might be true.

I wouldn't mind if it were, especially if Zara would want to *flow* toward Nina and away from William.

"So, you're saying you like girls too?" Cecile asked CJ. I had the same question.

"I mean, I wouldn't mind kissing you, for example," he replied to Cecile, who lifted a brow with a snort as a reply. "But yeah, I gravitate more toward men. Especially if they look like— *that.*" CJ brushed his nose as he scanned the server who brought our drinks back from head to toe.

CJ signaled the server to approach him and leaned in and whispered something in his ear, making him laugh. The guy walked away from the table, shaking his head with a grin.

"Miss Murphy," I heard from behind me. I turned around, startled, and saw David. His face tense, his jaw popping out, and his gaze burning.

Oh …

"Hey, David. Is everything okay?" I asked as CJ sat up straight in his seat and picked up his martini glass off the table, taking it to his lips.

"Just wanted to make sure everything's okay over here,"

he said, glaring at CJ. "And I also wanted to inform you that Amena's standing by in case you need to go to the ladies' room. She'll have to escort you."

I already knew that. Amena had been coming inside all public restrooms with me ever since I left the hospital. But I guess all David wanted was an excuse to approach the table.

"Mr. Jewel, may I have a word, please?" he said, looking at CJ, followed by a tiny, tiny smile.

I wouldn't want to be CJ right now. David must've seen him flirting with our server, and I didn't even know where David and CJ stood, but they had to be *something* enough to cause him to dart our way the second CJ did that.

CJ finished off his martini and made a face as he gulped the whole thing. He dropped the glass on the table and said with a big smile, "Maybe later, Dr. Scott?"

Doctor? I had to get a fact-check on that one later.

"Christopher," David said in a commanding voice. CJ tilted his head with a smirk and stared at David, who insisted on setting him aside to talk. "*Now.*"

"That's not fair. You know I love it when you get rough and feisty on me." CJ stood up. "I'll be right back, girls."

Ren made a face, and I laughed a little.

"You're one of us now," Nina teased.

"I see that," Ren replied, still chuckling. He then dropped a kiss on Sophie's lips. They were spilling honey all over the place. I was happy for them. But Cecile looked bored as hell. I had to fix that.

David and CJ walked away, and everyone turned silent on the table, noticing the apparent tension between them.

"Prom King has arrived," Nina said, breaking the silence. Sophie immediately looked around the place to see what Nina meant. Her eyes widened when she saw William. Sophie would forever be starstruck in William's presence. And damn … I was just in awe of him too.

He came walking out from one of the corridors holding a glass of red wine in his left hand and directing three servers who carried a big paella casserole each.

I covered my mouth in shock as I watched him instructing them what to do, how to place the things correctly on the table, making sure everything was perfect, I guess. But I lowered my hand from my face, attempting to appear normal again.

"Everything okay?" Nina chuckled as another server rushed out of the kitchen carrying two big baskets of bread. William patted one of the server's backs and glanced at me with the warmest smile I've ever seen on his face.

My mouth twitched up, and I turned around to take a long swig of my wine. "Ah, yeah. Why?" I replied to Nina a century later.

"Hmm," she hummed, pouting her lips to the side. "You went pale there for a second. It must be the wine, right? I'd tell you to take it easy, but it's your birthday, so drink away."

"Yeah, it must be," I said, taking another sip of it, trying to prove Nina's theory right. But I knew she was teasing me about William. Shit, shit, shit.

"Surprise," William's deep voice uttered behind me.

CHAPTER 14

Nemorino's

"HEY!" I SAID, turning around, almost dropping my wineglass. "Whoa."

William kissed both of my cheeks, and that little fire inside me that I usually kept at check turned against me, burning me with its rebellion.

William looked *incredible* on the nerve-inducing scale. He wore black dress pants with a thin, black, long-sleeved, crew neck sweater that hugged his upper body in all the right places. His face was clean-shaven, and not a single one of his golden strands was out of place.

"Zara told me about the dresses Enzio de Luca sent you. This one looks—made for you," he said, his gaze wandering down at my dress for a second.

"Thanks," I replied. "Did you have anything to do with this?" It wouldn't have surprised me at all if he did.

"I swear I didn't. Not this time," William said, lifting his right hand just slightly. "They loved you."

"They loved that the pantsuit sold out," I said with a laugh.

"Because *you* wore it."

Because I wore it and stood beside you, and people thought I was dating you.

It was best to change the subject.

"Are you supposed to be drinking?" I asked as he took a long swig of his wine. It'd been only three weeks since he got out of surgery. I didn't think it was safe for him to do so.

"No," he replied casually. "But it's a special kind of wine. I had to have one glass at least. I'd have an entire case of it if I could." He laughed a hushed smile, mostly to himself.

A server approached me. "You asked for the bottle, miss?" He showcased the wine's label. *Nemorino's*. William shot a crooked little smile at me.

"Can I—keep this?" I asked the server. I wanted to inspect the label. *Nemorino's*? I'd never heard of it before. I didn't know this wine existed, but it was the coolest thing ever. The server nodded and left after asking if there was anything else I needed.

"Nemorino's Love Boosting Potion?" I asked William with curiosity. "Where *the hell* did you find this wine?"

"This"—he took the bottle from my hands—"is the wine you drank at the cottage last summer. I remember you liked it. A *lot*." He laughed. "So I asked Alice to hire a designer to make this label, and then we just stuck it on the bottles. Well, Alice did. She'd kill me if she heard me taking any credit for it."

"William." I was impressed by how much he always paid attention to every little detail. It was such a thoughtful gesture. "Thank you. I—I love it. But shouldn't it be *Dulcamara's* Love Potion?" I teased him.

"No. I *was* paying attention at the opera, you know? Dulcamara's potion was a hoax, but Nemorino was the one who believed in it and drank it—made it real. Besides," he said, leaning in to whisper the following words, "when *you* drank this wine, you kissed me—a few times. So, I'd say it *does* work."

William's attention traveled to my lips and lingered there longer than I could endure without having a hot flash.

"Um—" I hesitated in replying. I looked down at the floor for a second and smiled. It was inevitable to think back on that night. How perfect it'd been. And about the said kisses.

"It's hard to forget, isn't it?" William said, sipping on his wine as he enjoyed reading my mind, as usual.

Time for another, *longer*, swig of my wine.

I cleared my throat because the words got tangled into a lump as I kept delaying a reply. "Well, the wine's delicious, and the branding's amazing. You should consider selling it for real."

"Well, we could be business partners," William said, his gaze trained on mine. "I'm not joking." He laughed, probably at my incredulous face. "We could do this. It would sell."

"Maybe in another life when we are both men, and we can be friends." I laughed. The wine had kicked in quite nicely. But that'd been a similar line he used when I asked him if we could be friends back in November. I don't think business partners would be any less complicated.

Back then, I thought that being friends was the answer, but I realized now that all I wanted was to keep him near me. I was terrified of losing him, and in my desperation, I was willing to have him in any available way, even if it was just as a friend. Even if it was the last choice I envisioned for us.

"I'd be gay for you, believe me," he said, laughing. "We'll *never* be friends. Not even if we're dogs or cats. Or wait … I'd probably come down as a Lab or a Golden Retriever, and those guys are legit friends with everyone, but I'd be a prick of a cat, for sure."

"You do realize you're being super friendly right now, right?" I asked with a chuckle.

"Of course I do. I know exactly what I'm doing."

He certainly did. And that's why it was time to change the subject … again. Because I couldn't speak my mind when my heart was whispering treacherous things in my ear.

"My father told me how you helped Nathan out with the party," I told him. "Thank you for that. And I see your debt is settled." I jerked my chin at the paella with a smile.

"Wait till you try the socarrat," he said, rolling his r's perfectly as he always did, taking a few steps back.

Where are you going?

"I'll have you *begging* for more." *William*! I shook my head at him feeling how my cheeks warmed up. Fast. It's the way he said things, with that *look* on his face that got me every time. "And I'll make sure to save a few of these"—he lifted the bottle of wine—"for you to take home. Have fun tonight, Guille. I'll see you around."

And with that, he left me. Standing there. Alone. Stunned.

I emptied my wineglass with the last sip as he walked over to his mother and kissed her cheek. He then approached a group of guys that I had no idea who they were.

"Hey, Bee," Nolan said behind me with my camera strapped around his neck.

"Oh, hey!" I replied as a server walked beside us, offering more wine. I immediately switched glasses with him. Nolan declined the wine. "Are you guys having fun?" Emily sat and talked with the rest of our friends from Parsons in the distance.

"Emily and Bryce won't shut up about Jordan Schreiber," he said, pushing his hair out of his forehead. He looked a little tipsy. I guess I was about to join him any second now. "They're *obsessed* with him. But when I said something about Lily and that little model gang sitting over there"—he pointed a lazy finger at them—"Emily pinched me."

I laughed. "Well, Jordan's not my type, but I mean, look at him. You can't blame them, can you?" Jordan wasn't the kind of guy who walks by unnoticed, especially if you're into that bad-boy-fresh-out-of-jail-on-a-million-dollar-bail kind of look.

"Yeah, I know your type," Nolan teased. "Tall, blond, and Nordic."

"Nolan!"

He laughed. "Am I lying here, Bee?" He was dead serious with his question. I puckered my lips to the side, thinking about how to handle this conversation.

"Well, we do call you Nolan the Liar at Parsons, did you know?" I laughed.

He chuckled with me. "Come on, Bee. I can see the way you look at him."

Shit.

"Nolan, I don't think we should"—I looked behind my shoulders—"have this conversation right now. It's not the place or time."

"I'm just trying to help. I know you're *happy* with Nathan," he said, air quoting the word happy. That threw me off. "Look." He pulled the strap over his head and turned on the camera's display. "Look at that. That. Wait … *This*." He zoomed in on my face. I was looking at William with a stupid smile on my face. And yeah, my eyes looked—weird. Glazed. Sparkly and shit.

"You should delete those," I suggested. "Please."

"Nah, you should keep them. You'll thank me later."

"I wouldn't want Nathan to see them."

"Why?" he asked, putting the camera's strap around his neck again.

"Nolan, come on." I laughed a nervous, uncomfortable laugh.

"I just want to see you happy, Bee."

"I am!"

"Happier. No … happiest?" He laughed. Yeah, he was tipsy and funny.

"Happiest?"

"The happiest you can be."

I peeked over Nolan's shoulder and saw Nathan laughing, drinking, having fun with Joel and his friend Aiden from work. It's as if he felt I was staring because he looked my way and winked at me with one of his cheeky smiles. Fuck. I loved him.

But …

"Nolan?"

"Yes, Bee?" He signaled one of the servers passing by to come over.

"I have feelings for William."

"Shit," Nolan said when the server arrived. "We'll have two shots of tequila."

There. I said it.

CHAPTER 15

Best Behavior

THE SERVER RUSHED back with a tray holding two tequila shots, a few chopped-up limes, and a small plate with salt as Nolan and I stared at each other in silence.

That's why it's hard to tell the truth. One rarely knows what to do with it once it stares back at you—taunting. Waiting.

Nolan tried to wring it out of me, and now that he finally did, he didn't know what else to say because, yeah, my situation couldn't have been any shittier.

I dropped my wineglass on the tray to make the switcheroo.

"Okay, let's do this," Nolan said. I licked the back of my hand where I'd previously tossed a pinch of salt, downed the shot, and chewed the lime. It reminded me of my Halloween date with Nathan. "Damn, Bee. I was gonna say *on three*, but you just dived in, didn't you?"

He followed suit, and I would've laughed at his remark, but I was busy shuddering and making a face as the tequila burned my throat. I would never get used to the fire.

The server nodded with a smile and left with the tray of our empty shot glasses after I grabbed my wineglass back.

"I wouldn't keep drinking wine," Nolan said. "Wait it out. See how the tequila kicks in. There's no rush."

He was probably right. But I didn't want the wine to go to waste. Even less so after William explained how much intention went into selecting it and designing the custom-made label. I would hold on to the wineglass and drink it later, as Nolan said … after I waited it out.

"So?" I said to him, as in *I just confessed something huge, do you have anything to say about it?*

"It's not like it's brand new information." Nolan laughed. "But hell, I wasn't expecting you to admit it so fast. What are you planning to do about it?"

I shrugged and shook my head a few times, my teeth nipping the corner of my lower lip for a second. "I don't know. It's weird to even say it. I've been trying to push it all away, but I can't now. I feel like I'm being torn in half. And yes, it's as painful as it sounds."

Two very familiar arms wrapped around my waist from behind me. "What's painful, love?" Nathan asked, kissing my cheek. His eyes looked a bit glazed, and he was all smiles. *That was painful.* To see him so invested in us. In me. And now I wasn't fully there with him. And I wished I could. I really, really did. But for the millionth time: how?

My feelings for Nathan weren't decreasing, but they were changing. And I didn't know what that meant. I was terrified of trying to figure it out. Maybe it was just too many things going on at once and it was getting hard for me to keep up with myself. But one thing I knew: Those feelings weren't alone anymore. New ones had made a last-minute appearance. Well, I wasn't sure as to how *new* they were. But me finally acknowledging them … that was new. I didn't even think that was possible. To feel so much. But apparently, it was.

Nathan left for London the day of the premiere, and when he came back the next day, I wasn't the same person I used to be. And him thinking that I was … *that* was painful too.

With him, I had this incredible sense of security, mutual

respect, love. What else could I ask for? He gave me everything any girl could dream of. And there I was messed up in the head for someone else who I wasn't even sure if the odds would be in our favor. If we could work. But I was so damn curious about the possibility.

William was like the sun. It shows up every single day, but it's unpredictable and unique every single time. Never boring. Like a perfect sunset that you can't stop looking at with awe, even if you've seen it a thousand times—right until you're sucked in by the first shades of dusk. And as I stand there, aching for more, yearning for the sun to rise again at dawn, the moon shines above, and it too reminds me of him. Every single time.

My sun and my moon.

But Nathan was my stars. Reliable, familiar, structured. Unfailing. Bright and comforting.

"She was telling me about her wrist," Nolan replied in my stead. And I thanked him for it. I was so in my head that I hadn't had the chance to snap out of my train of thought. To concoct a lie.

I couldn't. Never could.

"Oh, of course," Nathan replied. "Nolan, could you take a few shots of us?"

"Sure thing." Nolan grabbed the camera, and Nathan pulled me closer to him.

"Thank you," I said to Nathan. "For all of this. I thought I didn't want to celebrate, but I'm having fun." Nolan kept taking a few shots of us as we talked while I was wrapped around Nathan's embrace.

"I just want you to be happy—always. Because you deserve to be," Nathan replied. "I love you."

"I love you too." *And I do!* *I fucking swear that I do.* I didn't love him *less*. Love simply is. There's no measure to it. We either love or not. Right? I was still trying to decipher if there's such a thing as loving a little or loving a lot.

What I *did know* was how the heart has this weird expandable ability, like when a mother has a second child. You wouldn't love your first one any less. *But these are not your children, Guillermina.*

I knew I couldn't live like this, so torn. But I couldn't just end things with Nathan, especially when I didn't know for sure what to expect with William. And Zara jumping into the equation just complicated things even more.

Again, I wasn't the type of person who was willing to take risks of this magnitude. A risk that William wanted me to take. For him.

The truth is that I was afraid to end up with nothing. As ugly and selfish as it sounds.

"I'm sorry about the paella," Nathan said. *What?* He knew it's my favorite. Nolan excused himself and gave us privacy.

"Why?" I asked him, looking into his eyes with a puzzled smile.

"We just had paella last week. I didn't think you would want to repeat today," Nathan explained. "I told William to cook whatever the hell he wanted *but* paella." Nathan snorted. "I don't want to ruin your favorite dish by having it too often."

He obviously didn't know how William owed me a paella. That he'd promised to cook one for Easter this year. But I understood Nathan's frustration. He'd ask for a single request, and William dismissed it, as it was expected.

"I don't mind at all. I swear. You know how much I love it."

"I know. It's just annoying. William insisted on helping, on how he had a free schedule, and I needed the help, so I agreed."

"It's okay. Everything's perfect." I kissed him. Right there. With all I had. And I kept striking myself with a mental whip as I wondered why *this* couldn't be enough.

"You taste like tequila," he said to me with a weak laugh. "Don't mix, love. If you're going to switch, do the switch."

"I know, but I'm fine. I swear." I was fine, but I could feel the brewing sensation of the wine and the tequila building up in my head. And I wasn't thinking about Caleb, so that was already too convenient.

"I'm heading to the loo," Nathan told me, kissing my hair. "That dress ..." He shook his head. "I'll see you in a bit."

I nodded and smiled at him. Nolan stood a few feet away from me, shuffling through the images on the camera's screen. "Thanks," I told him.

"Sure, Bee, no problem. I'll keep taking care of the camera for you."

"I meant—" *For lying for me.* Nolan quickly picked up on that.

"Oh. Yeah—well. Try not to torture yourself with that right now. Just ... enjoy your birthday. You know we can talk about this any other time," he said, turning the camera off and letting it hang on his neck. "Also, um ... Emily and Bryce want to know if it's okay to ask William for a photograph. They're too embarrassed to ask themselves. I understand if—"

"No, no. It's okay. I'll tell him when I see him again. I'm sure he won't mind at all."

"Thanks, Bee." Nolan turned around and walked back to sit with my friends from school.

Cecile seemed bored as she chatted with Nina, Sophie, and Ren. And I didn't want to see her like that. I wanted her to have fun. CJ was still talking to David. I could see them near the main entrance—arguing, it seemed.

On my way back to cheer Cecile up, I heard a deep voice behind me, "Billie Murphy?"

I turned around, and it was Jordan Schreiber. "Oh, hey! Yes,

I'm Billie."

"Hi, Billie, I'm Jordan," he said in a deep voice. *Yeah, I know who you are.* "Nice to meet you." He had a *gorgeous* face.

"Nice to meet you too," I said. I couldn't offer my hand to him because of my wrist cast, but I saw him eyeing it, so we got that easily out of the way by avoiding handshakes. And I learned the hard way that I couldn't double-cheek kiss people around. Not everyone's used to it.

"I just wanted to introduce myself since a few of us are crashing your party. But we're all excited to see the band playing later tonight."

"Oh, so you're into jazz?" I asked him.

"Um, yeah. Besides, Tobias can't shut up about how great you are. I wanted to meet the little sister he never had." He laughed. *Tob*! He was the sweetest. "You're with William, right?"

"Ah—no. No, I—"

"Shit, I'm sorry. I just assumed, you know, from Tobias's premiere photographs a few weeks ago. I saw you together and— yeah, I'll shut up now." He laughed again. I tried joining him, but it wasn't the most genuine laugh in the world.

"Anyway," he said, looking at his drink. "Is—*she* your friend?" Jordan jerked his chin at my friends' table.

"Ah, yes. They both are. Which one do you mean?" I needed clarification on *friend*. Nina and Cecile both sat at the same table. And I knew he wasn't asking about Sophie, who sat on Ren's lap.

"The cute French girl with an attitude," he said, taking a sip of his whiskey and glancing at Cecile. "I heard her talking to the blonde girl beside her when I walked by, and she's so damn cute."

Cecile's left brow seemed to be stuck on a raised arch position giving off major *don't mess with me* vibes. So I understood where Jordan was coming from with the attitude remark about Cecile. But yeah, she looked classically beautiful as she always did.

"It makes me want to see what her problem is and maybe get scolded for asking." He laughed a deep rumble of a laugh again—harder this time. I couldn't help but laugh at that.

"You most probably *will* get scolded." I joked. "Her name's Cecile. And I'll introduce you to her, but you better behave. And yes, it's a warning. She's one of my best friends."

It didn't feel like a bad idea to introduce them. I wanted Cecile to have fun, and this guy seemed like the guy to take care of that. And something told me Cecile wouldn't mind meeting him.

"I swear I'll be on my best behavior," Jordan said, raising his hand. "Will *she*?"

"Not a chance," I said, just to tease him.

"Just how I like it."

"Right this way then."

CHAPTER 16

Various Introductions

"CECILE?" I SAID to her. She turned around and scanned Jordan, who stood beside me, with her signature lifted brow. "This is Jordan Schreiber. Jordan, this is my friend Cecile Dubois." She stood up and double-cheek kissed him. Jordan didn't seem to know what hit him. He drained his whiskey afterward and dropped the glass on the table with a side-smile.

Nina straightened herself on her seat. And although Jordan had made his interest perfectly clear, I introduced them just to be polite. They shook hands, but Jordan quickly focused his attention back on Cecile.

"May I sit with you?" he asked her. Ugh. His gentlemanly manners contrasted interestingly well with his tough exterior. Cecile would surely keep herself busy for the rest of the night trying to figure this guy out. I knew her well.

Nathan came back from the bathroom and joined me. We sat with Nina because I didn't want to leave her alone after introducing Jordan to Cecile, who'd been keeping her company. And CJ hadn't returned yet. He was still talking to *Dr. Scott.* I couldn't wait to ask David about him being a doctor.

"Jordan introduced himself to me and asked to meet Cecile," I whispered to Nathan, just to fill him in on what happened when he was gone.

"Tobias is going to be *gutted*," he said with a laugh.

"Shit." I'd forgotten all about Tobias. He hadn't approached Cecile, and I hadn't talked to him much. "He's gonna kill me."

"Tosh. He could've come to talk to her, and he hasn't. You did nothing wrong, love."

I hoped Nathan was right.

"So how are things with Juan Pablo?" Nathan asked Nina. "Is he coming tonight?"

Damn it. I hadn't told Nathan how they had broken up for good. They had been on and off for months now that I guess it'd been hard for Nathan to keep up.

"He's a lying, holistic, yogi—dick," Nina said dryly, the right side of her mouth slightly upturning as she pushed her long, dark brown hair behind her shoulders.

Nathan widened his eyes at me and sipped on his whiskey, probably regretting having asked about Juan Pablo.

"I just realized I haven't told you what happened, what I found out about him. But these past few weeks—well, it didn't seem like a good time to talk about any of this."

"What happened? Are you okay?" I asked her.

"Yeah, I'm *way* better off without him," she said, putting her glass down. "A few of his students from the yoga studio reached out to me. I knew he was sleeping around while we were dating, but he always had a perfect new-age excuse for it. Something similar to what you talked to him at your place, remember? I just didn't know there were *so many* women."

"Bastard," Nathan pitched in.

"Wait till you hear this," Nina replied. "He's actually *married* to this fifty-something-year-old millionaire. She's been sponsoring Juan Pablo for years. They have this—agreement of sorts where she pays for everything. The yoga studio, his apartment, food, clothing, *everything*. In exchange for, well, you know—keeping her *happy* whenever she wants."

"What?" Nathan and I said at the same time.

"You're kidding," I said to her.

"I wish I were." She laughed a sad, bordering on ironic kind of laugh. "I was an idiot for getting myself involved with him. I just—I don't know. I got all wound up with his words. Eating up all the lies he told me. And it's so sad because I feel like he *does* have a gift. I've seen it. But unfortunately, he chose to use that to manipulate women. Ugh! I don't want to judge him, but it's so fucked up."

"I'm sorry, Nina." I could relate in a way. When I dated Thomas, I didn't really know who he was. He always kept this other side to him hidden from me. It only makes knowing the truth, in the end, a bit more shocking.

"But yeah, I agree with you. You're better off. And you *will* find someone better," I continued. "I don't think that will be very hard to do."

Nathan stood up and excused himself for a second without telling me where he was going. Nina took a deep breath and let it out with a sigh.

"There's a bunch of things I just learned about Thomas, too," I told her. "Things that have been—hard to process."

"Billie, I know we haven't talked about what happened. But know that whenever you feel like talking—I'm here. And Caleb …" Nina looked away and shook her head. I knew she liked him. She got to know him somewhat. I could tell it'd been hard for her to process the news. But I didn't want to talk about Caleb. Not now.

"It's okay. If I'm honest, I haven't felt like going back to remember any of that, but we'll talk about it some other time, I promise."

Nathan came back with Aiden. I greeted him, and then Nathan introduced him to Nina.

"Nina, this is Aiden Hall. We work together. Aiden, this is Nina Lewis." They both smiled at each other as they shook hands. "Aren't you hungry, love?" Nathan asked. "They're already serving dinner."

"Oh. Yes. I'm starving. Let's go." I winked at Nina, and she chuckled under her breath.

Nathan and I walked away to allow them to get to know each other in peace. Aiden was such a good, wholesome guy. The opposite of Juan Pablo in *every* possible way. He was tall, elegant, and such a gentleman, just like Nathan.

We approached the area where dinner was being served. A few people were already eating, and it smelled delicious. I knew paella wasn't Nathan's favorite dish in the world, but it was the only choice for him tonight.

We stepped into the short queue of people waiting to grab a plate, and William appeared out of nowhere and walked around the table to talk to one of the chefs serving dinner. He kept pointing at the paella as the chef scraped the bottom part of the iron casserole. William grabbed the plated dish and tossed a piece of bread onto it as he walked back—in *my* direction.

I looked away.

"Come rain or shine," he said, offering the plate to me. My eyes went wide, and I gave Nathan my wineglass to grab the plate.

Nathan glanced at me with a puzzled face, probably wondering what that meant. I planned to explain later. If he asked …

"Will, can you get me a plate too?" Zara said behind me. There were three people ahead of us. It wasn't going to be a long wait. But she wanted William to pamper her or something. He lifted his hand and signaled one of the chefs for another.

Nathan's face was expressionless. I couldn't read him. Zara

stood in between him and William and linked her arms with both of them, resting her head on William's shoulder as we waited for Zara's paella.

The sight of that almost made me drop my plate. And I was sure Nathan agreed with me. His expressionless demeanor began to ooze with annoyance.

And I believed William, for a change, when he told me there was nothing going on with Zara. I'd learned from experience that William had never once lied to me about anything. But I felt like Zara was probably secretly in love with him. Or maybe it wasn't a secret and he already knew.

It didn't seem to me like Zara was trying to hide her obvious affection for him, not even in the presence of Nathan, who had been very vocal in disagreeing with them ever being an item.

And I didn't blame her, especially with how *splendid* William could be. There he was, getting her a spot in Juilliard and paying for her tuition? How would she not get the wrong idea? Or a dash of hope, at the very least.

"You're up, Nate," Zara said to him, pulling slightly on his arm.

"Nah, I'm not hungry," he said, taking a swig of his whiskey. "I'll eat later."

"Here you go, Chef," one of the chefs said to William, giving him Zara's plate. He nodded and passed it to Zara, who had to unlink herself from them to grab it. It was so weird hearing William being called *chef.* I kinda liked it. It suited him. It also reminded me of the simpler times when I met him and how I thought that's what he did for a living.

But William's face indicated discomfort after the chef's remark for some strange reason.

I looked around and saw my father sitting on one of the sofas in the lounge area by the bar with Nathan's boss, Mr. Chapman.

They were both eating and talking.

"Should we join them?" I asked Nathan.

"Sure, let's go," he replied.

"Thank you," I whispered to William, lifting my plate.

Nathan signaled one of the servers and asked for more whiskey when he approached us. I still had my glass of wine that Nathan held for me, so I was good.

"Good evening, Mr. Chapman," I said to him with a smile. I hadn't had the opportunity to say hi to him before. There were so many people. He greeted me back, and I asked them if we could join them.

"Of course, kiddo," my father replied. We took a seat across from them, and I rested my plate on my lap. Eating with my left hand was still a work in progress.

Nathan initiated the chit-chat with them, and a few involuntary *mmm's* escaped my throat as I tried William's paella for the first time. Nathan turned to look at me with a snort.

"Is it good?" he asked. I nodded and kept stuffing my mouth. It was freaking *delicious* as William promised it would be. A hundred times better than the one we ordered from the restaurant a few days ago. William's paella was different from my mother's, a bit more gourmet if you will, but they were both a ten.

Yes ... William's socarrat was the best I ever had. But I would have to find another way of rephrasing that to him, of course.

We kept eating, and the small talk quickly turned into a business meeting. Nathan and his boss discussed a client's case, and my father happily pitched in. But Mr. Chapman changed the subject after a few minutes of legal talk.

"I know we've been keeping you busy at the office, Nate, but try to relax tonight. We'll talk about the case on Monday on our way to London."

Oh.

I didn't know Nathan was leaving on Monday. He hadn't mentioned it. And by the look on his face, the office hadn't informed him about going to London either. Zara would still be in New York the entire week, and I thought Nathan would want to be here.

I wanted Nathan to be here too.

"Oh, of course. I—didn't know I'd be leaving for London on Monday," Nathan said to Mr. Chapman. "I'm sure we'll figure things out on our way there."

"Well, how else would you sign the paperwork for your new partner position? We need you in London for at least three days next week." Mr. Chapman replied with a grin.

Nathan shook his head once, fast, and licked his lips. He dropped his glass on the table and glanced at my father and me as if trying to make sure we all heard that.

"Congratulations!" Mr. Chapman said, standing up. He approached Nathan, who shot up from his seat and hugged him with a few pats on the back. "I've got to tell you, James, you've got one bright future son-in-law. We're never letting this one go." He laughed. Nathan chuckled with him, and my father immediately agreed with Mr. Chapman as he stood up to congratulate Nathan too.

Nathan was still in shock. He knew he was getting this promotion, but I don't think he expected it to come in a few months. I dropped my plate and stood up. I was about to hug Nathan when Mr. Chapman addressed me.

"You'll be glad to know that Nathan will be having more of a permanent residence here in New York. Surely, he'll still have to fly back and forth when needed, but you can count on him being here for the long run."

Nathan had mentioned how once he was made partner in the firm, the traveling would decrease. But that wasn't the case for what his boss was telling me. It was nice to hear he wouldn't be asked to go back to London anytime soon, though.

Ahh! I wanted to tackle Nathan and congratulate him, but I was trying to keep it cool in the presence of his boss.

My father looked so proud of Nathan. He couldn't stop smiling at him.

After dropping the big news, Mr. Chapman excused himself to *the loo*, and my father stood up for a second round of paella. Finally, alone, I was able to jump up and down with excitement. "Congratulations!" I said to Nathan as I hugged him tightly. "You're in shock, right?"

"Thank you! I—yes!" He laughed. "I knew it was coming, but I didn't think it would be happening *today*. I guess Mr. Chapman's having a good time right now. It was a great idea to invite him."

"I'm so proud of you," I told him, kissing his cheek. "I love you."

"I love you too." He kissed me back, and I rested my cheek on his chest for a second.

Oh, my God! I pulled Nathan's arm and whispered, "Look."

Jordan and Cecile were full-on kissing. They were still sitting on the chairs where I left them. Alone. Nina and Aiden were at the far end getting something to eat.

Jordan kept a firm hand behind Cecile's neck, the other gripping her waist. Her hands cupped Jordan's face.

I had to look away. That was one hell of a kiss.

"You're blushing," Nathan said with a laugh.

"I'm not!"

"You are," he said, leaning in to grab his whiskey. "I can kiss you like that if you want me to."

I laughed a nervous laugh and grabbed my wineglass from the table. "I know you can. You always do." I sipped on my wine, and Nathan met his lips with mine afterward. He then wrapped his arm around my waist and pulled me in. His whiskey-tasting tongue brushed slowly against mine.

"Like this?" he said, pulling away for a second, his gaze on my mouth. I wet my lips and nodded. He was about to kiss me again when someone cleared their throat beside us to get our attention.

CHAPTER 17

If You Wouldn't Mind

"*SORRY TO INTERRUPT,*" Tobias said to us. He looked upset and drunk-ish. "Liam just told me you introduced Jordan to Cecile. What the fuck, Billie? You know how much I like her."

Who the heck *is Liam?*

"Whoa, whoa, whoa," Nathan said to Tobias, tapping his shoulder twice. "You need to settle down, mate." He lifted a brow at Tobias as a warning.

"I-I'm sorry, Tob. I didn't—I mean, I know what *happened* between you, but I didn't know where you stood, and you hadn't even approached her all night. How was I to—"

"I was waiting for the right moment to do so," he interrupted me. "I know what I'm doing. I wasn't going to throw myself at her the moment she arrived. But now ..." He closed his eyes and took a deep breath. "Now Jordan's got his fucking tongue down her throat, and she—" he trailed off, dragged a rough hand through his hair, and gripped his neck.

Nathan said something to him in Swedish with a gruff voice, but Tobias didn't reply. Instead, he glanced at Jordan and Cecile with a scowl and met my gaze once again. "You *knew* how much I liked her."

"You said that in October, Tob! You haven't mentioned a

thing to me about her ever since. For all I know, you might be dating someone else. You never talk to me about these things. How was I to know?"

"We've kept in touch," he tossed in. "You're Cecile's best friend. I'm sure she said something."

She hadn't. But I didn't think Tobias would believe me anyway. He was pissed and wanted someone to blame.

Me.

"Jordan came up to me and asked to meet her, Tob. What did you want me to say? No, you can't meet her because she slept with Tobias six months ago?" I was getting a bit worked up because I didn't know shit about what was happening between them. Nathan kneaded my shoulder, trying to calm me down. But it wasn't working.

"Try two weeks ago," Tobias spat back.

"What?" I couldn't believe Cecile hadn't told me anything about this. And I'm sure Sophie didn't know either. She would've told me something if she did. And yes, Tobias had been in Europe to promote his film right after William was shot. I remember he wanted to stay here in New York, but he was obligated to go. I guess he went to Paris and sought her out.

"Stop acting like you didn't know, Billie." He turned around and walked away, taking an angry sip of his beer.

Damn it. "Tob!" I yelled at him. But he didn't turn around. "Tobias!"

"Let him be. He's drunk," Nathan said, standing behind me and kissing my shoulder. "You did nothing wrong. He'll be sorry tomorrow. And if not, I'll make him."

I blew out a breath. I'd never argued with Tobias before. And I didn't like it one bit.

"I swear Cecile hasn't mentioned a thing to me about it. Who's Liam, by the way?" I asked Nathan in an annoyed tone.

"Do you know him?" I thought it was absurd how Tobias was pissed at me because of some snitch-guy I didn't even know.

"Ah, yes. Liam Kelly. Actor. Australian. He's good friends with the Sjöbergs. He was at the Superbowl with us, actually."

"Shit," I said, looking over Nathan's shoulder. Tobias ambled toward Cecile and Jordan's table.

"What?" Nathan asked, turning around. "Shit, indeed."

Tobias stood between them and talked to them, but we obviously couldn't catch a thing. They were too far away. But he kept patting Jordan's back. And the lack of concern in Cecile's face was inspiring.

I want to be like her when I grow up.

She didn't seem to care. Or at least that's what she was letting on. But still, wow. I'd faint if I were in her position.

Nina and Aiden took a seat at another table. Sophie sat with Ren next to Cecile, but she observed their interactions with her big doe eyes.

I'd rather not watch.

"I'll be right back." I kissed Nathan's cheek. "I'm going to *the loo*," I said that in a terrible British accent.

"Oh, my." He laughed and kissed me back. "Why am I getting turned on by that?"

"Olive," I said an inch away from his lips, again in the best accent I could muster. "Do you remember?"

"Always. Now please leave, young lady, before I decide to follow you to the bathroom and lock the door."

I laughed. And it got me thinking … things.

"I'll cool off by making sure Tobias doesn't do anything stupid," Nathan said, walking away. It made me feel more at ease to hear that Nathan would be close by just in case. I didn't want Cecile to find herself caught up in the middle of a weird or uncomfortable situation.

My watch marked 9:55 p.m. That meant that there were at least two more hours to go before my birthday. I knew the party wouldn't be over at least until after midnight. And according to Tobias, I wouldn't be allowed to leave until dawn. But that was before our argument. He probably wouldn't mind if I left right now.

Whatever.

I emptied my wineglass, which took me a few seconds to do so, and dropped it on one of the cocktail tables as I walked toward the bathroom, feeling a bit rattled after my discussion with Tobias.

Amena's arm appeared out of nowhere, opening the door to the ladies' room before I could do so.

"Shit, Amena. You scared the hell out of me."

"My apologies, Miss Murphy," she said with a smile that felt like a bucket of iced water on me—a suffocating reminder of how I couldn't even pee on my own. Wouldn't want to get swallowed by the toilet.

Amena opened the wooden bathroom stall door and took a quick look, then nodded, as she always did, just to make sure there wasn't someone waiting for me inside to watch me do my business. We then proceeded to the usual *me peeing and pretending Amena isn't listening* scenario.

I stepped out and washed my hands carefully. Amena helped me with that too since I didn't want to get my cast wet. That was the convenient part of having her coming into the bathroom with me these days.

A couple of girls walked in when I was retouching my lipstick.

"Hi! You're Billie, right? I'm Lana, and this is Poppy. We're Lily's friends."

They were clearly Lily's friends. They both had the whole

model look going on. Lean, long legs, long necks, flawless skin.

"Hi! Yes, I'm Billie. Nice to meet you." They both went in for a hug, which caught me off guard and made Amena take a step forward. *Easy*, I said to her with my eyes. Geez.

"Happy birthday," Poppy said with a sweet smile. "Are you having a good time?"

"Yes, thank you." I smiled back.

"We can't wait for the band to come out," Lana said, pushing her short dark hair behind her ear. Apparently, everyone was very much into jazz these days. Poppy agreed with her as she checked herself in the mirror, tousling her blonde curls.

They both walked away toward the bathroom stalls as Lana said with a smirk over her shoulder, "Anyway, hope you keep having fun tonight, Billie. And say hi to Nathan for me."

I probably wouldn't have given that much thought to her comment if it weren't for Poppy shaking her head disapprovingly as she pulled Lana away.

"Ah, sure. See you guys later."

Ughhhh! Now my mind was inevitably thinking about *why* and *how* they knew each other. Why couldn't I be like Cecile? Dismissing the bullshit around me one raised eyebrow at a time.

Amena opened the door for me, and as I walked back to the party through the long corridor, "What Difference Does It Make" from The Smiths started playing. And that just did it for me. I was sure my father had requested the music. Or maybe Nathan did because he knew I liked them. But my legs stopped cold, refusing to keep walking as the memory of Caleb and me dancing and singing to that song in my apartment a few months ago invaded my mind.

His voice singing the song in his lovely accent was all I could hear inside my head. And a very real bummer about dying that no one talks about is how once you die you never get to listen to your favorite music ever again. And the thought of him being deprived of that—of life—broke my heart all over again.

"Shit, shit, *shit*." I placed my left hand against the wall and rested my forehead on it. *Someone get me out of here.* This was the type of thing that would merit an SOS beacon, and thinking about that just made things worse. Yeah, I could still use it. But it was Caleb's favorite thing, and now that he was gone, I would never get to see his excited face after I pulled an SOS.

This is how my mind works. I start pulling on a thin string, and a whole building collapses on top of me eventually. There was no way to stop the bullet train of thoughts from running me over.

"Miss Murphy, is everything okay?"

No.

"Yes." I took a deep breath and turned around. "Please ask David to come here. Quickly, please."

Amena immediately clicked on her earpiece and did as I asked her to. I leaned my back against the wall and looked up at the ceiling. Maybe if I looked up, my eyes would swallow back the tears by gravity.

David's silhouette appeared at the far end of the corridor. He marched our way and caught up with us in a few long and fast strides.

"Miss Murphy," he said with a sharp nod.

"Thank you, Amena. Could you give us some privacy, please?" I asked her. "And could you hold on to my purse for a while?" She took the purse and immediately turned on her heel and left.

I glanced at David and said, "Do you have my cigarettes?"

"Yes."

"Take me to the kitchen, and don't pretend like you don't know where that is because I know you've studied this entire venue's layout."

"Follow me," he said, adjusting the flaps of his jacket.

David was my go-to discreet agent of choice. He'd buy the cigarettes for me and carry them with him for situations such as these. I refused to carry my own box, fearing I'd consume them in a heartbeat. They were supposed to be for emergencies only.

We walked in the opposite direction of the party through that same long corridor and made a left. Then a right after a few steps where a white double door appeared at the far end of the space. The kitchen.

"Miss Murphy," David said before I stepped in. "I need to know what you're planning to do."

"There's always a backdoor in every kitchen. I need to breathe. And I can't walk out the front door. I just need a smoke. To clear my head."

"Okay. Let's go."

We walked right in, and I tried to avoid making eye contact with any of the kitchen staff as David led the way. My thought was if I walked right through with confidence, as fake as it might be, no one would ask questions or ask me to leave.

We made it through the huge kitchen without a problem and found the back door open. A couple of cooks smoked outside. I said hi to them, and they said hi back, returning to their conversation quickly after that.

David reached into his inner jacket pocket and took the cigarette box and a lighter out. He offered me a menthol cigarette, and I brought it to my lips. He lit it up for me as my hand slightly trembled.

"I'm sorry," I said, taking a long, slow drag. "I just needed to breathe for a second." I blew the smoke out, leaned against the wall, and crossed my left arm over my stomach, holding my right arm up with the cigarette in between my fingers.

It was one of the few things I could do without my cast

getting in the way. Hold a freaking cigarette.

"Do you want to talk about it?" he asked. He knew what my problem was. You didn't have to be too smart to figure it out, but David here was cunning and knew me well by now. He surely knew this was about Caleb.

"There's not much to say. I just fucking miss him." I shook my head slowly and stared at nothing. "Too much. I—I don't know if it will ever stop hurting. Well—I *do* know. And the answer is no." I laughed a short, wry laugh.

The death of my mother was evidence enough to know this. The pain would always be there. But the pain changes with time. It likes to play games. Sometimes it hides. Sometimes it lurks behind you. And at times, it steps right in front of you and demands attention like a child having a tantrum for no apparent reason.

But there's always a reason.

And you better figure it out or wait for it to pass because it won't ever leave your side.

I knew where I was headed dealing with Caleb's death. But I needed time. And time usually likes to be left the fuck alone. At least in that, we're similar, but we're not friends. It taunted me most of the time, especially at night.

David didn't reply. That's why I liked him. He was always one step ahead, observing, reading the place and everyone in it.

"So you're a doctor?" I asked. It seemed like the perfect time to do so. I needed to get out of my head. As if it were possible.

He snorted. "Yeah, I am. I enlisted in the Marine Corps when I was seventeen. After a couple of years there, I decided to pursue medical school within the military, which was the main reason why I enlisted in the first place. And I got in."

"Do you have a specialty?"

"I'm a General Medical Officer. I thought about doing a

specialty, but one thing led to another, and I ended up here. And I couldn't be happier right now."

"But why did you leave? Was it not what you expected it to be or …?"

"It's tough for a guy like me in the military—black. Gay. I was lucky enough to have finished medical school," he said, his jaw tense. His eyelids shuttered. "Um—yeah."

I frowned.

There must've been a story there, and I didn't know it, but I was already angry because the look on David's face told me it wasn't an enjoyable one. And as much as I would've loved to hear it, this wasn't the time or place to get into it.

"You know CJ's father is a renowned pediatric surgeon in the country, right? The famous Dr. Jewel," I said to him. "My father told me he has saved many lives. Including a former President of the United States' son when he was nine years old. But he wouldn't tell me who."

"I—yeah. I know that." He laughed under his breath. "One of my first options for a specialty was Pediatrics, actually. But it was *suggested* to me that it wouldn't be okay for a gay man to treat children," he said with a snort. That's the stupidest thing I've ever heard. "I have two nieces and four nephews. I'm good with kids. They love me."

A smile grew on my face, and I could feel my eyes getting smaller from the warmth with which he said that. I believed him. David's such a noble, trustworthy guy. And I'd never seen him interacting with kids, but if he said he was good with kids, then he was good with kids. Period.

"Anyway, right now, I'm good. I've never been more at peace," he added.

"And—CJ? Is he driving you insane or what?" I chuckled.

David looked at me from the corner of his eye for a second

and looked away. He rubbed his face with both of his hands. "Yeah. He is."

"Good insane? Or bad insane?" I asked, tossing my cigarette and stepping on it. I picked it up afterward and threw it in a trash container a few steps away from where we stood.

"A little bit of both, I guess. But I messed up a few days ago. That's why he's acting out. Flirting with the servers, etcetera."

CJ's specialty. I don't think he can help it. It must be automatic. Since the first day I met him, he's been on a mission to flirt with any and all servers that crossed his path. But I wasn't going to say any of that to David.

"He really likes you," I said to him instead. It was the truth. "He liked you from day one. Remember your first day with me? I met you both the same day, actually. And when he saw you outside the restaurant … he was immediately drawn to you."

David laughed. "Yeah, well, he drooled for Caleb for weeks."

"It doesn't count," I replied with a smile. "Everyone drooled for Caleb. I know I did. For *years*. The girls at school would faint as he walked by. He was a legend." I smiled a silly smile that quickly melted off my face.

An invisible hand knifed my gut like butter. The burning sensation stationed itself there and wasn't planning to leave. My hands moved to my stomach involuntarily as if trying to stop the pain somehow. But again, invisible. There was nothing I could do to defend myself.

My mind went to the day I met Caleb. He was 22 and out-of-this-world beautiful, so different from anyone I've ever seen. He was the first guy to ever give me butterflies. And he'd been so tender when we met. The way he talked and moved around me, as if afraid I'd break. And yeah, I was so fragile then.

Inside and out.

But I've toughened up since then. Not enough, though, I'm

afraid. Still a work in progress. My new goal was to be at a *Cecile* level on the *Harden the Fuck Up* scale.

David extended his hand and offered me a napkin, and that's when I realized I was crying. I didn't even notice him stepping away from me to fetch it.

I asked for another cigarette as I patted my face gently to dry it off. But the tears wouldn't stop the constant dripping. So I tossed the napkin in the garbage bin and let it be.

One more cigarette, I said to myself, and then I'd go back.

David lit me up again like the good chap he was, and I took a deep, lazy drag.

After deciding to stop fighting the tears, I closed my eyes and whiffed the smoke upward when a low, husky voice I could recognize even after a lobotomy said, "David, if you wouldn't mind, I'll take it from here."

CHAPTER 18

Go

MY BODY TENSED UP, sensing William's towering presence behind me. I quickly brushed off the tears, unsure about wanting to turn around or not, but I had to at some point—even if it was to escape him. And William wasn't going anywhere or allowing me to leave. That much I knew.

Having just admitted my feelings for William to Nolan made me panic. Almost afraid he would be able to notice that fact in my face if I allowed him to see me. And now more than ever, I had to conceal them from him because I didn't know what I would do yet. I didn't even want to think about it. Not when he stood so close to me.

It was probably wrong of me to confess my feelings to Nolan because by putting my thoughts into words, I gave them life. I made them real—official. And my fear was they would plot and turn against me or deceive me somehow.

"Could you have someone tell Nathan I'm okay?" I asked David. "That I'll be back in a few minutes?"

"Few minutes," William scoffed. He was damn right. With William, it could never be *a few minutes*. But at least I planned to keep this conversation as short as possible.

We're not even close to being done with this conversation; he'd told me at the hospital after saying how he wouldn't stop anymore. I didn't know when to expect him to throw more truths in my face. But he did every single time he could. And I was sure right now wouldn't be the exception.

"Yes, Miss Murphy," David replied. "I'll be right outside the kitchen." And with that, David left us, clicking on his earpiece. The cooks that were smoking beside us were gone too. It was just the two of us now out in the somewhat chilly evening.

"Hey," he said, walking around me, plucking the cigarette from my fingers and tossing it away, still looking impeccable from head to toe. "You have to quit this shit."

I know.

"And you need to come back to the party."

I know.

"Right now," he said, his tone businesslike and sexy as hell, and again … somewhat ruining the self-induced miserable state I found myself in.

My hands felt empty. I had no security cigarette or wineglass to hold on to. I'd have to use words to fill in the silence. It's so easy to put a cigarette on your lips or take a sip of your wine instead of answering someone's question. Those two simple actions are replies of their own.

But again, I had nothing but words as an option to deal with my exchange with William.

"I'm not ready to go back yet."

"What's wrong?" he asked, taking a step my way. "You've been crying." A statement.

I took my hands to my face because he said *crying*, and apparently, that's my eyes' cue to do their thing where they try to dull the pain by shedding tears. And yeah, that's the way it works, chemically speaking.

The next thing I know, William pulled me in against the

hard line of his body, his arms tight around my shoulders. The embrace too familiar and comforting to pull away from.

My left hand and my forehead moved to his chest, where, as always, I surrendered to him. To the warm solace.

"This is why I didn't want to go out tonight," I said, feeling his chest heaving. And I didn't want to be weak, but I didn't know how to be strong either. At least not all the time. It was exhausting.

I was tired of feeling like I was this fragile thing that needed to be handled with care. That's why it was easier to stay home. I didn't mind being pathetic in the comfort of my bed. But to expose myself like this … vulnerable. I began to feel like a broken record.

"Caleb?" William asked. I nodded against his chest as he took a slow breath in, his heart beating hard against my face.

William's hands traveled down my waist, locking me in after I tried pulling away from him. I looked up to meet his gaze and the overwhelming awareness of it, all fixed on me.

"You need to let me go," I said in a breath. I knew I couldn't fight him off or push him away because I didn't want to. And I needed him to meet me halfway. "*Please*."

"I swear I would if your body wouldn't be begging me to hold you."

I let my forehead crash against him again and said, "I need to get this off my chest right now, and I can't if you—"

William's hands dropped from my waist, shutting me up. His warm body flush against mine. *That's halfway*. All I had to do now was take a step back. So I did, ignoring my body's hissy fit while I was at it.

And I didn't want to think about how I pretended like time had stopped because it didn't. I stalled because I yearned for that closeness just like he did.

I hugged myself and rubbed my right arm to compensate for the sudden temperature change. William noticed. But he had no jacket on. I knew it would've already been over my shoulders if he did. He seemed annoyed to not be able to help with that.

I looked away and shook my head twice, fast, trying to shake off the distractions. I needed to get my thoughts and feelings about Caleb out right now if I wanted to go back inside.

"I don't know how I'll ever recover from this. *No one* knew me as Caleb did—cared for me in the way he did. And sometimes I wonder …" I didn't want to compare or give William the wrong idea. I had Nathan. He loved me and made me happy. But my relationship with Caleb was unique—unconditional. Eternal. And I lost that.

"And you think that what? That no one will ever know you more, care about you more … *love you* more than he did?" He asked, but I knew it was rhetorical. And he didn't give me the space to reply because he continued. "That's *not* your case. Or if it is, then why are you still with Nathan? Doesn't he—"

"I *didn't* say that." I stopped him cold. That was my fear. That he would think that I was implying this had something to do with Nathan when it didn't. "But if you want to talk about it, I have no problem unraveling this mess of a feeling and try to lay it out for you," I offered.

His silence followed by a gentle shrug and a bob of his head indicated he wanted me to continue. It would be awkward, but I couldn't afford to mix things up and confuse him.

"Nathan's my boyfriend, and he loves me, and he's great, okay. But he's *all* boyfriend. And Caleb offered me an unconditional friendship, a sense of protection that went above and beyond anything I've ever known. Oddly, complementing my relationship with Nathan."

William was silent. Observant. His face undecipherable.

"Ah! It's hard for me to figure this feeling out and even harder for me to explain it," I said, hoping I wasn't fucking this up. "I feel like there's this—cavity inside my chest that Nathan, as my *boyfriend*, can't fill because it belonged to Caleb. And I'm afraid to see what happens if that void is left untouched. So I want to acknowledge it because I know what it's like when you don't. It only gets bigger—more painful. And one can sometimes try to fill it out with the wrong things. Am I making any sense?"

"You are," he said instantly. "I know your relationship with Caleb was special. And you knew him from way back. But with time, you'll fill that emptiness with new feelings, and it's okay if you do. You're not replacing him by doing so."

"That's the point. Nathan gives me what I ultimately couldn't see happening with Caleb, and Caleb and I had finally reached this—perfect point in our friendship. A kind of friendship *I* need. And I fear I won't find that ever again."

"You think that because you haven't allowed me to be that for you. I *can* be both," he said with resolution. I stared at him for a few seconds, letting his words sink in.

"William, you've repeatedly said you're not interested in being my friend."

"*Just* a friend. That's different. I don't care to be *just* your friend. And I know you'll always love Caleb and cherish what you had. But I can give you much more than that. I never have before, but I know I want to. I know I can."

I parted my mouth to speak, but I let out a breath instead when my mind couldn't find any suitable words to reply to that. I was still processing it.

"And you—" He licked his lower lip and smiled with a tinge of exasperation and shook his head a few times as if changing his mind about what he was about to say at the last moment. "You'll always love Caleb. That will never change. But with time, your heart will heal. It's too soon, and it's okay for you to feel this way. And for some reason, you think that if you're vulnerable, that somehow means you're weak. But you're wrong."

I probably was wrong. About that and many other things because I had no clue of the full extent of what William could mean to me. Of what he was offering. I could only imagine, as much as I constantly tried not to. But even so, they were just speculations.

"And what about Zara? I know it's not my place to ask, but I swear I see *something* in her eyes when she looks at you."

William looked away for a second. "I know it's the worst possible answer in the world, but it's not what you think it is," he said, his brows drawing together and his tone suggesting the topic might be out of bounds.

"I can't help but wonder if you're too naive to see it." I brought the idea to his attention. "To realize that she might—" *Be in love with you.* I couldn't even finish the sentence.

"Could you live knowing that I might not be able to explain my relationship with her to you for a while? And that she'll always be around?"

No.

I don't know.

I could try.

Maybe she was to William what Caleb was to me. But with William, a raw, primal, territorial feeling always found a way to sink its claws on me. *If* something were to happen between us, I wouldn't want to share him like that with anyone. And talking about that "if" wasn't something I could make myself discuss with him.

"You don't need to explain anything to me," I said, retreating. I shouldn't have brought it up. It would only complicate things even more. I couldn't allow myself to show William how much I cared about him.

"But you still wished I could explain, right?"

"No, I—"

"You're just jealous. I get it. *Believe me*. But it's best if we don't get into that. We could be here all night."

I agreed.

"I'm not jealous. I'm … curious."

He laughed and crossed his arms at his chest, calling my bluff.

Yes, okay! I'm jealous! I'm so fucking heart-wrenchingly jealous that it makes me want to die twice. "You're lucky I've got nothing at hand to throw at you," I tossed in.

"Stay put," he said, still unwinding from the laughter. He rushed inside the kitchen and came out with a glass of wine. He offered it to me, and I took it without a second thought. "Drink up because this Nemorino's shit is not working. I fear you might've grown immune to it." He grinned, running a lazy hand through his soft, golden hair.

Oh, but it was working. And I wasn't immune to it. Never.

My head was already somewhat spinning, but I sipped on the wine anyway.

"Tobias *hates* me, by the way."

"Tobias *loves* you." He snorted with a faint but gentle smile. "What happened?" William let his body rest against the wall beside him, a foot crossed in front of the other. His hands slid inside his perfectly tailored pants pockets.

I loved how easily we could switch off those heavy conversations and just fade out into something so unrelated but helpful in balancing out the complexness.

"I um—introduced Jordan to Cecile, and they started making out. So, Tobias wants to burn me alive."

"Shit." He laughed.

"It's not funny, William. I didn't know Tobias and Cecile were, you know, in contact."

"Fucking?"

"William!"

"That's interesting," he said, the right corner of his mouth pulling up slightly.

"Ah, what's—interesting?" I sipped on my wine and looked away. And that's why it's good to have something to use as a distracting prop.

"That your cheeks react when I say *fucking* in that context," he said, locking his gaze with mine.

"It's the wine." I was trapped, immobilized. I've never stood a chance against the hypnotizing blue of his eyes.

"So Nemorino's works then?"

Obviously.

"You're not helping me sort this out!"

"Okay." He smiled. "So Tobias *hates you* right now because he's drunk, horny, and jealous, which seems to be the theme of the night, but he'll go back to loving you tomorrow when he's sobered up," he said. "Does that sort things out for you?"

"I guess."

William looked away and smiled. "You had to throw Jordan at Cecile of *all* people."

"What's wrong with Jordan?"

"Nothing. That's the point. He's a great guy. I like him. We all do," he admitted.

"Yeah, I bet he is," I said with a chuckle.

"Do you find him attractive?" William asked, tilting his head with curiosity.

"Well, I don't know. I guess he's—*okay*."

William laughed harder this time. "I'm just curious to know if a guy like Jordan calls to your attention." Jordan and William were like oil and water. So different in every way, physically speaking.

"He must call to any girl's attention, isn't that your point? But let's just say that if I were Cecile, I would probably lean more toward Tobias." Maybe that would clear things up for him.

"You do know who he is, right?" he asked, probably thinking I didn't know what he did for a living.

"Of course I do. I saw that movie he starred with Joel a few months ago." And I sipped on my wine again. There'd been some steamy scenes in there that Jordan had participated in. Cecile was in for a treat if that was something she wanted to pursue. It seemed to me like she did.

"Ah! So you've been acquainted with Jordan's ass."

I'd been, but, "Don't you use like butt doubles and stuff?" I laughed a nervous laugh.

"Some of us don't need them."

"So, your ass is out there for the world to see?"

"Yeah. Does it bother you?"

"Why would it? It's your ass. You can do whatever you want with it." I did think it was kind of awful that anyone could see him naked. I'd only glimpsed at his perfect behind at the hospital, and yeah, he didn't need a double.

Annoying.

But it shouldn't have been a concern of mine, and it certainly wasn't my business.

"Can I? Do whatever I want with my ass?" He tilted his head again and shot a taunting side-smile at me, the kind that used to get on my nerves. It still affected me. But it was different now.

"Your ass, your call," I said with a laugh, taking a few more seconds to answer than I should've.

"I kinda like it when you tell me what I can and cannot do, though," he said, standing up straight, displaying the full, powerful length of his body.

"How did we end up talking about asses?" I said, unable to withhold a smile.

"I needed to get you out of your head. To change the mood," he said, taking one step forward. "To get you to come back inside."

I heard a buzz, and William pulled his cellphone out of his pocket.

"Cheater!" I said as he took the call with a grin. There were no phones allowed at the party, but again, when did William ever follow the rules?

"*Hey man ... I know,*" he said, sweeping me with his gaze. "*Thanks, yeah ... We'll be there in a minute ... Not a literal minute, no ... How about I call you back and make that your cue ... Thanks again.*"

William ended the call and said, "I've got party planning perks," and tucked his phone back inside his pocket.

"I'm afraid to go back inside now. What are you up to?" I said, feeling a warm, relaxing sensation flowing through my veins.

I was now officially operating in *present* mode and not thinking about Caleb anymore or worrying about things that most of the time don't even end up happening like I usually did. *This* was the ultimate goal for the night, and I'd achieved it. Thanks to William.

"I'm ready," I told him.

"You say that now." He laughed a funny evil laugh and herded me back to the kitchen. "Wait," he said, just before we stepped inside. "Look up."

"Crescent moon," I replied, looking up. "I can't tell what kind, though. Is it—"

"Waning crescent." William bit his lower lip with a smile and pulled me back inside.

"Shit," I said, looking at my watch as we walked through the kitchen. "I've been out here for an hour."

"My point exactly," he said, rushing. "We have three minutes before eleven, and we *have* to go back."

"Wait." I pulled him to make him stop. I could feel the muscles in his arms tensing up, so I released him from my grasp.

He looked down at me, and his eyes widened for a second. "Yes?"

"Where's that bottle of wine you refilled me with?"

He snorted. "I think you've had enough."

Maybe. But all I wanted was to keep myself in that sweet spot—the eternal present. I feared that if I stopped drinking, that feeling would go away.

But you know how sometimes you're standing in front of that thin, blurry line, and you *know* if you take *one* more drop of alcohol, you'll cross it, and it's game over?

Well I didn't. But this night surely taught me that.

"You'll pour more wine into my glass," I said, waving a hand at him.

"No," he replied, his negative like a brick wall.

"Am I low on my midi-chlorian count?"

"Never." He laughed. "I would only agree to pour more wine in your glass if I were in charge of taking care of you."

"You always take care of me." *Flag! Someone shut me up.*

"In that, we can agree. But," he said, walking toward the kitchen staff. He asked for two shot glasses and the bottle of wine, which were handed to him mere seconds later, and came back. He placed everything on the stainless-steel table in front of us. "How about if we do a shot of wine and you close shop for the night."

"A shot of—*wine*?"

"I'm not giving you any hard liquor after all the wine you've already pushed down your throat. I saw you taking a tequila shot earlier with Nolan too. I don't know how you're still standing."

I honestly didn't know either. But I was reaching my limit. And I hadn't noticed at all that William watched me while I talked to Nolan. About him.

"Ah, right. The mixing thingie," I said, waving a haphazard hand at nothing. "But you shouldn't be drinking."

He raised a brow. "You shouldn't either. So," he said, pouring the wine into the shots, "you either drink this *with* me, or you walk out of here empty-handed."

"I can ask for another glass of wine outside, you know."

"You can. But once you take a step back into that party, wine's gonna be the last thing on your mind. So last chance. Yes or no."

What the hell does that mean? I had no time or mind to figure that out.

"Pour it."

William smiled an annoyingly triumphant smile and poured the shots.

"Here you go."

I grabbed my shot and said, "Thank you for—you know."

"I don't know. Be specific," he said, holding his shot glass in front of me.

"For cheering me up. For helping out with the party. For the paella and Nemorino's wine—everything."

"Well, I was bored and had a clear schedule." He teased. He shot a smile at me that almost made me fall to my knees. But I smiled a stupid smile back instead and cleared my throat. "We'll talk about the paella some other time because we *really* need to get back. But just tell me how much you loved it."

"Best I ever had. The socarrat had me begging for more," I said with a laugh, just to tease him, remembering how he promised that would be my reaction after trying it.

"Ha-ha," he countered.

"It's true!"

"Focus. A toast?" he mused, bringing his shot closer to mine.

"I thought we were in a hurry."

"We are, so you better think of something quick." He lifted his brows and jerked his chin at my shot glass.

I brought it closer to his and said, "May our worst nights be like this one."

"Damn it, Guille." William shook his head slowly with one of his smirks, bumped his glass against mine and said, "Skål."

"Skål."

We emptied our shots, and William's phone buzzed again. He took the phone out and read the screen. "Shit. We need to start moving," he said, placing his phone back into his pocket. He grabbed my hand and pulled me out of the kitchen. *Whoa.*

David was right outside as he said he would be and followed us as we made our way back through the corridors. I had a hard time keeping up with William's long and swift strides. But we were almost there, making our way through the long passageway that led to the bathroom.

The DJ's music that poured our way stopped dry, and the lights went out. Everyone cheered, screamed, and whistled.

"Can you run?" William asked without looking back, still pulling me.

"I'm already running!" It was the only way I was able to keep up with him. "*You* shouldn't be running!"

An electric guitar became audible, and ten seconds later, drums joined in, and they made up a song I instantly recognized. "William!" I increased the pace as much as I could.

We finally reached the event area, and William stopped, released my hand, and turned to look at me. It was Dave Matthews band playing "Bartender." We shouted the first three words of the song at the same time: "*If I go!*"

"*This* is the jazz band?" I was panting.

"I'm afraid so." He laughed. That explained everyone's excitement about *the jazz band*. Figures. "Your first concert." His mouth twitched into a smile.

"It is," I replied, not minding him wanting to tick off another first. William kept surprising me. And I couldn't believe this was happening.

Everyone swarmed in front of the stage. Nathan saw me in the distance and walked my way. I turned to look at William, and my stomach shrunk. "William, I have to—"

"Go."

CHAPTER 19

First Concert

WILLIAM SHUFFLED AWAY toward the crowd with his brows pulled down. And I was left there standing with a pit in my stomach.

"You okay, love? You were gone for a while." He looked over my shoulder at William. "Where were you?" Nathan asked with a certain—tone. But his eyes looked weird. Drunk? Probably the first time I'd seen him like this.

And that little run from the kitchen back here had my head spinning a lot more. So I guess we were both sauced up, as Nathan liked to say.

"I—smoking. With David. William came looking for me. He was trying to make me come back for the show."

"Amena told me you needed a bit of space," he said, pushing a strand of hair behind my ear with a slow hand. "What's wrong? No, wait … Let's go. We'll talk later. You're going to miss the show."

He threaded his fingers with mine and pulled me toward the crowd, where my friends' faces began to pop up everywhere. Once we stood in the front and middle, Nathan wrapped his arms around my waist from behind me, our hands still holding.

He held me like that for the rest of the song as I sang "Bartender" to the top of my lungs. I *loved* that song.

Cecile walked up and stood beside me just as the song ended. "Hey!" We hugged each other.

"You okay?" she asked in French.

"Better now, thanks," I replied in French too and kept it that way. "You've been keeping secrets from me."

She raised her brow at me as a reply, and Jordan appeared behind her with drinks as the band played "#41" next. I raised my arms and let out a loud *woo*! as many others in the crowd did. Cecile laughed, and Nathan pulled me in and kissed my cheek.

The music didn't precisely cater to Cecile's taste. But she seemed to be having fun with Jordan, who also kissed her cheek as he handed over a wineglass to her.

This only reminded me of how Tobias was furious at me. With good reason. Jordan didn't seem to plan on letting Cecile go anywhere for the rest of the night.

"We have a lot to talk about tomorrow," I told her. She nodded and squealed after Jordan basically snatched her away from me. Jordan mouthed "thank you" and winked at me. I shook my head at him in return with a smile. *You're welcome*, I thought, but at what cost? At that moment, I couldn't worry about Tobias because I was having too much fun. But the concern was stuck at the back of my head.

The band played "Satellite" and "Crazy" next. I saw my father standing next to Nathan's boss with a big smile, watching from an uncrowded distance away. Nolan and Emily joined us and sang "Crazy" with Nathan and me. Nina, Aiden, and CJ approached us too and sang the last minute of the song with us.

"Where Are You Going" played next, and the slow tune made me feel all mushy inside. It'd been a roller coaster of a night, and it wasn't over yet. Nathan hugged me from behind again, resting his chin on my shoulder.

"I love you," he whispered in my ear.

I turned my neck and looked up at him and whispered back, "I love you too."

He kissed my lips softly and lingered there for a few seconds. He then pulled a black, somewhat long but narrow jewelry box out of his inside jacket pocket. "I was going to wait until tomorrow," he said, handing it over to me. "I should've given this to you earlier today. I feel like it's going to look great with your dress."

"Nathan," I said, turning around to face him and grabbing the box. "But the party—you must've already spent a lot of money on it and—"

"Nonsense. Please just open it, love."

I did. It was a ruby pendant necklace with a thin rose gold chain. It was so beautiful.

"Oh my God, Nathan," I said with a gasp. "I love it." I trailed my finger along the chain and around the stone.

"Do you want to wear it?"

"Yes. Yes, could you—"

"Of course." He took the necklace out of the box and made me turn around again. He fastened the chain around my neck, and I looked up and saw William standing beside stage left. Zara was cuddled up with him, swaying from side to side to the rhythm of the slow tune.

I couldn't seem to look away from them. As much as I tried to remember William telling me how it was something he could never explain—that it was *nothing*—it served no purpose.

I wished I could feel *nothing*.

"They seem cozy," I whispered to Nathan as he tucked the jewelry box back inside his jacket pocket. And I know I shouldn't have said that, but yeah, I was drunk, jealous, and confused. Probably the drunkest I'd ever been in my life. But I was still standing and able to talk to people, so I thought I was good.

Nathan looked at them but said nothing, and that was so unsettling. I wanted him to say something, but he didn't, and now there was no way to know what he was thinking.

Tobias joined them, and Zara placed her arm around him too. And for some reason watching that also hurt. To see how great her relationship was with all of them. It made me crazy jealous.

I looked away.

The band was done playing "Where Are You Going," but a soft flute kept playing, and that's when Dave addressed the guests. Everyone reacted by screaming, whistling, and clapping. He wished me a happy birthday and mentioned how they couldn't leave without playing the next song. And I knew what song that was going to be.

The band started playing "Crash Into Me" as everyone kept making noise, and I felt a fire burning inside me. My gaze wandered toward William, and I caught him watching me too. This was our song. And he'd made this happen, brought Dave Matthews Band for my birthday because he knew how much I loved them. I just couldn't. I looked away but found myself unable to keep it that way.

William sang the song with his arm around Zara's shoulder, but his gaze aimed my way. And I felt like he was singing it to me.

Lily appeared next to me and hugged me. Joel stood next to Nathan, ran his hand around his shoulder, and said something to him in Swedish. They both laughed and chit-chatted—the bromance.

Lily and I sang as we stood next to each other with my arm around her waist, and her arm around my shoulder. "Your favorite song," Lily whispered. I saw her glancing at William next, and he was singing the chorus, no ... shouting it at the ceiling with such emotion I could feel my skin reacting. Lily knew all about it being our song and the meaning behind it.

The song ended, and I had to let a slow breath out through my mouth just to chill the fuck out.

"We haven't been able to talk, just you and me. You know, after everything that happened," Lily said to me. "I'll be in New York for the rest of the week. I think we should have one of our sessions. What do you say?"

Yes, please.

I nodded, and my wide eyes made Lily laugh. I was desperate to sort things out.

The band went on to play all kinds of percussion instruments like drums, bongo drums, and others I didn't even know their name. The guys were doing an improv on the spot for what it seemed. You couldn't tell what song was going to be next. Then a flute joined in.

Dave stepped out of the spotlight as the band kept jamming. He walked over to William, who was still standing just beside stage left with Zara, Tobias, and my new best friend AKA *snitch-guy:* Liam Kelly.

Ugh. He was cute, though.

William kept nodding as Dave leaned in to talk to him. Dave then walked back, grabbed his guitar, and took the microphone to say how they couldn't say goodbye without "Say Goodbye." The crowd cheered again as he invited William to join him.

The band vamped as William jumped up on the stage and was handed a guitar.

"Oh, my God!" Lily shouted, laughing.

Joel shouted something Viking-ish behind me. And Lily and I burst out laughing. And when William shot a sharp nod at Dave, the song exploded, and the crowd too.

Tobias and Eric came looking for Joel since we stood in the

front row. They kept cheering and whistling at a performing William.

I looked over my shoulder, and Nathan seemed anything but happy, but still, he smiled at me. I extended my hand to him, and he took it. I pulled him closer to me, and Zara shouted, "Sis!" as she darted our way.

She hugged Nathan and me and said, "Are you having a good time?"

"I am, thank you!" I shouted back through the noise.

"He's *bloody* brilliant! Look at him!" she shouted, staring at William on stage, stars bursting out of her eyes. She sang along, standing in between Nathan and me. And I had no other option but to stare at William as he sang and played that freaking song.

And I wanted to shout and cheer too, but I couldn't. I sang, though, and I thanked the Norse gods that William never once looked in my direction.

☾

The show was over, and the band stepped off the stage after thanking the crowd a few times. William idled with Dave, talking. Zara unlocked herself from us and placed her hand on Nathan's cheek. "You alright, Natey? Your eyes look wonky."

"Amgood," he shot back with a smile.

"Right. Well, I'll see you guys later." Zara smiled at both of us and walked away.

"Thank you. For putting all of this together," I said to Nathan, placing my arms around his neck as the crowd dispersed. "The necklace is beautiful too. I loved it."

A handful of brave souls dared to go up the stage and ask for a photograph with Dave, to which he agreed. Bryce was obviously one of them. I still owed her a photo-op with William.

And … no. No, I didn't owe her anymore. Bryce took care of it herself by asking William directly. Nolan carried Emily by the waist and helped her up the stage. She joined Bryce for a selfie with William, and then they took one each with him.

I laughed.

"Well, as you can imagine, the show thing was all William's idea," he said with an edge of bitterness in his words.

"But you organized the whole thing, so it wouldn't have happened if you hadn't," I reminded him.

"I guess so," he said with a forced smile. He looked at his watch and said, "Shit. Twelve-oh-two. Happy birthday, love!" He ran his arms around my waist and lifted me as I held on tight to his neck. "I love you." He attacked my lips with a bunch of kisses.

"Billie!" Lily shouted as she hurried our way. Joel followed close behind. Nathan placed me back on my feet.

"Happy birthday!" She hugged me tight and swayed me from side to side in a rough but full of love kind of way. Joel hugged me next, and then Eric came along. And then everyone I knew approached me to say happy birthday. One by one, I hugged them all.

This was all very new to me. I'd never had this many friends. It felt weird. Last year, there were plenty of people at the surprise party, but they were mostly Embassy staff. I'd made a lot of great friends in New York, and it felt kind of great to realize that.

"Kiddo," I heard my father say behind me. Nina was hugging me. She smiled and stepped aside. "Happy birthday. I can't believe you're twenty-one already. The show was great. Did you enjoy it?"

And I don't know if it was all the hugging or just a matter of time before it happened, but a horrible, shuddering chill crept up and down my spine, finally stationing itself on the pit of my stomach. My forehead felt moist with tiny droplets of cold sweat, and I held on to my father's arm with one hand. I knew what was about to happen, what *needed* to happen so the discomfort could find its release.

"Kiddo?" My father searched for my gaze, but I couldn't make myself look at him. "Amena!" he shouted.

I turned around and held on to Nina. "Bathroom. Now," I pleaded. She linked her arm with mine, and Nathan took my other arm. I heard people talking around me, but I was done registering what they were saying.

Amena opened the bathroom door, and in we went Nina, Amena, and me. I couldn't hold it in any longer. Nina helped me get on my knees and held my hair back. I'd never felt so disgusting and embarrassed in my entire life as I threw up in the fucking public toilet.

CHAPTER 20

Right Behind You

April 11, 2010

I PRESSED THE ruby pendant tightly against my chest. I didn't want it to get dirty with my vomit. Nina kept running a hand up and down my back, trying to comfort me. I finally felt like I was done and tried standing up, but Nina helped me.

Amena stood outside the bathroom stall, holding a glass of water. She offered it to me, and I almost snatched it away from her hands.

I drank deep, trying to get the awful acid tang away from my taste buds.

"Please, don't let anyone inside the bathroom right now," I begged, addressing Amena. I dropped the glass on the long marble sink and rested my left hand on it as I let my head hang. I intended to find a cozy spot in this bathroom and spend the night here. I didn't have the courage to step out.

"The bathroom's locked, Miss Murphy," Amena said with a firm bodyguard stance in place. "We're the only ones inside right now."

Perfect.

"Who's got my purse?" I asked.

"David's got it. Just a second." She clicked on her earpiece, nodded a few times, and aimed at the door. She unlocked it and opened it just a tad, enough for David to hand over my bag. I washed my hands with Nina's help as Amena retrieved it. "Here you go, Miss Murphy."

I grabbed a hair tie from my purse and fastened my hair in a low pony. That was the only way I could wear it up since it was too short. I threw water at my face a few times, feeling how the sweat beads stuck on my forehead dissolved away. I rinsed my mouth with water and chugged down the rest of the glass Amena had bought for me.

"Thank God," I said, looking at the mouth wash dispenser on the far end of the countertop. I filled a small paper cup and shot it inside my mouth, spitting it after I swished it for almost half a minute. I tossed the paper cup on the waste bin and grabbed a mint from a small basket of goodies just to make sure my breath was minty fresh.

Damn, I was so dizzy. That dreaded ice-cold sweat wanted to creep up on me again, and I'd sell my soul twice just to avoid having to throw up again on that bathroom, as fancy as it was.

I spotted two sofa chairs to my right just beside the door, and I hurried to throw myself back on one of them. That scared the chills away.

"Shit, Billie," Nina said, squatting in front of me. "Do you need to go back to the bathroom? Maybe you still—"

"No, *no*. I'm fine now. It helped, throwing up before. I just need a second."

A knock on the door.

Amena approached it and opened it just a tad. It was my father, and he stepped right in.

"I'll be outside," Nina said, abandoning me to my father. She didn't want to wait to be thrown out because that's exactly what was going to happen next if she stayed.

"Amena, could you bring my daughter more water please," my father said with his commanding voice. The one that only ever makes an appearance on rare occasions. Amena nodded and stepped out. I wondered if she would actually bring the water or not. Maybe it was my father's polite way to ask her to leave.

My father paced in front of me as if gathering his thoughts. I tried sitting up as straight as I could at my malaise's expense but focused on taking slow and steady breaths through my nose.

He finally stopped, but I didn't dare to meet his gaze.

"We're leaving right now. You're to be taken straight home. Nathan can ride with you, but he will be driven to his apartment afterward," he said. "I've already informed him about this. He's in no position to be taking care of you right now either. He's too intoxicated for my liking. One thing is to have a few drinks, and a whole other is to—"

He cut himself mid-sentence and shook his head a few times.

"I'm sorry," I muttered. "I got a little excited with the wine, and I swear this is the first time this has ever happened. Nathan never drinks like that either."

"You were smoking too. You reek of it," my father snapped back. "It took me a while to get your mother straightened out of her—pleasures. The drinking. The smoking. She was the one who asked for help, by the way. She would get too carried away at times. Always alone, she drank. Never at functions. It was all too stressful for her. Being the ambassador's wife. She never wanted that life, and I was too selfish to oblige to her wishes."

What? It was the first time I ever heard about this.

"You're just like her, you know," he continued. I planned to let him speak. "You might look like me, but you're all *her*. In every possible way. It's painful to watch." He shut his eyes and looked slightly away, his mouth a tight line.

A constant reminder that she's gone. And how he probably thought it was his fault.

He took a deep breath and addressed me once again. "I know

that I've restrained you and that you must feel this—constant *urge* to break away. I know your mother did. But you need to know that it's been necessary. I tried giving your mother some sense of normalcy by having discreet security around her and look at what happened. I can't—*won't* allow it again."

"What happened?" I dared to ask. "I'm old enough to know." This seemed like the best opportunity to ask. He was rambling. He never did. Perhaps he'd finally tell me the truth or maybe I could find a way to lure it out of him.

"You know all there is to know," he said.

"Don't you mean all *you want me* to know? Is it that bad that you can't tell me? I'm not a child anymore. I can't take it. Just say it."

He paced back and forth again, slower this time. And I didn't know if he was finding the courage to finally talk to me or if he was just disappointed in me for wanting to know so much. His face dripped with frustration.

"It's time to go home, Guillermina," he replied instead. "I'm sorry your celebration has to end this way, but you're in no condition to step out like this."

"Just tell me!" I shouted. His eyes widened at me, and his features quickly blazed up into anger. I'd never spoken to my father that way. Never raised my voice like that before. But my patience grew thin, just like his. But we'd been bottling things up all these years. I know I had. And it only got worse the older I got because nothing made sense to me.

My father didn't enjoy me screaming at him like that. That was perfectly written on his face, but still, he said nothing. He gave me a pass because, for some reason, he thought I deserved one. I thought so too.

"Is someone—coming to get me as they did with mom?" I asked in a low, controlled tone.

"You've got nothing to worry about. You're safe. That's what I'm trying to tell you. I couldn't keep your mother safe, but I won't make that same mistake again with you. Look what happened with Thomas the moment I let my guard down with that kid."

I wanted to say so much. How Thomas had been this awful thing that happened but totally unrelated to whatever "danger" he thought my life might pose. And yes, they'd been lax with his background check because my father wanted to change—to trust again.

And once more, all of it led to an unfortunate series of events that had driven me back into a cage I feared might be permanent. Because there I was at the dawn of my 21st birthday, still feeling like a helpless child in my father's presence.

I knew it was useless to say any of those things to him, and I didn't know how much longer I could resist even sitting in this chair. I needed to lie down and get some sleep.

And after more than a few scared-shitless seconds fled the scene, my father said, "He's been given a sentence—Senator Hill. He'll spend a long time in prison for murdering his son."

I took my hands to my face and covered my eyes for a couple of heartbeats.

Justice, after all.

"Let's go," my father said, offering his hand.

"You're never going to tell me, are you?" I asked with a slight grimace drawing itself on my face.

"There's nothing to know. Just know that you're safe." His hand was still extended toward me. I finally took it.

Did I have a choice?

And just when we were about to leave the bathroom, he added, "And the fact that you live alone doesn't mean you're independent. You're still living under *my* roof, which means there won't be any alcohol allowed inside that apartment from now on.

"And I don't even need to tell you that you can't smoke either. I don't care if you're twenty-one. Those are the rules you are to abide by if you wish to remain there, yes?"

I nodded. I knew what Option B consisted of if I refused to comply: Going back to his apartment.

Never.

"With time, you'll understand it's all in your best interest. You are trying to drink and smoke the pain away. Just like your mother did, and I know you still miss her and Caleb—"

Stop!

"Please," I said, raising a hand in front of my chest. "I don't want to talk about—him." I didn't even want to utter his name. I'd just recently been able to talk about my mother without bursting into a bawl. But Caleb ... I couldn't promise I wouldn't. And the night had been humiliating enough. I refused to walk out that door crying and making a fool out of myself.

He opened the door, and Nathan, Nina, Aiden, Zara, Lily, and Joel stood there waiting for us to step out. David and Amena flanked the bathroom door with a firm bodyguard stance in place. Amena never went for that glass of water. I wouldn't have either if I were her. My father could be very intimidating when he wanted to be.

Thankfully, William wasn't there. At least he was thoughtful enough to spare me the humiliation because there was *no way* he didn't know what happened. The Sjöberg grapevine ran a tight network. I knew that much.

The party seemed to continue outside. Good ... because the show must go on and all that crap. It would be easier for me to sneak out that way if people were still having fun—distracted.

Sophie and Cecile were right outside the corridor that led to the bathroom. I guess they heard I felt ill too but didn't want to cram up outside the bathroom door.

I quickly approached them and whispered, "I feel like *shit*, and my father has pulled the plug. He's making me go back to the apartment." I looked behind them, and Jordan talked and laughed with Ren, most probably waiting for Sophie and Cecile to return. "You should stay."

"No, of course not. We'll leave with you," Sophie said.

"No. *Please* stay. You never get to see Ren. You seem to be having fun. You too," I said to Cecile. I took my keys out of my purse and handed them over to her.

"Are you sure, Billie? It feels wrong to stay," Cecile replied.

"Please, do it for me. Tomorrow we'll spend the entire day together."

They both hugged me, and I said goodbye.

Nathan walked up to me and reached for my hand to lead me out. Every step I took felt as if my feet were two chunks of lead, trying to fuse with the floor. It'd been the most exhausting day ever.

The servers quickly took our laminated numbers to retrieve our phones. Once outside, I realized Lily, Joel, Nina, Aiden, and Zara had followed Nathan and me out.

"What are you guys doing? You should all stay," I said to them, shooing them with a limp hand.

"Do you want me to come home with you?" Nina asked. She seemed somewhat worried. "You know, to keep you company and make sure someone puts you to bed." She laughed, and I couldn't help but laugh a weak laugh back because, yeah, I wouldn't mind the company. And Nathan wasn't coming with me. My father had already delivered that warning.

"I can help too," Zara joined in.

Nathan smiled a tight smile back at them. He was surely grateful for them offering to help when he couldn't.

"You stay," I said to Lily and Joel.

"But—" Lily began to say.

I hugged her to make her stop from making up an excuse to leave when she didn't have to. "Your friends are all still in there. You can't leave."

Zara's phone rang as we walked toward the SUV. She said yes a bunch of times and hung up the phone. William showed up in his Porsche a few seconds later and parked behind us. I quickly looked away. I was a mess and a half. I'd never want him to see me in this condition.

"I'll meet you guys back at the apartment," Zara said, rushing toward William. "We'll be right behind you."

I laughed bitterly on the inside. Zara could be bathed and in her pajamas by the time we arrived if she wanted to. That's how fast I knew William liked to drive his car.

Zara was barely closing the door when William's engine roared as he sped off into the night.

Behind you, my ass.

CHAPTER 21

Come Here

DAVID JUMPED ON the third-row seat of the SUV, and Nina, Nathan, and I sat together in the second row. Aaron, whom I hadn't seen since I arrived, drove the car alongside Amena. He'd stayed outside this entire time, posted at the entrance.

"Where's CJ?" I asked Nina, trying to keep my voice down.

"He—left. Right after he congratulated you for your birthday after the concert," she replied, widening her eyes at me. Yeah, it was best to talk about that later. David sat right behind us, and something told me it had something to do with him.

"I wish you could spend the night at my place," I whispered to Nathan, resting my head on his shoulder.

"Oh, I'm staying, love," he said confidently. "There's no way I'm leaving you tonight. Thank you for offering to come Nina, but I'm staying."

"Mr. Saunders, we have to comply with Mr. Murphy's request," Aaron said from the driver's seat in a stern tone. "We can't allow you access to Miss Murphy's apartment tonight. I apologize."

"Aaron, come on. We're all grown-ups here. And Billie's not a child anymore. For God's sake, she's twenty-one years old."

"Nathan, I think it's—" I began to say.

"What a sack of bollocks," he said, cutting me off. He took a deep breath, trying to reel in his temper, or so it seemed. I had to reassure him.

"Nathan, I'll be fine. Nina and Zara will be there with me," I said, my voice sluggish. "I just need to sleep. I'll see you all day tomorrow."

Nathan replied with a snort and turned on his phone. A ton of notifications dropped in, filling his screen. I let him be, hoping that would distract him. He was drunk and in a bad mood, it was evident.

I shut my eyes, unable to keep myself awake any longer, but Nathan woke me up a few seconds later, saying, "What the bloody hell is this, Murph?"

He startled me, probably unaware that I had just shut my eyes. "Wha—what's, what?"

Nathan scrolled through pictures that had been sent to him through iMessage. I focused on the screen and saw Lana was the sender. She'd sent him all the photographs from Tobias's premiere. Well, the ones with William and me on them.

I scrunched up my nose and ran the palm of my hand up my forehead. His reaction made it clear it was the first time he looked at them.

He tucked his phone back inside his jacket pocket and looked away.

I was more asleep than awake. Perhaps I was already sleeping in my bed, and the nightmares had chosen a different direction this time. But it wasn't the case.

"Nathan, it's—nothing. They're just photographs from Tobias's premiere. We all got photographed."

Nathan laughed, still looking out the window. "Lana was right."

"You take advice from *Lana* now?"

Yeah, we were going at it in the car. In front of everyone. At first, I thought we could wait it out until we got home and talk about it privately, on the curbside, that is, since he couldn't come up. But once he said Lana, I lost it. I couldn't stop seeing that little smirk of hers drawing on her face when she implied she *knew* Nathan.

The car came to a complete stop, and Aaron and Amena shot out from their seats, opening the SUV doors on both sides. Nathan stepped out on his side, and I followed Nina out.

"I'll go find Zara," Nina said, walking inside the building. David escorted her.

Nathan and I moved away from the main entrance. I leaned against the wall and said, "So? What about Lana? Is there anything I'm missing here?"

"I saw you, you know?"

"You saw me—where?"

He arched his neck back with a sad laugh and loosened his tie. "You thought I wouldn't go looking for you? When you went missing during the party?"

He still needed to clarify what exactly he saw, and I wouldn't say a word until he did.

"Amena told me that you were okay and that you needed a minute, so I waited. But a minute turned into ten, twenty, thirty minutes. She finally told me where you were, and to my surprise, you weren't alone." His eyelids were heavy, and the way he bit his lip, with such disappointment, just destroyed me.

Nathan didn't deserve for me to be this torn. And seeing him like this made me panic. The thought of losing him was unbearable.

"We were just talking," I replied. It was the truth. "I was having a hard time about Caleb, and he came looking for me because the show was about to start. It's not like I sought him out to talk or something."

"I know you were just talking. I heard you both talking about Jordan. That's why I went back." He sighed. "I've been trying to be—*patient* with you. After William got shot, everything changed. I can see the way you look at him, and I don't know if it's guilt. If somehow you feel—I don't know, responsible for him getting hurt or if you bloody bonded over that, but I'm not an idiot."

"I—no. I mean, I do feel guilty about what happened, of course. He *did* get shot because of me. But I'm with you it's not like—"

"His relationship with Zara makes you jealous too," he threw in. I stared at him because I didn't know what to say. Here I was, feeling like a sheet of glass. Transparent. And for some stupidly naive reason, I thought Nathan was the exception to being aware of my translucency.

But he wasn't. I guess everyone could see right through me all the fucking time.

"What? Why do you seem so surprised, Murph?"

"I'm not jealous of Zara," I lied, too quickly that it almost burned my tongue. I had to. "She's your sister, and William's just my neighbor."

"Neighbor of the year, that is," Nathan said with a snort, looking at me, analyzing my every gesture. "I'm *sick* of him. Everything revolves around him. Everyone. It's like none of you can't help yourselves. I've been trying to figure out what this— awestruck-filled admiration means. And I try to tell myself how it's nothing because I know that you love me. I can feel it. It's just that I've never felt this—insecure before. It's not quite like me to feel this way, and I *hate* it."

"I do love you, Nathan. You know that. I adore you." *So much*. And I kept wishing he didn't ask if I had feelings for William because I loved Nathan too much to lie to him about it.

My reply seemed to put him at ease. His eyes were still wonky, as Zara noticed before, and that wouldn't change until he slept the drunkenness off.

His brow furrowed again as he asked, "What about those photographs?"

"I was furious when that happened. You have *no* idea. You see me smiling, but I was asking him to let go of me through my teeth. I was so worried about what you were going to think. I discussed it with Caleb afterward."

It seemed like a million years had passed since then, but it'd only been a few weeks since that happened. When Caleb died, it was like the end of an era. Anything before that felt so far away— distant. Yet the pain was still so achingly raw.

"Lana approached me when I came back alone after I went looking for you. I was at the bar refilling my drink, hoping to stop thinking nonsense. And she asked about you and said how everyone is saying that you and William are secretly dating. And she said she had proof, but I know how she likes playing games like that, so I ignored her."

"And you guys used to date or …?"

"No. No, we never dated."

"So just sex then?" I queried. That look on Lana's face didn't mean *nothing*. And the thought of them together drilled a hole through my stomach. The idea of her scheming her way back to Nathan made me want to puke again.

"Yes." He shot a lazy grimace at me. "But what does this have to do with anything?"

"It's got everything to do with everything! I'm shocked that you can't see it when you know *how much* she likes to play games. It seems to me like you know her so well, so you tell me. What does she have to gain by making you think that I'm 'secretly' dating William? I met her, by the way. Earlier tonight. She says hi, but I'm glad to see that you don't need me to pass on the message since you've already been reacquainted."

"You're jealous," he said, not a hint of a question in his remark.

"Crazy jealous."

"Come here." Nathan took my mouth and kissed me like he never had before. Each brush of his tongue against mine filled with a primal claim. And I met him, stroke for stroke. He'd pinned me against the concrete wall behind us, and all I wanted was for him to come up. I didn't care if I'd find myself fainting from exhaustion the next day because of it.

I needed to convince myself that Nathan was *it*. That William was and would always be an object of awestruck admiration, as Nathan said before. To me and everyone else, so it seemed.

I wasn't too crazy to feel that way about him. Apparently, everyone did too. I knew Zara, my friends from school, and half the female world population did.

Everywhere and anywhere William went, people loved him. He would always be the sun that rises every day and fades out into dusk. Get too close, and you'll burn. I knew that already. I just had to wake up. William was and had always been too much for me to handle. The things I felt for him felt so ridiculously out of proportion that they couldn't be real.

Nathan was real, and he was standing right in front of me, kissing me with all he had. And I did too, after days of feeling like I couldn't give all of myself to him again.

Nathan stopped kissing me abruptly and said, "I have to have you tonight. I want you spread on your bed in nothing but that necklace."

Listening to him saying that made me burn and yearn for him in a way I hadn't before. As if realizing for the first time how I probably couldn't live without him. The way he kept talking to me with such untamed desire sparked things up inside me that made me think these feelings had to be answer enough.

He broke away from my lips again and said, "Tell me what I have to do to come up, and I'll do it."

I turned toward the apartment building's green shade, and Amena was gone. However, Aaron and David still lingered there, not entirely giving their backs to us but rather standing at an oblique angle, offering us the most privacy they could.

"Come. I'll talk to Aaron." I grabbed Nathan's hand and pulled him.

"Hey," I said to them. Aaron and David acknowledged me, ignoring Nathan's presence. That wasn't good. Aaron must've wanted to keep a distance from him, and I could only imagine why.

"Ready to leave, Mr. Saunders?" Aaron said to him, looking at me. *That's why.* I was having a hard time leveling with the intense indigo of his commanding gaze.

"Nathan's walking me up," I said casually, ignoring his authority. An authority that was bestowed upon him by my father and that I was expected to comply with.

Aaron lifted a brow in return, and by the look on David's face, I knew he was most definitely going to stay out of this conversation.

"Miss Murphy, we've discussed this. No access for Mr. Saunders, and you are to go straight up to your apartment."

There was nothing left for me to do but beg. But the thought of doing so felt out of place and humiliating. I guess Nathan caught up with that, or the lawyer in him was out of service because he didn't argue his case like I thought he would.

"I'll see you tomorrow, love."

With that, Aaron darted toward the SUV and climbed in the driver's seat. David opened the door for Nathan, and I walked him over to the car to say goodbye. Nathan pulled his phone out, unlocked it, and deleted the messages Lana had just sent him. He then blocked her number.

"I don't take advice from that girl," he said. "But I can unblock her from time to time just to watch you get riled up like you did before and make you forget about it in a million different ways."

I tugged on Nathan's jacket and pulled myself against him with a giddy smile, and said, "That'll teach me."

"It certainly will." He placed a soft kiss on my lips, and he leaped into his seat. "Happy birthday, love."

CHAPTER 22

A Choice

"HEY, BRUCE," I said to our door guard, who seemed in a great mood despite the hour.

"Happy Birthday, Miss Murphy," he replied, holding the door open for David and me. I summoned a smile and thanked him as I ambled toward the elevator.

"David, I'll walk up on my own. I'm good," I said to him. He raised a brow in return, probably not believing I *was* good. And I know I must've looked like shit, but I wasn't feeling ill anymore, just exhausted. "I swear."

"Okay." He waved his keycard for elevator access. "Happy Birthday, Miss Murphy."

"Thank you, David. And … thanks again. For everything."

Talking to him earlier had been helpful. He'd listened to me, and I also got to know him better. I hoped he and CJ could work things out.

"Anytime, Miss Murphy. Have a good night."

I stepped into the elevator and said, "You too, Dr. Scott."

The elevators shut as David laughed, making me smile. I texted Nina next to let her know I was coming up. It was best not to knock on William's door. But she replied quickly, saying she'd meet me in a second.

As I walked out of the elevator toward my apartment, William's piano filled the hall.

Nina opened the door and stepped out. Zara followed her. She had changed into a comfy outfit, although her hair and face were still done. "Hey, sis. Feeling better?"

William's piano came to a halt.

"Yeah, thanks. And don't worry. I'll just take a shower and go to bed," I replied. "I'm sorry you had to come, Nina. I feel like I probably wasted your time."

"Don't be silly. Come on. Let's go," she said, herding me toward the door. "I'll make sure you're good before going to bed, and then I'll leave."

William was now leaning against his doorframe, his piercing blue gaze directed at me, testing my resolve. I swear I picked up a bit of annoyance on his pretty face too.

"You're welcome to stay if you want to," I said to Nina, trying not to look into William's eyes. I knew how easy it was to get lost in them. He still watched from a distance without emitting a sound.

"Or I could have the guys drive you back to your place," I offered Nina as I opened my purse, looking for my keys. "Shhhhit." I let my forehead rest against the door, feeling defeated.

"What's wrong?" Zara asked as I listened to her steps approaching me.

"Nothing. I—gave my keys to Cecile," I replied with frustration. "Aaron carries a copy, but he left just now to drop Nathan off at his place. We'll just have to wait for him to return."

William disappeared into his apartment as Zara said, "Doesn't Nate live a few blocks away? I'm sure Aaron will return in a few minutes. Why don't you come inside and wait for him to arrive?"

I parted my mouth to reply when William stepped out from his apartment and marched toward my door holding a set of keys in his hand. He unlocked my door and opened it just a tad for me to understand and process the fact that, yes, he'd *actually* unlocked my apartment.

"Your father gave me this set of keys—for emergencies," William explained, walking away. I hadn't asked for an explanation—yet. But I was going to, of course, and he knew that.

I was in shock and unable to believe my father would trust someone with keys to my apartment after what happened.

"Yeah, I made that same face when he first suggested the idea," William said, sliding the keys inside his pocket. "He made me sign a bible of paperwork, as you can imagine."

"What kind of paperwork?" I asked. Nina and Zara remained still—attentive.

"Could you guys give us a couple of minutes?" William said to them.

"Sure," Nina said quickly, walking toward my apartment. Zara crossed her arms at her chest and shot William a side-glance but followed Nina into my apartment and shut the door behind her.

This was the last thing I needed right now—*another* conversation with William. I'd walked up to my apartment feeling hopeful after Nathan left, having decided a lot of things. But it was impossible to keep moving forward with my decisions and realizations if William kept showing up in front of me with that look on his face.

I took a few steps away from the surveillance camera's reach. I didn't need this interaction to go on the record.

William parted his mouth to speak, but I took the floor instead. "I just wanted to say I loved the show. It was great. Thank you." I didn't know how this conversation would end, but

I wanted to make sure he knew how much it meant to me that he did that for me. "You were great up there, by the way."

"I'm glad you enjoyed it," he said with a relaxed side-smile.

I looked away and shook my head twice, fast, just to brush off that mood off me, and asked him about the paperwork my father made him sign.

"I signed off on an NDA, which I've already breached by telling you this." He laughed a low, lazy laugh. "And another contract, stating I can hold on to the keys for twelve months unless the contract is renewed. With rules and such. I don't want to bore you to death with the specifics."

"And what are the consequences of having breached the NDA?" I was worried. Not that I would tell on him, of course, but what if my father had a way to find out William told me about this? And now Zara and Nina knew too.

Zara could easily mention it to Nathan, and he was my father's bestie. But after tonight, my father made it clear that yes, he loves Nathan, but there's a line of authority that no one can step on. Not even Nathan.

"Aside from losing your father's respect? An economic penalty," he said, not a pinch of worry on his face.

"What? How much money are we talking about here?" *What the fuck.*

"Nothing I can't comfortably pay off," he said with a frown. "Not that I'm looking forward to it, of course."

My father never ceased to amaze me—the things he did behind my back. I wonder what *things* had gone back and forth between him and Nathan, because I was now convinced there had to be at least something there, a contract, an agreement, a pact, or something. Like the good lawyer he is, Nathan would never admit to any of it, even if I begged for him to tell me. So I would never know. William, as always, didn't give two shits.

And I'm not going to lie; it *was* reassuring to know that William had a key. I knew there was no way something like what happened with Thomas could happen again, but if William had access to my apartment that day, maybe things would've been different. Maybe Caleb wouldn't have died.

"Why are you telling me this?"

"Because it's *ridiculous*," he spat back the words. Almost furious. "It's just a spare key. And the fact that your father gave it to me means that he trusts me or else he wouldn't have even offered it to me.

"I literally took a bullet for you," he reminded me as if somehow I'd be able to forget about it. "That should've been enough for him. But it wasn't. He needed paperwork." William laughed again and ran a hand up and down his face. "This made me realize how deep his fears are ingrained when it comes to you. And I don't like it."

"It's okay. I'm used to this kind of stuff." Or better said, I was getting used to it.

"You shouldn't."

I know! But what was I to do? I depended on my father economically. I was still studying, and I didn't even have to ask him to know that I wouldn't be allowed to work while I got my degree. I didn't even know if I would be allowed to work at all after graduation.

I was trapped, and I had made my peace with it. Living here on my own, under his terms, was the best available choice for me until I graduated and found a way to become financially independent, whether he agreed to it or not.

But I didn't share my thoughts with him. Instead, I said, "I won't say a word to my father about this. Or anyone else," just to reassure him. "I'll talk to Nina, and you should probably talk to Zara."

"Zara wouldn't dare tell a soul."

Right.

"Well, you're safe then, I guess." I hoped. "Thanks for getting the door. I'll send Zara over to you in a minute." I turned around and walked away.

"Are you feeling better?" he asked. "I heard you were sick."

"I'm—yeah," I said, looking over my shoulder. "I just had too much to drink."

"It pisses me off that I can't take care of you," he said, sauntering my way. I looked away but froze in place, careful not to go into the surveillance camera's detection area.

"I'm fine. I don't need to be taken care of."

"Why isn't Nathan here?" he asked. I turned around because I was sure he would walk around me and position himself in front of me anyway. "Why would he leave when you were sick just before? I don't get the guy. And on your birthday?"

"He wasn't allowed access tonight, that's why," I replied, not wanting to give him an extended explanation, but just enough for him to stop grilling me with his questions. I didn't need William to trash-talk Nathan either. Not when Nathan wanted to be here if he could.

"Denied access? Why? What did he do?"

"William ... *stop*."

"Then *what* happened?" he asked, his gaze moving from my face to my necklace, spotting it for the first time.

"Nathan's drunk, and my father didn't want him coming up because of it, okay. That's it."

My thoughts were boiling up into a scorching temper.

"I wouldn't have given a shit if *Daddy* didn't give me access. I wouldn't have left you alone on your birthday. Period. I would've—"

"You say that," I cut him short. "But I'd like to see you try going against Aaron someday. It's not that easy."

"Nathan keeps doing that. Leaving when he shouldn't. Or should I remind you how he left for the Super Bowl and left you crying?"

"That was two months ago! And that was a completely different situation. *I* asked him to leave. And if it were up to me, I'd want him to be here right now."

There I said it.

He needed to know where I stood with Nathan. He needed to know that I loved him and that I wanted to be with him, but William kept messing with my mind all the time. I had to put an end to it, as painful and challenging as it was.

"So … what? You're choosing *Nathan*?" William asked, glancing at the ruby pendant again with such fierceness I thought it would shatter to pieces. I looked down at it and instinctively ran a finger through the red stone.

My eyes went wide from the bluntness of his question.

Why would he corner me like this?

"You don't understand, it's—"

"You're shitting me, right?"

"William—"

"Save it." He snorted and shot a smirk my way, the kind that drove me crazy. Bad crazy.

His lips then went into a tight line, and he nodded a few times. He turned around and walked away. "I would've chosen an emerald … your favorite color. To match your eyes. Too bad the guy doesn't even know what you like. Good luck with that."

"William. Wait—"

"I'm done." He slammed the door behind him, and I shut my eyes as I processed what had just happened. Half of my body wanted to go after him, to tell him I didn't know what I wanted yet, to give me time. But the other half pulled me back in. It was time to grow up, wake up, and start owning my choices.

I walked back inside my apartment and found Nina and Zara talking casually in the living room. The room went silent as I approached them. They both glanced at me.

"Hey guys," I said, coaxing a smile. Zara looked away and stood up.

"How are you feeling?" Nina asked. What a question, and how to begin to answer it?

"Exhausted, but I'm good. Thanks. Um—I could ask the guys to drive you home, or if you want to stay, you're welcome."

"No, of course not. I'm pretty tired too. It's best if I go home," she replied, standing up too.

"I'll let Aaron know, okay?"

"Thanks, Billie." She hugged me. "Happy birthday. I had a lot of fun tonight. The show was amazing."

"It was. And you need to tell me all about Aiden some other time. He's cute, right?"

Nina laughed a nervous laugh. "I will, and yeah, he's a great guy."

"Very well, then!" Zara said, approaching me. "I guess I'll see you tomorrow, birthday girl. Rest up that pretty head of yours. Will and I will be right next door if you need anything, sis."

Will.

"Thanks—sis," I replied. I still couldn't make myself sound legit when I called her that. It was so ridiculous.

They both left, and I was finally alone, so I took an uncomfortably hot shower to avoid my mind from wandering and collapsed in my bed. But a nagging thirst invaded me during my sleep. My throat was dry, and I craved a glass of water.

With my eyes still closed, I sat on my bed and reached out for my phone. My head was threatening me with a monstrous headache that would surely explode in the morning. I looked at the screen through shuttered lids. 3:45 a.m.

I threw myself back on my bed to gather the courage I required to walk out of my bedroom and grab the water I desperately needed. And in that stillness, I heard a faint laugh across the wall. The laughter eased into a moan. And another. And another.

No. No. No. No. No.

This isn't happening.

Hadn't William's doctor requested him to abstain from *exerting himself?* But when has he ever done as he is told?

I grabbed a pillow and held it against my face trying to smother the moans of pleasure that filtered to my room, but there was nothing I could do to stop listening. And I remembered what William said about wanting to fight the wall when he heard me having sex with Nathan, and I'd never related to anyone or anything as much as I did at this moment because I wanted to *demolish* it.

Maybe Sophie and Cecile had arrived already. I needed backup, so I bolted out of my room and opened the guest room's door only to find it empty, but the thirst was still waiting to be satiated.

After chugging down two large glasses of water in the kitchen, I dragged myself to the living room and collapsed on my couch, lacking the guts to go back to my room and keep listening to how William had also made his choice.

It surprised me how shock didn't overtake me. It's as if I knew to expect it. I suspected there was something going on between them, so why would I be caught off guard? I was furious, disappointed, destroyed. But stunned? Blindsided?

Never.

A bit of denial, maybe. It wasn't like I had a hard time with pretending like shit didn't bother me all the time.

Yes, denial wasn't a half-bad idea most of the time. So I started by shutting my eyes and welcoming the nightmares. At least those weren't real. They'd vanish as soon as I brought myself to a wake.

CHAPTER 23

An Understanding

MY EYELIDS FLUTTERED, and my head rested on a pillow. A light blanket covered the lower half of my body. There was a fresh glass of water set for me on the coffee table. Outside my window, the day was deceiving, somewhat gray. I couldn't tell the time, but it must've been early because it all felt too quiet—still. The city hadn't woken up.

Sunday.

This time I wouldn't make the same mistake again. I planned to have an insanely dark coffee with a side of ibuprofen for breakfast. There was nothing much on my schedule for the day aside from: hardening the fuck up, forgetting about the moans beyond the wall, and lobotomizing William. For the hundredth time. *For good*, I promised.

Three simple tasks, but essential, nonetheless.

Oh yeah, and it was still my birthday. I'd probably wait for Lily to fulfill her promise of bringing over those almond croissants and stuff my face with them throughout the day. Jot that down as the fourth item on my to-do list, please.

Anyway, it was time to get my ass up from that couch, which became my new best friend after the unnamable events of the wee hours of the night. It was my good luck couch now because no nightmares occupied my dreams as I slept there. Even my subconscious was too fed up and drained to concoct any terrors.

I allowed myself one last long, slow, annoyingly unpunctual train of thought that consisted of self-inflicted mental torture. I didn't know how *the hell* I was ever going to be capable of looking at Zara again, knowing she'd shared William's bed, listening to her reacting to him.

And now I needed a big fat cake because I knew what my wish was going to be when I blew those candles out: *Ctrl + alt + delete William* because I had no idea of what my reaction would be like when I saw him again.

My fear was that if they became a thing, then what? We'd all somehow become in-laws? Attend each other's weddings? Suffer in silence through eternity? It'd be like constantly picking a wound and denying it to heal. And perhaps with time, it would. But an ugly scar would surely remain—a constant reminder of what could've been but never was and never will be.

And my father wanted me to stop drinking? Pff. I shook my head at the outrageous inconsideration of his request. Not that I wanted to drink anytime soon, but I couldn't promise I wouldn't want to some other day. It usually takes a few days to forget a nasty hangover, I learned.

My mind wouldn't cease the internal chatter. And another prouder part of me delivered me this disapproving look of, *how dare you mope for William when he turned around and fucked Zara a sliver of a wall away from you when he'd promised there was nothing going on between them. When he knew you'd be able to listen. When he said he wouldn't stop pursuing you anymore.*

That last statement didn't age well, didn't it?

As much as my blood boiled, my head shook, and my fists clenched with powerlessness, I couldn't blame William. I pushed him into Zara's arms, delivered him to her on a silver platter.

But it was still so heart-achingly devastating to see how easily he allowed himself to be driven away. To move on and invite her to his bed.

It'd probably been the right call then.

That realization showed my heart a kindness that I held on to like a lifeline—that I so desperately needed. But my thirst brought me back to the physical realm, drove me out of my head, and demanded—*what about me?*

After emptying the glass of water that either Sophie or Cecile had laid for me on the coffee table at some point during the night, I decided to brew a delicious pot of coffee.

And as I waited for it to be ready, I walked over to the guest room to check on Sophie and Cecile just to make sure they were both home and okay. Carefully, I pushed the doorknob down and opened the door just a tad.

Hello, Jordan's ass. We meet again.

I shut the door as slowly and cautiously as I could and ran back to the kitchen to stare at how each drop of coffee fell into the pot. If only to wipe out the image of Jordan's body sprawled on the bed naked beside Cecile—his tattoos slithering up his arm and fading onto his shoulder blade. Another long, black, geometrical tattoo ran down the length of his spine.

Tobias was going to *murder* me, not if, but *when* he found out about this. It was a matter of time before Jordan mentioned something to Tobias. They were friends, but I assumed he hadn't told Jordan a thing about liking Cecile or sleeping with her in the past. And I didn't know if Cecile would even mention it to Jordan.

The coffee was still brewing at a glacial pace, so I went to my room and changed into jeans and an oversized black t-shirt, slightly tucking it in the front. I grabbed my phone from my nightstand and two ibuprofen from the foyer closet on my way back to the kitchen and slipped them into my back pocket.

It was 8:15 a.m., and the coffee was finally ready. I grabbed a cup and filled it up as the rich smell of it invaded my nostrils. I took the first sip, and suddenly, I believed that everything was going to be okay, that I'd done the right thing in choosing Nathan. I just had to allow things to fall into place, like an ocean settling after a level-five storm.

A faint knock on my door interrupted me from drinking my authorized stimulant of choice. They could take wine and cigarettes away from me, but never coffee.

I grabbed my cup and took it with me to open the door. When I peeked through the peephole, I saw the last person on Earth I wanted to see right now: Tobias.

"Hey, Billie," he said, twitching his lips to the side. "Happy birthday." His eyes looked tired—remorseful.

Hell no.

I reached for the pills and pushed them down my throat with a long drink that almost drained my coffee and scorched my esophagus in the process. *They better kick in fast.* Then, I stepped out to talk to Tobias in the hall. *Let there be witnesses*, I thought, looking up at the camera.

It wasn't going to be a lazy Sunday.

"Thanks, Tob," I said with a smile, wondering if it would conceal the mini panic attack that was about to surface.

"I'm so sorry about yesterday. I was drunk, and I messed up," he said, rubbing the overnight scruff on his face. "I know I haven't talked to you about Cecile, but I honestly thought you knew something. She's your best friend, I mean, how is it that she hasn't—" he trailed off, taking his hands to his face and rubbing it with exasperation.

"Don't worry about it," I said reassuringly. "I feel like shit because you know I wouldn't have introduced them if I knew something was going on between you guys. And I don't know why she's chosen not to tell me about it. After her breakup with Paul, she—well, Sophie says she hasn't gotten over what happened. And *how* it happened. She hasn't been able to forgive herself for it."

"I know that. We've talked—a lot. And she's been clear with me from the start. It's *just sex* and nothing more, but I keep hoping she will warm up to me, you know?" He dragged a hand through his light brown hair.

"The conversations we've had it's like nothing I've ever experienced with anyone else before, Billie. It's like I can't help but open myself up to her. Like I want to bare my soul to her. And when we're together, I feel like we're on the same page. That we want the same things, but the moment she walks out the door, she's *gone*."

I loved them both so much, and nothing would've made me happier than to see them happy together. But I also knew Cecile, and I knew what Tobias was talking about. She could put up thick walls when she wanted to—the kind of walls that are impossible to take down.

"I'm in a bit of a hurry. My flight leaves at ten-o-five, but I assumed she's here, and I just want to talk to her real quick before I go. I don't know when I'll get to see her again."

I looked over my shoulder at my door and bit my lower lip, thinking of what to say that wouldn't give away the fact that Cecile was *indisposed* at the moment.

"She's sleeping, Tob. I don't think it's—"

"Please, Billie," he begged. His puppy eyes were going to be the death of me. "I know I fucked up yesterday. Wake her up and tell her I'm here, and if she doesn't want to talk to me, then fine. I'll leave."

"Give me one second." I went back inside my apartment, not knowing how to fix this mess. I didn't want to lie to Tobias.

He didn't deserve it. But I also wanted to protect Cecile. I didn't know what to do!

Tobias pushed the door open and caught me pacing in the foyer.

"Why aren't you waking her up?"

"Um, yeah, it's—that's what I was about to do."

Tobias locked his gaze with mine and angled his head. "He's in there, isn't he?"

I swallowed and gathered up the words to say, "Yes, he is."

"I'm going to fucking kill him," Tobias said through his teeth, aiming at the guest room. The creamy skin on his face and neck built up in color and his fists were clenched so hard his knuckles were white.

I dropped my mug on the foyer table and ran after him, pulling his arm with my single functioning hand. "Tob! Tob, look at me. Please, wait!"

He didn't look at me, and he didn't wait. He dragged me with him with every step he took. And then the guest room door flew open.

Jordan jumped up from the bed like a warrior ready to strike and covered himself with his hands, but I guess his hands weren't big enough. And he realized that too because he took a pillow and covered himself with it. Yeah, I planned to offer that pillow to him as a souvenir. It was definitely going to be a memorable event.

"Hey, man," he said to Tobias, his face blank. He then turned to look at Cecile, who remained in place, half her body under the sheets, her arms hugging a pillow. She didn't do as much as open her eyes and stared at the scene before her. She glanced at me, and I pleaded for forgiveness with my eyes.

She raised her brow and pulled herself up, tugging the sheet with her. She rolled the sheet sloppily around her body as she got out of bed and wandered off to the bathroom. Jordan and Tobias followed Cecile's movements with predatorial gazes. She then shut the door with a loud thud behind her.

I stepped away from the scene and leaned my back against the wall beside the guest room's door.

"What can I do for you?" Jordan finally said to Tobias. I could only see Tobias's profile from where I stood, his teeth almost bearing.

"How about you get the fuck out and let me talk to her," he replied to Jordan. "Seems to me like you're done."

"Not exactly," I heard him say, followed by a deep, short laugh. "But how about *you* step out and let me throw some clothes on so you can tell me what's your fucking problem."

Tobias was like a tiger about to pounce on Jordan. And even though they were the same height, Jordan was massive, broad, mighty, whereas Tobias was all muscle too, but lean and long.

"Get dressed," Tobias ordered, throwing a shirt he picked up from the floor at him. "And no, I'm not stepping out."

"Suit yourself," Jordan replied. I ran to the kitchen to retrieve my phone. I needed reinforcements. I couldn't allow them to get into a fight. Not when Cecile would be caught up in the middle of it.

The easiest and fastest solution would've been to call William and have him put the fire out. But I couldn't make myself look at him. Not even if his presence was necessary here. And I didn't want to involve Aaron, who could single-handedly take care of the situation before anyone could even know what hit them.

This episode couldn't be reported. I had enough on my plate with my father as it was. The last thing I needed was to get Cecile and Tobias blacklisted.

I imagined Lily and Joel had probably stayed up late last night because that's how they rolled, and Joel was a heavy sleeper and a late riser, Lily always complained. But he was my only hope.

Luckily, Lily took the call with a raspy voice after a couple of rings.

"Lily. I need Joel down here. Now."

"What's wrong?" Her voice sounded alert now.

"Tobias came looking for Cecile, and Jordan's here so ..."

"Shit. Baby. Baby, wake up. Joel!" I heard a groan through the phone. "I'll send him over." She ended the call, and I walked back out to see what was happening.

Jordan was dressed now, thank God. And Cecile hadn't stepped out of the bathroom yet. I stood a safe distance away. And I would've escaped to my bedroom and seek cover, but the only reason I didn't was that Cecile was still in there.

"How could you?" Tobias said to Jordan with the deepest frown of disappointment. "I pulled you aside yesterday. I told you *everything*. You said you'd find a way to slip away from her. What in the actual fuck, man?"

"Well, tough shit because I like her too. A lot. And I asked her about you, and she said you weren't exclusive and that she'd been clear to you about it. What did you want me to do?"

"To show some respect."

"Respect," Jordan scoffed. "I've known you for years, Tobias. Don't throw this next-level bullshit at me about being so self-righteous and shit. You would've done the same. Isn't that how you ended up sleeping together in the first place? You—not respecting the fact that she was some other guy's girl. That's fucking worse than this because right now, Cecile's single, and she has a right to choose who to share her bed with. It's not like you can claim her or some shit like that because you feel like you *like her more* than I do."

"That *guy*," Tobias said, pointing at the bathroom door

where Cecile was, "wasn't my friend, you idiot."

Jordan stared at Tobias as he ran his tongue through his teeth. I mean, Tobias had a point there, and I guess Jordan saw it too, but he seemed like the proud kind of guy who wouldn't just dip his chin and fold over his hands.

"You're just trying to turn things around and make this about *me* when you're this piece-of-shit-friend who can't keep his dick in his pants," Tobias continued.

Joel showed himself in, surveying the situation. Tobias acknowledged him and shook his head, glancing my way. He then shot some rough words in Joel's direction, who replied something back in a similar tone. All in Swedish, of course.

Tobias looked away and returned his focus to Jordan. Joel nodded once my way, and I immediately felt more at ease. But I was stressed about Tobias's flight. You know that awful feeling you get when you're late for the airport? I couldn't help but feel that anxiety in my gut, even if Tobias didn't seem to care about the time.

I heard Cecile walking out of the bathroom, so I stood behind Tobias and saw her hair dripping wet over her shoulder, a towel securely wrapped around her slim silhouette.

She then squatted in front of her suitcase, grabbed a few clothing items, and returned to the bathroom. We were all ghosts, spectrums, non-existent. She was living in a different dimension from us.

The apartment went silent enough that I could listen to Jordan's deep, heavy breathing and to how Tobias swallowed hard, his gaze still fixed on the bathroom door.

"I need to talk to her. Alone," Tobias said, almost growling. "So you better leave Jordan, or God help me, I'll drag you out of here myself."

Jordan laughed. "As much as I'd love to see you try, bro, it's in your best interest that you don't. Wouldn't want to ruin that pretty face of yours for the South America press junket." Jordan's features hardened up again as he looked over Tobias's shoulder, glaring at Joel. Perhaps he'd forgotten that Tobias wasn't alone, but he didn't seem oblivious now.

Cecile walked out of the bathroom, fully clothed and showered. She freaking *showered* because she couldn't give a rat's ass about these guys going at it as she lathered, rinsed, repeated.

"Are you guys done?" she queried, her crisp and melodic French accent slicing through the silence. She took a seat on the edge of the bed, crossed a leg over another, and rested her hands elegantly on her lap. She looked a little pale and probably needed a big cup of coffee and a few more hours of sleep. Heck, I knew I did.

"Can we talk?" Tobias countered, his features unclear as if he'd rather seem like a heartless robot instead of showing an ounce of discouragement. These guys knew how to switch things up fast—actors after all.

"Yes," she said coolly.

"Cecile, I thought that—" Jordan began to say.

"We have an understanding, don't we?" she cut him off with such gentleness one wouldn't imagine she was blowing him off. "And I have unfinished business with Tobias."

Damn. I needed to get on my knees and beg to become her pupil.

Jordan snorted and grabbed his phone from the nightstand. "We've unfinished business too," he said to her, heading out. Jordan bumped his shoulder against Tobias's, who was somewhat blocking the way.

Tobias pivoted and followed Jordan with the intention of—something. His glower begged for release as if he were glad that Jordan had shoved him on his way out so Tobias would have an excuse to reciprocate the gesture.

But Joel caught up with that and held Tobias's arm before he could reach Jordan, who apologized to me without turning back before he walked out my door.

That simple action of Joel grasping Tobias's arm had made it worth it for him to be here. He stopped Tobias from doing something that would've surely gotten out of hand—that neither Cecile nor I would've been able to stop.

Tobias released himself from Joel's grasp with a sharp sniff. He again said something to Joel in Swedish and disappeared into the guest room where Cecile was waiting for him, shutting the door behind him.

Tobias missed his flight.

CHAPTER 24

Tone

JOEL LEFT AS soon as Tobias joined Cecile inside the guest room. He said he'd go crash for a few more hours. I wasn't surprised, and I envied him—the bad kind of envy. My mind wouldn't allow for a morning snooze. I had too much shit going on in my head. But I was thankful that Joel stopped by to help out with the situation. He deserved to go back to bed.

I poured myself a second cup of coffee instead and texted Sophie and Nathan. I assumed Sophie stayed over with Ren, and I assumed right. Nathan was still asleep, or so it seemed, because he wasn't texting me back.

I'd just put my feet up on my good luck couch and a book on my lap when the doorbell rang.

Aaron.

"Good morning, Miss Murphy," he said to me. "Happy birthday." He went in for a hug that made my throat feel tight. I'd been keeping a certain distance from Aaron ever since he came back from Caleb's funeral.

It was so hard for me to look at him, and something told me it was mutual. His face was scarier than ever, not to me, of course. I knew what laid hidden behind that tough exterior. But I'm sure it was a threatening look for anyone else who didn't know him as I did.

I had to take a slow, steady breath in through my nose to avoid falling into that dark, bottomless pit that kept luring me in all the time.

"There were unusual movements flagged on the surveillance camera about an hour ago. So I went back on the footage and saw Cecile coming in with a big guy at around four in the morning," Aaron explained. "He wasn't authorized to come up. Bruce told us he said he was headed to Tobias's apartment, and since his name is on the Sjöbergs' list, he was allowed to come up."

"Ah yes, sorry. I was asleep when this happened, and I didn't realize he was here until this morning. Will this—be reported?" I asked.

"It depends. The recorded video shows Tobias barging into your apartment after you'd gone inside, and then Joel also stepped right in without knocking or ringing the doorbell. Then the big guy walked out with a sour face. What happened, Miss Murphy?"

Damn it.

"Aaron, this had nothing to do with me. Yes, it unfortunately happened inside my apartment, but I'm okay. Cecile's okay. Tobias is still in there talking to her."

Aaron lifted a brow and looked down at me as he kept his bodyguard stance firmly in place.

"I don't want to bore you with the drama. I'm afraid my father will make Cecile leave or something. Please don't report this. We're all okay. Joel was here to make sure that things didn't go too far with Tobias and Jordan."

Aaron didn't seem so happy with my request, but he agreed.

"Thank you. I promise it won't happen again." I hoped. "Oh, and I just spoke with Sophie. She's at Ren's. Could someone pick her up and bring her over?"

"Certainly. I'll go get her myself." He nodded and turned around, heading toward the elevator.

"Aaron?"

"Yes, Miss Murphy," he said over his shoulder.

I wanted to ask him how he was doing. If he was having a hard time as I was. To share the pain in the hopes of making it go away. Together.

But I couldn't make myself ask such an obvious question when I already knew the answer. And I didn't know if he wanted to talk about it, so I retreated.

"No, nothing. I—I'll see you later." I fled to my apartment, rushed to my bedroom, and grabbed Caleb's letter from my nightstand. I sat on the edge of the bed and stared at it. Two fingers grazing the three letters written on the simple, white envelope.

RED

I closed my eyes, took the letter to my chest, and pressed it hard against it as if I could somehow suck whatever of Caleb's essence that still lingered on the paper. But I couldn't do it. I Couldn't make myself open it, let alone read it. And there was nothing more I wanted than to listen to him if only one last time. To be able to tell him how much I loved him. Still did.

To thank him for everything he did for me. For having merely existed. To tell him how infinitely grateful I was that our paths had crossed. And that he stayed, as long as he could. Right until the end.

That I would've never had enough of his beautiful soul and that I was so selfish to wish that I would've rather gone instead of him, just to avoid this excruciating pain.

How I wished for him to be able to keep living his life.

That thought burned my chest like acid dripping torturously on my heart. To think of the life he had ahead of him and that he'd given up because of *me*. For my mistakes.

What I would give for one last hug; one last look at Caleb's sincere and loving hazel eyes that I cherished so much.

My mind gave in to deep sleep as I nestled into my bed and rested my head on my pillows, my body in the fetal position, and Caleb's letter still pressed against my chest.

☾

I opened my eyes and saw Cecile sleeping next to me, my hand still holding on to Caleb's letter. Her eyes opened when I sat up on the bed. "Hey," I said to her. She blinked fast a few times and stretched her arms above her head with a yawn.

She then sat up and hugged me. "*Joyeux anniversaire!*"

I hugged her back and quickly put Caleb's letter away on my nightstand drawer afterward. My phone showed a few texts from Nathan, so I called him. He said he'd be coming over in about an hour, suggesting we all go to brunch.

Perfect.

As long as my *sis* didn't show up. But I knew there was no way to avoid that. Nathan was leaving for London the rest of the week, and I was sure he would want to spend as much time with her as possible.

If Nathan knew what happened between William and Zara last night, he'd be setting the whole building on fire.

It was weird to know I had the power to sabotage whatever was brewing between them. But I would never do it. If that's what William wanted, if that would truly make him happy, I had to respect that. Even if it felt like a million toothpicks were stabbing my chest.

I told Cecile about the brunch plan, and she was in. She then told me Sophie arrived earlier, took a shower, and was now napping on the living room couch.

"I've never had a morning nap," I said to Cecile with a laugh.

"They are the best," she laughed back, her smile quickly disintegrating.

"Are you okay?" I asked her. "Do you want to talk about what happened earlier?"

"Um, yeah. I'm fine," she said, picking at her nails. "I thought I'd been clear with Tobias. That it would be easier that way—to be honest from the start. But I see now that it was all a mistake."

"I feel like shit, Cecile. I didn't want to cause any trouble when I introduced you to Jordan. And Tobias took me by surprise. I didn't imagine he would show up, and I didn't know how to stop him from going into your room. I tried. But when he realized Jordan was here, he just—lost it. He really likes you. I've never seen him like this. So affected by someone."

Cecile sighed. "I like Tobias too. Too much that it worries me—I don't know, it makes me want to run away. But when I see him, I just ... melt. And it's so hard to look at him because it reminds me of what happened with Paul. That something's wrong with me and with what I did.

"And I wonder if I did it once, will I do it again? And I don't want to—be that person. The cheater who goes around hurting people. And I'm so scared of hurting Tobias. I feel like it's not the way you want to start something with someone new, cheating *with* them.

"That's why I told him it would be nothing but sex because that way I thought I'd be protecting him. Hoping he would somehow think it didn't mean anything and make him stay away. But he keeps coming back, and I keep *wanting* him to come back." Cecile closed her eyes and ran her fingers up and down her temples. "I'm so fucking hungover."

"Wait here." I ran to the kitchen and poured a cup of coffee for her. Sophie was still asleep on the couch. There was some of the coffee I brewed in the morning left, and it'd been keeping itself warm on the heated base. On my way back to my bedroom, I grabbed the ibuprofen bottle from the foyer closet and brought it with me.

"Breakfast," I said to her, placing the cup of coffee and the pills on the nightstand next to her.

"Ah! *Merci beaucoup*!" She took the cup to her lips and moaned at the first sip she took. "So good," she said, lifting the cup slightly in a sort of *thanks* gesture. "Just what I needed."

The lightest shiver went up and down my spine. The last thing I needed was to hear any *moans* right now. I was still feeling disgusted about Zara's reactions to whatever William did to provoke them.

"You okay?" Cecile asked, taking another sip of her coffee, her brow lifting, analyzing.

"No." I was tired of saying *yes, I'm fine*, all the time. I wasn't okay, and I wanted to be able to say it. "But we're not done with you yet. We'll talk about me later. What about Jordan, then? If you like Tobias so much, why are you not allowing yourself to explore something with him?"

Cecile snorted and shook her head as if she couldn't come up with an answer for that either. "I thought it would be fun to tease Tobias a little bit. He'd been cold with me the last few days before the party. We saw each other in Paris a few weeks ago, and we barely left my apartment. He—" Cecile smiled, and I swear I saw her cheeks getting a little rosy.

"He was so great to me, Billie, and I—well, I was a cold-hearted bitch, as expected. And I didn't tell him I was coming to New York, so he was pissed at me for that, and he ignored me yesterday at the party when I arrived. So when you introduced me to Jordan, I thought I could use him to make Tobias jealous. To reel him back."

"Well, it worked, didn't it?"

"It didn't. I mean, it *did* because, yes, Tobias came looking for me right away, but I wasn't expecting to like Jordan. And I did. A lot." Cecile blew out a breath through her mouth and took another sip of her coffee.

She carefully placed her cup on the nightstand and took two ibuprofen to her mouth, grabbed the cup again, and swallowed them with a long sip of her coffee.

"I obviously said to him the same things I said to Tobias. That it was just sex, that I wasn't looking for anything formal right now, that I was just looking to have fun. He quickly agreed, so I brought him here. I told him about Tobias and asked him if he'd be okay with it, and he didn't mind."

Cecile pursed her lips and looked away. *Is she embarrassed?* I didn't want her to be. "I'm sorry, Billie. I know I shouldn't have, but—"

"I don't mind. I was just surprised when I opened the door earlier this morning looking for you and found Jordan there sleeping beside you." I covered my face feeling flustered, and Cecile's laughter roared through the bedroom.

"He's gorgeous, isn't he?" she said, biting her lip.

"He—um, well, he has a great body." I couldn't deny that. Even if the tattooed, bad boy look wasn't really my thing. "But he's so different from Tobias."

"Yes, he is. But they're both so great, and after today I don't know if either of them will want me anymore." Cecile seemed not sad but disappointed in herself. And I hated that look on her face. Like she could think for a second that she wasn't good enough or something. She was the best, and I needed her to be able to see that.

"Don't be ridiculous. They're both angry because they like you. And they both want you all for themselves. You're the one who has to figure out what you want." I felt like a hypocrite suggesting that to her as if I were an expert on choosing and figuring shit out.

"But what if I don't want to figure it out just yet?"

Wow. In that, Cecile and I were so different. She was so … free. Why would she have to rush to make a decision? If any, at all? On the other hand, I was constantly worried and battling myself. Rushing to make choices that I wasn't even sure if they were the right choice to make.

And I wanted to keep telling myself that I had done the right thing in choosing Nathan, but it still felt hurried. The truth is I wasn't ready to let go of William, but I did anyway out of fear of losing Nathan, and now after what happened with Zara, there was no turning back. I was too hurt to admit *I'd* been hurt after listening to them having sex. Wait, hurt? Try: completely devastated.

"What's your secret?" I asked her. She stared at me with a quizzical look on her face. "You know, how do you handle them so well?" I laughed after asking the second question, remembering how she didn't allow an ounce of worry or stress to leak out of her face when Tobias showed up wanting to kill Jordan.

She chuckled cutely, shaking her head. You'd never imagine the fierceness below that sweet smile of hers. "You can speak your mind and get away with anything if you only watch your tone," Cecile replied.

She looked away, drained her cup of coffee, and dropped it on the nightstand. "Well, at least that's worked for me in the past. But right now, I kinda feel—lost. I'll probably have to re-evaluate myself because I'm not sure I'll be able to handle Jordan and Tobias. Not after today."

"Well, I think you should keep being honest," I suggested. "With them, of course, and yourself. Not everyone knows how to feel comfortable doing that, and if you are, you should keep it going."

"Sometimes I fear it's too raw—the honesty. I feel like I'm hurting Tobias every time we have one of these talks, like the one we just had. But after what happened with Paul, I don't want to risk it. I don't want there to be anything I didn't say."

"So what did you guys talk about?" I was so curious to know. "You know, aside from the fact that Tobias will hate me forever. I'm sure he mentioned it at some point."

"Tobias loves you, believe me," Cecile said, raising a brow. "He's obviously upset that I met Jordan, but even if you hadn't introduced me to him, Jordan told me he would've introduced himself. So it was inevitable, I guess. And I made it clear to Tobias I hadn't told you anything, and for some reason, he was hurt about that too. He thought if I'd talked to you about him, that it would mean something. The only reason why I didn't tell you anything was precisely because I'm scared of admitting how much I like him. So I told him I needed time."

Cecile's words resonated deep inside me. Our situations were different, but she was torn between two guys she liked. And I could relate to that, of course. But I was way past *liking*.

I envied that she was still on time to make a careful decision about what she wanted—time I didn't have. And I was already so invested in Nathan that losing him would not only be tragic but heartbreaking too. The kind of heartache I didn't know if I'd be able to heal from.

I didn't have anything working in my favor, just a constant feeling that tugged and demanded to be acknowledged as much as I tried to ignore it, bury it, smother it. It was useless.

As always, Cecile caught on with the emotions I failed to conceal as my thoughts kept eating at me.

"Your turn," she said, jerking her chin at me. "Tell me everything."

And I did. I told her everything.

CHAPTER 25

Take Your Time

CECILE WASN'T SURPRISED at all by my entanglement with William. And she agreed with me regarding Zara.

"She kept hugging Tobias," she said with almost a snarl. "I was one hug away from jumping at her. I can't believe she slept with William. Why is she so obsessed with them? Do you think she might have slept with Tobias in the past?"

Cecile was jealous of Zara too. And I thought it was so tragically funny that Zara had the wits to make us both go nuts without even knowing. Although Cecile liked to think Zara knew everything and somehow enjoyed herself by making us suffer in silence.

A part of me wanted to think that Zara wasn't that bad. My conclusion was that who she truly wanted was William, and the love she showed for the rest of the Sjöberg brothers resulted from knowing them from years back, and in a way also admiring them, as they had achieved success in something she wanted to do too—acting.

"I hate her," Cecile said with an endearingly wicked chuckle. I knew she didn't mean it in a literal sense, but more in an: *I'm annoyed by her* kind of way. "She's so pretty, though."

Yes, I agreed with Cecile on that one.

The doorbell rang, and I assumed it was Nathan. Cecile followed me out of my bedroom and headed toward the living room where Sophie was dozing off, probably just woken up by the doorbell. I bet she didn't sleep at all last night, just like Cecile hadn't. And for the same reason.

"Hey, you!" I was excited to see Nathan. I *needed* to see him if only to reassure myself of the decision I'd made the night before about choosing him. And by the look on his face, I knew he wanted to pick up where we'd left off.

Seeing him always felt right. That's why it was so hard not to choose him. It was comforting, familiar—safe.

He stepped right in, shut the door behind us, and kissed me. I walked back as he led me to my bedroom, his hands on my waist and his lips attached to mine, unwilling to let me explain that my friends were right there in the living room, probably looking at us.

"Nathan," I whispered, unlocking myself from his lips. I looked over his shoulder, and he turned around to see what I was looking at. Cecile waved her hand once.

"If you'll excuse me, ladies. I'll have to steal her away for a few minutes," he said with the most charming smile ever.

"*Few* minutes?" I taunted him.

"I can make this last as many minutes as you want, love," he said, cupping my cheeks. "And I already wasted the entire night by sleeping alone in my bed, so keep in mind I'll have to make up for the lost time at some point during the day."

"We're starving!" Sophie shouted with a laugh, teasing us.

"We are! You better make it quick!" Cecile tossed in.

"Nathan will be as quick as Jordan was!" I replied as Nathan kept taking slow steps toward my bedroom. Cecile shared a few details on how good the sex with Jordan had been, how he'd taken his time with her, and how much she'd enjoyed it.

"We'll go for a smoke on the rooftop then!" Cecile replied, pulling Sophie up from the couch. I heard Sophie ask Cecile what I meant by the Jordan remark when Nathan finally pulled me inside my bedroom and shut the door. At least they'd be entertained talking about that in the meanwhile.

"Where's the necklace?" Nathan asked in a deep, demanding tone. I jerked my chin at the nightstand, and he moved toward it to get the ruby pendant he gifted me last night.

He picked it up and stepped behind me, pulling my t-shirt over my head in a swift move. His hands grazed my jaw and collarbones as he positioned the necklace around my neck.

"I can't get that image of you wearing just this out of my head," he said, softly kissing my neck. "It's the only thing I could think of last night."

He flipped me so I would face him, pulled my jeans off, and knelt before me.

"Did you think of me too? Like I did?" He kissed my thighs as I held on to his head for balance, my legs quickly turning into jelly.

"Yes," I lied. I hadn't, but I wasn't going to ruin the mood and say *no*. Not only was the William drama unhelpful, but I'd collapsed from exhaustion too. And then I had to deal with his sister's moans, which was a major buzzkill.

So it's not that I didn't think of him because I didn't want to, but because I didn't have the energy to do so. To go into that headspace.

"Good," he replied, standing up, and unbuttoning his shirt. My hands moved to his jeans, feeling how eager and ready he was for me. "So what's it gonna be. Fast and hard? Or should I take my time with you?"

I blushed at his words. But I savored the demanding need in his voice. And admitting that to myself made me blush even more. He smiled a triumphant and proud smile after noticing my reaction.

"How about a mix of both, and we don't set a timer?" I suggested as I laid back on the bed to grant him the image he so desperately wanted—me, on my bed wearing nothing but the ruby pendant.

"Let them wait then."

☾

If William was home or not, I couldn't have cared less. Not after last night. He'd set the tone, and finally, I was free of the anxiety of William listening from across the wall.

Nathan and I took a shower, and I asked him where we were going for brunch and if Zara would be joining us too while we got dressed and ready to leave.

"She's not answering my calls, which is odd," Nathan said. "And I'm not planning on calling William, but I will if she doesn't pick up the phone in the next few hours. Perhaps I should just knock and see if she's in there. She might be sleeping, though."

It was a possibility that they'd gone at it the entire night and were probably sleeping together in William's bed.

"I'm sure she's okay," I told him. "We should go. I'm starving. If she calls you, just ask her to join us." I'd prefer it if Nathan didn't go knocking on that door.

I hoped she didn't come, as we finally left for brunch.

Lily and Joel joined us too, and we were almost done when Zara called Nathan back.

"Hey-hey ... Well, we're having brunch, and I wanted you to join us, but we're done now. Why weren't you answering your phone? Are you okay? ... You're going where? ... Sagaponack? ... Zara ... I

*know I'm not Dad. And believe me when I tell you that I don't want
to be. But I'm still your brother and … No … You still have meetings
in the city … But … It's impractical to come and go almost every
day … You could stay with me, with Billie, or with Lily and Joel …
Okay, bye … Suit yourself … Bye … No … Bye."*

Nathan dropped his phone on the table with a thud. Joel
addressed Nathan in Swedish, and he replied with an angry and
exasperated tone. Lily looked at me with wide eyes for a second,
then looked away, thankfully.

I couldn't help but remember how William told me he never
took girls to Sagaponack, how I'd been the only girl to have gone
inside his room and slept in his bed. And I liked that. To not only
have been the first but the only one that had been there.

And now he'd taken Zara there too. To his sanctuary. To
keep doing what he finally decided on doing with her over there.
In the same bed I'd slept in almost a year ago.

I just hoped he'd taken that photograph he kept on his
nightstand of me down. I didn't want it to become an issue with
Nathan. I didn't care to know what would happen if Zara saw it
in case William still kept it there.

"What did she say?" I asked Nathan, placing my hand on the
back of his neck, slightly massaging it with my fingers, hoping it
would help him relax. I knew he was furious.

"Well, William decided to move to Sagaponack indefinitely,
and Zara will be staying there with him for the rest of her stay."

William moved *to Sagaponack? Indefinitely?*

I was sure it was easier for him to hide his face there instead
of confronting me when I was one hundred percent sure he was
aware of what he was doing with Zara. That I had listened to
them and was now familiarized with the decisions he'd made a
second after informing him of my choice. That with his actions,

he invalidated every great thing he'd ever said and done before because how was I to believe William was serious about *any* of it if he could so easily pivot?

He'd rather leave than risk seeing me again.

The coward. *Go hide in Sagaponack.*

CHAPTER 26

Showing Up

May 12, 2010

Me: Hey you! Have you boarded your flight yet? The event starts at 7:00 p.m. sharp, so if you come straight from the airport, you should be arriving at Parsons at around 6:30 p.m. I'll arrive at 5:30 p.m. so I'll meet you there, okay?

Nathan: I'm not going to make it, love. I'm so sorry. Can I call you in 15 minutes?

Me: You missed your flight?

Nathan: I'm stuck in a meeting. We're having trouble with the clients signing the paperwork we brought for them. They want to make changes. I can't leave until these papers are signed and everyone's happy.

Me: But you'll be here on the 14th, right? I need you here.

It was my mom's death anniversary, but somehow this year felt heavier with Caleb gone. I knew it would be a tricky day, and I wasn't on the best terms with my father.

Caleb was the one who usually comforted me on this day. He would come to church and sit beside me because my father never could. Never wanted, I assumed. He blamed it on his busy schedule. And everyone grieves differently, so I tried to be respectful.

This year, my support system was reduced to Nathan. I knew I had friends who would've gladly come with me to church if I asked them, but it was such an intimate and vulnerable part of me. Of my past. And even though they all knew that my mother was dead, I hadn't really opened up myself to everyone about the specifics of my experience.

That's why I needed Nathan. The only person alive who I'd opened up myself to about my mother other than him was William. And not only was he out of the question but he was gone. Vanished.

I hadn't seen him or heard from him since my birthday. And I would lie if I told you the ninth floor didn't feel hollow without him. His presence, even if we both lived our separate lives, was always felt, heard.

In a way, he'd done me a favor by leaving. But I missed him, knowing perfectly well that I shouldn't have. That's why I prayed he wouldn't return. Even when a part of me, as small as it was, hoped he did.

Someday.

He'd been gone for long periods of time when filming, but he always returned, or at least I knew he would. But now, there was no way to know if he would or not, or *when*, if he ever planned to.

He'd told me once how he wished he could spend more time in the cottage. To slow things down with work. And since he was still recovering from his surgery and taking things slow, I guess this was the best opportunity to do so.

I'd be there too most of the time if I were him. That place was next-level amazing.

Nathan: I know, love. I will be there. I promise you.
I'll call you back in 15. I'm so terribly sorry about today.
I feel like a proper idiot. I'll make it up to you.
Me: It's okay, don't worry. Call me when you can.

Today, I had my photography exhibit where a committee of professors selected a few pieces from students of all Photography BFA program levels. One of my photographs was chosen. It was a portrait of one of the ballerinas that I took when we went to the New York City Ballet a few weeks ago.

We were all given the allotted time that day to photograph each of the ballerinas. One of them stood out to me the most—Vivienne. Her light brown hair was pulled back into the tightest, most perfect bun ever. Her eyes were like molten amber, almost orange. And they were one of the saddest eyes I'd ever seen aside from mine in a while.

Do you want to reveal someone's essence? Photograph them.

I could see how the performer in her did a magnificent job hiding whatever it was that troubled her, but pain recognizes pain. Fairly easily. And every move, every look, every position of her slender figure was so ironically fragile and powerful at the same time. Very telling.

Twenty days had passed since the day Caleb died when I photographed Vivienne. And looking into her eyes felt like looking into a mirror, such profound sadness reflected upon them. I would've loved to tell her I could see her pain and that I was hurting too. But I focused on photographing her, and the portrait turned out to be stunning. My teachers agreed.

I developed it in black and white, and even so, you could see the fire in her eyes.

Nathan hadn't seen the photograph yet, and I was excited for him to see it. But he was officially a partner at Chapman

& Payne, and the promise Mr. Chapman made about how Nathan wouldn't be traveling as much after his new promotion was *rubbish* after all. He left the next day after my birthday and stayed in London for five days.

But I was unimpressed because Nathan traveled even more back and forth between London, New York, and Washington, D.C.

I tried to be supportive about it and focused on school, which was always helpful. But the truth is that our situation sucked. I felt like the more he grew in the firm, the less I saw of him. And I wanted him to be happy doing what he loved to do, but it unfortunately reminded me of my father and his work addiction.

Fifteen minutes later, Nathan called me as he said he would. He told me how the meeting hadn't gone well, how he needed to stay another day in D.C. But he promised to grab the first flight back to New York on the 14th and go to church with me. He said how proud he was of me, of my work being selected for the exhibit.

And I didn't ask for much. I just wanted him to show up when it mattered.

When I needed him. Just like I always did for him.

☾

My friends arrived on time to show their support at the exhibit. My father promised to be there, but I knew well enough what that meant. He'd show up in the last five minutes before the thing was over and congratulate me with squinty eyes and the biggest smile on his face that would typically disarm and melt me in the process. I would typically excuse him by thinking, *well, he's here, isn't he?*

He didn't disappoint this time either because it was 8:30

p.m., the event would be over at 9:00 p.m., and he hadn't arrived yet.

Nolan asked about Nathan's absence, and I brushed the question off with a somewhat icy tone. He frowned, and I quickly apologized afterward. But I was angry, and as always, I was having trouble hiding it.

I was annoyed about Nathan not being here, about my father letting me down as usual, and because that's how weird I was around my mother's death anniversary.

He pulled me aside. "You okay, Bee?"

"No," I replied in a neutral tone. My conversation with Cecile had been very enlightening. I was learning to say the things I wanted to say, to admit my feelings, and to use the right tone while doing it.

It was going to take some practice, but at least now, I was aware of how I usually wanted to pretend like everything was okay when it wasn't. And how exhausting that was. I was done with that. It didn't help solve anything or make things feel better.

The oddity about carrying out such a practice was observing how people react to your honesty. Not everyone wants it, and not everyone knows what to do with it.

Most people ask how you're doing, expecting a: *Fine, how are you?* And then the other person goes: *Fine, thank you.* But that's not a real conversation. It's just social protocol, and I sometimes wondered if I shouldn't want to try to change things. But it was an interesting experiment, nonetheless.

Nolan didn't shy away too quickly from an honest reply. And he was one of my closest friends. One of the few who knew the most about me.

"I'm sorry that we haven't been able to talk since your birthday. We've been so caught up with finals that I never asked again about—that *thing* you told me about *you know who*."

Ah. William. My feelings for William, to be exact.

Nolan and I were on the same page. We both were clueless because, just like him, I hadn't asked myself about those feelings either. And with the training I've had for years to lock things up and throw away the key, there was no easy way to have the courage to unlock the trunk and see what sensibilities still survived inside, especially after William disappeared.

"I think we've both made the choice to move on from whatever *that* was," I replied.

"What do you mean?" He asked, angling his head with curiosity, a subtle frown drawing on his forehead.

"We talked that night. I realized that the thought of losing Nathan was too painful to even consider, and William asked me directly if I'd chosen Nathan." I paused for a second, the memory of that scene biting at me. "I said yes."

Nolan nodded as he leaned in to listen. I kept my voice down, of course.

"Okay, but this is William we're talking about. He never actually believes you when you say that kind of stuff to him. He just laughs, you get super annoyed by that, and it all goes back to normal the next day, which consists of William not giving a fuck and doing all this crazy shit to win you over," Nolan said, a tiny smirk drawing on his face afterward. He really knew all the stories. "What's different this time? Aside from the fact that you've already admitted to having feelings for him. Not that I was shocked about it."

"Well, he slept with Zara that night, and I heard it through the wall. So I guess he's reached his limit."

Nolan cleared his throat. "What?" He lowered his chin. "Zara as in Nathan's sister, Zara?"

"Unfortunately, it's the only Zara I know."

"And you're *sure* it happened?" Nolan asked, his brows

bunching up, looking confused.

I snorted and shook my head. *I know what I heard.*

"Why is it so hard to believe? I saw how territorial she was and how she chased him around like a puppy all night long. And I have a feeling that's how it's been for years."

Nolan rubbed his jaw. His gaze drifted away, staring at nothing in particular. "I don't know. It's just—he must've been devastated for him to have done that. I just—fuck, that sucks."

My brows rose, and I shrugged. What did I expect? I was sleeping with Nathan on a regular basis, so why wouldn't he be able to do the same with whoever he felt like taking to his bed? He's William freaking Sjöberg! He can have anyone he wants. He's not going to wait around for me to make up my mind. He had enough.

And I wasn't an idiot. It was foolish to believe he hadn't had sex with anyone in the past months, but at least he wasn't bringing girls over to his apartment. I was thankful for that, but on my birthday, he made a statement. *I'm not going to guard your heart anymore.*

"And I don't think he's dating Zara because I googled him and—shit, I know I shouldn't have, but I've been doing it lately. I'm just curious to know what he's been up to, and he's been going out a lot. There are a bunch of photographs of him coming in or out of different bars, with different girls every time. The headlines aren't encouraging at all. And I know I shouldn't care but—"

"You do," Nolan finished the sentence. I'm not sure that's what I was about to say but yeah, basically. It was so maddening to watch, but I couldn't stop googling him. "You shouldn't be looking at those tabloids. I feel like most of it is bullshit. You're going insane for no reason."

"Well, I found this stupid website that posts paparazzi photographs with the date, place, and everything. And I mean—

they look recent," I said with a sigh filled with exasperation. "I know I can't complain. It just sucks to see him with a different girl whenever I type his name. I can't help but feel jealous, but I'm sure the feeling will fade with time. At least he's not bringing them over to his apartment." Yet ...

Nolan raised a brow. "Yeah, you know, as long as you never see him again in person, which is highly improbable since he's your next-door neighbor."

"He—moved out," I clarified. "He's living in Sagaponack right now."

"Hmm. I guess that'll be helpful to both of you. The critical distance."

"I guess—ugh! This freaking cast." I scratched around the edges of the rough material that wrapped around my forearm. But the itch came from deeper inside, and I was going nuts.

Thankfully, the wrist cast was finally coming out on Friday. It was an eventful day, May 14th. It was the anniversary of my mother's death, my wrist cast was coming off, and don't forget ... It's William's birthday too.

"Wait here," Nolan said, laughing. He stepped away and aimed at Emily, who took a pen out of her bag and handed it over to him with a smile. Nolan came back and gave it to me. "Scratch away."

"Oh, my God. Thank you!" I pushed the pen in between the cast and my itching skin and scratched away as Nolan suggested. "Ohhh, yes."

Nolan laughed again. "You might want to keep it down, Bee. That sounds weird."

I joined him with a chuckle and a slight grimace. "Sorry." My smile disintegrated promptly as I told him, "That's basically what I heard that day—across the wall. But louder. So you tell me." I extended the pen toward Nolan.

He squinted at me, obviously agreeing with my hypothesis. "Nah, you can keep that," he said, waving a carefree hand at me. "You should probably call Nathan and scratch your arm with that pen. You'll see how fast he hops on a plane and flies back to New York."

"Nolan!" I shoved him.

"I'm just saying!" He eased out of a laugh and asked, "So, has Nathan been like super busy all the time or what?"

"He has. I feel like his job is getting crazier by the minute. I'm happy he got that big promotion, and I thought he would delegate more of the work. But that hasn't been the case."

"Well, Nathan's a grown-up lawyer—man-person, so what did you expect? That's what you get for dating an old dude like him."

"Hey! He's only twenty-eight, and I'd like to see you tell Nathan that to his face." I raised a brow at him. Nolan was in a very playful mood. Or maybe he was just trying to cheer me up, and it was definitely working.

"Yeah, I'd rather not." He let out a low, breathy laugh. "Just don't let that grown-up, serious vibe get to you. Don't forget you're twenty-one. The guy's almost thirty. I mean unless that's what you want." Nolan pushed one of his brown curls off his forehead. They were longer now.

"I've told Emily more than a few times how I feel like you're just gonna step into school one day with a big ring on your finger."

"Oh, no. No, no. No." My eyes widened in panic. Nolan noticed my alarmed reaction.

"See what I mean? I say *ring*, and you get all high-pitched and panicky."

"No, I don't!" I almost screeched.

"I swear to God … the guy's not gonna make it to the end

of this year without proposing," Nolan said, crossing his arms at his chest, his fingers drumming on his bicep as he squinted at me, studying me.

"Nolan, you need to stop, or I'm going to need a sleeping pill tonight." I released a nervous, broken chuckle.

"Look, I'm sorry, but I can't get over that conversation we had at your party. How your eyes glazed with—something when you talked about"—he looked over both of his shoulders—"*William*. About having feelings for him. So I'm just having a hard time believing they've all gone away. And I know you're probably hurt after you heard him with Zara. You can't deny it."

Nolan was now helping me scratch a different kind of itch, basically saying, *hey, I found this key. Why don't you open that chest and see what happens?*

"And hey, it's okay not to know what you want at our age. As I said before, you're twenty-one. And for some reason, I get this vibe that you feel like you need to have all your shit figured out, but you don't. So I'm just wondering if Nathan pops the question in the next few months, or say a year if we exaggerate, would you be ready for something like that?"

Not in the very least. I felt like I had a million things I wanted to do, to experience, and it's not that I felt like Nathan was stopping me from doing things, but I wasn't sure if he would be down for the kind of adventure my soul was demanding of me. And I didn't even know if I would be able to get away with any of the numerous things that went through my mind—the possibilities. But I had to at least try.

I knew I wanted to travel around after graduation, to grab my camera and go places. And again, I didn't even know if such a thing would be possible with my father being like he was, but what if he agreed one day?

Nathan couldn't just drop everything and join me. And I

wouldn't mind going alone on a trip now and then. But how would that work with Nathan? Relationship-wise. I'd never been in a long-distance relationship, and I didn't know if that's something that would work for us.

That is why listening to Nolan speculate about rings and proposals was a level five on the anxiety-inducing scale.

"You told me how he keeps making marriage jokes and shit like that," Nolan continued. "You know he's measuring you up, right? Like he wants to see if you laugh or if you freak out on him."

"Well, I usually laugh, but it's mostly out of nerves, so I don't know what he might be picking up from that."

"Shit, Bee," Nolan said, shaking his head a few times. "And by the look on your *how do I get off this ride* face, something tells me you're not ready for any of that. And I swear to God I'm not trying to mess with your mind or something. I know Nathan wouldn't think twice to pull any of that Krav Maga shit on me because of this, but I just think you're a little too hard on yourself sometimes."

That's what Juan Pablo told me the last time I saw him, how I needed to stop being too hard on myself. And I didn't realize what he meant by that at the time. I mean, I understand the meaning of that phrase, but I didn't know in what context or in which cases it applied to me.

I kept battling the idea of Juan Pablo being full of shit or not, but damn, he always hit the spot with most of the things he said. I still wished I could bump into him so I could kick his ass for what he did to Nina. It's so unfair that she had to go through all that nonsense while dating him.

"I think you and Nathan make a great couple. You know I like him, and I know he loves you and that you love him. What I'm saying is just try to be honest with him about where you stand with everything. About your plans after graduation, about where you stand with marriage, and all that scary shit, okay?"

Nolan was right.

I'd never actually talked to Nathan about *any* of that. Like having an actual conversation about my plans or being honest regarding how I felt about marriage. And it's not that I did not see myself marrying him. I did. Actually, I thought it was like a given. Something that was inevitably going to happen at some point down the road. But I had to agree with Nolan in that maybe Nathan and I had a very different timeline.

"You're right." I offered him a small smile. "Ugh, but I still wish Nathan could be here and see the exhibit. I'm worried he won't make it for Friday."

"It's your mom's day, right?" he asked, tilting his head just a bit. I nodded. "You know Emily and I can—"

"I know. Thank you. Nathan already promised to be here, so I don't think it will be necessary. I'm just stressed out, you know. I always do around this time of year."

Nolan parted his mouth to speak, but he stopped himself when we both heard a voice from afar drawing in, "Kiddo!"

8:55 p.m. Right on schedule.

CHAPTER 27

Showing Up Part Two

May 14, 2010

NATHAN ARRIVED IN New York at 8:00 a.m., and I already felt like I could breathe easier. I only had to go to school to hand in a final project in the morning, and I was done with the semester. But I'd enrolled in two Summer Intensive Studies programs. One started on May 31st and the other on July 5th. They both lasted three weeks, like the one I took last summer.

As much as I begged Nolan to sign up with me, he only agreed to enroll in one of the two programs. He would take a break in June and join me in July. Keeping myself busy was important, especially with Nathan being so absorbed with work all the time.

That constant *need* of wanting to keep myself occupied to avoid overthinking scared me. I wondered if that's why my father did it, and perhaps there was a dormant gene inside me that had a tendency toward work addiction. I'd never want to fall into that kind of obsession.

Nolan and I handed in our last final project of the semester and were heading out.

"We're done, Bee!" Nolan said, walking beside me, pulling me in for a side hug.

"I know. I'll definitely enjoy these few weeks off."

"Lucky you," he said, breaking away from the hug. "I'll be taking an extra shift at the restaurant until the Summer Intensive Program starts in July. I need to make a few extra bucks to pay for the course since a little friend kept harassing me with the idea."

Shit. I never considered that paying for the course would require an extra effort from Nolan and that perhaps I'd pushed too much.

"I'm sorry," I said with a silly grimace. "I never meant to be too pushy about it, but you know you're my security blanket at school." I laughed. I loved taking my classes with Nolan.

"Yeah, yeah, yeah," he said, flicking my ponytail. "Since you're one of the few female friends I'm allowed to have, there's nothing much I can do but keep you around."

"You're kidding, right?" I narrowed my eyes at him, my head slightly angling. "Is Emily normally very jealous or …?"

"Nah, not really. I guess she was a little jealous of you when we first met. She asked me when we were starting out if you and I had ever, you know, dated and stuff. But she knows we've been friends since before I met her, and I mean, she knows Nathan, so I guess that's why she doesn't mind."

"Well, I'm glad we're authorized to be friends," I quipped, but it was the truth. I was glad Emily hadn't forbidden him to talk to me because I would've been devastated. I liked her a lot too. She was so sweet.

"Speaking of the devil," he said, jerking his chin forward. I glanced that way and saw Emily standing near the entrance holding a small bouquet of white flowers. "I asked her to bring those for you."

"Aw! Nolan, you shouldn't have." I planned to buy more white flowers at some point during the day to place around the apartment as I usually did.

Emily waved hello from afar and walked in our direction.

"Hey, Billie!" Emily said with a hug. "These are for you."

"Thank you, guys. They're beautiful." I could see Aaron and David standing in the distance. And something told me today was going to be a hard day for Aaron too. He was there with me when my mother died. We went through it together, as we had with Caleb.

Almost two months had passed since Caleb's death, but it didn't feel any better, and it all was still bundled up into a big, fat, ugly knot in my chest.

Something told me Aaron felt the same, but he never allowed a drop of emotion to show on his clean-shaven, expressionless face. Not even on a day like this.

"Nolan told me how Nathan was out of town and that you like going to church on this day every year. So, if you want, we'll be happy to keep you company," Emily offered.

"Thank you. You really are the best," I said to them. "But Nathan arrived earlier today, so he'll be coming with me."

"Oh, that's great, Bee. I'm so glad he could make it," Nolan replied with a smile.

"Anyway," I said, looking at my watch, "I have a doctor's appointment to finally get this thing off." I raised my hand. "Why don't we go out for dinner tomorrow? Like a double date."

Nolan and Emily agreed to the dinner plans. I hugged them both, and when I was about to walk away, Emily asked me, "It's William's birthday today, right?"

"Um, yeah. It is." Emily seemed genuinely oblivious about William and me. She wouldn't have asked about him if she knew something. That meant Nolan had kept his promise to keep the things we've talked about secret from Emily. I couldn't risk something like that leaking out, especially with how obsessed the tabloids were about anything regarding William's personal life.

"If you see him, tell him I said happy birthday. I know he won't remember me, but maybe he will," she said with a grin.

"You've got to be kidding me," Nolan said to Emily, rolling his eyes at her. "He obviously won't remember you."

I laughed. That was the William effect. As I said before, everyone loved him.

"William knows who you are." I chuckled. "He knows Nolan's a good friend of mine and that you're Nolan's girlfriend. He's good at remembering people's names and faces." I frowned and looked away for a bit, remembering the bunch of times he'd asked about my friends, about school, about the things I liked. He was always so curious to know everything. "But ... I haven't seen him in a while. I think he might be filming or something. He's been away."

I didn't want to give any details about him currently living in Sagaponack. Besides, I wasn't even sure if he was still there. I never dared ask about him, and Lily never mentioned anything about him either.

Tobias would've probably told me everything about William without having to ask, but I hadn't seen much of him either and I felt like he was still angry at me, probably avoiding me.

"But I'll let him know if I see him," I said, taking a few steps back. I needed to leave for my doctor's appointment. "I'll call you guys to set up a time and place for dinner. I'll see you tomorrow!"

"Thanks, Billie!" Emily shouted as I walked away.

☾

It was 5:50 p.m. when I walked up the short flight of stairs to St. Patrick's Cathedral. Not only was it close to my apartment, but it was a beautiful architectural masterpiece that I hadn't taken the time to visit until today.

Mass started at 6:00 p.m., and Nathan said he'd join me there since it was only a few blocks away from his office. We would meet my father for dinner afterward. I invited him to church, but he declined with a gracefully diplomatic reply.

As I sat there waiting for Nathan, I took my wrist splint off and made a few simple movements my doctor recommended. My wrist felt stiff and weak. It was the most uncomfortable feeling ever. It felt as if they had stuck it back together with glue.

I felt inclined not to use my right hand much, but the doctor said that the less I used it, the more time it would take to get the muscles around my wrist strong again. It could also get swollen if I kept it still all the time. He also suggested I go to physical therapy three times a week for a couple of months anyway.

The organ started playing, and the people attending mass all rose to their feet as the priest walked down the aisle. I checked my phone before standing up, and my notifications were empty—no sign of Nathan. I dropped my phone back into my purse and shook my head as I stood up.

The *one thing* I asked of him. Show up.

I took a deep breath. It was 6:00 p.m. sharp. Maybe he was running a few minutes late, and I'd be okay with that. But that wasn't the case.

6:45 p.m. The priest gave the final blessing, and still no sign of Nathan. He couldn't even text me to say he wasn't showing up. I swallowed hard and concentrated on my breathing because I felt so small and alone in this massive cathedral. And I didn't deserve to feel this way. Not when Caleb would've been sitting next to me, no questions asked.

Am I on my own now?

It sure did feel that way as I sat there in silence looking at how people shuffled out in a smooth, orderly fashion.

6:50 p.m. I left.

Aaron opened the SUV's door for me. David, who was behind the wheel, looked over his shoulder and nodded once in my direction with a sympathetic look on his face. Aaron walked around the car and sat beside me instead of in the passenger seat next to David.

"Let's go," Aaron said to David in a deep voice. He then looked at me with a solemn expression on his face, his indigo blue eyes almost gray and lifeless with obvious pain. He held his palms up and wiggled his fingers back and forth between us. I scooted over next to him and settled my face on his chest, where I allowed his arms to wrap around me.

I cried my heart and soul out all the way to the restaurant.

CHAPTER 28

Saunders & Murphy

MY FATHER WAITED at our table with a drink in his hand when I arrived alone to meet him. I didn't care to edit myself in front of him or try to hide the fact that I'd been crying. Let him feel the discomfort of it. I was done concealing my emotions to make others feel good about themselves.

Not only was I furious about Nathan not showing up or reaching out to me to explain why. But I was so *done* with my father's lack of empathy in general.

I mean, Nathan had an assistant now. Couldn't he have asked her to call me, just like my father did when he was too busy? I'd put up with this behavior for years now being my father's daughter, and I was finally growing tired of it. And how hard could it be as a father to set forty-five minutes aside from an entire *year* to sit with your daughter at church to commemorate your wife's death?

Un-fucking-believable.

I'd love for him to just tell me, *hey, I don't feel like going because it makes me feel like this or that.* But he never talked to me about Mom or told me how he felt about her death or anything for that matter. I knew it must've been devastating for him; I liked to assume.

I wished he would just tell me something. *Anything.*

The only feelings he would convey would be those of apprehension toward my safety. That's it. The conversation we had in the ladies' room on my birthday was one of the most enlightening I've ever had with him, and we all know how that went. What had to happen for him to start blurting things out?

I walked over to him, kissed him hello, and took a seat in front of him.

"Kiddo?" He leaned in with lowered eyebrows, probably wondering what was wrong as he analyzed my face, which was already too revealing. "Where's Nathan?"

Exerting more pressure than I should've, I bit my lower lip to avoid bursting into tears again in the middle of the packed steak house when my phone buzzed on the table.

It was 7:15 p.m. when Nathan finally called me.

"Hey," I said, meeting my father's gaze, as in, *try to catch up, because this is part of the reason why I've been crying.*

"Where are you?" Nathan whispered. "I can't see you. You said St. Patrick's, right?"

"Mass began at 6:00 p.m. I left twenty minutes ago."

Nathan cursed over the phone, and I reminded him he was inside a church. He told me to wait as he stepped out.

"Murph, I'm so sorry. I swear I thought you said 7:00 p.m. I arrived at 7:05 p.m., but I thought it weird that you hadn't arrived, and the place is practically empty. I mean, there's like tourists and such, but I—shit, love, I'm so terribly sorry. Are you at Sparks?"

"We are." I rested my elbow on the table and cupped my forehead.

"I'll be right there."

"Don't bother."

"I said I'll be right there."

I ended the call and tossed my phone into my bag.

"I'm sure he got caught up with work," my father began to excuse Nathan.

"*Please* … don't take his side." My voice was more of a warning than a request.

"Nathan loves you, kiddo," he said, reaching his hand out to me, grabbing it, that is. He squeezed it for a few seconds and released it. "I'm sure it'll be easier once Nathan and I open our firm. We've been discussing it this past couple of months. He's mentioned something about it, yes?"

"Your—firm?" I glared at him. "What *firm*?"

"I believe Nathan's a bright young man. Full of potential. I see a lot of myself in him. We've been talking about how he should hold on to his position for the rest of the year at Chapman & Payne before we partner up for our new firm.

"I have quite a lot of contacts. Contacts that I would love to hand over to him freely. To *our* firm. I believe we can make a great team, and you'll both have a secure future, too, economically speaking."

I signaled one of the servers to come and ordered a Coke from him. I literally felt like I was about to faint. My father was trying to turn Nathan into a revamped mini-him. And by doing so, he might as well be taking him away from me because if he didn't have time right now, imagine running an entire firm? How would that make things easier for Nathan?

In his mind, my father was supporting us—our future, in granting Nathan the opportunity to own a legal firm with him as a partner.

My father kept rambling about how it was a great idea. About how Nathan was like the son he never had, among other things I failed to account for as I kept thinking about how this could play out in the future. In part because I was focused on bringing my blood sugar up to an acceptable level that would allow me to remain seated instead of dissolving away on the restaurant's floor. And most importantly because I simply didn't want to hear any of it anymore.

To learn from my father that they wanted to become so involved with each other and not from Nathan felt exactly like when they ganged up against me to sign the restraining order against Thomas. They insisted on keeping me in the dark. It didn't surprise me coming from my father but from Nathan … why?

I was sure he would excuse himself by saying something in the line of, *well, the shooting happened, and Caleb died, and we didn't want to mess with your birthday, and your mother's death anniversary got in the way, so we couldn't find the right time to tell you.*

And don't get me wrong. I was glad to know that my father held Nathan in such high esteem. That he approved of him and thought he was a great match for me and all. But I felt like, again, my father was pulling the shadiest puppet master move to turn Nathan into someone "worthy" of his daughter in *every* possible way.

To keep controlling everything related to me.

To keep controlling—me.

And who said I wanted to be with someone just like my father? I wanted Nathan to be Nathan. I didn't want him to be molded or groomed by anyone let alone, James Murphy.

It became a tricky situation in which I believed Nathan was cornered in a position where he couldn't say no to him. I knew he respected and admired him, and what if deep down what my father offered him wasn't what he wanted?

Maybe Nathan envisioned something different for him in the future and felt obligated to agree to my father's proposal. Or perhaps it was all he ever dreamed of. I don't know which of the two options scared me the most.

All I knew was that I didn't want to live a life of being alone, waiting for Nathan to arrive, and being eternally disappointed. He'd already begun displaying carelessness in paying attention to me or simply becoming unable to show up for things that I considered important.

There was always an excuse—a tailored-made explanation for every missed event, every tardiness, every omission.

At first, when Nathan hinted at marriage and started joking about it, I thought it might be a solution to feeling trapped. As terrifying as the idea of marriage was to me, I thought, *well, if we get married, I get to unleash myself from my father's grasp.* That's the only reason why I considered that marrying young wouldn't be such a bad idea.

But I was so wrong. I didn't want *that* to be the motivator.

Nathan was the perfect vessel for my father to keep things going as usual. To keep me inside a perpetual cage. All he wanted was to hand over the key to Nathan.

My attention was pulled back to my father's voice after getting lost in my head for an undetermined amount of time. All I did was nod in the meantime to keep him talking as I digested the bullshit information he had just brought up to my attention.

And then Nathan arrived carrying a big bouquet of white roses.

"Good evening." Nathan kissed my cheek and whispered, "I'm so sorry, love." He gave me the flowers with a smile impregnated with regret. "James." He shook my father's hand with a grin and took a seat, signaling the server to approach the table.

"I was telling Billie about our plans for Saunders & Murphy," my father said, sipping on his drink. They had a name for it and everything. I mean, it was an obvious name, but still.

I placed the flowers in the empty chair beside me when the server walked up to our table.

"Good evening, sir. Welcome to Sparks. Can I get you started with something to drink?"

Nathan's blood had left his face. "Ah, yes. Laphroaig. Neat," he said to the server with bunched-up brows. He couldn't look at me, even when my gaze burned a hole through his face.

"This could be the start of many great things," my father continued. "I've told Nathan numerous times how I feel he'd be a great ambassador one day. I know people in the UK's diplomatic sphere, and I'm sure they'd love to have someone like Nathan in their corner. It could be something worth pursuing in a few years once we get the firm up and running. You know, just like I did with my father's businesses. They practically run themselves on their own."

I kept shaking my head now as my father spoke. No. This was officially a nightmare. Was he actually suggesting for Nathan to dive into the diplomatic world? And don't get me wrong, I know it's a harsh thing to say, but I'd rather be dead. So, no … Thanks, but no thanks.

Nathan was at a loss for words, which was weird to me since apparently, they did a lot of talking when they hung out without me.

"I'm ah—" Nathan let out a sharp snort with what seemed like a nerve-induced smile, his gaze trained on the empty plate in front of him. "Thank you, James, for the flattery, but I think they might find me too young for such a venture."

"It could be in a few years from now. No rush," my father replied. "And you know how I started out young as a diplomat. It's all about who you know."

I could tell Nathan was uncomfortable with the conversation. Or better said, with the conversation happening in *my* presence.

I was so disappointed. Not in my father, of course. To say I was unimpressed was an understatement. What I failed to understand, though, was how Nathan felt about it all. I needed to know, to ask him.

It was so heart-wrenching to feel, again, like it was so convenient for him to keep me around. Just like when Thomas benefited from my relationship with him to make his father "proud." Perhaps Nathan found it advantageous for his career to be with me. And I didn't want to think that, but my father made things out to feel that way.

Imagine a scenario of Nathan maybe tiring of me and keeping me around because of my father's proposals? It could be. And I didn't even want there to be a possibility for that to happen. Ever. That's why I hated the fact that my father got so involved with Nathan.

Again, I loved how great they got along, how my father wanted to support him. But he was never one to do things without a purpose. And more often than not, there always was one—a hidden one.

The server brought Nathan his whiskey and asked us if we needed anything else.

"I'll have a glass of red wine, please." My father raised a brow in my direction. "Wine's cheaper than therapy," I said to him with a controlled smile. "Isn't that a saying?"

"Never heard of it." My father kept staring at me as the server asked for my ID, which I pulled out of my wallet. He nodded after taking a quick look at it and asked if we were ready to order. My father looked away with a somewhat flat look on his face. He wouldn't make a fuss out of a glass of wine and certainly not in front of Nathan.

Our server took our food order and left the table.

"James!" A man tapped my father's back twice. He shot up

from his seat after seeing it was someone he knew. He introduced Nathan and me to his acquaintance and talked to the man for a few minutes, giving us a small window to speak privately.

Nathan immediately reached out for my hand. "Your cast is off," he said, realizing that as he grabbed my hand in between his. "Does it hurt?"

I couldn't make myself look at him. "No. It only feels—wonky."

Nathan laughed a soft laugh. "I like it when you use my words." But I didn't laugh back. I couldn't pretend like I was okay with everything. I wished I could, but it was something I couldn't control. It was all part of a deeply ingrained trauma.

I didn't want to be deprived of Nathan in the same way I'd been robbed of my father's time because of work. I refused to accept a reality where work always came first.

"I know you're furious with me about not going to mass with you. I know I promised to be there, and I swear that I got the time mixed up. There's nothing more I want but to be there for you when you need me. Just like you're always there for me. You have to believe me."

"I do believe you. It's not that. It just—worries me," I whispered back, "that you're not able to juggle your personal life with work. And I know how important your job is. How much you love doing it. That's why I never say a thing to you about it.

"But you couldn't make it for pizza night two weeks ago, and it's okay if you can't make it every time, but you canceled on me when the food was on its way. You missed Nina's birthday last week too. I showed up alone when we'd already RSVP'd. Everyone kept asking me about you. Even Aiden was there.

"You couldn't come to my exhibit either and it was kind of a big deal for me. And then today—" I looked away for a second and sighed, trying not to be emotional about this. It was a tough day for me, and I usually wouldn't be as touchy-feely with this type of conversation. But I couldn't help but feel so utterly alone.

The server brought my wine, so I took a sip and continued.

"It's been a month since your promotion, and you know how proud and happy I am for you—that you got it, but you've missed out on a few things already. And I wonder if this is how it's going to be from now on. And the fact that I'm used to it doesn't mean that's what I want for us."

I sipped on my wine again and placed it back on the table, staring at it.

"Murph, look at me." He cupped my chin and gently turned my face toward him. "I am *so* sorry—about everything. I know I've been consumed with work, and I want to stop making excuses, but I'm adjusting to this new rhythm. I'm sure it will get better with time."

That's where we disagreed. It wouldn't get better. Why would it? Not with all the plans my father had in stock for him. And it's not that I wanted him to be lazing around all day. I was proud of Nathan, of what he'd achieved. I just wanted him to be more self-aware of how his job could end up affecting his personal life because, at this rhythm, I wasn't sure I could keep up.

"And I find out through my father you want to partner up and start a firm with him? Why wouldn't you tell me anything about it?"

It all felt too formal too soon. And I have to admit the thought of them getting so involved did make me panic—a million *what ifs* invaded my mind.

"I didn't want to tell you until it became more than just chit chat over drinks. And I still feel like what he's offering me is too good to be true if I'm honest. I guess I couldn't believe it myself. I was waiting for it to be real, to tell you."

I parted my mouth to speak, but my father said, "My

apologies," taking his seat back on the table.

For the rest of dinner, I didn't bother to smile or fake a laugh. All I wanted was to leave. But I couldn't stand up and walk away, although the thought crossed my mind a few times.

My father kept looking at me funny as we ate dinner. He knew I was upset with Nathan, but I guess that in his mind, he couldn't understand *why* it bothered me that much that he didn't show up for mass. Maybe if he agreed with me—if he saw my point—he'd automatically admit to being wrong himself for blaming his job all the time too.

It even made me doubt if I was wrong for caring too much. And I refused to be a victim of my circumstances because the thought of leading this kind of life for the rest of my days felt like the most boring thing in the world. I'd always promised myself to break free someday.

I *had* to let Nathan know the things I craved for myself. The adventures I wanted to embark on, the sense of freedom I've been waiting to find my entire life, knowing perfectly well there was a high probability that it's not that he wouldn't want that too, but that he might've already lived like that growing up. And I hadn't. He was ready to be a grown-up, to get serious.

I … wasn't.

CHAPTER 29

A Safe Choice

"DO YOU WANT me to spend the night?" Nathan asked as we rode back from the restaurant. He dropped a gentle kiss on my neck. "I want to make it up to you."

"I don't know. I'm tired. It's been a long day." I didn't say that to be proud, but it was the truth. It'd been *the* longest day, and all I wanted was to collapse in my bed. And it wouldn't do me any harm to sleep off the discomfort of everything that happened. I was still processing all of it. And I'm sure Nathan wasn't planning to go straight to sleep.

"Is that what you really want? To partner up with my father?" I whispered to Nathan. I felt like we couldn't talk freely at the restaurant. There were still a few things I wanted to ask him—to know. "I don't want you to feel pressured into any of it just because it's him asking."

"Well, I've always dreamed about having my own firm. And I respect your father, his trajectory, so I feel like if I partner up with him, it would be something that could happen sooner rather than later, or at all, for that matter. But yes, it is a dream of mine, and to be honest, I don't know if I would be capable of doing it on my own. There's too much competition out there, but with your father's connections—"

I could see the spark in Nathan's eyes. How excited he really was about it. It was the opportunity of a lifetime for him; to own a legal firm in New York City. And I wouldn't be the one to crush his dreams. But why was I always so quick to crush *mine*?

And it's not that I didn't want to be with someone hardworking and successful, but I feared that he would get sucked into his job in a way that wouldn't allow space for anything else. Maybe something that would allow some balance.

I'd never gone on a proper vacation with my father. We've had the chance to travel a lot and know many places, but always for work. He would never disconnect completely. And it was disheartening to know that Nathan could go down that same path—never having the time for anything other than work.

I didn't know what it was that I wanted to do exactly, but I knew I wanted to try to live a different kind of life than the one I'd been living—to have the freedom to flow, to make plans out of the blue, to be more spontaneous. Everything had been meticulously planned, scheduled, observed. That's what I wanted to break away from.

"I can't tell if it's upsetting you," Nathan said. "So I'm going to need you to tell me if it does."

The look on Nathan's face when he asked me that simply destroyed me. I had the power right there to make his dreams come true or to shatter them to pieces. I couldn't do it. But I could get my concerns across.

"No, it—doesn't." It hurt so much to lie. But at least this was a lie I was willing to tell to make him happy. For his sake. I'd find a way to put my priorities first some other time. "I just want to make sure it's not something you would accept for the wrong reasons," I said to him.

We arrived home, and Nathan lifted a brow and jerked his chin at the apartment building, probably inquiring if he should come up with me or not.

"Could you guys give us a few minutes," I said to Aaron and David, who immediately jumped out of the car to give us some privacy. I was used to them always listening in to my conversations with everyone, but what I was about to tell Nathan wasn't something I wanted anyone to monitor.

"I don't want you to keep me around for fear of losing the opportunity to do that with my father. I'm sure he would want to partner up with you either way. He loves you. Respects you, too. But I hate that he's put you in that position."

I wasn't sure if starting the firm was a short or medium-term goal for them, but I assumed it would take some time in planning, which meant it was in Nathan's best interest to keep his relationship with me going smoothly to achieve that goal.

And I hated that. To be that much-needed piece of the *make Nathan's dreams come true* puzzle.

"I guess all I'm asking of you is for your honesty. If you ever tire of me just—"

"You're *mad*," he cut in with a snort before I could finish that sentence. His head shook. "It's adorable for you to think that, though—that I would tire of you. That's impossible, love. I'm in this with you—for good. You know how much I love you."

"I love you too." I smiled as anxiety sneaked up on me like a million invisible, tiny bugs that crawled up from my feet, trying to make their way up.

It's not that I was disappointed with Nathan's answer. On the contrary. I was happy to have his confirmation on the matter, that he loved me and that he was with me for me. And that, yes, there was an incredible opportunity being presented to him that he couldn't refuse, but that it was an unexpected bonus. I would hang on to that thought.

Sadly, I knew what it all meant.

It meant that I would have to compromise and set my hopes and dreams aside. Yet, another part of me kept whispering in my ear that it wasn't going to be very easy to make them come true anyway. That this was the life I was destined to live and that I shouldn't be ungrateful for the privilege of living the way I did, of having the things I had, of being kept safe from all the invisible *harm.*

What I'd never told anyone was how I would be glad and willing to throw some of that away just to be … free.

"What's going on inside that head of yours?" Nathan asked. "You seem so—sad. You don't believe me?"

"No. No, of course, I do. It's just a tough day for me. It always is. And it's been harder this year with Caleb gone. I can't seem to make any progress. I miss him so much that—" I took my hands to my face and took a deep breath. "I can't help but feel alone sometimes. He always came to mass with me on this day. It's been hard to accept that he's really gone."

Nathan wrapped his arms around me. The perfect amount of tight and gentle. "You have me, love. Always. All of me," Nathan said to my hair. "I swear it. I know I couldn't be there for you today, and I won't stop feeling like shit for it. But I promise you it *won't* happen again. Ever. And I'm right here, right now."

I wasn't sure if Nathan would be able to keep to his word, but I still needed to hear it. I needed to believe him, and I would hold on to that promise if only to keep the hope alive. Hope that we could find a way to stay together—always, as he said.

"Do you mind if I just call it a night? I want to go straight to sleep, but if you're free tomorrow, we can go for a run in the morning, and I also made dinner plans with Nolan and Emily."

"That's perfect," he replied. "I just need to take a look at some papers at noon, but it will only take an hour tops. So we can run in the morning and then I'll see you again once I get out of the office. And dinner with Nolan and Emily sounds great."

Nathan ran his fingers through my hair, down my neck. "Are you sure I can't help you change your mind? About staying?" Nathan's lips met mine. I allowed myself to get lost in the kiss that felt like an effortless apology, making things feel better. Lighter.

And even if it usually was the hardest thing to resist him, I wasn't in the mood for any of that. Not tonight. And a part of me thought it wouldn't do him any harm to miss me a little.

"You're cheating," I said, breaking away from his lips.

"I know." He kissed me again, but I guess he assumed that if I hadn't told him to come up by now, then it wasn't happening. And he was always such a gentleman. "Get some sleep, love, because tomorrow you are going to have trouble kicking me out of your bedroom."

"That sounds ... interesting," I said with a laugh.

"I'll make it as interesting as you like." He gave me one last peck on my lips and said, "Off you go. *Please.*" He dragged a hand through his brown wavy locks and leaned in over me to knock on the window twice. David opened the door for me. "I love you."

"I love you too. Aaron will drive you home. See you tomorrow." I smiled at him, and he smiled one of his charming smiles back.

I walked inside the apartment building, and David offered to walk me up.

"Any plans for tonight?" I asked him as the elevator moved up to the ninth floor. It was Friday, after all.

"Not really. I'm on duty, Miss Murphy," David replied. "Right until sunrise."

"But I'm staying in. You should go out or something. Please take the rest of your shift off." Aaron lived downstairs, so come on. I thought it was excessive for him to stay up all night doing nothing. "I'll talk to Aaron."

"Well, there's this party that Christopher wanted me to go to, but I told him I had work tonight, so—"

"You *have* to go. I don't want CJ to resent me." I laughed. CJ had never once asked me to switch a shift or anything of the sort to accommodate his plans with David. He was respectful of David's job, but it got me thinking how many times I might've ruined their plans.

"He understands, but yeah, he gets annoyed sometimes. You know how he is." David lifted a brow. I knew what he meant.

"Can you hold this for me?" I handed over the bouquet that Nathan had given me, and I fired a text to Aaron letting him know that I was staying in for the rest of the evening and that David would end his shift right now, not knowing if he would like it or not, but I didn't care. I wanted David to go to that party with CJ.

"I've already let Aaron know, so you're free to go," I said as I placed my phone back in my purse and took my keys out.

David gave me the bouquet back with a grin and said, "Thank you, Miss Murphy. Have a good night."

He walked away, and I opened the door to my apartment with a gasp.

What the hell is this?

The foyer was filled with different types of white flowers. Planters and vases of all shapes and sizes stood against every single wall, making a white trail of flowers toward the living room and another toward my bedroom. It was *breathtaking*. A delicious aroma filled my nostrils as I walked around the apartment.

The living room's coffee table was also packed with white blossoms. I couldn't even tell which ones I had brought before, but the person who did this probably used the few vases I had placed around the house to complement this elaborate design.

I unwrapped Nathan's bouquet and placed the flowers in different vases all around the foyer.

All of this had William's name written all over it. But I couldn't find a card anywhere, and why would he do this? Not only did I not deserve anything from him after telling him I'd chosen Nathan, but he had made it clear with his silence and his actions that he had made his choice too.

But I couldn't think of anyone else who would do something like this. I knew it hadn't been Nathan, and it's not something my father had ever done for me before.

I opened my bedroom door and found a single white orchid on a small silver planter sitting on my nightstand. There was a card.

For: Miss Guillermina Murphy
From: Lily and the Sjöberg Family.
"When the best is gone—I know that
other things are not of consequence—"

"Damn it," I uttered under my breath. William had to be the one who orchestrated this. In our conversation in the cottage last summer, I'd told him that I loved placing white flowers around my apartment on this day. And, of course, he must've remembered and took it to the next level. And adding that quote just … damn. It was hard not to reminisce and connect with a lot of things that had happened between us.

But I still couldn't understand why he would do this. It was also his birthday, and I hadn't even congratulated him. I'd been toying around with the thought all day, but I never made up my mind—until now. I had to thank him for the flowers, at least.

I texted Eric, Joel, and Tobias, to thank them for the gesture.

I wasn't sure if they knew they'd been added to the card, but I thanked them either way. Eric replied fairly quickly, saying he was glad I liked them, which meant they did know about it. I sent Lily a quick video showing her the flowers and thanking her as well.

My hands trembled when I decided to text William next. I was nervous about reaching out. A part of me didn't know if he would reply, and I wasn't yet sure if I wanted him to do so or not. But I had to thank him.

I erased and rewrote my message a few times before finally sending it.

Me: Hey, William. Happy birthday! I just got home and saw the flowers. They are beautiful. Thank you so much. I loved them. Emily wanted me to wish you a happy birthday too. I hope you're having a great time.

Lily replied when I was about to jump into the shower, so I turned off the water and threw my robe on. I hadn't told Lily anything about my last conversation with William and how I heard him and Zara having sex afterward. I couldn't risk her telling Joel, and if Nathan found out that I kept that information from him … It was best not to dwell on that thought.

Lily: Oh, my GOD! I had no idea that's what we were going to send you. Billy told us that Alice would take care of it. They are sooooo beautiful! I would've loved to go down to your apartment and see them, but I'm in LA. I couldn't make it to the cottage. They're celebrating Billy's birthday over there.
Me: I know, right? My apartment smells delicious. Thank you again. I'll see you when you get back. I'm sure they're having a great time over there.

Lily: Have you recently spoken to Billy?
Me: No. I haven't. I mean, I just texted him to thank him and wish him a happy birthday. But I haven't talked to him since my birthday. I didn't even know if he was in the US or not. He just disappeared.
Lily: Do you miss him?
Me: Lily!
Lily: Billie, come on. You know you can trust me. I feel like something happened, and Joel won't tell me much. But I just want to see if you're okay. I know Billy cares a lot about you, but I found it weird that he would leave like that. He did mention something to Joel about wanting to sell the apartment, but Joel convinced him not to because that's insane.

What! Sell the apartment? It was so frustrating to know he wanted to sell it just to avoid seeing me again. And his entire family lived here. He shouldn't have to sell his apartment because of me.

Me: I'm okay. And I'm sure he is too.
Lily: I don't think he is when he's considering selling his apartment. You know I wouldn't tell Joel a thing. I never have. I'll delete these texts after we're done talking, okay?

Damn it.

I told her what happened on my birthday. About how my conversations with William had been during the party. About Nemorino's wine, and how I got into an argument with Nathan when her friend Lana sent him the photographs of William and me. How scared I was about losing him. And how I told William I had chosen Nathan. I left out the part about Zara and William having sex, though.

263

Lily: I'm going to KILL Lana.
Me: Don't. I don't want to make a big deal out of it since Nathan and I are okay. He blocked her already, so whatever.
Lily: Well, if Billy left, then it means he must be having a hard time after you talked.
Me: I don't think he's having such a hard time. Believe me.
Lily: How can you be so sure? Unless there's something you're not telling me.

Just remembering that William and Zara had sex made my stomach churn. I so desperately wanted to share that with Lily just to vent—to get her two cents on it. She had proven to me that I could trust her.

Lily: Billie?
Me: I'm 99.9999% sure William had sex with Zara.
Lily: WHAT!!!!!! Who told you this? How did you find out? I mean, they've always been close, but they insist on how they're just friends all the time. I mean, Zara loves them all so much. They've known her since she was a baby. It took me a good while to trust her when I started dating Joel. She's somehow always been in the picture.
Me: Well, I guess she's gonna be stuck in the picture for a while longer.
Lily: How did you find out? Does Nathan know?
Me: I heard them, Lily. Well, I heard HER through the wall. Right after I talked to William, I showered and went to bed. I woke up a few hours later, and I heard her. They were having sex. There's no doubt about it.
Me: And no. Nathan doesn't know, and it's been eating at me that I haven't told him. I don't know how he would react if he found out. But I'm also scared that he will be angry

at me if he finds out later on that I knew about it and chose not to tell him.

Lily: He CAN'T know. I'm afraid to see what happens if Nathan finds out. I agree that it's best not to tell him. Not right now. Especially when we're not sure if they're in a relationship or not.

Me: Okay. Then pleeeeeease don't say a word to Joel about this. I don't want Nathan to find out. And I don't think they're in a serious relationship because I've seen a bunch of paparazzi photos of him with different girls every time he goes out, which is very often.

Lily: I don't want Nathan finding out either, so you've got nothing to worry about. And I guess you're right. Joel mentioned how Billy's been partying and drinking a lot lately, and he's a bit worried. I feel like Billy might be doing it because he's hurt about what happened between you.

Me: Well, now I'm worried too. I know it's been almost two months since his surgery, but I don't even know how he's doing or if he's been cleared to drink and party every other day.

Lily: Was it hard for you? To listen to them having sex?

Me: I wanted to break down that wall. I had to sleep on the living room couch. It was THAT bad. But now that he's left, I feel like it's been easier for me to block him out. But the flowers he sent today are messing with my head. It meant a lot to me that he remembered, but I'm so confused about why he would do it. I'm afraid that once Zara comes back, they'll rekindle their relationship or something. And it would be so awkward because I would have to see her all the time. I mean, she's Nathan's sister.

Lily: I feel like it was only a one-night thing. For Billy, at least. It could be that he was just trying to get you out of his head, and Zara happened to be there. But Zara might feel differently.

Me: Could be. But it doesn't matter anyway.

Lily: It does matter when I know how you feel about him.

Me: William's gone. He left. He wants to sell his apartment. He doesn't want to see me. He's going out with all these other girls. It's all very straightforward. And I'm with Nathan.

Lily: Why do you think that is? He's crazy about you. All the things he's done for you. I've NEVER in my life seen Billy do a fraction of that for anyone else. And I freaking love Nate too. But ughhhhh!!! I hate this.

Me: I feel like I should get real and just focus on my relationship with Nathan. That's what I've been trying to do these past few weeks. I can't risk what I have with him. And what if Zara is in love with William or something? How weird would it be? I hate this too.

Lily: I get it. Nathan's the safe choice.

The safe choice.

I guess Lily was right, but her remark kind of hit home, and it certainly didn't make things easier for me. It was a complete brain fuck, to be exact.

Safe. *Does that make me a coward?*

Me: I guess I never know what to expect from William.

Lily: And that's the reason why you're still curious about him.

William's reply came in.

Me: William just texted me back.

Lily: Shit, ok. Well, I'll leave you to it. I'm already late for dinner with friends. I'll see you in NY in a few days.

Love you, Billie!

Me: Love you too, Lily. I'll see you soon. Thanks for everything.

I clicked out of Lily's conversation and opened William's text.

W.S: Glad you liked them. Thanks for the birthday wishes. Emily is Nolan's girl, right? Tell her I said thanks.

That I wasn't expecting. There was no witty comeback, no sarcastic comment, no teasing me to the point of wanting to slap him all the way to Sagaponack. I wasn't used to William being so ... polite with me—cold. And it hurt more than I would've imagined.

But he did me a favor ... I guess.

I didn't reply. Instead, I tossed my phone on my bed and jumped in the shower. That's what owning your choices looks like. And it felt like shit.

CHAPTER 30

The Cottage

June 18, 2010

TODAY WAS THE last day of my Summer Intensive Program. I took a graphic design course as an elective for my BFA curriculum. It was a somewhat demanding course, and it kept me occupied during these past few weeks.

My hand was healing fast. Every day it felt better, thanks to the physical therapy sessions that I'd been attending. It didn't feel stiff anymore, and the swelling was gone completely.

Nathan kept traveling all the time, working late, working weekends—exhausted. It worried me to see him so stressed out. He insisted on how the workload would go back to a more acceptable rhythm once they were done with a tough negotiation. But there was always going to be a new client. *It never ends.*

I was still having good and bad days regarding Caleb. And the nightmares hadn't gone away. They weren't as frequent as before but still very much present—raw and vivid.

Nathan was making an effort to show up when he had to— to stay over when he could.

To be there for me.

He was finally putting his assistant to work. She would help him sort his schedule out, clearing it out for important things like this weekend.

The Sjöbergs invited us to spend Midsummer in Sagaponack. Nathan and I planned to leave today at around 4:00 p.m. and return on Sunday late in the afternoon. My father agreed for me to go because Nathan convinced him. My security detail would take turns to rest at an inn close to the cottage.

I know what you're thinking: What about William?

When Lily called to invite us, I immediately refused. There was no way I would spend the weekend at William's house. Especially when I knew Zara would be attending too. And I didn't even have to ask Nathan to know that he wouldn't want to go either.

Seeing William and Zara together wasn't something I wanted to try anytime soon. She moved to New York for good three days ago, and she would be staying in William's empty apartment, of course, until she found an apartment for herself. I'm sure she wasn't in a hurry to get that done.

Zara hadn't asked to stay with me, and Nathan was too busy to remember to offer her my place. Lily told me William was filming in South Africa. And *that's* the reason why I agreed to go to the Hamptons.

William wasn't going to be there.

Dating Nathan meant that I would have to learn to coexist with Zara. She had come to my apartment to say hi when she arrived, but we hadn't hung out. I was too occupied with the final project that I handed in today, and Nathan arrived from D.C. early this morning, so he hadn't seen her.

But we would both see her today once we arrived in Sagaponack and would hang out with her the entire weekend. There was no way to avoid that, and I wasn't one bit excited about it. She left early in the morning with Lily and Joel. Eric and

Tobias arrived yesterday, and I didn't know if Sivert and Nathalie, their parents, would be there or not since things had been tricky after the divorce. Lily told me they weren't getting along so well.

If one of them did show up, that meant the *only* available room for Zara would be William's. And the thought of her sleeping on his bed was fucking annoying. But who are we kidding? She would most definitely lay her pretty head to sleep on William's pillows either way.

I forced myself to make my peace with that thought as I closed the small suitcase I was taking for the weekend when Nathan called me.

"Hey, you! I'm heading over to pick you up in about five minutes. Are you ready?"

"I'm—not. That's why I'm calling. I'm not done yet, but I can arrive tomorrow at noon," Nathan said, his tone low and seemingly stressed.

"It's okay. I can wait for you if you want, and we'll leave tomorrow. Together."

"No, no, no. Everyone's already there. You're done with school—you should go. I'll see you there tomorrow. I promise."

Nathan had been keeping to his promises lately. I wasn't too worried about him showing up or not, so I agreed. I was looking forward to hanging out with Lily, and I had a pending chat with Tobias. We hadn't been able to talk after what happened on my birthday with Jordan and Cecile. I wanted to clear the air once and for all.

I wanted my friend back.

"Okay, I'll see you tomorrow then," I told him. "I'll miss you today."

"I'll miss you too. I can't wait to see you. I love you."

"I love you too."

☾

"Hey, Billie!" Eric said, walking up to me. We hugged each other, and then he peeked inside the car. "Where's Nate?"

"He'll be arriving tomorrow."

"Aww! Why?" Lily shouted from afar, darting our way.

Eric took my small suitcase out of David's hands and told him he would bring it inside for me.

Setting foot in this place again was nerve-wracking for a million reasons, starting with the painful fact that Caleb was here with me the last time I came. I missed his face, his eyes, his voice.

Him.

And William didn't have to be here for me to be reminded of him anywhere I fixed my sight on either. Like the freaking pool, for example. I wished it would've been drained, but no, there it was, looking at me funny like, *hey, hey, we meet again. Remember me?*

I ignored the pool and kept walking.

"Hey!" I hugged Lily. "Nathan couldn't get out of the office today. But he promised to be here tomorrow by noon."

"That's too bad. I'll send Joel to drag his ass down here if he doesn't show up at 12 o'clock sharp," Lily said, walking back to the house. I followed close behind.

"Please do." I laughed. That wasn't a half-bad idea.

"Hey, sis!" Zara shouted as she rushed down the stairs.

And so the sisfest begins.

Zara looked effortlessly beautiful as always—her long, tanned legs on display in ripped white jean shorts. Her shiny brown locks held up in a messy bun, and her eyes of the bluest blue sparkled from afar.

Why wouldn't William want to sleep with her?

"Hey—sis." I'd come to terms with the fact that I would

never feel comfortable calling her *sis* but that I didn't have a choice anymore but to keep doing it. I was sure I could make it sound more natural with time. And she wanted to be an actress, so I couldn't tell how genuine she was about the nickname. She was surely going to be a great one.

"Where's Natey?" she asked with a frown. "He's been hiding from me."

"Nathan's been hiding from me this past couple of days, too. Don't worry. He's been crazy busy. But he'll be here tomorrow."

"Ugh. Bloody workaholic," Zara grumbled, walking around the kitchen counter. "Fancy a cuppa?" She looked at her watch and placed a cup on the counter. "You're right on time for tea time. Lily, how about you?"

"Sure. Thanks," I told her. I couldn't stop staring at her moving around the kitchen—*William's* kitchen. She seemed to know her way around it very well, almost entitled. Like *I'm the woman of the house*, kind of entitled. Lily refused the tea and grabbed a wineglass and bottle of wine instead. *Is that Nemorino's?*

"Do you take it with milk?" Zara asked me. It seemed like she'd been brewing a kettle because all she did was pour it in the cup.

"Just a splash."

"Points for that, sis." Zara winked and placed the cup in front of me.

I sipped on my tea. It was delicious and officially my drink of choice for the rest of the evening. I wasn't in the mood for drinking any alcohol today because I planned on taking a mild sleeping pill at night. I'd figured out that it was less likely for me to have any nightmares when I slept more profoundly.

The three of us took our drinks to the terrace. Zara told us about how she was still undecided about a couple of great apartments she'd found as Lily uncorked the bottle of wine, which *was* Nemorino's. I guess there were a few cases left from the party. William never sent the ones he said he would, for obvious reasons. Maybe those were *my* cases.

Whatever.

"In what neighborhood are you looking to live?" Lily asked Zara as she poured herself a glass of wine.

"Well, I want to be close to Juilliard, and I also want to be close to you guys," Zara replied, twitching her mouth to the side. "I found a studio apartment in Lincoln Square, so I guess it's very convenient—location-wise. But there's also this *stunning* one-bedroom apartment in the Ritz Tower. And it's got the loveliest rooftop."

"Wow! So you'd literally be our next-door neighbor," Lily said.

Zara *really* wanted to be close to the Sjöbergs. The Ritz Tower is mere feet away from our apartment building—on Park Avenue as well. You can even see the Ritz's gray sunshade if you look left when exiting our building. It's *right there.*

"I know! And Nathan's apartment is also close by," Zara said, taking a sip of her tea. "I'm *in love* with the Ritz apartment. But it's only for sale. My realtor reached out to the owner and asked if he would be willing to rent it, but he refused."

"So what are you going to do?" Lily asked. "Are you renting the studio on Lincoln Square then?"

Why do I have the feeling that …

"Well, Will insists on buying it. He said it would be a great investment opportunity and that he would let me buy it from him later on when I start working."

Yeah, Juan Pablo can suck it. I could steal his fortune-teller job in a second because I *kneeeew it.*

Lily's eyes went wide as she drank from her wine. And I was sure we were thinking the same thing—William and Zara were officially a thing, right? Who gets you into Juilliard, pays for the whole thing, and buys you an apartment while they're at it?

She must've been great in bed. I had my doubts now if that was the first time they'd slept together—probably not.

"You're all set then," Lily said. I coughed to stop a nervous laugh from escaping my mouth. The way she said it, with such shock, was so disturbingly amusing.

Fortunately, Zara didn't appear to notice my reaction. She was grinning, seemingly excited about her new life in New York City. I hated all the parts of me that felt jealous of Zara. Everything was working out so perfectly great for her. And that, I didn't mind—good for her. What bothered me was that it was all because of William. *He* was responsible for her happiness, and I resented that.

I wondered if she was aware of William's extracurricular activities in South Africa. The latest headline indicated he'd been seen on a couple of dates with an insanely gorgeous South African actress. I saw the photographs. They looked real fucking cozy on their dinner dates. But William had to come back from filming at some point, so I guess buying Zara an apartment was his way of keeping her warmed up for his return.

"Good evening, ladies," Tobias said, walking over to the table—shirtless and sweaty. Joel was right behind him in the same attire as him. Shorts and sandy tennis shoes. "Glad you could make it, Billie." Tobias smiled at me. "Where's Nate?"

"He's working," Joel replied in my stead, "but he'll be here tomorrow. He called me earlier to let me know. But don't worry, Billie. He's been warned. He'll be here."

Tobias kicked off his tennis shoes and socks and jumped in the pool.

"That's disgusting!" Zara shouted at him. "You're mixing your sweat in the pool."

"It's just sweat, Zara." Joel laughed and removed his tennis shoes and socks too. He took a few steps back and winked at Lily, who was shaking her head at him. Joel turned around to join Tobias in the pool. He then shouted something to Zara in Swedish.

"Get your own beers!" Zara replied to them.

"Any volunteers?" Joel shouted back.

"I'll get 'em," I said with a laugh. I went inside and grabbed a couple of beers from the fridge. When I came out, Lily followed me to the pool, took one of the beers off my hand, and gave it to Joel. She sat on the edge in front of him. I leaned in and gave Tobias his beer.

"Tob, can we talk?"

"Sure," he replied. We moved a little bit away from Joel and Lily. Zara walked over to the pool too. She sat next to Lily and chatted with them. "What's up, Billie?"

I sat cross-legged, took a deep breath, and said, "I just—I don't know if you're still angry at me, but I wanted to apologize again. I miss you, Tob."

Tobias sipped on his beer and dropped it on the edge of the pool next to me. "No, of course not. It wasn't your fault. I've just been busy traveling back and forth from LA. I miss you too, Billie." He ran a hand through his hair and looked at me from the corner of his eye. "You know you're like the sister I never had."

"I heard that!" Zara shouted from afar. "I'm getting jealous!"

Why am I not surprised?

Zara wanted to be the center of attention with the Sjöbergs all the time.

"We're having a moment over here!" Tobias shouted back at her. "You're like my *other* sister, too, okay?"

"Fair 'nuff!" She stuck her tongue out at him and went back

to her conversation with Lily and Joel. But apparently, we weren't far enough for her to eavesdrop on our conversation, so I planned to make it as swift as possible.

"So—we're good?" I asked him.

"Of course we are," he whispered back with a warm smile.

"Do you want to talk about Cecile, or ...?"

He frowned and looked away. "There's—nothing much to talk about right now anyway."

"Okay. Well, I haven't spoken to her about—anything. So I really don't know what has happened since that day. But—"

"It's okay." Tobias seemed disturbed. Like something was eating at him. I kept quiet—my usual method of getting people to talk. "A friend told me that Jordan flew to Paris last week to see her," Tobias whispered. "Ah! I fucking *hate* him. I can't believe he's doing this. We used to be so close, him and me."

"I'm sure it sucks, but I know Cecile likes you, Tob."

"And she likes Jordan too, *believe me.*"

Tobias was getting annoyed, and I didn't want to ruin the good mood he was in just before. He just came from a run, he was still high on the endorphins, and here I was, ruining it for him by mentioning Cecile.

"So have you been training with Grant?" I changed the subject. Tobias snorted a weak laugh. He grabbed his beer again and drank deep.

"You don't need to do that," he said, raising a brow. I widened my eyes as in, *do what?* "Change the subject."

"Well, you were smiling, and then I opened my mouth, and now you're all serious and frowning. So yeah, I had to change the subject," I explained. "I honestly just want to know if you're okay. That's all."

"I am." He smiled at me and drained his beer. "It's just complicated, you know. But thank you. I know how much you care, and—I really appreciate it."

"Thirsty?" I laughed. He finished that beer in a few minutes.

"You have no idea." Tobias laughed. "I should be drinking water after my run, not beer, but fuck it."

"Do you want me to get you another one?" I offered. "It's Midsummer weekend after all."

"See?" Tobias said out loud in Zara's direction. "That's why Billie's my favorite sister!" He was trying to tease Zara about it. And she took the bait because I heard her complaining as I walked back to the kitchen. Joel shouted that he wanted another one too.

I walked back, handed them their beers, and sat next to Lily.

We were all just hanging out and talking when Tobias finished off his second beer in under five minutes.

"You should try mixing it up with water," I told him with a laugh.

"I know," he replied with a burp—a loud and long burp.

"EW!" Lily and I said at the same time. I waved my hand in front of my face, trying to fan away any suspicious smells before they reached me.

"That's absolutely *disgusting*," Zara said with a grimace.

"That's it," Tobias said, jumping out of the pool. Lily and I pulled back reactively, and before I even blinked, Tobias had Zara by the waist and dropped her into the pool. The scene was all too familiar to me. But I was mostly glad to be dry.

"ARE YOU MAD?" Zara yelled, completely drenched. "The water's freezing!"

Tobias jumped back into the pool. "You called me disgusting twice," he said to Zara. "I couldn't let this one slide." He laughed and closed the distance between them. Zara splashed him, and he splashed her back.

"Stop!" Zara cried. She was chuckling too—somewhat. But she seemed annoyed.

"Well, you started it," Tobias said, getting closer to her, still laughing. Joel asked Lily to bring towels, so she fled into the house. Joel and I couldn't stop staring at Zara and Tobias's dynamic in the pool.

Tobias looked like he was enjoying making Zara angry. He splashed her again and kept walking in her direction, basically cornering her against the far wall of the pool. But again, it all seemed harmless, like he was just playing around with her.

"Back. *Off*," Zara warned in a grave tone. She pushed Tobias back and tried swimming away from him. But he was on a mission to tease her, and he probably thought she wasn't serious because he grabbed her arm and pulled her back.

"Get your bloody hands off me!" she yelled.

"Whoa!" Tobias returned, raising his hands. "I was just playing around."

Zara didn't reply as she moved toward the stairs. She looked over her shoulder at him as if about to say something, but she turned around and walked out of the pool.

"I know you're into Billy okay, it's not like I was hitting on you or anything. I was just messing with you."

"You know *nothing* about my relationship with him," she spat back, pointing a wet finger at him as she stood at the edge of the pool, glaring at him.

Shit, this was getting tense and uncomfortable.

Lily came back with the towels and offered one to Zara, who immediately used it to wrap herself with it as her gaze dropped to the floor.

"Why are you being weird about this?" Tobias asked with a grimace.

"As I said … because *you* know nothing." Zara stormed into the house, and we didn't see her again for the rest of the night.

"She's sleeping in William's bedroom, and she wants us to

think nothing's going on between them?" Tobias said to Joel. "I don't get why it's such a huge fucking deal. And then she acts like I was trying to come on to her or someshit like that. We've always gotten along like that. So what's changed?"

Yeah, I was most definitely going to need a full dose of my sleeping pills if I were planning to fall asleep at some point. And that's precisely what I did because knowing Zara was getting her z's upstairs in William's bed was enough to keep me up at night.

Seeing how obvious it was for everyone that she was so into him … it's what nightmares are made of, and I didn't need any more horrors invading my dreams.

CHAPTER 31

Sous-Chef

June 19, 2010

THOMAS HAS ME *pinned to my bed again. His full weight on top of me, the tight grip of his hands on my wrists, crushing them. He leans in and grazes my jawline up to my ear with the tip of his nose. I cringe but try for my reaction to go undetected. I fail—miserably. He notices my rejection and his crushing grip snaps my wrist.*

I scream as the pain cripples my entire arm.

Thomas uselessly tries to make me stop, but I keep screaming. William walks in, and he's roaring my name. Thomas asks him to stop, and he doesn't. He never stops.

Thomas pulls out a gun, and he shoots. Twice.

Head. Heart.

William's down, and I scream again in between sobs.

The scene melts away. I'm alone now, and I sit up in my bed. The room is pitch black, and my eyelids are heavy. I can't seem to keep my eyes open.

"It's okay. You're okay," a soothing, melodic voice whispers in my ear. I feel two hands on my shoulders. They gently push me back in the bed and cover me with the comforter. I'm crying again, but it's a soft and constant weeping—a realization that I'm safe. Dreaming. "It's okay, Guille."

"William," I whisper back. My eyes are closed, and as much as I try to open them. To see him. I can't.

"Shh. Just breathe."

I'm sleeping again, and this time I'm sucked into the dark, welcoming nothingness.

(

A sliver of sunshine squeezed into the guest bedroom through both sides of the blinds making my eyes fly open. I reached out for my phone on the nightstand. 10:04 a.m. A sense of panic kicked in when I couldn't find Caleb's letter. I'd slept holding on to it last night, but I exhaled with relief when I saw it on the floor beside my bed.

Damn it. I overslept. I'd never taken a full dose of my sleeping pill, only half, sometimes even a quarter. I realized just now that taking the sleeping pills didn't turn off the nightmares. It'd just been a coincidence that I had no bad dreams the last few times I took one. I wasn't taking them very often, only when I absolutely had to like last night.

Nathan said he'd be arriving around noon, so it was best for me to get up and start my day. So I jumped in the shower, got dressed, and walked out of the guestroom.

The smell of different herbs and spices hit me as I stepped out. Outside, I spotted a big truck with five guys unloading furniture and a wooden pergola like the one that they used last year during the Midsummer party on the rooftop.

Aaron and Amena stood near the front door with firm bodyguard stances observing the scene before them. I guess they were apprehensive of the furniture guys or something. They always lingered around the SUV.

I followed the delicious aromas coming from the kitchen, and William was there. Cooking. He had a beard now. It was neat and well kept, just like in the paparazzi photos of him with that South African actress. It looked great on him, of course.

I froze. *Was William really in my room last night soothing me back to sleep?*

No, no, it'd all been a dream.

"Feeling better?" he asked as he kept doing his thing, chopping stuff, for what I could tell. His gaze fixed on his knife and cutting board.

Uh-oh. *Was he, then?*

"Hey. Um … yeah. What do you mean? Where's everyone?" My feet were glued on the spot where I stood, unable to move as I waited for the effect of seeing him again to settle.

William dropped the knife, wiped his brow with his forearm, and focused his blue gaze at me. He scanned me with a frown and turned around to take a few things out of the fridge. Vegetables. He resumed the chopping and finally started talking.

"Zara went out for a run with Eric. Lily and Joel left to get some stuff I need from the grocery store. Tobias is upstairs taking a call in his room, and you were screaming in your sleep as usual when I arrived a few hours ago," he explained. "Do you want some coffee, or are you gonna stand there all morning?"

Both. He was back to being Midsummer William: cocky, analytic, and hot as hell. And I don't even have to mention he was wearing a white V-neck t-shirt with gray joggers.

"Yes. Coffee—I mean. Thank you." I coaxed my feet to respond, so I walked over to the kitchen counter and took a seat on one of the stools in front of William. "Sorry about last night. I didn't realize you were in there. That you heard me."

"I suspected that. You never opened your eyes," he replied. "Here you go. Milk, right?" I nodded, but he was already pouring a dash of milk into my coffee. "So tell me, why is Nathan never around when you need him again?" William asked as he placed the milk carton back inside the fridge.

"He's on his way, actually," I said, my brows pulling in and a portion of me going into panic as I realized William was here when he wasn't supposed to be. I feared what would happen if or *when* Nathan found out about the speculations regarding the nature of Zara and William's relationship.

"I—thought you were in South Africa," I tossed in. "I wasn't expecting you to be here." I was so nervous about talking to him. And his attitude wasn't helping at all to soothe the tension.

Deja vu.

"I was. But Lily said they were ordering take out from Mockinbird's a few days ago, and I can't allow that," he said with a laugh. He grabbed a couple of empty food containers and placed the vegetables in there. "Besides, family comes first. I realized it would be the first Midsummer I'd be missing out on. Can't allow that either."

William rinsed his hands and dried them off with a small towel he grabbed from over his shoulder. He tossed it and said, "Make yourself at home. And—could you keep an eye on the potatoes?" He walked away and left me sitting there in the kitchen with my coffee staring at the huge boiling pot of new potatoes.

I peeked over my shoulder and saw him sitting on the wooden bench in front of a digital piano in the living room that I failed to account for the last time I was here.

William placed his headphones over his ears, and started playing the piano, so I turned around and sipped on my coffee, wondering what song he might be playing. I'd never actually heard William playing the piano in the same room as me, although I'd heard him numerous times through the wall.

That wall.

After a few minutes of me listening to William's soundless song and me staring at the potatoes as instructed (not that I would know when they'd be ready), Tobias rushed down the stairs.

"Hey, Billie!" I was glad to see him being his usual self with me again.

"Hey, Tob. What's up?"

"Nothing much. Just done with a few calls, so I'm officially open for *Midsommar* business." He pulled the refrigerator's handle and scanned the contents of it when I heard William dropping his headphones over the keys with a thud. I tensed up as I listened to his footsteps approaching behind me.

"Drop the gravlax. And the cheese too," William said to Tobias. "That's for later."

He turned around and met William's gaze. "Don't start with the moody chef thing," Tobias replied, ignoring William and pulling out a large Tupperware with cheese. "Where'd you hide the bread?"

"I don't hide things. It's in the oven. You can grab *one* piece."

Tobias popped up a beer out of the fridge, and I instinctively looked at my watch.

"It's almost noon, Billie," Tobias said to me.

"I didn't say a thing."

"You didn't have to." He laughed. "It's already 5:00 p.m. in Sweden."

"Well, in that case," William joined in, opening the fridge and grabbing a beer for himself. He twisted the lid with the kitchen rag, and I heard his beer fizz open. I was still working around my coffee and couldn't fathom the thought of drinking a beer right now.

Tobias grabbed a plate and poured a few cubes of cheese on it.

"I'll make you eggs or something. Just put the damn cheese away," William said to Tobias, seemingly stressed about the cheese situation.

I couldn't help but laugh, as much as I tried not to. I thought it was cute that William wanted everything to be perfect. Tobias opened the oven door, pulled out a piece of bread, and took a bite. William looked away and rubbed his nose. He then took an angry sip on his beer with the most annoyed look on his face.

Tobias placed the cheese Tupperware back in the fridge and said, "Ah! *Smultron*." He took out another bigger Tupperware filled with strawberries. "Want one, Billie?" He offered as he opened the lid.

William glowered at Tobias but didn't say a thing. His death-threat-filled stare should've sufficed, but Tobias didn't seem to care. He took a strawberry to his mouth and chewed away.

"Thanks, but I don't like strawberries," I replied to Tobias, draining my coffee and dropping the cup on the counter.

Tobias stopped chewing and stared at me with a grimace. William grabbed a strawberry and said, "That's impossible. You must try one of these. We fly them in from Sweden every year. They're handpicked to be perfect."

"Ah—sure," I replied, sticking my hand out. I feared their reaction if I refused to try one. William placed the small strawberry in my hand, and I inspected it between two fingers. "Is this like a different type of strawberry? It's um—prickly. Seedy."

"Just take a bite," Tobias said to me. They both stared at me, waiting for me to try it as if they were the creators of this fruit, and wanted so desperately to know if I approved of their conception.

I took the strawberry to my lips and took a bite. It was sweet but less juicy than a regular strawberry. The texture of the seeds in my mouth made me shudder. I closed my eyes and stuck out my hand as I swallowed it. Tobias placed his beer in my hand, and I took a sip.

"Ah! The seeds," I said, my mouth twisting to the side. Maybe

I didn't get enough sensory stimulation as a child. "I can't. I'm sorry. I really don't know what it is." They shook their heads with disappointment, and I couldn't help but laugh at their genuine frustration on the matter.

"So you didn't try the strawberry cake last year?" William asked with a frown as if it were a crime.

"I did, but I pushed the strawberry pieces to the sides," I explained, giving his beer back to Tobias. "I'm—sorry?" I laughed again, mostly out of nerves. "I liked everything I tried last year. I mean, I'm not a picky eater at all. I usually like everything new I try. It's just the texture. The seeds and the acid aftertaste. I don't know."

"Dad's here," Tobias said, looking out the huge floor-to-ceiling window. He dropped his beer and went outside to greet him. *Thank God.* That way, we could put the strawberry issue behind us.

William took a deep breath and dropped his beer on the kitchen counter too. He seemed weird—on edge.

I leaned in and dared to ask, "You okay?"

"Ah—yeah," he replied without looking at me.

"Is your mom coming too?" My guess was that his mother might be coming and that he was stressed because of it.

"No—no, definitely not. She's—*not* coming."

Guessed wrong. Well, then maybe *that* was the stressful part. Perhaps it was the first year of them not spending Midsummer together as a family. I had a few follow-up questions, but I bit my tongue. It wasn't my place to pry.

Sivert walked into the house, and Tobias followed him, rolling in his suitcase. I stood up and greeted Sivert after William hugged him. His father made a few remarks about William's facial hair as he made his way to the kitchen and picked a couple of strawberries from the Tupperware.

"Ah, ripe and perfect," Sivert said after tossing one into his mouth.

Zara and Eric stepped into the house, both red-faced and sweaty from their run.

"Shoes outside," William warned. "Both of you." Eric and Zara stopped cold and went back out to kick their sandy tennis shoes off. Tobias frowned at the sight of Zara. It'd been an awkward little scene, the one at the pool yesterday evening. It seemed to me like they hadn't spoken about it yet. The vibe was still tense between them.

Eric greeted his father with a hug, and Zara said, "Hey! You made it!" Sivert opened his arms in her direction. "I'm all sweaty!"

"I don't mind. Get in here." Sivert took Zara in his arms and gave her a warm hug and a kiss on the top of her head. Damn, they *really* got along, didn't they? I forgot how she was basically a member of the Sjöberg family. It was annoying to witness.

"Is um—Nathalie coming?" Zara asked Sivert.

"No dear, she's not," he replied as William popped the lid back on the strawberry-filled Tupperware and returned it to the fridge.

Eric fled upstairs to take a shower when Sivert said to William, "I spoke to Zane earlier this week. He tells me you've been seeing a lot of his daughter Rachel lately. In Cape Town."

Oy.

Rachel King is the beautiful South African actress William had been casually seeing when filming out there. Zane King is Rachel's father—an actor too. And now I realized he's friends with Sivert.

Perfect.

"I have," William replied with one of his fake, studied smiles. I had to bite the inside of my cheek just to keep my out-of-service robot face in place.

William was about to say something else when Zara interrupted their exchange with a demanding tone, "Will, I need to talk to you."

Yeah, join the club, sis, and take a number. I'm sure she hated it as much as I did to have confirmation that he was dating another girl.

Tobias shook his head and looked away. Was she going to tell William what happened at the pool too? Tobias seemed to think so.

"Sure," William said, grabbing his beer. "Let's go outside."

I looked at the boiling pot of new potatoes and freaked out. They'd been there for a while. I didn't want to ruin them.

"What should I do with the potatoes?" I asked William as he walked away.

He looked at his watch and said, "Could you take them out of the water? There's a strainer in the second drawer below the stove. And try not to set my kitchen on fire while you're at it." He winked at me and followed Zara out. "Oh! And if you want to cut those in half and transfer them into a bowl, I wouldn't mind at all!"

I wished I could've thrown a potato at him. He knew I was useless in the kitchen.

William and Zara took their conversation to the garden, way past the pool, and I wondered what the hell Zara wanted to talk to him about as I looked for the damn strainer.

There it is.

Tobias chatted with his father as I analyzed the fancy industrial-looking stove, searching for the correct dial to turn it off, and I did. I placed the strainer in the faucet and heard, "Incoming."

Tobias carried the huge pot for me and emptied it into the strainer.

"Thanks, Tob." I couldn't help but glance at Zara and William through the window as they talked. Their conversation appeared to be a heated one. Zara kept gesturing with her hands as William stared at her with his arms crossed at his chest, lifting his beer now and then to take a sip.

William pinched the bridge of his nose and nodded a few times. And there I was staring at them when I had a few pounds of new potatoes to start chopping in half. It was best to jump right into the task at hand.

William had left a cutting board and a knife on the counter, so I was planning to use those. I just needed to look around the cabinets and find a large bowl, which I did, eventually.

I brought the strainer to the counter and began with my chore, transferring the potatoes into the big bowl once the cutting board was full of halves. I've got to say that working in the kitchen was somewhat therapeutic.

Nathan *finally* arrived, and I was halfway done with the potatoes, but I dropped my knife and went out to greet him.

"Hey, you!" Nathan put his duffel bag on the ground and hugged me, lifting me off the floor.

"God, I missed you," he said, kissing me.

"I missed you too."

He put me back down, and I instinctively looked in Zara and William's direction. They were still arguing.

"What's he doing here?" Nathan said, jerking his chin at them.

"Apparently, he decided to come at the last minute," I replied. "He arrived early in the morning."

"And what's *that* about?"

"I've no idea, but they've been arguing over there for a while. Sivert asked William about this Rachel girl he's sort of—dating in South Africa, and then Zara asked to talk to him, and that's all we know."

I could've ended the sentence in *I've no idea*. But I guess we can all be a bit toxic at times. I knew I would probably regret planting the seed that could easily sprout into chaos.

Nathan didn't say a word.

"Let's go inside," I said to him. He picked up his duffel bag, and we walked into William's house, wondering if we should've just grabbed our things and asked the guys to drive us back to New York.

Spoiler alert: That's what he should've done. And we didn't.

CHAPTER 32

Sleeping Arrangements

"HEY MAN," Tobias said to Nathan as we moved into the house. "Glad you made it." They shook their hands with a loud clap and pulled themselves in for a hug with a few firm pats on the back.

"Glad to be here, mate," Nathan replied. "Sivert, nice to see you again. It's been a while."

I shuffled back behind the kitchen counter and resumed the potato task. Nathan grabbed a beer and offered one to Sivert and Tobias, who obviously accepted.

"You're cooking, love?" Nathan asked, standing behind me, dropping his beer on the counter. He ran a hand around my waist and kissed my cheek.

"Well, I'm chopping potatoes," I replied as he rested his chin on my shoulder. "Just don't ask me to use the oven." I kissed him back.

Zara and William sauntered back to the house, his arm around her shoulders as she wiped what I assumed were tears under her eyes. He kept whispering things to her while she nodded. Nathan still stood behind me, holding me tight.

"Natey! Hi!" Zara rushed our way. Nathan kissed my cheek one last time and released me to hug Zara.

"What's wrong?" He asked her in a stern tone. "Have you been crying?"

I lifted my gaze for a second and saw William staring my way, so I looked down at the cutting board again. All I had to do was keep chopping those potatoes. But I could see from the corner of my eye that William was approaching the kitchen.

"Nothing. I'm fine," Zara replied to Nathan with an overly cheery voice. I heard William opening the fridge behind me. He then placed a few bars of butter and herbs on the counter.

Nathan lowered his voice and asked Zara, "Do you want to talk?"

"No, no. I'm fine. I think I should go upstairs and take a shower."

"Upstairs?" Nathan returned as William placed another cutting board beside me. I was almost done with the potatoes. Was he going to make me do something else? "Where did you sleep last night?"

Shit. I felt nervous for Zara. I knew this was going to be an issue for Nathan.

"I'm afraid to ask you to use the stove. Do you know how to use the microwave?" William asked me since Zara was apparently trying to find the courage to reply to Nathan. I answered William's question by glaring at him. "I'll take that as a yes." He chuckled under his breath.

"Zara?" Nathan insisted. Sivert and Tobias drank their beers in the living room, comfortably away from the drama.

"I slept in William's bedroom last night," she said in a hushed voice.

"Okay, but now that William's arrived, I think we should talk about the sleeping arrangements," Nathan replied, brushing his forehead. "I'm sure Tobias can sleep with William, and you can grab one of the bunk beds in Eric and Tobias's room."

"Or," William said, "you both can have my room, and I'll sleep in the guest room with Zara where there are two beds."

Is he high?

"Thank you, but we couldn't take your room," I Immediately replied. "We don't want to impose. I think Nathan's idea would work just fine."

Me and Nathan sleeping in his *bed?* Never.

Besides, couldn't William understand that Nathan didn't want them sleeping in the same room together? Neither did I, but my opinion wasn't going to be taken into consideration. And the fact that there are two beds in the guest room didn't assure any of us they wouldn't just share one of the full-sized beds. The best option was for Zara to sleep with Eric on one of the bunk beds. Yes.

"Oh, but you love my bed, Guille," William added as a bonus. *Son of a bitch!* His hands were focused on chopping dill like the pro he was, not a single care in the world.

My bones turned into gelatin. My stomach simmered and shrank at the sepulchral silence that followed William's last statement. But he wasn't done. No.

"You slept like a baby the last time you stayed over."

"I beg your pardon?" Nathan interjected.

Asshole!

William must've had a death wish because he had the audacity to say that when I held a knife in my hand. I couldn't find the courage to look up, but I felt Nathan and Zara's million Fahrenheit gazes burning me to a crisp—waiting for my reply.

I wasn't sure if William said that to get me into trouble with Nathan or if he was so desperate to sleep in the same room as Zara that he'd rather yield his bed to us.

Both, for sure.

Or maybe he thought that saying that would get me to leave

so he could have his room back to share freely with my *sis*.

Sorry, I'm not leaving. I was sure William was trying to get under my skin. I refused to believe he was genuinely offering his room to us. He knew I would never accept to sleep there with Nathan. Maybe I should've plot-twisted his ass and accepted his offer.

I didn't care that it was his house. I wasn't going to allow him to provoke me like that. If Nathan and I stayed, he wouldn't be able to bunk up with Zara, so tough shit. Although mentioning how I slept in his bed wasn't going to be a turn-on for Zara. But only God knew what was going on in that mind of his.

The only thing *I* was sure of was that I had to say something. So I thought of Cecile and tried to channel her with my reply.

"The pillows are too thick for my taste, if I'm being honest. But the mattress is nice," I said in the most nonchalant tone I could come up with, transferring the last potato halves into the bowl like I couldn't be bothered by what William just said. I wasn't planning to succumb to his taunts.

"And I only slept there because you insisted. So thanks, but Nathan and I will be fine in the guest room." I looked up and met William's gaze. "Do you need me to melt the butter?" I held up one of the butter sticks in my hand.

William raised a brow at me and replied, "I'll take it from here. Microwaved butter is a sin." So I dropped the butter and the knife and rinsed my hands in the kitchen sink.

The amount of energy I had to summon just to appear confident while talking would surely take a toll on me and earn me a spot in Juilliard's drama program with Zara. But it was necessary because I felt like if I acted all jittery and nervous, it would only make the situation seem worse.

Nathan and I could discuss whatever happened that night in William's room in private. I had nothing to hide because *nothing* happened other than kissing, and Nathan already knew that. Besides, it all happened before I even met him.

I still hadn't dared to look in Zara's direction, but she spoke next. "I'll sleep with Eric," she said, marching away toward the stairs.

Thank you.

Joel and Lily walked in carrying a bunch of grocery bags.

"Hey!" she said with the biggest smile, unaware of the drama she'd just walked into. She dropped the brown paper bags on the counter with a thud and approached Nathan for a hug. "There are more bags in the car. We could use some help."

Nathan greeted Joel and immediately went out to help with the groceries. I followed him.

"Can we talk?" I whispered as we each carried a couple of bags.

"Sure." He nodded once but didn't look at me. I didn't blame him. Not after William implied we had probably been intimate. In this house.

We left the bags on the kitchen counter and excused ourselves to our room.

Nathan shut the door behind him, dropped his bag on the floor, and went straight to the point. "Did you have sex with William?"

The phrase alone was mortifying and nerve-inducing, to say the least.

"No, I didn't. We kissed. He offered me his room that night, and he slept here in the guest room. He's just trying to mess with us. But I'm not going to be bullied into leaving. I know it's technically his house, but Joel and Lily invited us, and he wasn't supposed to be here. But if you want to leave, I've got no problem doing that."

"Okay." Nathan sighed. "We're staying. I'm not leaving

Zara alone with him. He's a player, and I don't want her to do something stupid she'll regret later on," he said matter-of-factly. If he only knew …

How I hated listening to Nathan call William a player.

Nathan closed the distance between us and pulled me in. "I'm going *nuts* just thinking about him kissing you"—he cupped my cheek and leaned in to kiss me—"in this house."

I locked my arms around his neck and melted away in his arms. He laid me back on the bed, and his hands moved to my jeans, unzipping them as his lips met mine again. The thought of having sex with Nathan in William's house felt off, especially when he was outside, mere feet away from our door, cooking in the kitchen.

But I couldn't make myself care. I missed Nathan, and I wanted to reassure him. He was jealous, and I didn't want him to be.

Another part of me was furious at William for saying that in front of Zara and Nathan. I was having trouble shaking the feeling off, and then someone knocked on our door.

Nathan cursed under his breath and threw himself on the bed beside me as I shot up from the bed, pulling my jeans back up. I rushed to open the door, and it was Lily. She needed help setting a few things up, and I told her I'd be right out.

"We should get ready," I said to Nathan, shutting the door. "Lily needs help."

"You're right. I'm going to take a quick shower," he replied. He gave me one last peck on the lips and disappeared into the bathroom. I opened the closet and pulled my dress out.

It had a high, round neckline with intricate lace design all over the beautiful white fabric. The somewhat flared sleeves went up to my elbows. It was fitted at the waist, and the straight skirt fell right up to my ankles. Lily helped me in selecting this dress.

She also asked me to bring comfortable shoes since we would do the frog dance around the maypole and other silly games and dances in the garden. So I paired my outfit with lilac low-heeled wedge espadrilles.

My hair was down since I didn't have a lot to play around with it. And I didn't have Mimi with me to have her braid my hair. It wasn't as short now. It fell right under my clavicles, but I felt more like myself with long hair.

I applied apricot-colored blush, mascara, and a peachy gloss when Nathan stepped out of the bathroom with a towel tied around his waist.

"Oh, wow, you—God, you look stunning." Nathan eyed me from head to toe and extended his hand to touch my dress. He kissed my cheek and whispered in my ear, "I love seeing you dressed in white. It makes my imagination run wild."

My heart ricocheted against my ribcage. I never knew what to say to Nathan's marriage insinuations, so I always smiled as a response. And I knew the normal thing would've been to feel giddy about it, but it always made me panic—an inner battle of wanting so bad to feel excited about it but feeling guilty because I didn't.

"Well, that towel looks great on you," I said with a nervous laugh that was triggered more by his previous statement and less by the fact that his body was on full display and looked *amazing*. Well, maybe a little bit of both.

"You better leave this room then, before I decide to toss the towel and remove that pretty dress off your shoulders," Nathan replied, pulling me against his bare chest. "Not that I'm not doing that later tonight anyway."

"I like where your head's at."

He kissed my cheek and said, "Off you go. I'm going to trim my beard and get dressed. I'll see you out there."

I smiled at him with a nod and walked out of the guest room to help Lily. She had a ton of flowers spread on the dining room table. Zara was helping her sort them out. Outside, Tobias, Joel, Eric, and Sivert were placing the wooden maypole.

"Ready to help," I told Lily, who was still in her sportswear. But not Zara. She wore her long brown waves down and a lovely pale blue lace dress that made her eyes pop and her tanned skin glow beautifully.

I had to look away.

What can I say? Zara's gorgeous. And I couldn't look at her without inevitably remembering what I heard on my birthday—imagining her hands all over William and his hands all over her, making her react and enjoy herself as *I* listened.

Anyway … There was stuff to get done, and there was no turning back now.

We both helped Lily make a few short, simple flower arrangements to place as centerpieces on the long table that had already been set up in the garden by the furniture guys. There were two larger flower arrangements with various kinds of flowers placed on the terrace table that served as a bar from what I could tell.

Someone hurried down the stairs behind me, and I didn't have to turn around to know that it was William. His stupid cologne gave him away as he left a scent trail of delicious ripe oranges, freshwater, and spicy amber as he aimed straight for the kitchen.

Well, shit.

I had already forgotten about that damn cologne. And I preferred to keep it that way.

William asked Zara for help, and she immediately dropped what she was doing and went to assist him. That's when I dared look his way. He wore blush pink linen slacks with a light blue linen jacket over a white button-down shirt. Needless to say that he pulled that cotton-candy-colored outfit off wonderfully.

I looked away, even though I wanted to inspect that Midsummery ensemble of his.

"I think we're done. These we'll use for the flower crowns," Lily said, setting some flowers aside. "Everything we need to make the flower crowns is inside this box. I'll take a shower and get ready. See you in a bit."

Lily left, and Nathan hadn't come out yet.

William and Zara spoke in Swedish, which was extremely annoying. Especially since she kept laughing at whatever William said to her. She helped him plate the food from what I could see before I stormed out with the flowers and the box. I couldn't hide my annoyance at seeing them interact, but I'm sure they didn't notice since they were busy getting along so great.

I took a seat on one of the chairs at the long table in the garden and decided to distract myself by working on my flower crown. Eric, Sivert, and Tobias chatted beside the maypole drinking their beers. Luckily, Nathan arrived at that moment, but Zara was with him.

They both carried a plate of food in each hand and placed them around the table. Zara rushed back inside.

"That's gonna look lovely on you," Nathan said, looking at my flower crown. I was barely getting started on it.

"You look so handsome," I told him. He wore khaki pants and a white button up shirt. He looked fresh and clean—elegant as always.

"Why, thank you." He kissed my cheek, and Tobias shouted his name. "I'll be right back, love. Are you okay here?"

"Oh, of course. I'm going to finish the flower crown. Go ahead."

Zara walked back out, and William followed close behind

her. They both carried two more plates of food each. Everything looked and smelled delicious as expected.

"Can I get you ladies something to drink?" William offered.

"Um ... yes. Wine, please," Zara replied, taking a seat in front of me. "If you've got any of that Nemorino's wine that we had at Billie's birthday, that would be lovely."

"I've plenty," William replied, somewhat annoyed. That wine did wonders for Zara on my birthday. And now I *hated* that wine. It only made me vomit the last time I drank it. The wine's formula needed to be re-evaluated for sure. "And for you?"

"No more Nemorino's for me, thank you," I said with a forced smile. "But I'll take one of those aquavit spritzer thingies."

"The one with the berries?" William asked. "Like last year?"

"Mhm," I replied, looking at my hands working on my flower crown.

William left, and Zara got curious as she worked on her crown too. "So, how was Midsummer last year?"

"It was fun," I replied. "I'd never been to a Midsummer party before."

"I couldn't make it last year because I was invited to this *amazing* Midsummer party in Gothenburg," she told me. "But I thought that's when you stayed over. You know, from what William said about you sleeping in his bedroom. Was that not on Midsummer then?"

Damn it, Zara.

"Um—no. That was about a month later," I replied, my eyes fixed on my crown. But I didn't have to look up to know that she was staring at me. "Last year's party was on the apartment building's rooftop. Not here." Zara probably knew that, but she was surely playing dumb to get the information she so desperately seemed to want to get out of me.

"So, did you guys used to date?" she pried. That made me

look up to meet her gaze. "You and William." She looked over my shoulders to where Nathan stood with the guys, talking and laughing.

Why couldn't Zara ask William directly about these things? Or maybe she already had and wanted to corroborate the information? She was ruining the vibe—making it awkward.

"William and I have never dated."

"True," William said behind me, placing my drink in front of me. He handed Zara her glass of Nemorino's. "But you already knew that, Zara. So stop harassing your *sis* with questions."

I *knew* she'd already asked William about it. But I can't blame her for being jealous. William's comment about me liking his bed so much was out of place for so many reasons. And I was still fuming because of it.

"I'm sorry, Billie." Zara's mouth twitched into a smile as she took her wineglass to her lips to take a sip.

"Zara, could you bring the iPod you borrowed earlier for your run?" William asked her. "I want to connect it to the speakers by the terrace table. We need music."

"Ah, yes. Of course. I'll be right back." Zara took one last sip of her wine and stood up.

"And could you bring me a beer on your way back, please?"

Zara walked away without replying, and William added something in Swedish, to which she didn't respond either.

Swedish was one of those languages where I couldn't pick up a single word when they talked. It was infuriating.

I texted David if he could come over.

"You're furious, aren't you?" William said with a laugh. "About the bed thing."

"Beyond. And it's not funny." I sipped on my spritzer for the first time since William brought it. "Damn it, this is good," I said under my breath.

William chuckled again and shot one of his signature smirks my way.

"Miss Murphy," David said, standing beside the table.

"Hey, David. Do you have my menthols?"

William took a sharp breath in through his nose and looked away. David took the cigarette box and a lighter out of his inner jacket pocket. He then handed me a single cigarette and lit me up.

"Leave the box, please. The lighter too," I said, turning away and breathing out the smoke. He did. "Thanks, Doc." David smiled and walked away.

William used to hate seeing me smoking. But now, I guess that wasn't a priority for him anymore.

"Don't you dare pluck my cigarette away," I cautioned, just in case. He lifted his hands as in, *I would never*—when he always did. "This is my *one* act of rebellion toward my father, so I'm gonna work with what I've got."

"We should all be afraid," he said, taking a seat in front of me. The only reason why I didn't stand up and leave was that I wanted to finish the damn flower crown. I liked them.

"Afraid of what?" I asked. "Can you hold this?" I extended my fingers for him to grab my cigarette. I needed both hands to fasten that last flower on the crown and be done with this."

He held the cigarette between his fingers and took a drag.

"Afraid of *you* when you finally find the guts to break free from your father. You'll be unstoppable—what the heck is this?" he asked, tapping his lips. "It tastes like peaches."

"Well, it's a peach gloss," I replied. I was finally done with my flower crown, so I placed it on my head and swiveled two fingers back and forth for him to return my cigarette. He did.

William licked his lower lip and said, "Yum."

My body shrank at the sight of him doing that and the way

he said *yum*. So I took a drag on my cigarette because, again, it was my best friend in situations like these. You smoke instead of replying, and it fills the silence.

Zara stepped out of the house in the distance, so I stood up to join Nathan. I saw her struggling to connect the iPod to the speaker.

"Wait," William said in that deep, husky voice of his.

"No. Zara will be back any second now, and I don't want her getting any more jealous than she already is. Besides, she's drinking Nemorino's, and we both know it does wonders for her."

"I wouldn't know," William said with an expressionless face.

"I'm sure she can pull a last-minute switcheroo with Tobias," I replied in a hushed voice and a wink. "Besides, the walls here are thicker, so you don't have to worry about anyone listening."

"Sit."

I laughed and pointed at him with my cigarette. "No."

Zara finally managed to connect the iPod, and the loud house music flooded the garden. She went back inside the house, probably to get William's beer.

"I don't know what you're talking about, and something tells me you don't either," William said, standing up, his palms rooted to the table. He leaned in and said, "You're so jealous you can't even stand yourself." *True.* "It's as if you wanted a tailor-made excuse to help you choose between him and me. But I'm sorry to tell you this as much as it burns and makes your mind want to flip. I'm *not* a dick. Deal with it."

I picked up my spritzer and said before walking away, "Zara's gonna be here any minute now, and I need to go back with Nathan."

"Guillermina." William's commanding voice made me stop after a couple of steps and look over my shoulder. I lifted my brows as in, *what can I do for you*? "Don't you fucking dare have sex with *him* in this house."

I laughed, just to piss him off. But it wasn't funny at all. Besides, for all I knew, he was taking that Rachel girl to bed back in South Africa, and knowing how he was, he would probably find the way to get Zara into his bedroom tonight. So it was more than infuriating for him to ask that of me.

William walked around the table and closed the distance between us. He leaned in to say, "I will *burn* this house to the ground if you do."

"That would be a shame," I said with a blank smile.

"I'm dead serious. If you ever have sex in this house, it's not going to be with him." His jaw popped, and his hands clenched into fists. "Now go use that creative mind of yours to make up an excuse when Nathan tries to take you to bed tonight."

"I won't make promises I can't keep." Let him burn on the thought and the possibility just as I would. I lifted my glass and said, "But thanks for the drink."

CHAPTER 33

The Vasovagal Syncope Convenience

THE REST OF the evening was pretty uneventful, William-wise. But I sensed a shift in his saucy attitude after our little talk. He'd turned it down a few notches. Or better said, he ignored me.

We all managed to get through the diverse activities that Lily had planned for us without any issues and getting along just fine.

Everyone drank as usual except for Lily and me. I still hadn't forgotten the vomiting episode on my birthday, so I tried to be aware of my alcohol intake today. And Lily was busy playing host and making sure everything was perfect. I only saw her having a single glass of wine while eating.

Nathan was in a cute-drunkish, still-very-much-operational level. I was happy to see him relaxing and having fun since he was so busy and stressed out all the time. I thought it'd do him good to blow off some steam.

Zara was *comfortably numb*, to put it mildly. But at least she mingled with everyone and didn't follow William around like she usually did.

It was 8:00 p.m., and the sun was beginning to set. I chatted with Lily when I felt Nathan's arms wrapping around my waist. He kissed my hair and said, "Lily, can I steal her away for a minute?"

"Sure." Lily smiled and walked away.

"What's up?"

"Nothing, I just wanted to tell you that I have to travel to London this Monday," Nathan said. "For a week."

Damn it. We had tickets for a Broadway musical next week. Nathan had to convince my father to allow me to go since he was apprehensive about me going to the theater.

When I asked for permission to go to the Metropolitan Opera back in December, he agreed because we had boxed seats, but we didn't this time. My father's mind worked in mysterious ways. It was hard for me to understand his judgment sometimes.

"Don't worry about it," I said, cupping his face. "I'll see if I can change the date on the tickets."

"I'm so sorry, love. I just got confirmation about the trip." He pulled me in flush against him. "Are you sure it's okay? I hate canceling our plans because of work."

"It's okay. Don't worry about it," I insisted. "But I was wondering if maybe we could find a way to go somewhere in August before the semester begins."

"Like on a trip?" Nathan asked, surprised.

"Yes. Even if it's only for a weekend," I proposed. "I'm sure we can trick my father into letting me go. Maybe I could tell him I'm going with Nina and CJ." Nathan stared at me with wide eyes. "You don't think it's a good idea?"

"You know I'd love to, but I don't know if your father will buy it. And what about your security detail? They have to report everything to him."

"I'm sure I could talk to Aaron and explain. Maybe they'll be willing to make an exception. If he finds out, then I'll deal with him. I don't mind blaming it all on me."

Nathan took a deep breath and rubbed his jaw. "Look, I swear there's nothing more I would want than to travel anywhere, just you and me. But your father and I—we're in the middle of planning everything to get the firm up and running next year, and I feel like it's not a good idea to upset him right now."

"Nathan, you promised that partnering up with my father wasn't going to get in the way of our relationship," I reminded him. I didn't want him to worry about my father's feelings more than he did about mine. I wanted to experience other things. To feel *normal* at times, even if it were for a few days. And I needed a partner in crime. "You could use the time off."

Nathan licked his lips and looked away as if thinking what to tell me. "I feel like I'm disappointing you again. I hate to see that look on your face."

"You know what. You're right. Forget about it, okay?" I persuaded myself to smile and gave him a quick peck on the lips. I didn't want to make a big fuss out of nothing. I wanted to enjoy the weekend, especially now that he was leaving on Monday for a week. A lot can happen in a month and a half, and I was just stressing Nathan out with the conversation.

"All of these things will get easier once we get married," Nathan said, leaning in to kiss my temple. "I'm sure your father will ease up on your security, and we'll be able to travel alone."

So it was official? My only way out of my father's grasp was marriage? And even so, who knew how much he'd be willing to let go, especially since it was in Nathan's best interest to keep my father happy. Also, I had my doubts about being allowed to travel.

That's what I wanted to do more than anything. To travel and experience new things without my security detail *before* I got married. Nathan had probably already done plenty of that, but I hadn't.

This smothering topic was weighing on me mentally and emotionally. It all felt like a big trap, and Nathan didn't even realize it, but he was standing at the door of the next big, beautiful cage. But a cage, nonetheless. And my father was only handing over the keys.

My relationship with Nathan was too attached to my father, and the only way to break away from that was to ask him not to partner up with him. And I didn't have the heart to ask him to forsake his dreams—for me.

It was all my fault because, again, I didn't have the guts to tell him how I felt about marriage. I could've told him right then and there that I wasn't going to be ready for at least a few years. I could've opened myself up to him about my plans and *my* dreams. But I didn't.

It was devastating to think that we couldn't both be happy. It was either his happiness or mine. And I hoped that if I stalled, maybe I could find a way to make both our goals and dreams come true. That's the reason why I held back from being honest— that and the fact that I'm a wuss. I was afraid to lose him.

"Everything's going to be okay, Murph," Nathan said reassuringly. "I promise you."

I nodded, wanting so bad to believe him. And I did, but not entirely. I didn't know why but I just felt trapped.

We walked over to the terrace table, where everyone gathered around as a few of them refilled their drinks. Zara laughed with Sivert and Tobias. They kept insisting on her to choose her seven flowers to place below her pillow that night. Zara and Tobias seemed friendly again.

"You've got to choose your flowers too," Nathan told me. William leaned against one of the terrace columns, observing. He'd been mostly quiet, and I didn't have a problem with that.

Nathan moved on to explain about the flower ritual and

all the things I already knew because I'd done it last year, but I allowed him to explain.

"She knows all about the flowers," William interrupted Nathan, still leaning against the column with that eye-catching outfit, his arms loosely resting at his chest and a foot crossed over the other.

The last rays of sunshine disappeared into the horizon. Dusk settled in, and apparently, so did William's politeness and the serene façade he'd been carrying around the last few hours. The sour look on his face was anything but stoic.

"Oh, right," Nathan replied. "You told me on our first date about how you tried the aquavit shots on Midsummer last year."

"She even chose her seven flowers and placed them under her pillow. Didn't you, Guille?" William added, his gaze fixed on me. A direct taunt. He elegantly rubbed his well-kept beard and crossed his arms again.

Why he bothered, I didn't understand. He seemed happy doing his thing with that South African Rachel girl, even if it wasn't too serious. I was sure once he came back to New York after filming, there would be other girls on the dating roster. And either way, Zara was always eager and available to match his affections—that I already knew.

My point is he seemed to have his hands full, and he didn't mind everyone knowing about it. So why keep messing with me?

Everyone seemed to find our conversation interesting because they all focused on our exchange.

"You placed the flowers under your pillow?" Nathan asked with a curious-filled glance aimed at me. "Did you dream of me?" He joked, pulling me in for a hug.

I was afraid of what William would say next—that he would reveal my dream to everyone. He didn't mind saying that comment about me loving his bed, so why wouldn't he mention my dream?

I quickly replied before allowing William to speak. "Nah, they don't work. I'm sorry to ruin it for you guys. I know it's kind of a big deal."

"Well, we hadn't met yet. I'm sure they'll work this time around," Nathan said with a chuckle, kissing my cheek.

William laughed a bored kind of laugh and said, "I agree with her. I don't think they work either." He excused himself and walked inside the house. Zara followed him; how strange.

William looked annoyed, but what did he want me to say? That I dreamt of him after putting the flowers under my pillow? In front of *everyone*? That he still lingered in my subconscious and made himself present every other day, even in my nightmares? Because I was certain that he was somewhat aware of that too.

Nathan caught me staring at William as he walked away, and I couldn't even smile back and pretend otherwise. I unlatched myself from his embrace, took a step forward, and poured sparkling water into a glass.

Everyone resumed their chatters. And Tobias, bless him, turned the music up, filling up the gaps of silence that remained from the previous interaction.

The show must go on.

Zara and William came back out ten minutes later, carrying a plate of snacks in each hand. Eric tried to attack one of the cheese plates, but William lifted it away from his grasp, laughing. They walked over to the long table by the garden and placed the plates there.

The rest of us followed them and lingered near the table to enjoy the evening snacks. William wouldn't keep his fiery glare off me. Even when I dared glance his way, he didn't look away. He made me feel uncomfortable, mostly because Nathan was sitting next to me, but that didn't stop him.

"Everything all right, mate?" Nathan asked William in a

rough tone after realizing the staring wouldn't stop. William turned to look at Nathan with a world-weary face and a slightly raised brow as if he couldn't be bothered by Nathan. "I asked you a question."

Joel walked over to Nathan and said something in Swedish to him, tapping his shoulder, to which Nathan replied, "Well, he's making her uncomfortable."

"Am I?" William asked, looking at me. I bit my lower lip, not knowing what to respond to him. I parted my lips to speak, to tell Nathan that I was fine, that there was no need to engage with William, but I guess I took too long to reply because William stood up, grabbed a couple of plates, and an empty wineglass, and sauntered back to the house.

William climbed a couple of steps up to the terrace, but he must've slipped or something because I saw him stumbling on the wooden deck. A loud clatter of shattering glass accompanied the fall.

"William!" Lily and I shouted at the same time. We stood up and rushed to see if he was okay. He was already standing up when we reached him, but his soft pink linen pants were stained with blood that poured out of a deep gash from his left hand right below his thumb. A long, sharp shard of glass from the wineglass stuck out from the cut.

"DAVID!" I shouted. Everyone else rushed to see what happened. Some stared at William's hand with wide eyes, looking at the blood flowing out. Others at the blood-stained deck and the shards of glass on the floor.

"I'm fine," he grumbled, looking at me. I could only shake my head. He wasn't okay. The blood poured out like an open faucet.

"David's a doctor. You should let him see your hand. You're probably going to need stitches."

"Oh, my God!" Zara said, gaping at William's hand. "Shit, I'm—" She clung to Nathan, who guided her inside, and Sivert followed them. Nathan told me later that night that Zara would usually faint at the sight of blood. I guess it would be best not to cast Zara for any gory horror movies in the future.

David and Amena darted our way and evaluated William's hand as he grimaced from the pain. But he was *fine*. Right.

"The cut is too deep. I can stitch it up for you," David said. "We carry a comprehensive first aid kit in the SUV. I've got everything I need to do it. Or you could go to a hospital, too."

"No," William replied instantly. "No hospitals."

"Let's do this, then," David replied. He asked Amena to get the first aid kit, and she rushed back to get it. David asked Lily for a few things he needed like water, towels, and such and asked William to take a seat inside on one of the kitchen stools.

Amena came back with the first aid kit, and David got to work. William hissed and looked away when David removed the pointy shard of glass from his hand. Another gush of blood flooded from the cut down his wrist when the glass came out, but David seemed to have everything under control.

David asked me to apply pressure to the wound while he prepared an injection of lidocaine to numb the area around it and make the stitching more bearable for William—or so he explained. Joel and Tobias checked on Zara while Lily and Eric watched how David worked on William's hand with curiosity.

"Are you okay?" I asked William, meeting his pain-filled gaze. He nodded at me with a furrowed brow and mouthed back, *thank you.*

☾

Zara fainted, so after David was done with William, he tended to Zara. She finally woke up, but Nathan and Tobias helped her upstairs to rest. Lily went up with them to help her change out of her dress while Joel, Eric, and I helped get the kitchen and the deck cleaned up after the stitching.

William wanted to help, but I shooed him away. He joined his father on the living room couch after realizing I wouldn't allow him to do anything. I thought it was best if he rested his hand. We wouldn't want the stitches to burst open.

We were done with the kitchen and almost done with the deck when Nathan walked down the stairs.

"How is she doing?" I asked.

"She's better now," he replied, looking tired. "She crashed on her bed, the poor thing. Sleeping will do her right."

I looked down at my dress, and it was blood-stained here and there, again, with William's blood. The sight of that reminded me of the shooting. There was something primitive and protective that ignited inside me whenever William got hurt. It brought back this tidal wave of feelings that I'd buried way down in the depths of my being.

I could still *feel* the adrenaline of it pumping through my veins.

"We should go to bed," I suggested, not that I was going to be able to sleep. At least not until the rush settled.

"Come." He pulled me out of the house and took me to the terrace table. "Choose your seven flowers." He smiled.

"Oh, of course." I leaned in to choose them, grabbed my seven flowers, and we walked back into the house. The brothers sat with their father in the living room. Lily must've stayed upstairs after helping Zara.

"Off to bed?" Joel asked us.

"Yeah, I'm knackered," Nathan replied, placing an arm around my shoulders. I saw William eyeing the flowers I was holding, and he looked away after that.

Nathan and I said good night to everyone, and we disappeared off to the guest room, feeling how half of my soul wanted to reach out to William.

That damn feeling was back. Or was it ever gone?

Never.

CHAPTER 34

Us

NATHAN LAUNCHED at me as soon as we shut the door behind us. He unzipped my dress and pulled it down in a pro move, but I wasn't in the mood for sex for a few reasons.

First of all, I felt like I needed to shower to wash off William's blood splattered on me. I didn't feel clean. Secondly, they were all still sitting out there, just outside our room in the living room, and I wasn't comfortable with that. Sivert was sitting with them, for crying out loud. What if somehow they listened to us having sex? The thought mortified me beyond reasonable measure.

And last but not least, I couldn't stop thinking about William telling me how he'd burn this house down if I had sex with Nathan here. Not that he would ever find out about it. But this was his guest bedroom, and he was out there sitting a few feet away from my door. I didn't know if I'd enjoy having him sleep with someone else in my house.

Well, I did know. I'd hate it, even when I shouldn't have because the last time I saw William, he made it perfectly clear that he didn't give a shit about me anymore. That he was William Sjöberg, and he had immediate access to any girl of his choosing at a snap of his fingers.

And I'm not going to pretend like I wasn't glad that Zara had to call it a night. That way, I'd have one less thing to worry about when trying to get some sleep at night because I didn't want to take another sleeping pill. I was afraid to become dependent on them, so I tried to leave a few days in between takes. But I trusted I was tired enough to hopefully collapse on the bed.

Nathan kissed me, and I was having trouble stopping him because I didn't want him to stop, but I had to. After explaining points one and two, he understood and agreed with point one completely. Nathan even ran the shower for me, but he didn't agree as much with the second point.

He didn't care that everyone was sitting out there or thought that anyone would listen to a thing. And he was probably right, but I'd left out point three out of the equation.

We agreed that I would take a shower, and he would go out with the excuse of wanting to grab a glass of water and check if they were still out there or not—to give me peace of mind. So I relaxed and agreed. Maybe if they had all gone upstairs, I would have nothing to worry about. And stressing about William was a waste of time. I refused to let him affect my relationship with Nathan.

I showered and removed the excess humidity from my hair with the blow dryer. When I came out, Nathan was sound asleep and snoring. I couldn't help but laugh a little when I saw him spread out over the bed like a star.

The other empty bed asked me to come forth, so I jumped inside the covers and rested my head on the delicious pillows where I'd previously placed the seven flowers before taking a shower.

These were the same kind of pillows William had on his bed. And they were great. I just wanted to piss him off before by saying they were too bulky. They weren't. They were perfect.

My eyelids felt heavy, and I was exhausted, but I couldn't make myself fall asleep. I dozed off for a few minutes, but then I found myself tossing and turning in the bed again.

Naturally, my thoughts attacked me and entertained themselves at my expense. So I watched them as if it were a movie, trying to let them pass and avoid engaging with them, just as my therapist recommended.

Writing my thoughts down was the other recommendation, and I would try everything and anything that would help me go back to sleep. So I grabbed the Moleskin notebook I carried around with me and jotted down a few things as I usually did every day. But when I left the notebook on the nightstand, the sleeping pills winked at me. I ignored them and picked up my phone to check the hour.

4:08 a.m.

I tossed my phone on the bed beside me and gave up. Maybe a glass of milk would help.

Yes.

I walked out of the guest room looking like a zombie on a mission. My eyelids were shuttered as I headed toward the kitchen and grabbed a short glass where I poured some milk. I was exhausted and so desperate to get some sleep that I couldn't understand why I couldn't allow myself to drift away.

"Off to dream of him?" William's grave voice spoke from the living room.

"Shit," I muttered, stopping cold. He scared the hell out of me. I hadn't seen William sitting in front of the piano when I walked out of the guest room. There wasn't a single light on. "Well, the flowers are under my pillow, but I would have to be able to get some sleep first to get to the dreaming part. So no."

William took his headphones off and placed them around his neck. He'd been playing the piano when he shouldn't have. It could've snapped his stitches.

"I can't sleep either," he replied. "Come. Sit."

I had nothing better to do but stare at the ceiling if I went back to my bed. It was hard to say no to William when he addressed me in that way. So I walked over to the piano and sat next to him. The wooden bench was long enough to fit us both sitting side by side.

"I didn't see this piano the last time I was here," I told him as he connected a second pair of headphones.

"Well, it's been here all along. There's a piano in every place I own. There just has to be, for situations like these."

"How many places do you own?"

"Just three," he replied, placing the headphones around my neck. *Just three.* "You know my grandfather used to say, *the more buttons, the more buttonholes.* So I try to keep things simple."

"That's a good saying but having three places to live isn't as simple as you think," I told him.

"That's why I said, *I try.*" He laughed under his breath.

"Where's the third?"

"Stockholm. It's a small apartment that serves as a *pied-à-terre,*" he said, carefully placing the headphones over my ears as if afraid his fingers would graze my skin. He was probably trying to be careful about his hand, but I was thankful for the lack of contact between us. I didn't need him touching me right now.

"You shouldn't be playing the piano. Your hand—"

"And you shouldn't be sitting here with me," he cut me off before I could finish scolding him. "But here we are, breaking the rules like we love doing."

"*You* love breaking the rules," I clarified. "No … You don't even get to break them because you don't have any." Those last words oozed with bitterness as I remembered a few things I wished I could forget. Things that made my soul ache. But he noticed because he angled his head as if trying to decipher why that was.

"I do have rules. The only difference is that I make them myself," he said. "For example, if I didn't have any, I'd kiss you right now."

I panicked.

"But I'm not going to do that. Not because I care about Nathan being your boyfriend, but because I won't be able to stop myself. And I don't feel like getting slapped right now, although maybe if we schedule that activity for some other day that I'm not as annoyed as I am right now, I might definitely enjoy you slapping me."

"You've got enough mouths and lips to choose from," I replied, faking confidence. "So I'd say that you wanting to kiss me right now is just plain greedy." But my blood had fallen to my feet. Having William sit so close to me and saying he wanted to kiss me made my limbs evaporate. Yet another part of me was still furious, and I was having trouble hiding it from him.

"I can't help but love when you get jealous." He placed the headphones over his ears and placed his fingers over the keys to start playing the piano.

He played "Moonlight Sonata" for a few minutes and then switched to "Clair de Lune." He played beautifully, but I was afraid for his stitched-up hand. As long as his bandage didn't turn red, we were good.

"Play that song," I told him after he was done with the previous song. "The one you used to play all the time in your apartment."

"You heard that, didn't you?" he asked with a laugh. "Do you like it?"

"I do. It's sweet at the beginning, and then it rises and intensifies, and then it drops again—slows down," I explained.

"I can't tell if it's melancholic, but it definitely gives off nostalgic vibes, and I guess that's why I love it."

"Hmm," he mumbled with a soft side-smile. "I love it too."

He played it from the top, and I heard it loud and clear for the first time since I initially heard him learning it back in December.

"What's the name of the song?" I asked once he was done. He took his headphones off, so I did too and returned them to him.

"I don't know. You tell me," he said, standing up and putting the headphones away. He took a few steps toward the living room couch.

I flipped around the bench to see him. "What do you mean?"

"I wrote it," he said, taking a seat just across from where I sat. "For you."

"William." I shook my head, unable to fathom what I just heard. It was the most beautiful song ever, and that he would do something like that for me … it made my heart unhealthily skip a few beats.

"I named it *Us* back then, but the song's yours, so you can change the name if you want to." He leaned back and stretched his arms open on the sofa's backrest, his body language screaming self-confidence at me—*power*. Power he had over me, and he knew it.

I frowned as I twisted my fingers over my lap, careful not to meet his gaze.

Us. I liked the name. Shit.

"What are you so angry about?" he asked. "You've been raging about something all day, but I can't tell exactly why that is."

"I'm not."

"Bullshit," he called my bluff. "And I'm not letting you stand up from that bench until you tell me why." He readjusted his posture once again, leaning in as he rested his elbows over his knees.

I looked away and bit my lower lip with a smile—the nervous kind of smile. "I'm not mad. We're just … even."

"I need you to explain yourself, Guille. It's almost five a.m., and I'm not in the mood for wordplay," he warned. "Are you jealous about Rachel King?"

Enough with keeping myself locked up inside my mind. I wanted to break free from my father's grasp, but I couldn't free myself from my thoughts?

"Yes. About the others, too. But not as much as I am about Zara." There I said it. And it felt so great.

"And why is it that we're even?"

Okay, so freeing my mind had to be done in a phased manner. I wasn't ready to tell him I heard them having sex, but I could express my jealousy toward Zara. I was sure William was smart enough to put two and two together.

I brushed my forehead and continued, "You came here with Zara when you said you never brought girls to the cottage. And she slept in your bedroom before you arrived. You got her into Juilliard. You're paying for everything. She told us how you want to buy her an apartment," I rambled on. "I know you're generous, but doesn't it seem like a lot for someone who's *just* a friend?"

"You've got it all wrong," he said, standing up. He took a few steps forward, squatted in front of the bench where I sat. "I did bring Zara here, but it's different—we're friends."

"With great benefits," I scoffed. "The only reason why you're down here right now with me and not upstairs with her is that she's dysfunctional after passing out earlier."

He snorted and shook his head with an angry laugh. "You really *don't* know what you're talking about."

"Well, you asked why I was pissed, and that's the information

I have to work with."

"You're pissed off and jealous because you insist on forcing things with Nathan—because you think you know what to expect with him. And you're used to that. Yet you're terrified to try things with me when you know you want to." Now William was angry. "I'd take that jealousy away from you in a second if you'd only allowed me to."

"Of course I am!" I shouted back. I composed myself and modulated my voice. "I know I feel like I've been cut in half ever since you got shot. And it's been the hardest thing to deal with because you *know* that I love Nathan, but I—" I stopped myself because I became aware that I was about to say something that I didn't even realize I felt strongly enough to say out loud.

I played dumb and switched it up. "I've been struggling to put my thoughts and feelings in order. So when we talked after my birthday party, I felt like you were so easy to turn around and just—give up. And then you were back to dating a different model every weekend, and that Rachel actress, and I didn't want you to give up."

"Well, what did you expect, Guille?" he said, sitting on the coffee table behind him, our knees touching. "You told me you'd chosen Nathan. And I've been"—he closed his eyes and took a deep, annoyed breath in—"*patient* with you—waiting as I've never had in my life because I thought you just had to get Nathan out of your system. But I realized that night how much of a coward you are, so yes, I gave up. I can't wait for you forever."

"I'm *not* a coward." Yeah, I was. He didn't mind calling my shit to my face.

"Then come with me to South Africa," he threw at me. "Because I can't stop thinking about you as much as I want to pretend like I don't anymore. As much as I try to forget you with others. It's useless. So let's just cut the crap and come to South Africa with me."

"William, I-I can't. I—"

"You said you're not a coward. And you've made it clear that you feel the same way I do—that you can't stop thinking about me either," he said, staring into my eyes so intently that I basically allowed him inside my mind. "So why don't you kill two birds with one stone and fly back with me to South Africa so we can finally see how great we can be together and piss your father off in the process. You know you want to do both."

I did. Both. So much. But how?

I couldn't!

So I would break it off with Nathan and hop on a plane the next day with William? I just wanted to understand how doing that was possible in my world.

I *was* a coward, just as he said. And I'd never heard of a more perfect plan than the one William was proposing. But my mind was lifting four iron walls around me, trapping me, and laughing as it reminded me how I wasn't free to make that choice, how I didn't have it in me to hurt Nathan like that—to break his heart. But why shouldn't I listen to mine and allow it to feel the things it wanted to feel?

"Guille," William whispered, making me take a deep breath in and snap out of the thought-trance I was in. "Look at me." He grabbed both of my hands and kissed the back of them. "I can keep you safe. You know I can. We don't need them." He sighed. "Will you come?"

"I'm scared," I whispered back.

"What if I told you that I love you?"

CHAPTER 35

What If

IT DIDN'T MATTER if William loved me because my heart had stopped beating when he said that anyway. My rioting thoughts protested about the oxytocin that flooded my brain and startled my mind.

William's reassuring gaze met mine. His hands moved to my shoulders, and he squeezed them, reanimating me with his touch.

"I *bloody* knew it," someone said in the distance. William dropped his hands from my shoulders, and we both glanced toward the stairs to see Zara shaking her head at us with disgust drowning her face.

"Zara." William stood up.

"Don't," she replied to him, holding her hand up.

I didn't know what to think or what to do. But this was my boyfriend's sister standing in front of us, letting us know she'd listened in to our conversation. How much of it? Who knew.

Zara stormed off back up the stairs.

"I'll be right back, okay?" William said, rushing behind her, and that just did it for me. Something raw combusted inside of me. To see him going after her like that. It made me doubt him—again. Why did he have to follow her?

So she's angry. Let her be.

"I heard you," I said to William as he climbed the first few steps. He stopped cold and turned to look at me.

"Heard me—what?" he asked, tilting his head. He walked back to me as I gathered the nerve to tell him what I was about to say. "Talk to me."

"You had sex with Zara on my birthday, and I heard you—*her*—through the wall when you'd been telling me all day that she was just a friend and that I had nothing to worry about."

"Excuse me, *what?*" He grimaced.

"I heard you, William." A few tears streamed down my face. He'd just told me he loved me, and I still couldn't trust him. "You keep telling me how I got it all wrong, how she's just your friend. And now you're running after her? What do you want me to think when it's so obvious something's going on between you?"

"You're never going to trust me," William muttered. I didn't know what hurt more, the speculation of them being more than friends or the disappointment on his face. "The *only* reason why I can't tell you the truth is that it's not my truth to tell. And I don't know what else to do to get you to trust me. I've proven it to you in so many ways, but it's never enough for you."

"Well, someone had sex that night in your bedroom, on your bed, and you're going to deny it was you? I had to sleep on the living room couch that night because I couldn't bear it."

"At what time did this happen?" William asked with an exasperated tone, making me feel like I was wasting his time having this conversation.

"3:45 a.m." I remembered perfectly well.

"Well, I left at 3:30 a.m. for an early morning call. I had to be at the GMA studios by 4:00 a.m. because I was interviewed on the show that day. So no, I didn't have sex that night."

What? But I heard …

"It *was* me." Zara walked down the stairs, wiping her tears off with the back of her hand. She stopped right at the last step and said, "I convinced Nina to stay after we left your apartment. She came in for a drink, and the three of us talked for a while. William left for the GMA interview, and you know how the story ends."

Shit. I was an idiot. An insecure, jealous, doubting idiot.

"When William came back from the interview, we decided to come here for the rest of the week because he doesn't have a guest room in his apartment. He's turned it into an office. So we were going to be more comfortable here," Zara kept explaining. And the more she talked, the shittier it made me feel. "Besides, William told me everything that day and how he wanted to keep his distance from you, which I didn't mind since you'd already chosen Nathan. And I thought that was a great idea because I didn't want Nate to get hurt by this. He loves you."

"I—I'm sorry. I thought—"

"Well, you thought wrong," Zara snapped back at me. "And I just *hate* seeing you toy around with my brothers."

Brothers?

"Zara," William said to her. "You don't have to—"

"I'm a Sjöberg too," she revealed, taking a few steps my way. *She's a what?* I was so confused. "I'm Nathan and Will's half-sister."

William rubbed his face and ran both of his hands through his hair.

"Sivert, *my father*, got my mum pregnant with me when my family first arrived in Sweden. It was a short affair, but it caused many quarrels between my parents. I'm sure Nathan must've told you about how my parents constantly argued when we were growing up. So now you know it was all because of me."

It broke my heart to see the pain in Zara's eyes. Her Sjöberg signature-blue eyes. It was all too evident now—the certain resemblance.

"My parents told me everything when I was thirteen, and William found out a few months after that and reached out to me to let me know he knew. But I asked him and my parents not to tell anyone else. Not until I was ready to reveal it to the rest of the family.

"I was afraid everyone would look at me differently—of not being accepted. I still am," she said with a sad smile. "So I've been relying emotionally on Will all these years. He's been my support system. And we were finally going to let everyone know today. My sisters found out last week. I talked to them before moving to New York."

I fucked up bad. My jealousy blinded me and made me think the worst of William—of Zara too. I've been judging her without knowing *anything*. But I understood everything now. And now I couldn't stop thinking about Nathan and what he would make of all of this when he found out.

"Nathalie found out last year, and that's when they decided to get divorced—because of me," Zara continued.

"That's *not* on you," William said to her. "We've talked about this. They've had issues for years."

"I know," she said, her voice breaking. She took her hands to her eyes and started crying. William immediately placed his arms around her and kissed the top of her head in the sweetest and most protective way ever. "I just can't help but feel like an inconvenience. Like I ruined everything for everyone."

"Stop. Everything's gonna be okay," William said to her softly. He wouldn't look at me. He seemed so angry and disappointed in me—with fair reason.

"You lied to me," she said to William. "You told me in April that you were done with her. I told you I didn't want Nathan to get hurt."

A door shut in the distance. "What the bloody hell is going on in here?" Nathan asked, approaching us. He seemed like he was trying to take in the scene before him—to understand it.

"Don't worry," William said to Zara, releasing her from his embrace. "I'm *done* now." He blasted off toward the front door and picked up a set of keys before stepping out.

"William!" I ran after him without a second thought. He got into his car, but I reached him before he could shut the door. "I'm sorry. I didn't know. How could I—"

William gripped the steering wheel and let out an exasperated grunt.

"We're never going to work because you're *never* going to trust me," he said looking at his hands. I've never seen him like this. Not even when he saw me kissing Thomas. It was different this time. His words were heavy with feeling, and his face was the grueling image of anger and disappointment—the balance swaying more toward the latter.

He turned to look at me over his shoulder and said with a slow shaking movement of his head, "The things I've done for you … For almost *a year* now." He looked away and I lost his gaze as he ran a furious hand through his perfect golden hair. "I'm done proving shit to you. Nothing's ever going to be enough."

I couldn't let William slip away from me. Not now that we've come this far. I gathered my courage because all I could think of was him and how I hated the discouraged look on his face. But he was right. I kept sabotaging myself with my insecurities because, deep down, I didn't think I deserved him—or think I was good enough for him.

Say it! Don't let him get away!

"What if I told you that I love you back?" I blurted out, my eyes wide and my soul hopeful.

William glanced at me from the corner of his brilliant blue eyes with suspicion, his hands back to being firmly placed on the steering wheel. The right corner of his mouth twitched up for a second into a smile. I swear it was a smile. But he bit his lip and said with a frown, "But what is love without trust?"

He rendered me speechless, and the Porsche's engine thundered as he turned on the ignition.

"Goodbye, Guillermina." He pulled the door shut, backed up on the driveway, and sped away with a roar of his engine and a screech of his tires.

CHAPTER 36

Half Of What You've Got

WILLIAM WAS GONE ... again. But somehow, this time, it felt real. He wasn't playing around. Deep inside me, I knew he meant those last two words he said to me because the crater that appeared on my chest and the emptiness that swallowed me whole rendered me useless—desolate.

I had to somehow drag myself back inside that house and talk to Nathan, knowing perfectly well that there was no way to deny my feelings for William to him. And I knew what that meant. I had to brace myself for the big leap into the final abyss. To put that light out.

I was about to lose everything.

And I deserved it.

I squatted on the floor and took my hands to my face, gathering the scattered pieces of myself to confront Nathan.

"So is it him you want?" Nathan said in a dark, grave tone. I stood up, and he stared at me with red-rimmed eyes and a broken, discouraged gaze.

I closed my eyes and turned away, pinching the bridge of my nose, trying to shield myself from the pain and hide from the shame, and a sob escaped my throat. "It doesn't matter anymore," I said in between low, breathy gasps, looking away. I couldn't make myself look at him.

"For how long have you been going behind my back with William?" The question alone destroyed me.

David, Amena, and Aaron had front row tickets to Billie's Reality Show, but I didn't have the energy to care.

"It's not like that. Nothing's happened, Nathan. I swear," I told him in between sobs. I wanted to tell him everything I ever felt and thought, but I couldn't even breathe. I needed to calm myself down first.

"Do you take me for an idiot?" I'd never seen Nathan so angry before. "That I turn a blind eye because I trusted you doesn't mean I'm not aware of everything that's happening around me," he said, pointing a finger at the cottage as if it were William. "Every stolen look, every frown, every nightmare where you screamed his name, how he sang those songs at your birthday, every witty banter between you. I saw it *all*."

"I'm sorry," I muttered, taking a step forward, but he took a step back. "I never meant to hurt you. You know how much I love you."

"You love me?" he scoffed. "You love me with half of what you've got to give. Maybe less. But I love you with *my entire* heart. And the only reason you never had the guts to leave me was that you were afraid of how it would be with him, am I right?"

Damn, that hurt. The blow landed straight in my gut.

"And just the thought of you together—" he trailed off.

"I swear he hasn't touched me. I would never—"

"He doesn't have to," Nathan cut me off. "I see the way you look at him. That's enough. I just didn't want to see it—to accept it. It hurts even more to know there's something going on between you. You can't deny it."

"It all changed after the shooting," I confessed. "I won't look you in the eye and lie to you. William and I have always had a special connection. And I tried to ignore it—to put it aside because *I* chose *you*.

"But the thought of William dying—of losing him forever was so painful that it fucked with my head. He almost died because of me. So I can't deny that I've been struggling with all of that. And losing Caleb only made things worse. I feel like I'm missing that part of him in me. And William—he's shown up for me, as a friend, when I've needed someone to talk to."

Nathan ran a hand down the length of his face and rubbed it for a few seconds. "And why not talk to *me* about these things?"

"Well, you've been busy. And when I do get to see you, I just want to make the best of the time we've got. I don't want to make it all about me and my drama," I told him. "All I want is for you to be happy, Nathan. So much that I've held back on telling you a few things about how I really feel because I'm afraid to lose you. And I thought *I* could fix those things for us."

"You're not afraid to lose me," Nathan replied with a scowl. I felt a change in his tone again. He was enraged. "You're afraid to end up with nothing. You just wanted to keep me around enough for you to figure your heart out. But I'll make it easier for you. Go after him. I'm done—*we're* done."

Nathan left me standing there as he darted inside the house. "Nathan!"

Everyone was up now. Some were in the kitchen grabbing themselves a cup of coffee while others sat in the living room. Everyone's gazes followed us as I rushed behind Nathan toward the guest room. Nathan tossed the few things he'd brought with him back into his duffel bag. I did the same. If he was leaving, so was I.

When we stepped out, everyone was seated in the living room.

"Nathan, would you join us, please?" Zara said to him,

making him stop cold. "I need to talk to all of you."

Nathan stared at her with a frown. Zara was about to drop the bomb, and I wished I could've stayed to be there for Nathan. I knew the information was going to be shocking and hard to assimilate. But he'd just told me he was done. And I had no business staying any longer. So I left after a quick thank you and goodbye to everyone.

"Billie!" Lily shouted. But I didn't stop.

I stormed out of the cottage, and David had the engine going. They couldn't have read the situation more perfectly.

"Let's go," I said as I climbed into the car.

I took Caleb's letter out of my bag and pressed it firmly against my chest as I laid down on my side. I hadn't slept one bit, and my body was operating on instruments.

This moment made me suffer and grieve for Caleb like never before. I needed him right now, and that letter was the only thing of his I kept that still had a pulse. So I clung to it like I used to do with my mom when she returned from a trip, realizing that faint flickering glow would expire after I read it. And I needed that last, tiny drop of hope.

I loved them both, and I didn't even know how that happened—that it *could* happen. But the feelings were strong and true.

Nathan made me feel safe and loved. I trusted him blindly. I loved how ambitious he was, even if it scared the hell out of me that he would be like my father. Deep down, I knew he wasn't. I knew that if I talked to him and let him know how I really felt that he would do everything in his power to make me happy. But I never did because I was a coward, just as William said I was. I just didn't want to feel any more pain. And losing Nathan was going to be painful. It already was.

He was perfect.

But he wasn't William.

The connection I had with William was undeniable. It was something so powerful but unexplainable at the same time. From the moment I met him, something immediately captured my attention. Still, as time went by and he allowed me to see more glimpses of the real him, I was infatuated—completely fascinated by him.

It hurt when he was away. I missed him beyond any comprehensible reason, and when I saw him again, the feelings only grew and reacted to his absence—manifested by replicating themselves.

There was so much more to him for me to discover, and I wanted so bad to be the one to do it—to reach deep within his heart and allow him to do the same with mine.

I'd been paralyzed by fear, pain, cowardice, and comfort. I knew that exploring a relationship with someone like William wasn't going to be an easy experience. Him being a public figure and my father wanting to keep me so shielded was the most perfect and explosive combination for disaster. And still, I wanted to throw myself into that.

I was left with nothing but the remains of two extinguished lights that once burned and twinkled inside me.

One for William.

One for Nathan.

They had both blown their kindling sparks out, and I had to let them be.

CHAPTER 37

Fortfarande Levande

July 25, 2010

Lily: Hey Billie! Are you done with your summer course?
Me: Hey! Yes. Just finished last Friday. What's up?
Lily: I have this photo shoot tomorrow at 6 am, and I was wondering if you could come with me. I know it's super early, and I understand if you don't want to. I would've asked Joel to come with me, but he's out of town, and I really don't want to go alone.
Me: Absolutely, don't worry about it. Is everything ok?
I just have to ask.
Lily: Well yeah, I guess. The photographer's my ex, and things didn't end up well between us. I'm just nervous about it. I don't want to show up there alone.
Me: Got it. Ok. Don't worry, I'll ask Aaron to be himself, and we'll be fine.
Lily: LOL! OMG yes!!! That's perfect. See you downstairs tomorrow at 5:45 am?
Me: Sounds good. See you tomorrow.

"Your food's going to get cold, kiddo," my father said. "Is it urgent?" I dropped my phone with the screen down on the table and apologized. We were celebrating my father's birthday since he was out of town on the 21st. I'd been listening to him rambling on and on about how great Nathan and I were, how he wished we could patch things up between us. And my patience was running thin.

"He misses you," my father told me. *What? Are they still in contact?* It wouldn't have surprised me at all. My father thought our breakup had been silly, and he was sure we would eventually get back together. He didn't know the real reason why we broke up, and I didn't think Nathan would tell him.

"I wouldn't know," I replied, looking at my plate and stabbing a piece of broccoli with my fork. "You know I haven't seen or talked to him since the day we broke up, right? So that's over a month now." I took the fork to my mouth and chewed the broccoli. "Please don't tell me you have been keeping up with the usual *liquid lunch* Fridays."

My father took a deep breath. "Of course we have," he said, taking a swig of his wine. "We're business partners."

You've got to be fucking kidding me. I thought that venture would go south when Nathan and I broke up. I was glad for Nathan that it didn't, but it would be the weirdest and most awkward dynamic ever if they went through with it.

I sliced a piece of meat and swiped it through the bordelaise sauce. My appetite had rushed around the tables and out the front door. But the only reason why I took the fork to my mouth was Spark's Bordelaise sauce—it's one of the best out there.

"You'll get through this hiccup," my father insisted. That's all he wanted to talk about. Nathan. Not a single question about my summer program or my plans for the rest of the summer. No. He wanted to talk about *my ex*—his business partner and BFF. "I really can't think of anyone who's better suited to be with you than him."

He'd been prepping and grooming him for months. Of course, he thought there wasn't anyone better suited to be with me. Nathan was kind but ambitious at the same time, and he admired my father. That's all he needed to mold him into a mini-James.

My father kept making it seem like Nathan was out there begging me to get back together and that I was refusing him. That wasn't the case. I was sure Nathan was probably entertaining the idea just to keep their plans going for the firm. And I didn't blame him. I knew I fucked up with his plans, and maybe he wasn't as ready to give up on them as he was to break up with me.

And I missed him. I missed that unique language we'd created between us. I missed his face. His kisses. Just ... him. But I was an expert in numbing out the pain.

At first, I thought he would reach out to me a week later after returning from London, but he didn't. I'd hurt him badly. And I was hurting too, but I tried to give him space.

Another part of me felt lighter. Not because I was okay with us being broken up but because I didn't have to worry about the things I did before when we were together. And that helped my overall well-being somehow.

I only wished he was okay, and I hoped for his happiness—every single day.

A part of me felt like I still needed closure. I didn't enjoy how things ended between us. It'd been too sudden and unexpected. I just missed him, but I already said that a few times.

And William. Shit, I couldn't even think about him. Sometimes it was easier to believe he didn't exist. That I made him up. But then I googled him. And I googled him again. And his name and his face kept showing up in the search results.

He existed.

He was living and breathing, still having fun with Rachel

King, and still filming in South Africa, as per the paparazzi photographs. He'd shaven off his beard, but his hair was a tad longer. I liked him best with a clean shave. Not that the opinion of an online stalker mattered.

Rachel appeared to like his face too. She couldn't seem to take her hands off it on every other photograph. And I kept scrolling through the images every day, trying to train myself to feel nothing. But I failed miserably every single time. My entrails burned, my jaw clenched, my heart ached, and my poor laptop was a shove away from shattering.

New thoughts kept me up at night. Mostly questions I asked myself on a loop to which I didn't have an answer to like: *What happens when William comes back from filming? Is he coming back to his apartment? Will Rachel come with him? And if she does … will I have to* listen? *Will there be others?*

That's why I kept practicing with the paparazzi photos, see? It was necessary. I had to be prepared if I ever saw them together waltzing into William's apartment.

At least, that's what I liked telling myself. It was better than accepting how I very much still wanted to keep loving him. Hoping the feelings were still alive somewhere in there for him too.

So I kept diving into a far, dark corner of my mind, promising myself in secret how one day I'd be brave enough to knock on the wall that divided our bedrooms—a few times. For a while. Hoping it crashes down and falls apart. Just to let him *know*.

He'd know … and I'd let him do whatever he wants with the rubble.

CHAPTER 38

A Chance

July 26, 2010

I DRAGGED MYSELF down to the lobby and met Lily at 5:45 a.m. as we agreed. She looked great, and come on, look at the hour. That's why they paid her big money to photograph her beautiful face.

I couldn't pull a smile out of her. She didn't look happy. Lily seemed nervous, and her body language was insanely telling. Her shoulders were rolled to the front, her gaze was lost, and her words were null. We didn't talk much on the way there, and I was thankful. I needed coffee to function, and she said there would be plenty on set, so I held on to that promise. Not that I wouldn't have sent the guys on a coffee run if for some reason there wasn't any. But luckily, there was.

The only thing Lily mentioned on our way there was that she was going to be photographed for Haute Magazine. The biggest and most influential fashion magazine in the world. No pressure. It was a swimsuit edition, so she didn't have to say anything else for me to understand how *that* was part of the complications of having his ex being the photographer. She had to be sexy in her swimwear for the guy. My mood was already declining.

We walked inside the studio, and it might as well have been

noon in there. Hyperactive people walked all around the place, setting up the lighting and getting the set prepped. It was so exciting to witness.

I spotted a coffee break table that'd been set against the wall on the far left, right beside two doors. "That's the hair and makeup room," Lily said, pointing at one of the doors. "Come on." I looked around, trying to spot *the guy*, but no one struck me as an asshole just yet, so I assumed he hadn't arrived.

I wandered over to the coffee table and poured myself a big cup of joe *because it's 6:00 a.m.* while Lily talked to a few people on set.

Aaron, David, and Amena had come along because I was hanging out with Lily, and *it's your father's orders* and all that crap. And I didn't mind this time. I'd fired a quick text last night telling them to be extra creepy on set today. Mentioning briefly how Lily's ex would be present and he couldn't sit with us.

Aaron immediately asked for his name. And I laughed because that was a total Caleb move, and I know he would've enjoyed this particular field trip. I could see his hazel eyes in my mind brightening up with amusement.

Damn it.

Anyway … I didn't have the guy's name, and I didn't want to ask Lily. Besides, I didn't think it would be necessary to check him out. I was planning to be Lily's emotional support for the day, and Aaron, David, and Amena would be the muscle.

Amena was on a mission to remove Aaron's title as scariest bodyguard alive because damn, she looked tough this morning. That's how you know their job was tedious, and my father was overreacting with my security; when things like these got them all excited and committed.

Lily grabbed a cup of coffee and pulled me into the hair and makeup room.

"Hey, mama!" Caro said to Lily. "Billie! It's been a while."

Caro and Frankie were there. They'd done our hair and makeup for Tobias's premiere. They were the best.

Lily and I greeted them with big warm hugs. I took a seat on the couch, and Lily climbed on the director's style chair to get started.

"Girl, what's wrong. I know you," Frankie said, shutting the door. "It's about that emmer effer, isn't it?" Lily burst out into tears as soon as Frankie said that.

Lily covered her face as she cried. "I tried to get out of it, but I couldn't," she started to say. "I talked to my agent, and I explained things to him, but he said he couldn't say no to Haute. That they'd requested me and *only* me. They even changed the photo shoot date to match my schedule. What was I to do?"

"We won't let him engage in any conversation with you outside of the photo shoot," Caro said matter-of-factly. "We'll stay till the end, mama. We'll make sure of it."

"I swear to God if he as much as looks at you funny, I'm gonna—"

"No, please," Lily cut Frankie off. I kept quiet as I got a gist of the situation. "It's—I don't want to cause any trouble right now. I'm just nervous to see him. And if Joel finds out about the photographs … I'm not sure if—"

"What photographs?" I asked Lily. "What's wrong?" I didn't like the sound of that.

Caro sprayed thermal water on Lily's face. Frankie looked away and tousled Lily's hair.

"Shit," Lily said in a breath, letting her head hang. She closed her eyes and shook her head. "He took some very—*explicit*—nudes when we were together. And when we broke up, I asked him to delete them. He even showed me when he did it. But he obviously had a backup, and he's been threatening to reveal them after I started dating Joel. I was such an *idiot*."

"*He's* the idiot," Caro said, arching a brow.

I hated the guy already, and I didn't even know his name or had seen his face.

"And what's his problem?" I asked.

"He's pissed that I started dating Joel a few months after we broke up," she said. "But I was miserable. He was the worst. He always had girls over at his apartment with the excuse of it being *work*. And every girl starting out as a model would do his bidding just to have him take their picture. I don't even want to imagine how he abused his power over them."

I guess I understood why Lily was so jealous and insecure in her relationship with Joel. She'd been traumatized by the asshole of her ex.

"But what does he want from you? Is he asking for something in exchange?" I pressed.

"At first, he wanted me to end things with Joel, and when I didn't, he started sending me the images at random hours during the day to make a point. I was afraid he would send them to Joel, so I begged him to stop. He then asked for money in exchange for not revealing them to the public. Every now and then, he asks me to wire him money. Sometimes a thousand dollars. Sometimes two, in exchange for his silence."

Fucker.

"That's blackmail, Lily. And it's a criminal offense. What's his name?" I asked.

"Billie, no." She immediately understood why I asked.

"I'm going to find out either way, and I'm not going to let this fly, Lily," I replied, standing up. "And you say Joel doesn't know about this, right?"

"He doesn't. Leonard says that if I tell Joel, the photographs will get out."

Joel would probably chew the guy's head off before that could even happen, but sure. "Leonard … what?" I insisted for her to spill the last name.

"Roux-Bertrand," Lily said with a sigh.

"You're going to have to write that one down for me," I said with a chuckle.

Lily grabbed her phone and texted me the last name. "What are you going to do with it?"

"Ask Aaron to run his name, of course," I said with a smirk. "Come on. It'll be fun."

"Fuck yeah, run it," Frankie said with a laugh. Lily couldn't help but laugh too.

"I don't know," Lily said anxiously, kneading her hands. "What if he finds out or something?"

I shook my head twice with a slow blink as in, *no, he won't.* Lily nodded once in agreement.

"I don't know if there'll be anything else we can use against him, but I suggest you report the blackmail to the police. I could ask my father for help. I'm sure one of his lawyers can help us get this settled. Fast. You could also file an order of protection against him. There's enough evidence to support the need for it."

"Gurl, you a lawyer?" Caro asked as she applied under-eye patches on Lily's face.

I frowned and said, "Used to date one …" Lily and I locked eyes, but I couldn't hold her gaze. I wasn't yet immune to the feelings that involved Nathan.

"Let's see what Aaron has to say about this, and then we'll talk about the lawyers," Lily said, taking a deep breath. "Shit, I'm so nervous."

"Don't be. Everything's going to be okay," I promised her. "But you can't keep living like this. Always afraid. He needs to be held accountable for his actions."

"I like her," Frankie said. "And I agree, Lily. This has gone for far too long."

"Okay. Do it." Lily said, seeming a bit more convinced about it. I stepped out of the hair and makeup room, and there he was. It had to be him. Leonard's frame was slim and tall. He wore an all-black ensemble and slightly tinted glasses. He held a camera with a big telephoto with both hands while another person stood beside him holding a second camera for him. His shoulder-length hair was slightly wavy and of light, golden-brown color.

I saw red.

Aaron, David, and Amena idled near the studio's entrance.

"Hey, guys. I need to talk to you," I said, looking at Leonard as he tested the light around the set. We stepped outside, and I explained the situation to them. David then stepped away to make a call and run a quick background check on Leonard.

"I'd like to take a look at some of those e-mails," Amena said. She had a background in IT. "People are usually sloppy in their digital communications and often leave other pieces of information that can be helpful for an investigation. And we need them as evidence of the blackmail. We would also need the wire transfer receipts."

"Well, we'll need her laptop for that. Let me ask her if you guys can go pick it up at her place." We were a few blocks away from the apartment building. If Lily agreed, they could have the laptop back in a jiffy.

C

Lily agreed for them to fetch her laptop. Amena and I were inside the hair and makeup room. Caro and Frankie were taking their time getting her ready. Stalling.

Amena had full access to Lily's e-mail with her permission.

She made a folder on the desktop where she downloaded all the images that Leonard sent. Including those in her iMessage app. She then ran the information window for each of the files. I wasn't sure exactly what Amena was looking for, but she went one by one.

"Are these all the files he's ever sent you, Miss Young?" Amena asked with a frown. "These are all screenshots from the original files."

"Well, yeah. Those are the ones he's been sending," Lily replied. "But initially, he gave me a USB with his five favorite photographs." She scowled with disgust.

"And did you keep those?" Amena asked quickly.

"They should be in there somewhere," Lily replied. "Let me take a quick look at it." Amena handed over the laptop to Lily, and she began her search. "Here. I hid them inside this random folder because I was afraid they would be too easy to find. I don't even know why I kept them. You should delete them."

Amena took the laptop back and inspected the files. "What is your date of birth, Miss Young?" Amena queried.

"January 1st, 1987."

"And how old is he?" Amena followed up.

"He's um—eight years older than me."

"Well, you weren't eighteen when he took these," she said. Lily covered her mouth with a gasp, probably just realizing what that meant. "These are time-stamped for December 16th, 2004. You were a minor, and that's considered a *serious* criminal offense. I'll be right back. Don't touch the laptop, please."

We all stared at each other in complete silence. There weren't any words to describe the outrage toward Amena's discovery. It didn't matter if Lily was less than a month away from turning eighteen. She was a minor, and those photographs were considered child pornography. And Leonard knew that. He wasn't stupid. That's why he sent the screenshots instead of the original files to her. He probably thought Lily would've deleted the original files by now, but she hadn't.

Leonard couldn't make the photographs public either for the same reason, but he used them to keep disturbing Lily with them. Or if he were stupid enough to do so, the repercussions would be catastrophic for him.

There was a knock on the door after a few minutes. Aaron and Amena asked me to step out. They explained how Leonard's background check came out clean, but the evidence of blackmail and the original files were enough to make a strong case against him. Aaron mentioned how he talked to my father about this and would escalate the issue with his lawyers.

"I'm going to have a little chat with him," Aaron said with a subtle but wicked smile. "He won't be able to bother Miss Young after this. Not anymore."

I nodded once in agreement. Amena asked me to go inside the hair and makeup room and informed me she would be just outside if we needed anything. Damn it. I wanted to see when Aaron talked to Leonard.

Lily asked me what was going on when I stepped back inside, and I told her everything. She started crying again, and her makeup got ruined.

"Shit, shit, shit!" She grabbed a tissue and patted her face with it. "I'm so sorry, mama," she said to Caro.

"Hey, it's okay," she said reassuringly. Caro hugged Lily. It was a long, warm, and protective hug. Frankie paced inside the room. She looked pissed. With good reason.

Caro waited for Lily to compose herself before fixing her makeup.

About twenty minutes later, someone stepped inside the room without knocking. "Leonard left, and so did his assistant," the woman said in a rush. "He didn't say why. He just did. We tried getting a hold of someone else, but no one's available right now on such short notice. We're going to have to reschedule. We'll let you know."

What! I wanted to jump up and down and hug Lily. I was ecstatic about the news. Leonard leaving meant he was scared shitless about everything Aaron said to him. And I was glad.

The tall, brown-skinned woman, with long, straight, platinum hair, turned around to leave.

"Billie's a photographer!" Lily shouted back.

The woman turned around and said, "Who's he?"

I bit the inside of my lip to avoid a laugh escaping me before realizing Lily was suggesting *me* as the photographer for the shoot. The smile melted off my face as I went into a panic.

"*She*," Lily clarified. "Her." Lily pointed at me. "Billie's a photographer. And I'm not just saying this, but she's a badass, Becca. She's photographed me before. We work great together."

Becca scanned me from head to toe with a pout—analyzing me.

"I mean, yeah, we could reschedule, or you could have Billie take a few shots to see if you like them," Lily continued. "We're already here. Won't it be a nightmare to reschedule?"

"I remember you," Becca said to me, squinting her eyes, pointing a finger at me, and taking a few steps my way. "You wore that beautiful Enzio de Luca ensemble to the premiere with William Sjöberg."

"Ah, yes. That was me," I said, feeling how my heart tightened on me at the mention of William's name.

"You guys dated?" she asked with a crooked smile.

I was about to deny it when Lily said, "Yes."

Crap.

"Interesting." Becca tilted her head. She gave me one last

look and said, "Let me talk to Joaquín. He needs to authorize this." She stepped out, and I dropped myself back on the couch.

"Lily, I'm about to hyperventilate here. What the fuck."

She jumped down from the chair and tackled me. "Thank you, thank you, thank you!" She kissed my cheeks a few times. "I can't believe Leonard left! You have to thank your father for me. I—I have no words. Thank you!" She hugged me again. "I'm sorry about the William thing just now. But I know how these people operate. The fact that they think you dated William has already sparked an interest in Becca. They will accept if only because of that. And I *know* how great you are. They'll be impressed with your work in the end."

"What if I make a fool of myself? This is Haute Magazine we're talking about."

"My point exactly! What if you don't?" Lily mused, climbing up to her chair again. Caro would have to redo her lips after kissing my cheeks. "Don't you want to see what you're capable of? Besides, I owe you big time. It's the least I can do. I'm sure you'll do great. And you've already photographed me before. You know all my good angles." She chuckled.

There weren't any bad angles on Lily's face, but sure.

"Billie," a man said with an accent, stepping inside the room. "Nice to meet you. I'm Joaquín Serrano." He extended his hand, and I shook it and greeted him back. I was sure he was Spanish, so I asked him. He was.

We switched to Spanish as Becca lowered the corners of her lips and nodded a few times, looking impressed as he asked me a few questions.

"*Vamos a intentarlo, vale?*" Joaquín said. He said *try*, and I could do that. I could give it a try. We agreed that I would leave to grab my camera. The studio provided plenty of the necessary equipment for the shoot, and I was familiarized with almost everything since we did a lot of studio practice at Parsons.

My security detail drove me hastily back home. I wanted to choose which cameras to bring over. I had a few. And when I came back, Lily was ready and wearing an amazing all-white one-piece swimsuit. A woman was styling her look with different accessories, and Caro and Frankie made sure she was good to go with her hair and makeup.

My hands trembled. I positioned myself on the set while Joaquín and two more women rambled about the concept, the lighting, and their general expectations for the shoot.

Breathe.

I took a few lighting tests and showed them to the creative team. I could sense how they wanted to micromanage me, and I didn't blame them. They knew nothing about me. They were giving me a chance, and I had to prove myself to them. To earn their trust.

After a few adjustments, they were happy about the lighting and allowed me to start shooting Lily. I had all the information I needed to get the shots they wanted. I just needed to relax.

Joaquín and what felt like a small crowd of people swarmed around the monitor where the shots I took would appear one after the other. I could hear them commenting on them with praise. That gave me the confidence to loosen up and start directing Lily a bit more with what I thought would look good.

"Yes!" Joaquín shouted. "That's the shot. Right there, Billie. Take a few more like that, please. Lily, you're looking great!" I did, and then they switched Lily's outfit.

Frankie winked at me from afar, and I could feel my face getting warm. I couldn't believe I was shooting for Haute Magazine.

The team allowed me to shoot the rest of the outfits they had on a rack for Lily, which meant they were pleased with my work.

We were there for a few hours. It'd been exhausting, amazing, surreal, and the most fun I had in a while.

"Someone from the office will contact you later today to get your bank account information," Becca said as we were leaving. I nodded a few times with a slightly furrowed brow like I knew the business and she let out a soft laugh. "You didn't think you were working for free, right?" I honestly hadn't thought about the money. I was just happy to have been given the opportunity to collaborate. It would be the first time I earned any money for work. And I didn't even know how much they would pay me, but the feeling was so rewarding.

Lily and I left, and I realized I hadn't had anything to eat, so we celebrated with sushi.

Exhaustion hit me hard when I returned to my apartment, but I was thrilled about the shoot. I took a shower with stupid smile on my face. I couldn't wait to tell Nolan about it. He was going to flip.

I threw myself back on my bed with a towel wrapped around my body because it's just the best feeling ever to chill out for a few minutes right after showering before putting clothes on.

That's when William's piano became audible, and my smile melted off my face.

He was back.

CHAPTER 39

Curious

July 31, 2010

NINA AND I went for a run this morning. We've been seeing a lot more of each other ever since I was single again. I invited her to my apartment for breakfast afterward. Mimi said she'd cook a few things for us, and I wasn't ever going to pass on that.

We stepped out of the elevator on the ninth floor and saw Eric and Zara rolling a few suitcases out of William's apartment. Eric jerked his chin with a smile to greet us. We both waved him hello. I freaked out for a second but relaxed once I saw Zara locking the door. William wasn't with them. He was back, but I hadn't bumped into him yet.

It was best to keep it that way.

Nina clutched my arm as we approached my door.

Zara and I had crossed paths more than I would've cared to during the summer since she was staying at William's place until her new apartment was ready, but we always pretended to be ghosts and basically ignored each other after a simple *hey*.

She hated my guts, and I still couldn't deal with the embarrassment of my immaturity regarding everything that happened the last few months. I wished I could've apologized, but I just never found it in me to approach her when she'd pulled up a thick wall around her.

My guess was that her time as my next-door neighbor was up.

"Oh, hey guys," she said, turning around. Her gaze darted at Nina. She was rolling two more suitcases aside from the ones Eric had in his grasp, plus a backpack and her bag.

"Hey," Nina and I said at the same time. I offered an attempt of a smile in their direction. "Is your apartment ready?" Nina asked.

"Yeah. It's finally ready. We're just going to roll these suitcases over there." Her apartment was only half a block away from here. Lily confirmed to me that William bought her the one-bedroom apartment at the Ritz Tower.

"Do you need any help with that?" Nina offered. Her voice was shaky. I could tell she was nervous about seeing her.

"Um—no. We're good, thanks," she said, pulling her long hair into a pony.

"Aaron and David are downstairs. I could ask them to help you," I told her, but I knew she was going to decline. I still wanted to be polite.

"That would be great, Billie, thanks." She actually smiled at me. *Wow, okay.*

"Sure, no problem. I'll let them know you're coming down."

She offered me a quick nod and resumed walking toward the elevator.

"See you around, girls," Eric said to us.

Zara stopped and said to Nina over her shoulder, "I'll call you."

Nina bit her lip and nodded. Zara smiled and left.

I walked toward my apartment and texted Aaron about helping Zara with her things. Nina followed me. I dropped my phone and keys on the foyer table as she shut the door and leaned back on it with a grin.

"What did I miss?" I asked with a laugh as I washed my hands in the guest bathroom. "Have you guys been in touch? I thought you said you weren't talking to each other."

"No! We haven't!" Nina said, laughing back. "I hadn't seen her since your birthday. We texted a bit for a few days after—*you know*, but it kinda faded off as I'd told you already."

"Right." I walked out, and it was Nina's turn to wash up. "So? Aren't you sort of dating Aiden?"

"I mean, he's great. I like him, but it's not like we're exclusive," she said, drying her hands with a towel. "We have great conversations, but he's too serious sometimes. If I were older, I'd probably be all in, you know what I mean?"

I knew exactly what she meant.

"You like her, don't you?" I pried as we both made our way to the dining room, where Mimi had everything set up for us. We were both starving.

Mimi stepped out of the kitchen to greet us, dragging the back of her hand along her forehead. She offered us coffee and went back to the kitchen since she had a few things on the stove to look after. She always left me food for the weekends.

"So?" I insisted, adding a spoonful of cottage cheese over my bowl of fruit. "Are you curious about Zara?" Nina hadn't really given me any details about her little escapade with Zara that night, although I did want to kill her for not telling me sooner. I'd been pulling my hair out just thinking it'd been William, because why would I ever think it was Nina?

The only thing Nina mentioned was that she had a great time, which I don't doubt at all from what I heard, and that Zara's bisexual.

"I don't know. Maybe?" she said with a shrug, bringing her cup of coffee to her lips and taking a sip. "It's weird. I'm not really attracted to girls. It's not something that had ever crossed my mind before, but that night I don't know what got into me. And she—" Nina trailed off, took another sip of her coffee, and placed it on the table.

"She—what?" I chuckled. "Come on, you're killing me!" I took a piece of cantaloupe to my mouth and chewed away as I waited for Nina to spill the beans.

"I guess I don't like girls, but I like *her*," she finally admitted. "She's fun and interesting. And I mean, look at her. She's beautiful, right?"

Yeah, I've already covered that before. Drop-dead gorgeous.

I rolled my eyes because all the Sjöbergs were impressive, and she was half a Sjöberg. And her Saunders genes weren't half bad either.

"So, what's the verdict?" I pushed.

"I'm gonna take that call."

C

My phone buzzed when we were done with breakfast. It was an unknown number. I walked over to the living room to take the call and gestured for Nina to come to sit with me.

"Good morning. I'm looking for Billie Murphy."

"This is she."

Nina jerked her chin with a frown, inquiring who I was talking to, but I still didn't know, so I shrugged in response.

"This is Mel from Haute Magazine. I am calling on behalf of Joaquín Serrano," she said. "We have an opening in our internship program, and we believe you might be a great fit for it. Joaquín was very pleased with the results of last Monday's photo shoot, and he definitely wants someone like you in our corner."

OhmyGodohmyGodohmyGod!

I took my hand to my mouth, and Nina shook my shoulder.

I widened my eyes at her. *Wait*! I wanted to mute the call and jump up and down on my sofa, but I needed to compose myself and actually accept the offer.

"That's—of course. I'd love to. How long does the internship last? When do I start?"

Mel chuckled. I guess my response wasn't as controlled as I thought it would be. I just made a fool out of myself with my overenthusiasm.

"We would love for you to start next Monday. And the internship lasts the entire month of August. You would be coming in from Monday to Friday on a part-time basis during the morning schedule. Occasionally, if there's something else that might be a right fit for you, we'll ask you to stay through the afternoon. Does that work?"

"Yes. That sounds great."

"Joaquín liked your work, so if you meet his expectations on the internship, there's a possibility to keep you on the roster for any eventual projects once the semester at Parsons starts," Mel explained. "It's a highly competitive work environment, I'm not going to lie. But if you keep Joaquín and his team happy, they might ask you to collaborate on other projects too."

This opportunity couldn't have arrived at a better moment. I needed this. Not only was I sure it would be a lot of fun, but I would learn a lot and keep myself busy during the rest of the summer, which was something I desperately needed after everything that happened lately.

I grinned at Nina and squeezed her arm, making her know this was a good call. She seemed desperate to know what was happening.

Mel went on to explain how someone would call me tomorrow to explain everything in further detail. Her call mainly was to offer me the position and make sure I accepted, which I did, of course.

I thanked Mel for the millionth time and ended the call.

"It was Haute Magazine. I'm starting an internship with them this Monday." I squealed.

Nina screamed and tackled me with a hug. I burst out into laughter. "Congratulations! They must've loved your work, Billie!" she exclaimed. "We need to go out and celebrate."

"We do."

And hell yeah, we did.

CHAPTER 40

A Counterfeit Shade
of Red

CJ HAD ME LAUGHING hard as I talked to him on the phone on my way back to my apartment. We had a great time that evening. We went to a bar at around 6:00 p.m., just Nina, him, and me. He was ecstatic when he heard the news about my internship, and I allowed myself to let loose a bit tonight.

My father surprisingly approved of me to go out with my friends right away. It was encouraging to feel like maybe he would start to ease up on me as I grew older. The last time I went to an actual bar was in Paris on the night I met Thomas, so I guess it was time to make some new memories.

I hadn't really drunk this much since my birthday, but I didn't mix this time. I stuck to tequila, so I was "good."

CJ and I couldn't stop laughing as we remembered how we forced David into downing a shot with us. I had to tell Aaron I couldn't find my phone and asked him to look for it in the car, and that's when we made him do it. He was terrified when Aaron waltzed back into the bar, especially since Nina said, "*Hey, Aaron*," looking over David's shoulder the moment he drank the shot. He almost choked on it. It was so funny.

Nina gave David a couple of spearmint gum afterward, so no biggie. I didn't think Aaron would notice. I know it was wrong to ask David to do that, but he found it especially hard to deny CJ, of course.

My good mood drained to the floor when I saw William's apartment door open as I approached my place. There was a mini-party going on in there, from what I could see. A guy I didn't know stood just outside his door, leaning against the wall, making a call. He looked at me and shot a two-finger wave in my direction.

"I'm gonna have to call you back," I said to CJ.

"Wait, Billie, what—"

I ended the call and tossed my phone back into my purse. It was best for me to flee the scene, but I couldn't find my keys, and the alcohol flowing through my veins wasn't helping my case.

"Hey, Red."

What the ...

☾

I spun around thinking I was officially going mad, but instead, I saw Liam Kelly sauntering my way with a drink in his hand. Liam was the Australian actor who was at my birthday party. How could I forget him?

"Hey, snitch," I said, focusing my attention back on finding my keys. I was a second away from emptying my bag on the floor. I shot him a death glare and said, "Don't call me Red."

He laughed and closed the distance between us. "Why?" he asked, amused.

He was damn cute. Liam had big brown eyes, heavy eyelashes that any girl would kill for, light-brown hair, and the obligated celebrity-white smile that went great with his golden sun-tanned skin. He was like a polished surfer boy.

"You told on me. At my party," I said, pointing at him with a lip gloss. He stared at it with a frown. "Tobias wouldn't speak to me for almost two months after you told him I introduced Jordan to Cecile. That's why you're on my permanent snitch list. Right next to Tobias. He's proven to be a snitch in the past too. I guess like calls to like."

Liam laughed. "Yeah, that was fun," he said, sipping on his drink. I was getting annoyed, and all I wanted was to get inside my apartment. Quickly. "But what I meant is why can't I call you Red."

I rubbed my face with exasperation. "Just—*don't*."

"Locked out?" he asked, lifting a brow, watching me struggle with my things.

"Not really." I pulled my phone out. "I must've left my keys in the car." Aaron had a spare set of keys, so this wasn't really an issue. I was about to unlock my phone to text the guys for help when Liam seized my phone and walked away. Back to William's apartment.

I was going to kill the guy. "Liam!"

He walked right in, and I halted at the door as if I'd crashed against an invisible wall when I spotted William. Fuck. At least he was alone. *A proper sausage fest.* Good. But not really. I needed my phone. And I needed to leave.

"Why don't you join us for a drink, Red?" Liam shouted, pouring himself another. "It might help you relax and remember where you left your keys." He chuckled.

William's apartment was configured differently from mine. He removed the gallery wall, which gave me a clear view of his apartment's social area. It felt bigger.

"Guys, this is Billie. William's next-door neighbor, and you know … Nathan's ex. But I'm sure you all know who she is since most of you crashed her birthday party in April just to see Dave Matthews Band performing." A thoughtful introduction.

About six other guys, including William, sat in his living room, and they were now all looking at me. They greeted me, and I greeted them back. William didn't partake in this interaction. Well, only if a subtle jerk of the chin counts as such.

"So, what can I offer you to drink, Red?"

"You need to stop calling me Red, and I want my phone back." I extended my hand and swiveled my fingers, but a smile escaped me. I swear it was the tequila because I knew I was pissed, but Liam calling me Red was bittersweet. It was nice to hear it again, but not from him.

The guys laughed and mocked Liam after I blew him off, but he only joined in with the laughs.

William was already burning a hole through my forehead with his blue laser-beam glare. Us women are blessed with exceptional peripheral vision. Cursed, I would say.

"Just give her back her phone, man," one of the guys said. My eyes couldn't take it anymore. I glanced at William for a second, and yup. He was indeed staring at me and sipping on a beer as usual. My presence didn't seem to agree with him.

Liam left my phone on the coffee table and said, "Here you go. All yours."

"Keep it." I walked away, intending to find Aaron downstairs, and ask him to open my door. Not only did I refuse to set foot inside William's apartment, but it was physically impossible for me to walk through that door. I just … couldn't. I could retrieve my phone later.

The elevator doors opened for me, and someone grabbed my bare arm, stopping me from leaving. I didn't have to turn around to know whose hand that was because the way my skin reacts to him is abnormally pathetic—a cruel joke.

"You're locked out," William affirmed. Not a question. *Nice to see you too.* He dropped my arm once the elevator doors almost pinched my nose. His face was clean-shaven, just how I liked it. And as much as I tried not to evaluate his overall appearance, I did. And yeah, I preferred him this way—his perfect masculine bone structure on display.

I tried breathing in through my mouth, but it was useless. His cologne had me cornered.

"Your phone." William handed it over and walked away, pulling a set of keys out of his perfectly pressed pants pocket. He was dressed a bit more elegant than usual and headed straight to my apartment.

He's got keys to your apartment, remember? And you'd think I'd forgotten about that little fun fact, but I hadn't. It was a thought that was best not to pull from my mind.

Not a single facial gesture escaped William as he unlocked my door and pushed it slightly open for me. Androids could be crafted after him.

"Thank you," I said with a frown, my hand removing the keys that hung from the last lock.

Two guys rushed out of William's apartment toward the elevator, and the doors opened when they were still halfway there. Five girls walked out of it. One of them was Rachel King. She wore a beautiful terracotta silk dress with thin straps and a cowl neck. A high but elegant slit displayed her toned legs. Her dark chestnut hair was done in soft waves that bounced against her golden-brown skin.

William looked in their direction, and Rachel dispatched the biggest smile at him. He freaking smiled back.

"Good night," I said, stepping inside my apartment, dragging my heart on the floor behind me. "Thanks again."

I pushed the door, but William stopped it with his foot, and I can still taste the frustration I felt when he said, "My keys, please," because a part of me thought he would say something more in the line of a taunt, a claim, a statement of disagreement. Anything other than that. Something to show me that underneath it all, an emotion awaited—ached to resurface.

But I just replied, "Right," and handed them over to him.

"Wait," he said, a second before I shut the door in his face, feeling my blood pumping aggressively through the veins of my neck.

"Yes?" I peeked through the small opening.

"Joel and Lily just got engaged. There's going to be an impromptu engagement party on the rooftop right now. You're invited. Check your texts." And with that, he left, and I almost collapsed on the floor because not only would I have to watch William and Rachel there, but Nathan was going to be there for sure.

My phone was boasting with text messages from Lily where she told me about the news. Tobias had texted me too to let me know about the engagement party.

I needed backup.

Me: Joel and Lily got engaged. There's a party on my apartment building's rooftop. Nathan's going to be here for sure. William's here with Rachel King. I'm sending over someone to pick you up right now, so you better get your ass into something pretty because you can't leave me here to die.

I fired Nina that text as I walked to the kitchen and grabbed a glass of water. My head spun in a melodic way brought to you by Don Julio 1800, and I needed to find something that would overshadow Rachel.

Nina: Shit! This is gonna be goooood!
Me: Nina!
Nina: What? Hahaha. You're delaying me. See you in a bit.

CHAPTER 41

Getting Experimental

NINA AND I stepped into the engagement party on the rooftop escorted by Aaron and Amena. David's shift ended, so he was going to meet with CJ. Probably to drink more tequila. My keys were in the car. I must've dropped them at some point.

The rooftop was packed. And the party didn't seem impromptu to me. Everything was beautifully decorated in white and silver, and there were flowers all around the place. We greeted Tobias and Eric first, who were the closest to the rooftop's entrance. They both looked great as expected.

I wore one of the Enzio de Luca dresses they sent me on my birthday. It was the short, bright watermelon color one with a one-shoulder asymmetrical design and a somewhat flared futuristic shoulder. I should've worn black and tried to blend in with the night, but a part of me wanted to stand out too.

The pathetic side to this unnecessary thought was that I didn't even know the reason *why* I wanted to be seen. Or by whom exactly because William had his hands full with Rachel, and I didn't even know what to think about Nathan. My neck went stiff just thinking about seeing him tonight.

Nina looked hot. I bet she realized Zara was going to be here, so she went all in. She wore a dress too—beige and tight around her curves. But it wasn't too short, which made her look elegant.

The first person I saw next in the distance was Lily. She was beaming with joy. I quickly approached her and Joel.

"Congratulations!" I shouted at her and went in for a hug. Lily squealed as we embraced each other, and she immediately showed me her left hand. The ring was *gorgeous*—a perfect round (and huge) solitaire with a thin micro pavé band. "Oh, my God, Lily! It's beautiful! You need to tell me everything."

"I promise I will," she said, but someone stole her away from me. I congratulated Joel afterward. I've never seen him smile that much. He seemed elated. I was thrilled for them.

"Billie, I wanted to thank you for what you did for Lily the other day at the photo shoot," he told me in a hushed voice. "It means a lot to me that you would protect her like that. She shouldn't have kept that from me or gone through that alone as she did and for so long. But I'm glad that things are falling into place."

Joel dragged a hand along his face and scratched his neck. He seemed stressed about the situation. "I really wanted to find the guy and murder him, but Nathan—" He cut himself short from finishing that sentence.

"Joel, you don't need to do that," I reminded him. "I know he's your best friend, and you can mention his name."

"Yeah, I'm sorry. It's just weird that you're not together anymore."

I know. I missed hanging out together, just the four of us.

"So? What were you about to say?"

Nathan hadn't arrived. He was most probably at the office. But Lana, Poppy, and the rest of Lily's model friends were here.

Hurrah.

"Nathan's been monitoring the case alongside one of your

father's lawyers, so that's giving me some peace of mind. But I can't promise I won't mess up the guy's face if I see him walking down the street. I would gladly serve a few hours in jail to have the pleasure to do it."

"Joel, you need to stop thinking about that right now," I told him. That's when I spotted William at the far end of the rooftop with Rachel and some of the guys who were downstairs at his apartment just before. I shook my head twice and said, "You should just go back to smiling like a kid with a new toy."

He laughed. "You're right."

"Hey, Murph."

I widened my eyes at Joel and felt Nathan's lips on my cheek as he kissed it. Joel offered me a pursed smile when I greeted Nathan back with a simple, "Hey, Nathan."

"*Grattis, bror!*" Nathan and Joel hugged each other with heavy pats on the back. They both wore big grins on their faces. I couldn't help but smile and nod a couple of times. But it was best to walk away.

I didn't know what to do or how to act around Nathan. I hadn't seen or talked to him since we broke up. The fact that he kissed my cheek just now threw me off. I wasn't sure how he felt about me after everything that happened.

Time to figure out what to do with myself for the rest of the night.

Zara had quickly intercepted Nina, or perhaps it was the other way around. Who knew? I was undecided about approaching them, but I had no one else to hang out with.

"Hey, Red," Liam whispered in my ear, startling me, of course.

"You're just like my nightmares."

"How so?" He chuckled and stood right in front of me, stopping me dry.

"Because you won't go away." I tried walking around him, but he placed himself in front of me again.

"Your lips are chapped. You need a drink." I was wearing lip gloss, so that was impossible. He lifted his hand and signaled for one of the servers to come. "What's your poison?"

"Sleeping pills," I said with a forced smile. Not that I was kidding.

"Can I get you anything to drink?" The short blonde server asked in a sweet voice.

"You're funny," he said to me with a smile, angling a finger at me. Liam turned his attention to where the server stood, waiting. "I'll have another whiskey, and she'll have a tequila with club soda and a dash of lime since I'm guessing you don't serve narcotics, correct?"

Our server widened her eyes for a bit but laughed a nervous laugh under her breath.

"He's joking," I clarified. "But if you do happen to have a sleeping pill to spare, you can go ahead and smash a couple into his drink."

Our server walked away to get our drinks with a smile and a puzzled look on her face.

"How do you know I like tequila?" I asked Liam.

"Well, I could smell it when you arrived earlier, of course. Tequila is quite the betraying bitch, if you ask me. A *snitch*, if you will, since you love using that word. So yeah, I could tell you were drinking tequila."

I looked around and spotted Nathan talking to Lana. She was all over him and probably excited about his new relationship status. My blood boiled, and I didn't even want to look where I knew William hung out. And I guess my scowl had unstable magic powers because it made Nathan glance at me, but I quickly brought my attention back to Liam.

"Want to play a little game?" Liam asked, lifting his brows a couple of times and brushing a rogue strand of hair off his forehead.

"Honestly? No. Not in the mood for games," I replied.

Our server delivered our drinks and hurried away. I took a sip, and then another because I desperately needed it. My head was starting to pulse. I needed to delay the hangover symptoms by drinking more alcohol.

"All I want is for tonight to be as uneventful as possible."

"Pshhh. Come on, Red. I have a feeling you're going to enjoy this particular one I have in store for you."

The worst part of all was that Liam was my best and only option to hang out with because I didn't want to interrupt Nina and Zara; she already hated me enough as it was. And I wasn't going to sit down alone somewhere watching everyone have a great time. I'd rather leave than make a fool of myself, but I knew Lily wouldn't have appreciated it if I did.

Liam had to do for the night.

"I'll play your stupid game if you stop calling me Red," I proposed.

"And why do I keep getting this … low-key vibe from you that you love the nickname, then?" He sipped on his drink and clicked his tongue. "I'm getting so attached to it. But look here, I'll counter offer you. We'll play the game, and I'll *reduce* the number of times I call you Red."

"Fine." I had to work with what I had, which wasn't plenty. And I was sure the next time I would see Liam would be at Lily and Joel's wedding, so whatever. Caleb would've loved for me to punch Liam in the face for stealing his nickname.

"Glad you agreed, although we're already kind of playing the game," he said, draining his glass and placing it on the nearest cocktail table. "We'll just amp things up, if you will. And that's where the real fun begins. Let's call it an experiment. So drink up that snitch of yours because I'm going to need you to free your hands for me."

Snitch. I laughed. This guy was growing on me.

I brought my glass to my mouth to give it one last, deep drink before setting it down on the table, but Liam placed a finger under my glass and lifted it, "Drink up. You'll thank me later."

He made me down the whole thing and seized the glass from my grasp.

"Perfect," he said, leaving the empty tumbler on the table. He grabbed my hands and pulled me against him.

"Liam, what the hell are you doing?" I asked as he placed my hand over his shoulder and grabbed my waist. He started swaying me to the rhythm of the Bossa Nova beats. *Dancing.*

"Fact number one." He leaned in and whispered in my ear, "I'm not hitting on you, I promise." I lifted a brow as in, *explain yourself then.* "I've nothing against redheads, believe me. But I'm more of a brunette kind of guy. *A* brunette if I'm being specific. But she's away right now, and I'm not sure yet if we're an item or not. I know she fancies me, but she's always training, and she's got a major attitude problem if you ask me."

"Why?"

"Well, she's somewhat mercurial and a tiny bit hot-tempered. But I'm willing to do the work if you know what I mean." He winked.

"*Mercurial?*" I asked with a raised brow and a teasing laugh.

"What?" He laughed back. "I don't know. A reporter at the Australian Open said that about her and I knew I had to google it. I've been teasing her about it ever since. Let's say she's … volatile."

Liam was keeping me entertained, for sure. "So, who's the lucky girl?"

"I'm not supposed to tell you because it might be an issue if it gets out. But since I'm *a snitch* and you don't look like one, I'll share the little secret with you."

I snorted because, come on, he couldn't even keep his own secrets to himself. He *was* a snitch. "And something tells me everyone you know already knows about this, right?"

"Oh, yeah, definitely." He laughed. "Her name's Belén Freeman." He lifted his brows as if waiting to get a reaction out of me.

"I *looove* that name. Where's she from? Spain? Should I know her?"

"You're messing with me, right?" he asked. "She's Belén *Freeman.*"

"You're barking up the wrong tree, mate," I said with a terrible English accent. Liam rolled his eyes at me. "You know I didn't know who William was when I met him, right? I'm the worst for this sort of thing."

"Ah, yes! I've heard the stories. But unfortunately, I still don't buy it." Liam twirled me as I gaped at him with a laugh.

"It's the truth! Why would I lie about it?" I replied with indignation as he pulled me back in.

"*Because* ... with a lad like William, you'd be poking at his ego. It would make you seem more appealing, somehow," he said, looking in William's direction. "You're a smart girl, eh? But your secret's safe with me, Red. Don't worry." He winked.

He was so infuriating, and I wasn't going to beg him to believe me. So I let him think whatever he wanted to think. "Tell me who Belén is. Is she an actress?"

"She's Belén freaking *Freeman*! The tennis pro. Jesus." He shook his head with disappointment. "I promise to invite you to the US Open in a couple of months. It'll do you good to get out and such. I've got a few tickets, of course. And I know she's going to win it this time, so I'll take you to the women's final so that you can get a taste of the glory. That Kruschenko girl has a bad knee, and she's Belén's only real opponent right now."

"I've no idea what you're talking about," I said with a laugh. "I'm guessing Kruschenko is a Russian tennis player?"

"She is. Zoya," he said with an exaggerated annoyed look on his face. "And we don't like her. We *hate* her. She's the bad guy— the villain. You get the gist."

"Okay," I chirped. "I'll make sure to remember that." I officially liked Liam now. "Okay so, you mentioned fact number one. And something tells me you're going to start rolling out more facts on me, so carry on."

"Right. Fact number two: I *am* a snitch, a busybody, and all that rubbish," he said, flapping a hand in a carefree motion. He placed it back on my waist and continued. "But not by choice. It just happens that Tobias is all the above, as you very well mentioned before. And he tells me *everything* because we love each other dearly and have nothing better to do at times in between jobs. And it's a tough competitive industry, so we do find ourselves with quite a lot of spare time in our hands." Liam looked up and laughed at his own joke. I couldn't help but laugh a little bit too, either. "We can't all be William Sjöberg. Heavily booked all the time—acclaimed."

I tensed up when he mentioned William.

"Ah!" he exclaimed. "There it is. On to fact number three. My favorite one of all." He looked over my shoulder and met my gaze again with a laugh.

"Please, just tell me what you're doing."

"Just fact-checking."

"Liam."

"I swear that's what I was doing," he said, still easing out of a chuckle. "Fact number three consists of how I know all about you and William. And my fact-checker went nuts right now. That gnarly look on his face only confirms to me that he's got his knickers in a twist because of—this." He gestured with his hand back and forth between us.

"No, he doesn't. That's his—*resting William face.*" *He doesn't care who I talk or dance with anymore.* "And I'm going to kill Tobias for this."

"Cht, cht, cht." Liam twirled me again and pulled me back in flush against him. "I figured that one out on my own, thank you very much—a proper snitch move. Are you proud?" He smiled.

I shook my head at him, but he just laughed and said, "I'll take that as a yes."

"You don't know what you're talking about. If somehow you think that by doing this, you'll get on William's nerves … you're wrong."

"Yeah, well, he's very well-tended to if you ask me," he said, twisting his mouth to the side. "But I'm not one to shy away from a challenge."

I rolled my hand into a fist and tapped his shoulder.

"Ow!" he yelled with a grin. "Aren't you a wee bit heavy-boned for a petite girl like yourself?"

I was about to hit him again for the heavy-bone thing he just said, but I was more annoyed about the way he talked and the expressions he used. "Aren't you Australian? Why do you sound just like Nathan?"

"My mum's English, so I'm a fabulous mix of both."

"I bet you're a middle child."

"How'd you figure that one out?" he asked with a silly face. "I am, of course." He laughed. "Anyway. Now that you mentioned Nathan, that's where the real experimentation begins—the game I'm proposing."

I could see now where this was headed.

"We are going to keep pushing these guys' buttons for a bit, and you and I are going to bet on who's going to be the first to come kick my ass." He *revealed* with a grin, bending me backward and pulling me back in with a thrust.

"Liam!" I complained, pulling my dress down. "My outfit is not made for that kind of move."

"Nonsense. It's all been sharply calculated." He winked at me again. Ugh.

A part of me was curious about going through with this. It was a silly game that didn't prove anything, but they were both very much entertained with someone else, so why shouldn't I be allowed to do the same.

"So what racehorse are you betting on tonight?"

"None."

"Oh, come on! Don't be boring, now. Just pick one."

"I'm not trying to be boring. I truly believe that neither of them will care that I'm with you right now. That's my bet, and I'm sticking to it," I said, lifting my chin and feeling convinced about my choice. "How about you?"

"Well ... I'm torn. I was going to go with William because I've never seen him cook paella for one hundred plus people or set up a mini concert for a girl's birthday before. *But* ... Nathan's looking at me like he could chew my head off any second now." He snickered. "But now that I think about it, I wouldn't want the universe to think I want Nathan launching at me. He'd surely send me flying off to the dodgiest side of Hunts Point on a single blow. The guy's deadly, or so I've heard."

I laughed. *He is.*

"That being said, William's definitely my horse. Besides, didn't you break up with Nathan because of him? I'm sure we can reel him back in for you in a jiffy," he said looking in William's direction again. I clutched Liam's face in between my fingers and turned him away from William.

"Liam, please stop staring at him. You have no clue—" I shut my eyes and sighed. "This was a bad idea." I dropped my hands off his face.

"I can assure you it's not." Liam stopped dancing, caught my hand, and pulled me toward the area that had been set up as a bar. "Let's have one shot, and I'll make sure the agony ends in less than thirty seconds for everyone involved. What do you say?" He kept making way for us to go through the small clusters of people here and there. Saying hi to people. "Two tequila shots, please."

We were closer to Nathan now, and I couldn't help but stare at him as we waited for our shots to be served. He was still talking to Lana, which was the most *annoying* thing in the world. It hurt, actually. I wasn't ready to see Nathan with someone else, but that meant shit because he was free to do whatever the hell he wanted. I messed everything up, and now I had to deal with the aftermath.

"Poor thing. You're so torn, aren't you?" Liam laughed.

"Um—what? No!" I don't think I was. I knew my relationship with Nathan was over. I just needed time to let that sink in. To mourn *us*. It was hard to know that as long as I was friends with Lily, Nathan would always be in the picture. And I knew that with time I would probably stop feeling sick to my stomach whenever I saw him with someone else. But it was still too soon, and the feelings were raw.

And William … I couldn't even put my thoughts into order when it came to him. He messed me up every time. I shoved the thought of him back to my *Shit I'll Eventually Figure Out* folder.

"Here you go." Liam placed my tequila shot in front of me, lifted his, and said, "Here's to learning how to make good choices."

"Sounds about right," I said, pressing my lips into a line. "Cheers."

We downed our shots, and I was impressed by how my throat was getting used to the burn. I welcomed it.

"Let's end this thing then," I said to him, rubbing the palms of my hands a few times. "What did you have in mind? And just to be clear, there won't be any kissing."

"Psh. We don't need to go that far, *believe me*," Liam said, covering his mouth as if telling a secret. "I know these guys. They're territorial as fuck. Their insides must be poisoned by now from the bile that's oozing off their livers. I'm sure they're pissed that you're not sitting in a chair on your own, sipping on tea with a sad look on your face. But such is life, I guess." He ran his arm around my shoulders and walked lazily toward the rooftop railing beside me, far away from both William and Nathan.

"Just lay your back on the railing and look at me," he instructed. "Don't you *dare* look at any of them, okay? This is of the utmost importance."

I nodded.

Liam placed a hand beside each of my arms and held onto the railing. "Now smile." I did. "Keep smiling while I talk, okay? I'm going to pinch your waist next, and you're going to shove my shoulder, and then we'll both laugh, and I'll lean in to whisper a 'dirty little secret' in your ear. You'll shoot me with the cheekiest smile you can come up with, and I'll say it's game over by then. Sounds good? I'll improvise if for some reason that doesn't get either of them fired up."

I took a deep breath and said, "Okay. I'm ready." I don't know why I accepted, but I could always say the tequila made me do it.

"3, 2, 1, and …"

Liam did precisely what he said he would, and I did too.

He was about to go into the "dirty little secret" portion of the choreography, mind you, when I heard, "Liam, I'm going to kindly ask you to get your bloody hands off her."

"Oh! Hey, Nate," Liam said to him, turning left to look at where he stood. Waiting. "Sure, mate. No problem. We were just talking."

"Right. Bugger off," Nathan said, jerking his chin toward the bar.

Liam lifted his hands beside his face and walked around Nathan to leave. He winked at me and said, "I'll text you, Red."

"No, you won't," Nathan growled at him. "And don't call her that." But Liam placed his hands inside his pants pockets and sauntered away with a stupid smile on his face.

That's when it hit me—a disappointment of sorts. I was relieved that at least one of them cared enough to approach me, but I realized once Nathan did that I was bugged about it not being William because I looked at him, and he wasn't even aware of what was going on over here. And I wasn't used to the lack of attention on his part.

Anyway, it was a good thing that Nathan approached me because it was time for us to have that dreaded after-breakup talk once and for all.

CHAPTER 42

A Bluefin Tuna

"HEY, MURPH," Nathan said with a smile, looking as breathtakingly handsome as he always did. "So, what is Liam up to? Was he trying to—"

"No. We're just friends," I told him.

"Since when?" He grimaced. "You didn't even know who he was at your birthday party."

"Since today, actually. I like him. He's fun." Nathan was getting territorial on me, but he was talking to Lana just now, and he knew I wasn't a fan of hers. So why care about who I talk to or not?

"He's twenty, you know," he said, looking at him. Liam had joined Tobias to get drinks at the bar. "Just a lad."

"*Twenty?*" I was in shock. He looked older. Ha! "Well, he's closer to my age actually. And I don't know what that's got to do with anything."

"Just saying."

Right.

"How's Lana doing, by the way?" I asked him. He was getting worked up about Liam, and I hated seeing him with Lana, so I guessed he wouldn't mind me pointing out that fact for him. "Unblocked and back to being friends?"

"Not exactly." Nathan snorted and crossed his arms at his chest. "Does it make you jealous?"

I don't know.

"I object." It was best not to answer that.

"Overruled," Nathan said, taking a step forward. "Yes or no."

"Yes." What was I to say? I was overruled. And I'm not a liar either.

"Could we go somewhere a bit more private? To talk?"

"Ah—sure. Do you want to go downstairs? To my apartment?"

"Sounds good," he said dryly. He seemed a little nervous, though, and I was right there with him. "Let's go."

He grabbed my hand and pulled me toward the door. I risked one last peek at William, and we caught each other looking, but I couldn't hold the weight of his gaze. It wasn't blazing as it normally would in a situation like this. It was just … empty. Like he had nothing else to offer me other than that flat, vacuous, but heavy exchange.

My heart ached.

William watched me leave with Nathan. Hand in hand. And even though Rachel was right next to him, I still cared too much. I was still hopeful that things would somehow magically fix themselves. That he would trust me and open the door for me again.

I unlocked my apartment and remembered I still had Nathan's portrait hanging on one of the foyer's wall. I don't know why I hadn't taken it down. It's not that I was expecting to get back together with him, but I didn't hate him. On the contrary, I cared about him deeply, and I *loved* that portrait of him. Taking it down would be painful, and I was trying to avoid any more pain. It must've been awkward for him to come in and see it, though. I didn't know what he would make of it.

Fuck it.

I offered him something to drink, but he refused. He said he just wanted to talk, so we sat in the living room to do that.

"Hey," he said once we took a seat. He rubbed his legs and rested his forearms on them afterward. "I'm so terribly sorry about how things went down in Midsummer. I'm embarrassed about my immaturity. I feel like we could've talked more about everything—that I should've listened to you and acknowledged your feelings. But I was so insanely jealous that it blinded me."

My hands wouldn't stop shaking, so I placed them underneath my thighs just to conceal my nervousness from him.

"I know you saw me talking to Lana just now. But I don't care about her or anyone else. I swear I don't remember a single word that came out of her mouth. I couldn't stop looking at you and thinking about how *I'm* the one who should be standing beside you. Not Liam, for Christ's sake." He sighed.

"You've been going through a lot these past few months. The shooting, losing Caleb, learning all those things about Thomas." He closed his eyes for a second and took a deep breath. "And I've been too busy to be there for you. Like *really* there. But I know I love you more than anything in this world, and I believed that working the way I have would grant me the opportunity to secure a future for us so that I could give you everything you deserve and more. But I see now how wrong I was.

"Nothing's more important to me than you. Not my job, not my clients, or any other future endeavor. It's just *you*. And it's only natural for you to want to have that closeness, that connection that I know I was stupid enough to neglect even when you talked to me about it—several times.

"And William"—he snorted with a tortured smile—"was *there* for you. He understood you better than I did because he went through the same horrors as you, and your door was open because you *needed* someone to be there for you. But I see now that I was at fault for all of that. And if you give me another chance to allow me to right all the wrongs, believe me, that's all I will ever do from this point forth. I will make it my priority."

He cupped my cheek, and I nestled into the comfort and familiarity of his hand. "I miss you, Murph."

"Nathan—" I couldn't help but cry. His words were full of love, and the way he said them with such meaning and tenderness—it made my heart swell. But ...

"Will you let me be that person for you? Always?" Nathan asked, standing up. "Losing you was the most awful thing that's ever happened to me. It showed me how much I truly love you. How much I'm willing to do for you. To change, to improve, just to have the opportunity and the privilege of calling you mine. I can't lose you again, Murph."

I was speechless. I could only stare into his eyes and listen to him.

"I don't want to steal anyone's thunder," he said with a weak laugh, "but I've had this for months now. I've been carrying it with me, trying to find the perfect moment to do so. And I promise I will make everything right again."

Nathan got down on one knee before me and reached inside his jacket pocket. He pulled out a small black box, and before he could present it to me, I placed my hand on his chest and stopped him. He was going to propose ... and I was going to say *no*.

His eyes shifted from mine to the box he held in between his fingers. I could listen to his heavy breathing and his heart pounding against my hand on his chest. We were both shaking.

The things he said were perfect in *every* way.

He was perfect, and I was probably the biggest idiot on the planet. But I didn't even want to look at that ring. I was afraid I would give myself into the situation and say yes in the spur of the moment because I loved him! So much.

But it wouldn't be fair to him for me to say yes, knowing that I wasn't there entirely with him, even if he would've agreed for us to get married in five years. I wasn't ready to take this step. It was too much for me, and I didn't want to ruin the engagement for him. To have to say no. Even if by stopping him, I was already doing so, it wasn't the same.

Once he offered me that ring and I rejected it, the situation would've become even more painful for both of us.

I didn't want to see the ring. I couldn't.

"Nathan, I'm so sorry," I said in between short, constant gasps. I took my hands to my eyes and sobbed my heart out. My heart wasn't entirely his, and I'd been trying to be honest with myself about it these past weeks. Even if I knew William was waning me away. Even if he was trying to find happiness with someone else, I refused to lose hope.

It was the scariest feeling in the world to admit and accept those feelings for him because the road ahead promised nothing. Guaranteed nothing. But if there were even the slightest sliver of hope, I would hang on to it. And Nathan didn't deserve that.

He deserved *everything*. And I couldn't give that to him.

Not anymore.

I had nothing.

Nathan placed the box back into his jacket pocket and knelt with both of his knees. He slid his arms around me and pulled me in against his chest, where I heard the firm but fast beating of his heart—knowing perfectly well that I'd just shattered it to a million pieces. And yet, there he was comforting *me* after doing so.

I didn't deserve him.

"Nathan," I whispered, pulling back to see his face. "I'm so sorry. I know I'm hurting you, and that's the last thing I want to do. But I can't—I—I'm not ready, and I do love you. I've loved you more than anything during the time we had together. But—"

"William?" Nathan asked, standing up. He sat beside me, his grayish-green eyes dark and heavy with pain. I stared back at him. It *was* William, but the reality was that I had nothing but a one-sided feeling. And it wasn't just him.

"I feel like there's a lot I need to do for myself—to figure out," I started to say. I needed to tell him some of the things I felt while we were together, and I never did. "I want to travel. I want to find a way to have and know more freedom. To be *me* and someday break free from my security detail and my father's apprehensiveness.

"And I know that it might be hard to understand, but it's something that I *need* to experience. I owe it to myself. And how could we make us work if you have to be here, and I crave to be … free? I would unintentionally make myself stay here to be with you, because why would I want to leave if we're together? And you wouldn't be able to come with me either."

Nathan nodded as I spoke, but I wasn't making the pain go away. I knew that. His eyes let me know. And I still hadn't answered his question.

"Yes," I said after a moment of silence. "I do think about William, and I don't know why, because nothing's going on between us. And nothing happened when you and I were together. I haven't really interacted with him since he arrived from South Africa, and he's dating someone else. But it's not fair that I can't give you my all because it's true … I do have feelings for him, and I'm hoping and waiting for them to fade away. And it's not fair for me to figure that out while being in a relationship with you."

"Shite." Nathan let his head fall in his hands. "I wish I could've been the one to make you happy. But I guess there's nothing left for me to say after that." He looked up at me and smiled the saddest smile in the world. He blew out a sharp breath through his mouth and stood up. I stood up too.

"I think it's best if I get going." He tucked my hair behind my ear and said, "Goodbye, Murph." He took a few steps backward, nodded once, and left.

I walked over to the gallery wall and took Nathan's portrait down.

☾

Nina knocked on my door a couple of hours later. I didn't return to the party on the rooftop and texted Lily to apologize for leaving and promised to make it up to her. She didn't reply, and my guess was that she didn't even have her phone with her. But I was sure she'd understand.

"Hey. What's wrong?" Nina asked with a sweet voice. She hugged me as soon as she stepped in. I was already in my pajamas and lying on my guest room's bed before I stood up to open the door. I was afraid to sleep in my bedroom. Afraid of listening to anything beyond the wall. I'd had enough to deal with tonight. I wouldn't be able to take it if Rachel spent the night with William, so it was best not to find out if she did.

The farther away from William's bedroom, the better.

I asked Nina to spend the night in my place because I didn't want to be alone. She agreed, and I told her everything that happened with Nathan. All I needed was someone to talk to.

"Is Nathan still up there?" I asked her once we were done mincing every single detail of what happened earlier with him.

"He's not. He didn't return once you two left," she replied. "I thought he would be here when I arrived."

I let out a heavily charged breath through my mouth.

"So what happened with Zara?" I asked her, hoping we could change the subject now. I was done talking about my drama.

Nina's expression shifted. She bit her lower lip, looking uncomfortable. "I'm just—not feeling it. I mean, yeah, she's gorgeous, but I can feel myself forcing it because I know she likes me, and I feel flattered and all these other weird feelings I've never experienced before, you know, from being liked by another girl. And we had a great time that night on your birthday, but I was drunk … and mostly curious."

Nina ran a hand through her hair and played with it

"And I really like her, you know. She's funny, and I love talking to her. I mean, I wish we could like, hang out—as friends. But I don't know if that's possible after what happened between us."

Nina straightened herself in her seat. "Anyway, it's not like she's expecting anything from me. I guess I just need to relax." She chuckled. "It's all too new to me, but I guess I'm sticking to guys for now."

We both laughed. "Great choice," I said in between laughs. "But how about we stay single for a while and just enjoy ourselves?"

"Well … yeah," Nina said with a smile, looking at her hands.

"What?" I frowned. Curious.

"Nothing, it's just that Liam approached me when you left since I was waiting for Zara to come back from taking some family photos with the Sjöbergs."

"And?" I asked, hugging a pillow.

"Well, he wanted to let me know that you'd left, which I already knew since I saw you walking out with Nathan. And we talked for a bit, and I kinda liked him?" Nina shot a silly smile at me. "I asked him for his number, and, well, he—gave it to me."

She covered her mouth and laughed.

"You—oh, my God!" I squealed. "I *swear* Liam's my favorite person right now. I had so much fun with him tonight. He really cheered me up."

"Right? I couldn't stop laughing either." She agreed. "And what the hell is going on with those lashes? I even asked him if they were real. He's got the most *insanely* cute eyes I've ever seen."

Nina seemed excited about Liam. And with good reason. He's handsome, funny, and interesting.

"You know he's twenty, right?" I know age is just a number, but I felt like she was clueless about it just as I was because Liam looked older.

"What!" Nina stood up from the bed and asked me to unzip her dress. "I mean, not that I care, but he doesn't look twenty."

I wasn't sure if Nina was aware of what Liam told me about him liking Belén Freeman and how there was something going on between them. Something complicated, for sure. But I didn't want Nina to get wrapped up in that drama. But I couldn't meddle. I had to let it be. Let them figure things out on their own.

Nina grabbed a set of pajamas from my closet and returned to the guest bedroom. "Do you mind if I take a shower?" she asked.

"No, not at all. Go ahead," I replied with a yawn. She yawned too. "But you're sleeping in my bed tonight. And I'll be sleeping here."

"Obviously." She smiled. I'd already talked to her about my concern with listening to William and Rachel over the wall. I made her swear not to tell me anything the next morning. If she heard something or not, I wouldn't want to know.

Nina disappeared off into the bathroom, and I grabbed my phone to check on my messages before going to bed.

Talking to Nina was helpful and distracting. But the truth is that I was completely devastated on the inside. I had to concentrate on keeping myself from falling into that awful place where all I do was cry my heart out.

There was a message from an unknown number that was time-stamped from an hour ago.

Unknown: Why'd you have to bring Nina over to the party tonight? Didn't I tell you I have a weakness for brunettes?
Me: You better sort your shit out with Miss Attitude Problem before you get anywhere near Nina. She seems excited, and I don't want you to hurt her, Liam. I'll go after you if you do.
Unknown: Note taken, I guess. How'd you know it was me? ;)
Me: I could almost hear your voice through that text.
Liam: Aw! Aren't we cute? We're like besties now who threaten each other.
Me: Yeah, yeah. You've been warned.
Liam: So, I guess we both lost the bet lol. I swear to God I thought William was going to be the one to jump me first.
Me: I guess so. We're both losers then.
Liam: Why am I sensing a wee bit of disappointment in our experiment's results? Is it William you want?
Me: No.
Me: I don't know.
Liam: Now, now. There's plenty of fish in the water. I mean, William's one hell of a good-looking bluefin tuna, if you ask me.
Me: NOBODY asked you.
Liam: Haha! I guess I deserved that. Anywhoooo, we're on for the US open, yes? I'll text you. That'll give you a few weeks for you to miss me. ;)
Me: Sounds good. I had a great time tonight, Liam.

Thank you. For cheering me up and all.
Liam: Don't get sappy on me, eh. We'll get that horse
to the finish line, you'll see.
Me: Good night, Liam.
Liam: GN, Red.

The truth is, you can like a lot of people, just as Liam said. There's plenty of fish in the water, but even after all that happened with Nathan tonight, all I could think of revolved around one specific bluefin tuna.

CHAPTER 43

Can't Win Them All

September 11, 2010

MY INTERNSHIP AT Haute Magazine was out-of-this-world amazing. I had a great time, I met a lot of interesting people, and I got to collaborate on plenty of fun projects. The routine was therapeutic and helpful for my overall mental state. Working there was so incredibly fast-paced that it didn't even give me time to think about any other bullshit that usually found its way to the top of my mind.

I still had to deal with the awkwardness of bringing my security detail with me to work, but they kept more of a distance, and sometimes I even forgot about them being there at all. Nobody seemed to care either.

The first few nights following my final breakup with Nathan were tough, though. More than a few times, I double guessed my decision to reject him. But I knew I had to simply observe those emotions and watch them slide away from my mind.

I had to be strong and remember the reasons why I made that choice in the first place. But it was so hard to remember when my heart was just as destroyed as his. I was slowly picking up the scattered pieces of mine, hoping I wouldn't lose a bit in the process.

Ever since Lily and Joel's engagement party, I'd been officially sleeping in the guest room. I was still trying to avoid listening to any after-hour activities—if they ever did happen in the first place. But that was the point. Ignorance *is* bliss. I was happier that way—at peace. Out of sight, out of mind. But in my case, swap sight for hearing range.

School had started, and all in all, I was feeling better now. I found myself enjoying the sweet rhythm that school and the occasional call from Haute provided. I rarely bumped into William, and if I did, we would say hi, and that's it. But I would always feel like my blood sugar dropped to an unhealthy level after any sort of interaction with him, and I hated myself for it. For being too responsive to him.

Liam made me skip school today. He was taking me to the US Open Women's Final match, as he promised, and the event began at 11:00 a.m. Belén Freeman had made it to the finals, as Liam very well predicted, and was competing against her nemesis, Russian tennis player, Zoya Kruschenko.

Liam: I'm on my way to your place, and we'll leave together, sounds good?
Me: Hey! Sure. I'm at Lily's. I'll meet you here.
Liam: Brilliant. AND a little bird told me (Tobias) that William and Rachel have called it quits. So I'm guessing we'll have to start plotting something. We need to get him while he's fresh out of the newly single's oven.

Shit. I couldn't say my stomach didn't heat up from the shock. Was it nerves? Excitement? I couldn't stop staring at Liam's text as I allowed for the news to sink in. Not that it would in any way change my null relationship with William.

"Where'd you go?" Lily asked, waving a hand in front of my

face. "Everything okay?"

"Uh, yeah." I smiled. "Liam's on his way. I was just thinking about an assignment I had to turn in today, but I'll send an email to my instructor." *Right.*

I dropped my phone on the coffee table, and Lily and I resumed our talk about her wedding plans. They wanted to get married next spring. They still didn't know where or how many people would attend.

Joel wanted something small and intimate, and Lily wanted to go crazy with the wedding. I was #teamjoel on the inside, but I had to support Lily, especially since she'd asked me to be her maid of honor. And I had *no idea* of what that meant or the responsibilities that went with the gig, but my common sense told me I had to agree with Lily on everything and keep her as happy as possible. I could google *maid of honor duties* any other day.

Liam arrived fifteen minutes later. "I get so anxious when she plays, and I can't stop peeing every five bloody minutes!" He complained, rushing to Lily's guest bathroom. "Don't let me have a single beer in the stadium! Plus, they cost a bomb!" he shouted as he shut the door behind him. Lily and I laughed.

Joel walked out of his bedroom with a grimace. "Who keeps shouting? I was trying to take a nap."

"Joel, it's the middle of the morning," I reminded him. He was such a sleepyhead. "Aren't naps usually taken in the afternoon?"

"Not when you're a newborn baby." Lily joked, sticking her tongue out to him.

"Ha-ha." Joel stretched himself as he walked in our direction. He threw himself beside Lily with a grunt and kissed the top of her head.

There was a soft knock on the door, and Lily shouted, "Liam, would you get that!" Liam rushed out of the bathroom and saw to the door.

"So where are you guys going?" Joel asked.

"US Open," I replied. "That Freeman girl Liam likes made it to the final."

"Isn't she like sixteen years old?" Joel asked with a frown.

"Seventeen," Liam corrected, walking toward the living room. William followed him, and I almost sank into the couch.

He pulled his Ray-Bans down the bridge of his nose and greeted us. He then addressed Joel in Swedish. I couldn't stop staring at him. His face was scruffy again—growing his beard back. He wore grey joggers, a white t-shirt, a navy-blue New York Yankees cap, and his chunky headphones around his neck.

I was a sucker for that outfit.

And the fact that he was single again almost made me start drooling, but Liam placed his hands on my shoulders and said, "We should start heading out."

William directed his attention our way for a fraction of a second when Liam said that, but he quickly resumed his chit chat with Joel.

"Come on," Liam said, pulling me up from the couch, as if knowing I was entranced by William. "Let's go." He widened his eyes at me.

"I'll—see you guys later," I said to them, waving an awkward hand to say goodbye.

Liam placed his arm around me and shouted as he guided me out, "I promise to bring her back before midnight!" He laughed and shut the door behind us.

I gave Liam the side-eye, but he whispered, "I know what I'm doing."

There was a large suitcase, a carry-on bag, and a backpack right outside the apartment.

William was leaving, and it was the worst feeling in the world. It's as if every cell in my body ached when he was gone.

I hated it.

On our way to the stadium, I was too quiet. Liam did most of the talking, and I inevitably laughed a few times, but I couldn't help but wonder where William was going now and for how long. I needed to text Lily. I needed to know if he would leave for a day or a month. I was sure Joel mentioned something to her about it.

Lily: He's going back to South Africa. They need to reshoot a few scenes.
Me: Do you know for how long he'll be gone?
Lily: 2 weeks. Why?
Me: You know why.
Lily: Joel just told me that Billy ended things with Rachel.
Me: I know. Liam told me.
Lily: I'm sure Tobias told him. They're worse than us.

I laughed out loud. It was funny because it was the truth.

"Why don't you share the joke?" Liam said, trying to pry on my phone's screen. I shooed him away.

Me: I miss him. He won't talk to me or acknowledge me at all.
Lily: He'll come around. You'll see.

I clicked out of the conversation and put my phone away. There was nothing much I could say to that. I disagreed with Lily, and I know she was only saying that to be nice. Besides, we had arrived at Flushing Meadows.

"Here's your pass," Liam said, placing it around my neck. "And I need to pee. Again. Stay put." Liam rushed toward the restrooms, and I couldn't help but laugh. His friendship had been a wonderful surprise. One I didn't know I needed until it arrived.

☾

"Oh, my God!" I held on to Liam's arm and couldn't help but cringe. Belén lost to Zoya after a grueling match that ended with a drop shot by Zoya's hand, and she wasn't taking it too well. She banged her racquet against the court's surface a few times.

"Well, fuck me sideways," Liam muttered, dragging a hand through his hair. Belén was pointing at the chair umpire as she shouted a few things to him in Spanish. Awful things I could perfectly understand, hoping the umpire wouldn't. A man shouted her name as he approached her, and she stopped talking but gave her racquet a few more hits against the hard surface of the court. She couldn't seem to damage it.

Liam told me more about Belén on the half-time break. Belen's mother is former tennis pro superstar Addison Freeman and her father is Mexican former major league baseball player José "Joey" Batista. And I'd just been introduced to her *attitude problem* just now.

Finally, Belén tossed her racquet on the ground and fell on her knees, letting her head fall over her hands. We could all hear the inconsolable sobs as they flooded the silent stadium.

Liam cursed under his breath. "This is going to require some serious damage control—*shit*. And I don't even want to know about the fine she's gonna get for this." He stood up and said, "I'm going to try to talk to her. Do you mind?"

"No, not at all. Go—do your thing."

"You're a doll." Liam kissed my cheek and left in a hurry. I could see how much he cared about her. He looked genuinely worried.

Some of the spectators began clearing the stadium, but most remained on site, trying to catch a glimpse of the drama and the award ceremony that would follow, of course.

I left. It was painful to watch Belén coming undone in front of everyone. As I walked out, someone apparently from her team had already reached out to her. And I was sure Liam would try to comfort her too. I didn't know Belén, but I felt for her. I guess we could all taste the crisp bitterness of her frustration just by watching her reaction.

You can't win them all. That much I knew. And as much as my heart threw a tantrum, I made that my new motto.

CHAPTER 44

C. xx

September 17, 2010

EACH SECOND OF William being away tick-tocked like a constant drip of water leaking off a ceiling crack—reverberating on the back of my mind. If you focused on it, you could hear it, but if you didn't, it became white noise.

I missed him.

But I was doing just fine. I'd found a certain peace in my life that I hadn't felt in a long while. I used to be constantly stressed out, worried, and anxious. And now, only a warm feeling stirred up inside me. It was a comforting feeling that I was yet to identify. But I inevitably allowed myself to wallow in it.

Haute hadn't called me in for this weekend, so I was free. I intended to grab my film camera and take a few shots out in Central Park at sundown. Alone.

Well, you know what *alone* means in my world. Amena and David would be joining me today.

As I packed my things to go, I realized I was out of film. I kept extra rolls on my nightstand drawer, and when I took one of the rolls out, Caleb's letter flew out and fell on the floor.

Having refused to read it for so long made me forget about it altogether. And as I picked it up, I knew it was time to read it. There was never going to be a perfect time to do so, but this moment was as close as it was going to get. So I dropped my camera bag on the bed and laid on my stomach to read it.

I tore it open and braced myself for impact.

September 10, 2009

Hey Red,

I'm writing this letter hoping that you never have to read it and that I will rip it up into pieces and set it on fire one day. Probably the day you get married, and I won't be able to stomach it, so I'll be far away from you by then because I'll be in the foulest mood that would surely last a few lifetimes, and you won't be able to stand me anyway.

I've just walked away from your door. We just kissed goodbye. I can still feel your soft lips brushing against mine. It took all the strength I have in me to walk away and refuse your invitation to go inside and keep kissing you until you begged me to stop.

But I'm a coward. And I won't be able to tell you this, but I love you. I've loved you for years. It's all I've known and it's everything I lived for. So fuck yeah, I'm a coward because I walked away from you without telling you. But you're a smart girl, aren't you? I can't believe you wouldn't know this, and it's not like I've been doing a great job at hiding it from you lately. I wear my fucking heart on my sleeve.

And I'm going to write the next thing down because I need to let it off my chest. The way you look at William is the way I'd look at you if I were allowed to. It's filled with this awestruck fascination, and it makes me want to die twice. From the moment you met him, I saw the stars in your eyes, and they've only grown brighter with time. And that's why I'm a coward about telling you how I feel about you, because I can't fucking compete with that.

You know my job consists of watching you, watching everyone around you, watching you watch everyone around you, and hell yeah,

I'm the best at that. And as much as it pains to admit it (but not so much because again, you're not going to read this), I can see that William feels the same way about you. The fascination is mutual, but my guess is that neither of you knows what to do with so much. It must be overpowering. I know it's painful to watch.

I don't know what's going to happen. I don't know if you'll ever have the chance to be together or not, but hey, I love you so much that I wish you do, if that's what you really want. Even if it makes me want to break shit up or punch someone in the face, I just want to see you happy because:

YOU SAVED ME.

But I promised I would never leave, so don't worry. And now I don't know how I'm gonna be able to keep my promise knowing I'll have to endure watching every day how you look at William. I've also promised a few times that I would never lie to you or keep things from you, but I hate to say that I've been keeping something from you for years.

It's about your mother.

I know why she died, and again I write this because I know that you won't have to read this ever and I hope that your father one day will look you in the eye and tell you exactly what happened that day because we've always known. And you deserve to know.

*Fuck, this is hard to write even knowing you're not going to read it, but here it goes: Your mother was mistaken for a drug lord's wife that had their three daughters enrolled in the same school as you in Mexico City. They often drove her in the same brand and type of car as your mother was. **IT WAS A MISTAKE.** No one's after you or your father. You've never really been in actual danger. What happened to your mother could happen to anyone else regardless. The hitman fucked it up. He only had to look at the license plates, and he* *clearly didn't. It makes me want to go look for the guy and take my time killing him, but I'm sure he's dead by now. Hitmen don't often have a very long lifespan.*

Your father knows all of this, of course. But he loves you, Red, and he's been trying to deal with the guilt, the paranoia, and the pain of losing your mother. And in a poor attempt to make things better, he's kept you in the dark because if you knew you weren't in danger, that it was a mistake, you wouldn't have accepted your security detail for so long. And he justifies it by saying that if it happened once, who says it can't happen again? But I'm a firm believer that lightning doesn't strike twice in the same place.

Your father made a deal with the government when your mother passed away, consisting of having your security detail covered and paid **FOR LIFE.**

That's what your father has in store for you, and it's the most ridiculous thing I've ever heard in my entire life. I know it's protocol and justifiable when you're an ambassador's daughter. It makes you a target. But you're back in New York, and you should be living a normal life. You deserve it.

If you ever read this, which you won't, you'll probably be furious at me because I never told you about this before, but you know the answer to that, don't you? Your father made us sign a bunch of tight NDAs, and believe me ... it's cheaper for me to die than to comply with breaching those contracts.

It kills me to see you every day, knowing how desperately you wish for that freedom, and you're not allowed to taste it. I hope he'll reconsider one day. And if that day comes, I will have to break my promise of staying because I will have to leave. And so, in a way, I'm glad I've signed that NDA because it keeps me from telling you the truth, and I can keep you for a while longer. Yeah, I'm selfish. So what? It's bittersweet, you know? But if I could tell you, I would. Believe me, even if it means that I have to go.

*Red, when I met you, I was broken. But when I saw how fragile you were, you gave me the courage to be strong for you. To pull you out of the darkness. But the truth is that you're the strongest person I know, and **YOU** saved **ME**. I really want to drop this fucking pen and knock on your door and shout that in your pretty face because you really don't have a clue about how deep this shit goes. **YOU SAVED ME.** A million times more than I ever saved you, and you will never know it.*

Lead from the heart. Let the feeling take over and crash against you. I know I wish I had the guts to do it.

Love you forever,

C. xx

CHAPTER 45

Let it Crash

CALEB'S LETTER WAS still between my fingers, but my mind had checked out of existence. It's as if he had been here with me when I read it. I could listen to his voice and imagine every perfect line of his face as if he were standing in front of me.

I hope he knew how much I loved him too.

I was a fucking mess, but I found myself smiling too.

Pure, unadulterated shock invaded my system as the realization hit me: I was safe. I've always been safe. For years all I could think of was how there was someone out to get me, and as I grew older, the theories became darker and more elaborate.

One of my more sinister theories consisted of my father being involved in something illegal. That he'd somehow had associated himself with the wrong people, and things had gone south. That they were now after his family—after *me*. But that wasn't the case. And I was so glad it wasn't.

But all of this meant one thing. I was free, and Caleb was right—as always. There was no way for me to accept living like this after knowing the truth. I couldn't believe how Caleb managed to keep taking care of me, even after his death.

Hundreds of times, I daydreamed about walking out of my apartment and going for a walk alone, just to see what it feels like to do things on my own. But I always chickened out because the truth is *I was afraid*. What if there was someone out there waiting to catch me alone?

There was nothing to worry about anymore. I wasn't even angry at my father. It must've been hard for him to lose my mother and fear that something could happen to me every day. He had the option to take care of me forever, and he took it. But it was too much. And Thomas only fed his apprehensiveness even more—it fueled it and justified it.

And no, I don't want to imagine what would've happened that day if Aaron and Caleb hadn't shown up. We'd been lucky. William would've probably died that day.

William.

Caleb knew me better than anyone else. His opinion was one that I deeply valued, and for him to say the things he did about William and me made me want to take chances.

Lead from the heart. Let the feeling take over and crash against you.

With those words, Caleb made me want to grab a plane and fly to South Africa to tell William how I feel and do the things I've always been scared of doing—for him. To show him how much I care about him. How much I *love* him.

I was tired of being afraid, of being a coward, of playing it safe. I had to take control of my life. It was now or never.

And that's *exactly* what I intended to do. *Let it crash.*

But I couldn't do it alone. I needed a plan—a solid one. And I knew who to call.

Alice.

Something told me she might be #teambillie, and I would put all my eggs in that basket.

I called Alice as I pulled a small carry-on suitcase from the foyer closet to pack a few things for my impromptu trip. I didn't even have time to be scared of what I was about to do. I was running on pure adrenalin, and it felt so fucking great.

"Alice. Hey, it's Billie."

"Hey, Billie!" she said enthusiastically. "What's up? How's everything?"

"I need your help."

CHAPTER 46

Luna

ALICE SCREAMED WHEN I told her what I wanted to do. I explained everything that happened with Nathan a few weeks ago, that I knew William had ended things with Rachel, and how all I could think of was him.

She was ecstatic.

Alice texted me all the information about where William was staying in South Africa and his schedule. I opened my laptop and found a United Airlines nonstop flight to Johannesburg that would leave from Newark a few hours from now—at 8:00 p.m. I would then have to connect to Cape Town with an additional two-hour flight with another local airline. An odyssey.

I bought the tickets with my credit card, knowing it would leave a breadcrumb trail for my father and my security detail to follow. I didn't want them to worry and think someone kidnapped me or something, but I knew I couldn't ask for permission either. I wanted them to know where I was, but I wanted to go alone. Since it was a long flight, I knew it would give me enough time to do whatever I had to do and talk to William before they found me.

My father would surely go insane once they informed him that I went missing, and it's not that I didn't care, but I had to do this—my way. I needed to show William I wasn't a coward, and that I was willing to do all of this for him. He'd done and proven so much already in the past. And now it was my turn to win him back.

It was a few minutes past 5:00 p.m., and I was packed and ready to go. I needed to leave as soon as possible. But I couldn't just walk out the door with a piece of luggage without raising any suspicion. And what if any of my bodyguards were still lingering in the lobby?

Me: Hey, guys. I'm not going to Central Park anymore. I'm staying in, so if you want to call it a day, that's fine with me.
David: Noted. Good evening, Miss Murphy.
Amena: Thank you, and enjoy the rest of your day, Miss Murphy.
Aaron: I'll be downstairs in the apartment if you need anything, Miss Murphy.
Me: Thank you! Have a good evening.

When I confirmed to them that I wouldn't go out for the rest of the day, they usually scattered. But I needed help to verify they weren't idling in the lobby. New York Fashion Week ended yesterday, so Lily was in town. I just needed to see if:

Me: Lily, are you home?
Lily: Hey! Yes, I am. Getting ready to leave for a party. I'm so exhausted. I'd rather not go, but I have to. What's up?
Me: Thank God. I need you to go downstairs to the lobby and tell me if the coast is clear.
Lily: Hahaha, what do you mean? Like from your bodyguards?
Me: Yes. Please. I'm in a hurry. I also need you to ask

Bruce or Senad to hail a cab for me.

Lily: Where the hell are you going, and why am I not invited?

Me: I have an 8:00 p.m. flight to South Africa. I'm going to see William. Please hurry!

Lily: WHAT!!!!! OMW downstairs. Billie, what the fuck! Ah!!!!! I'm screaming. You HAVE to tell me everything.

Me: I'll call you once I'm at the airport and past security. I'm about to collapse from the nerves.

A couple of minutes went by, and my palms were sweaty. I stared at the screen, waiting for Lily to reply.

Lily: Coast is clear. Senad is hailing a cab as we speak. You need to get down here right now because he's great at it.

Lily: Yeah. He's got a cab waiting. Run. Now.

Me: On my way. Don't let that taxi get away.

Lily: Yes, ma'am ;)

I froze right before locking my door, waiting for that awfully dreaded feeling of having forgotten something to go away. I quickly reviewed the contents of my bag. Passport: check. Cash and credit cards: check. Sleeping pills: check because there was a sixteen-hour nonstop flight waiting for me, and I was flying coach for the first time in my life. The plane was almost full. I was lucky enough to find a seat.

With the door locked and my suitcase in hand, I looked up at the surveillance camera, winked at it, and hurried toward the elevator.

Lily waited for me just outside the building's door. Senad had the cab's door open for me. Lily hugged me and kissed my cheek. "Go!"

I jumped into the taxi and said, "Newark Airport, please."

Damn, that felt good. So liberating.

I wasn't sure if I would make it to the airport without getting caught. Maybe the surveillance camera would get triggered. Hopefully not, but I couldn't stop smiling anyway. I'd never been allowed in my entire life to even go around the block on my own. The feeling was unexplainable.

All I could think of was how, before the next 24-hours elapsed, I would see William. I didn't have a clue of what I was going to say once I got there. Probably best not to plan ahead of time.

Lead from the heart. Let the feeling take over and crash against you.

It seemed to me like I was on to a good start.

☾

September 18, 2010

I took a full dose of my sleeping pill three hours into the flight, and it knocked me out for ten hours. There were three more hours to go, so I ate a few snacks and watched a movie.

It finally hit me that I had escaped, and it was 9:00 a.m. in New York, which meant that I had a few hours before Aaron started wondering why I hadn't checked in for my usual morning run. My anxiety rose by the minute.

Lily called me when I was at the airport. I'd forgotten to call her. I told her about Caleb's letter, which I'd obviously brought with me. I read it a couple of times on the flight, which helped me to keep shoving the uneasiness aside.

Lily understood my reasons for wanting to go after William when I told her everything. She was heartbroken for Nathan, but she always knew how much I cared about William too. And she swore William felt the same. But I didn't want to get my hopes up. All I wanted to do was to *show* him my feelings. And as much as I wished for those feelings to be reciprocated, I had to make myself believe that I wasn't expecting anything from him.

But I was. I wanted so badly for him to feel the same way.

☾

We landed in Johannesburg on time, so I had a couple of hours before I boarded my next flight. I'd been careful to keep my phone on airplane mode. I knew they could easily track it. And even though they would find out I flew to South Africa five minutes into their investigation, I mostly didn't want to look at the thousands of messages and missed calls that would surely pour into my phone once I turned it on.

I needed to stay focused.

We landed in Cape Town somewhere around 11:00 p.m. It had been the most exhausting feat I'd ever been involved in. The trip destroyed me. But I couldn't believe I was finally here.

Walking out of the airport alone made me feel empty. I kept looking over my shoulder, somehow still used to having someone following me around all the time. But I can't say I didn't love the feeling of doing this by myself.

"Ellerman House, please," I said to the friendly looking cab driver when I took a seat inside the car, trying to seem casual. I felt like a pro at living life on my own already. And everything had gone so smoothly that I couldn't help but think Caleb and my mother had something to do with it. I knew they were taking care of me. I could feel it in my bones.

The nerves and the anxiety had drifted away. I was too tired to feel anything. Or so I thought, right until the cab parked in the motor lobby of the hotel where William had been spending the past few days while filming. Alice mentioned this is the same hotel he stayed at during the summer when he asked me to come with him and I refused.

I swiped my card and paid for the cab, keeping the breadcrumbed path alive. The night was chilly, so I rushed inside the lobby after a bellhop offered to help with my luggage.

The hotel was beautiful. It seemed more like a house than a hotel—a huge house. Yet, still intimate for a hotel. It was the perfect place for William to stay. The hotel staff was friendly, and they immediately invited me in. It's as if I were walking into a spectacular house.

I thanked them and took a seat in the lobby. My phone had to be turned on because I needed to ask Alice a few questions, so there was no way to avoid it.

My phone buzzed as I texted Alice, but I sent it to voicemail. It was an unknown number from the United States. I knew it was *them* looking for me, so I turned off the cellular data and asked for the hotel's Wi-Fi password to one of the hotel employees while I waited in the lobby.

Alice finally replied.

Alice: William's in his room. But I don't know if he's alone, Billie. I didn't want to be creepy asking about it.
Me: Ok. Don't worry. Thanks.
Alice: I'll call the hotel right now and let them know you've arrived and that you're authorized to go up to William's room. I'll ask them not to let him know you're coming. I really want you to tell me all about the face he makes when he sees you standing outside his door.
Me: Shit. I'm freaking out. It's late. Do you think I should book a room and find him tomorrow morning?
Alice: NO!!!! Get your ass in there right now. You gotta keep the momentum going. I'm on the phone with the hotel staff as we speak. Wait a second.

I sighed and laughed under my breath as I imagined Alice enjoying doing all of this with me, holding her phone with her shoulder, probably typing on her laptop like a maniac, too, doing whatever being William's assistant required her to do.

Alice: Done. Ask for Arno at the front desk. The password for you to be allowed up is LUNA. Haha.

Luna. I knew she chose that password because of her girlfriend Luna, but still, Luna means moon. My heart warmed up—a good omen.

The sound of crashing waves was heard throughout most of the place as Arno guided me to William's room—it helped ease my nervousness. He explained how there were only thirteen individually styled bedrooms in the hotel. But they were fully booked. I was sure Alice could help me find another nearby hotel in case everything went to shit.

We walked through a hallway that was basically a colorful, modern art gallery with walnut parquet floors. Incredible. The place smelled delicious too. You could tell every detail had been meticulously taken care of in this place. It was a mixture of homey and luxury with a lot of local inspiration.

We arrived at William's room, and Arno nodded once and excused himself.

I knocked on William's door and crossed myself. I swear it was my mom who made me do it.

CHAPTER 47

Dentist

WILLIAM OPENED THE door, holding what seemed to be a script in his hand and wearing his black acetate glasses. It was the first time I saw him wearing them. Do I even have to say how cool and strikingly handsome he looked?

"Guille?" William leveled me with a panic-filled look. He'd left the door wide open, and I could see his room, but no signs of anyone else in there. There was a single chair out on the balcony, a bunch of papers, and a bottle of wine on a small round table beside it. A soft, cool breeze blew in through his room. I could hear the waves crashing against rocks beyond the cliff.

He didn't invite me in. Instead, he said, "What are you doing here?" rolling up the papers in his hands and crossing his arms at his chest.

"I came here to tell you that I love you," I said, dropping my bag over my suitcase and looking straight into his eyes. "I'm here to tell you that I miss you. That I can't stop thinking about you as much as I've tried for over a year now, and I'm finally able to accept it."

William stared at me in silence. I kneaded my hands and looked down for a second, trying to collect my thoughts. To allow the nerves to settle.

"You're it for me, William. So that's what I'm doing here. I'm here, all alone, to ask you if there's still a chance for me to be *it* for you too."

William dragged a hand through his hair and asked, "Where's your security detail?" He stuck his head out and looked at both sides of the corridor. "Are they downstairs?"

That's not what I wanted to hear at all. I could already feel the courage I'd manage to summon melting away from me. I knew that it wasn't going to be easy. William wasn't going to start jumping up and down once I poured my heart out to him. He'd done it in the past a few times, and I was stupid enough to doubt my feelings.

I sighed. "No, they're not." I looked up to meet his sky-blue eyes again. "I'm here *alone*. And I'm sure they must've figured it out by now that I came here, so it might be safe to say someone's on their way to get me."

"You're shitting me." William let out a breath through his nose and pulled off his glasses, shock taking over his features. I shook my head twice. Slowly. *I shit you not.* He grabbed my bag and rolled my suitcase inside with a frown. "Come in."

I walked in, taking in the place. His suite was huge and impressive. The view from what I could see from afar was breathtaking. But I stopped cold right after closing the door behind me.

"Aren't you—dating Liam?" he asked with an incredulous, almost guarded tone. "I thought that—"

"Never," I muttered, "because all I ever think about is you."

William pinched the bridge of his nose and dropped the script on a table beside us, but he didn't say a word back, so I continued with my speech.

"Liam's just a friend. I like him." My mouth twitched into a small smile that was filled with hope, but William's face was still harsh.

"And what about Nathan?" he asked with a stubborn frown that was still stationed in between his brows as he ran a rough hand through his golden hair. "I saw you at the engagement party. One second, you were flirting with Liam, and the next, you left hand in hand with Nathan. I don't even know where you stand with him."

"Liam was just bored and trying to mess with you guys. You know how he is. And Nathan and I had a pending conversation. So we went down to my apartment to talk."

"He proposed, didn't he?" William asked, sweeping me from head to toe as if scanning for bullshit. "Joel told me."

"He was going to. But I couldn't let him go through with it. It would've been too painful—for both of us," I explained. "I knew I couldn't say yes to him because, as I said, all I've been doing this entire time is nothing but think about you." I took a careful step forward. "I miss you, William."

Something I could only recognize as pain took over William's features.

"I hated seeing you with Nathan," he said in a dark tone, "especially after everything that happened with Thomas. After Caleb died. Knowing how deep down you felt something for me. Something strong. And every single time you kissed him, hugged him, smiled at him in front of me ... I fucking *hated* it. And then you both came to my house on Midsummer and did all of that there and rubbed it in my face—" He laughed a soft, angry laugh under his breath. "And then Zara ... you kept doubting me, thinking the worst of me.

"I thought I'd been upfront with you—several times," he continued. "And I get it. It's not easy to be with someone like me. It takes a strong woman to ignore the chatter, the media, the paparazzi, and fully trust me, especially when I'm away for a while, working. And I thought that was you, that you and I were strong enough to deal with that. Together." William sighed and shook his head a few times. "I guess I was wrong."

I could feel my face crumbling, but I had to push through. Break through the new wall between us. I had to.

"I *know* you don't trust me anymore, and I deserve it. You've done nothing but prove to me time and time again that you've been honest with me from the start. And I—" I closed my eyes and gathered as much courage, confidence, and humility as I could. "I'm sorry," I said, looking up into his eyes, listening to his deep breathing. "I'm so sorry about everything."

William's chest heaved, but he said nothing. I couldn't read him!

"You were right. I *am* a coward, and it's cost me a lot not wanting to accept it—to be honest with myself. And I know you've probably moved on from the feelings you expressed to me on Midsummer, but I wanted to come here, alone, without any expectations, and just let you know how stupid and immature I was and how much I still care about you. How much I love you."

The greedy lump in my throat had me cornered against its sharp, pointy knife. I took a few deep breaths to compose myself and an actual step back from William, giving him space.

Telling William that I loved him over and over again without getting any feedback was the hardest and most painful thing I've ever had to do. But it was also liberating. I could finally tell him how I felt this entire time. And not having had the guts to do it before was destroying me. It was a feeling that I could no longer keep to myself.

I couldn't stop myself from letting it all out. He needed to know.

"I checked the weather every day when you were gone just to see what kind of day you were having," I confessed, brushing away a tear that had escaped my eye and rolled down my cheek.

"And I daydreamed about how it would've been if I had said yes—if I had accepted coming here with you in the summer."

William ran a hand over his forehead. His body language wasn't encouraging at all, but I wasn't backing down.

"I can't stop wishing how you won't give me that spare set of keys to my apartment back either. And how whenever I have a nightmare, all I hope is for you to be the one to comfort me back to sleep."

William licked his lips and looked down at his feet.

Please say something.

He sighed again, and I couldn't tell if it was a sigh of relief or a think-about-how-you're-going-to-blow-her-off kind of sigh. So I pulled out the ace from under my sleeve.

"You're a dentist," I told him.

William looked down at me with a puzzled face. "I'm— sorry. I don't understand."

"You're a *dentist*," I said matter-of-factly. "That's my third guess from our bet. I never took it." I took a step forward. "I lost." And another. "You won. Now take me on a date, or are you not a man of your word?"

William shook his head and snorted with a weak smile. I'd finally knocked down those thick, heavy walls of his.

"You will take me on a date," I said, Jedi-hand waving him with a smile. He stared at me without saying a word, so I held my hand in front of me and looked at it with a frown. "It's not working."

"Works every time." He pulled me in against him running his fingers through my hair. And before I had time to register what was happening, his lips met mine. I was going to pass out any second now just from the closeness between us, let alone the feeling of his soft lips against mine. It'd been a long time waiting for this moment.

All I ever wanted for so long was for him to kiss me like this, and I've been too blind and stubborn to accept that it was *him* I wanted all along.

"I can't stop thinking about you either," he said, taking a short break from kissing me. "I never had. Never will. I just—refuse." His mouth lingered a breath away from mine, and his comforting arms remained tightly locked around me as I rubbed my nose against his. "I love you, Guillermina."

I cupped his cheek, and my thumb wandered to his lower lip, brushing it. "I see you." I kissed the corner of his mouth a few times. "I always have."

He pulled my jacket off, grabbed my legs, and picked me up from the floor. I locked them around his waist and kissed him. This time he let himself go completely, letting me know he did want me as bad as I wanted him. In every possible way.

He walked toward the bed and dropped me gently on it, leaving a trail of kisses down my neck.

"I was going nuts just thinking about you ever getting back together with Nathan," he whispered in my ear. "And when I drove away from the cottage that day, all I could see was that look on your face—" he trailed off and laid on his side beside me, sweeping a few strands of hair off my face. "It *destroyed* me."

"I almost made a fool of myself and ran behind you," I said with an almost sad laugh. "I swear it physically hurts when you're away." I pulled myself closer to him. "Just being here with you—like this … it's perfect. I feel like I have everything I need."

"I feel the exact same way," he told me, kissing my cheeks and taking his time doing so.

"When Thomas shot you—" My face scrunched up, and I closed my eyes, trying to shove the memory away. "That's when I realized I couldn't keep pretending. I just couldn't imagine my life without you." I ran my fingers through his silky, beautiful golden hair and kissed him. "I love you, William Sjöberg, and I know the whole world loves you too, but I love you the most." We both chuckled, our breaths colliding. "And I know it might feel rushed for me to feel this way, but—"

"Rushed? Really?" He laughed, pulling me closer against him. I rested my face on his chest, and he ran his fingers through my hair. "It's been almost a year and a half since we met, and when we first kissed at the cottage, I swear I knew all I wanted was you." He kissed my hair and cupped my chin to meet my gaze. "I love you too, Guillermina. And yes …You still are, were, and will be *it* for me. Always."

I brought my lips to his and kissed him with everything I had, with *all* of me, and I never knew it could feel like this, so perfect—complete. All my heart was his. Every single part of it.

"William?" I asked, looking into those beautiful blue eyes I loved so much, unable to believe that I could freely stare into them now. "Will you be my boyfriend?"

William laughed hard, his belly rising and falling with each gasp. "You're *unbelievable*." He poked my nose with his finger. "No one's ever asked me that before."

"Is that a first?" I said with a grin.

"It is." He dropped a peck on my lips. "And I don't remember when's the last time I asked anyone to be my girlfriend either. Maybe in high school? All my agent does is send contracts to any girls I date."

"Contracts? That sounds romantic," I teased. There must've been a mean stack of dead files lying around somewhere in William's agent's office. "And don't you dare send one my way."

"Oh, I wouldn't risk it," he said, arching a brow. "You'd probably send it back in ashes."

"Something like that." I sat up on the bed and placed my hands on his stomach. "I hate contracts." My fingers brushed his perfectly chiseled abs up and down over his t-shirt. "And that's—not fair."

"What? This?" he lifted his t-shirt, and I had to look away as his six-pack made my blood warm up. "You're blushing?"

"I'm not!"

"Yes, you are. Guille, look at me." I raised my brows and looked at him, faking an annoyed look on my face as in: *see, I'm not blushing*.

"Come here." He grabbed my hand and placed it over his bare stomach. "All of this is yours, so get used to it. And all of this"—he grabbed my waist and pulled me on top of him—"is mine." I nodded with a smile. *All yours*.

"Is that a yes?" He hadn't answered my question.

"Shit, you're right," he said with a laugh. "I accept."

"Shut up." I shoved his shoulder. "I'm serious about this."

"Baby, I'm yours," he said in his low, husky voice. "And you're mine."

"Yours." I kissed him, and I didn't know how to stop doing it. All I wanted was to kiss and stare at him. I never knew I could know such happiness, and I was more than certain that he felt the same way.

Every graze of our skin was electric—intense. My body and soul recognized his and took pleasure in the familiarity of him. A part of me was scared to feel this much. I only hoped I never stopped feeling like this. It was almost addictive.

"So why don't we seal the boyfriend-girlfriend deal by going on that first date you Jedi-mind-tricked me into?" William stood up from the bed and offered me his hands to help me up. I replied with a nod.

"And … you're definitely done with Rachel, right?" I was so jealous when it came to William. He quickly noticed and set me at ease.

"I love it when you get territorial," William said with a laugh. He placed his hands around my shoulders and embraced me. "But there's no reason for you to feel that way. And I'll make sure you never do."

"Did she sign a contract too?"

The contract thing was so ridiculous to me. I understood why he did it. Not everyone out there was as good intentioned as one would think. And not every girl wanted to date William for the right reasons.

"Everyone does," he replied, dropping a kiss on my head.

"And you're sure you feel comfortable with me not signing one? If you need me to sign one, I can—"

"Never," he said, lifting my chin. "Come on. It's getting late. You can grill me with your questions over dinner. I know how curious you are."

"Won't the hotel's restaurants be closed by now?" I asked, walking toward my luggage.

"Not for me." He threw a wink my way.

"You're so spoiled." I rolled my eyes at him. "I'll see you in a bit then. I'll take my stuff to my room, shower there, and come back."

"You're insane to think you're walking out that door right now," he said. I laughed. "Don't laugh. I'm serious." He was. "You're staying. Here. With me."

"Well, thank God because I didn't book a room," I said, rolling my suitcase toward his bathroom. "I was just kidding. You're stuck with me."

"You were *that* sure I'd cave, huh?" He followed me. "That's what I call self-confidence."

"That's what I call stupid," I replied, laying my suitcase on the floor and unzipping it. "But Alice convinced me not to book a room."

"Why am I not surprised that Alice was involved in this?" William leaned against the bathroom's door frame, crossing his arms at his chest and his foot in front of the other. "I can't believe you're actually here." He smiled at me but frowned quickly after that. "But why is your suitcase so small? When are you planning to leave?"

"Well, I'm not sure I'll be able to stay for long," I said, standing up, grabbing a few things I needed from my suitcase to shower and get ready. I placed my toiletries and a perfume beside one of the sinks on the beautiful double-vanity covered in Carrara marble. "I'm sure someone's already on their way to get me."

I lowered my brows as reality kicked in.

Being here with William was a temporary oasis, one from which I'd be plucked out of the minute someone came for me. And my gut told me that someone was going to be Aaron. I knew it was going to be very uncomfortable between us. I put my security detail in a difficult position by escaping. But I had a pending and undoubtedly tough conversation with my father.

"You're practically moving in already," he said, looking at my stuff on the bathroom counter. "I like your things here."

I spotted William's cologne on the counter. "I *love* this," I said, removing the lid and taking a deep breath in through my nose to smell it.

William laughed. He took the bottle away from my hands and sprayed himself with it.

"You have no idea how obsessed I am with it," I told him, standing on my tiptoes to smell his neck.

"I do have an idea. That's why I dipped my hoodie in it." He laughed again.

"How could you know I love it so much?" It was so annoying to know he'd been able to see right through me this entire time.

Even when I thought I was doing a great job at hiding my affections.

"I don't know." He shrugged. "You seemed more annoyed with me when I was wearing it, so ... yeah. It kinda reminded me of the day we met. It pissed me off that you were wearing your gym clothes and still smelled like heaven when you shouldn't have. And I didn't want to like you, but you were making it *very* hard for me when I saw you walking away with those tight yoga pants that almost made me want to die."

I smiled and looked away, remembering how William couldn't stop frowning that day. It was funny to find out part of the reason behind his cocky attitude. I kissed his delicious neck and walked over to where I'd left my bag on the counter. My cellphone was drained. Even if I didn't intend to use it, it was best to have it fully charged, just in case.

As I pulled my phone out of my bag, I spotted Caleb's letter.

"There's a lot we need to talk about," I said with a sigh, reminding myself of the things I learned from reading it. I wanted to tell William what I found out about my mom so he could give me his advice on how to handle things with my father.

"Well, hurry up then. And do yourself a favor and lock this door. I won't be able to stand the thought of you being naked a few inches away with water running all over your body."

I bit my lower lip, just wondering ... things.

"So, just like back at home?" I laughed, trying to distract myself from my thoughts involving the shower and William there with me. "Always a few inches away from each other."

"I'm tearing that fucking wall down when I get back. I'm not kidding."

"Please do." I placed my hands on William's chest and pushed him away. "I'll see you in a bit."

I'd already shut the door, but I opened it again, just a tad, and said, "I'm leaving it unlocked just in case you want to test your resolve."

"I don't have any. That's why you need to lock it." He winked at me. "Unless you want to skip the date and go straight to—"

I shut the bathroom door in his face and locked it. I heard him laugh as he walked away. I've been waiting a long while for this date to finally happen. It was important for me—symbolic. I could go back to daydreaming about him as I showered. It's not like I wasn't a pro at it.

CHAPTER 48

A Year To Think

MY SHOWER TOOK longer than it should've, but the water pressure was on point. It was so relaxing. And the last twenty-four hours had been insane. It'd been too much to process that I guess I hadn't even started doing so, but I knew I felt lighter. Finding out about the details of my mother's death opened up a whirlwind of feelings and insights.

My fear now was that I wouldn't be fighting against a real threat but against my father's notions. And I knew how resolute and narrow-minded he could be when it came to what he thought was best for me.

Not only would he probably faint when he learned about how I came to Africa on my own, but he was probably not going to appreciate the fact that William and I were a thing now. I just had a feeling he wasn't going to be pleased.

The difference was that this time I had enough information to object and defend my case. I knew my father was scared shit-less after my mother died, and his mind flipped—turned against him and constantly fed him with doubts about how I wasn't safe, how I needed to be followed 24/7 to avoid *anything tragic* from happening to me.

He had to put the past behind him. I know that's all I've

been trying to do for years now. Still, some days are easier than others, but at least I'm constantly trying to acknowledge my feelings and avoid allowing them to eat me alive.

It wasn't going to be easy.

I had a few hours before I had to deal with any of that, starting with the imminent wrath that was surely brewing deep down in James Murphy's gut. But even if the retaliation would be severe, I'd do it a thousand times again because, ironically, I'd never felt happier and more filled with hope in my entire life.

I was so optimistic that I packed a nice outfit for this date, even when I didn't know if it was happening or not. But it *was* happening, and I couldn't hide my excitement as I finished getting ready, even if it was after midnight and I was collapsing with exhaustion. It seemed to me like I was still running on pure adrenaline.

I finally stepped out of the bathroom wearing the perfect little black dress with a heart-shaped neckline.

"William!" I gasped and covered my mouth at the scene before me. His suite was beautifully set up for our date. Candles filled the space, and a small table for two had been placed right beside the terrace. A small vase with different kinds of flowers decorated it.

William smiled at me as he watched me marvel at the improvised but stunning and intimate setup for our date. "You look—beautiful."

"Thank you," I said, rushing to hug him. "I love this." I kept looking around at everything.

"It's the best we could do on such short notice," he said, kissing my hair. "That's why I'm not complaining about how long you took in there."

"I'm sorry. But the shower's awesome."

"It is, right?" William laughed. "Come." He offered his arm

to me, and I linked it with mine as he guided me toward the table. "The restaurant staff left this wine for us, and I ordered some food. They'll bring it up as soon as it's ready."

"Perfect." I smiled. "I'm sure everything here is delicious." He pulled the chair and helped me to my seat.

"It's insanely good. You have no idea. I snuck into the kitchen a few times and cooked with the chefs here when I was filming during the summer." He sat next to me. "I learned how to make a few dishes, so be ready to eat a shit-ton of South African food when we get back." He laughed as he grabbed the bottle of wine to uncork it.

I couldn't stop staring at William and marveling at him. Not only was he the most beautiful thing I've ever seen in my entire life, but he had the biggest and kindest heart too. And it made me feel so special that he would share it with me.

He changed from his white t-shirt to a floral, vintage-style, short-sleeved button-down shirt that looked great on him. Ugh! He could pull anything off.

"You've been into pastels lately, haven't you?" I teased as he poured red wine into my glass.

He laughed under his breath and said, "Ilaria insists on how pastels are hot this season. Once we go back to NY, we'll see what she has in store for the fall. And you met her. I do whatever she tells me to do—*mmm*, you need to try this wine."

It seemed to me like William had *her* eating from his hand, not the other way around as he said. I remember her trying to please William when he expressed his opinion about my outfit for Tobias's premiere. But yeah, I would probably do whatever Ilaria told me to do, too. She was scary as hell, but she had a great taste in fashion.

I sipped on the wine, and it was divine, just as he said.

"Can I just say your Midsummer outfit was the most *perfect* thing I've ever seen you wear?" I liked calling it the cotton-candy outfit. "Please tell me you sent it to the cleaners right away to get the bloodstains off of it."

"Actually," he said with a silly smile, "it's rotting away in my closet in Sagaponack." He laughed. "I left in a hurry, as you might recall. And I've just been crazy busy these past few months. I haven't been able to go down there. So let's say it's your fault."

"What?" I gaped at him. "We need to save it when we get back. I really want to see you wearing that number some other time." I laughed.

"You loved it, didn't you?" He laughed with me.

"Obviously."

"Well, I loved that little Enzio de Luca dress you wore on your birthday," he said, sipping on his wine and looking up and down at me with that fiery gaze that always made me nervous. "What do you say we take my Midsummer outfit to the cleaners so I can wear it again while you wear *that* dress so I can tear it off you afterward. And I'll let you do whatever you want with my suit, of course."

My face warmed up, and William smiled at my feedback. He had this power over me, to make me feel things in such a heightened way that it was impossible for me to hide my reactions from him.

William teased me all the time but knowing that the things he said would actually happen made me feel nervous—an amazing kind of nervous. Things were real now. We were done with taunts and games. I still couldn't believe it.

"All I really wanted to do at Midsummer was stare at you, but I couldn't," I confessed. "I guess that's why I was in such a bad mood. Well ... that and Zara, of course. But now I feel like an idiot." I dropped my wineglass on the table and reached out for William's hand. My finger grazed the thin scar from when he cut himself that day. David had done a great job with the stitches.

William frowned.

"I'm sorry about what happened with Zara," I said, looking at our laced-up hands. "I'm so embarrassed about how I acted, about my stupid jealousy, and … I don't know. I was so immature, and I know I doubted you, but it was so hard not to feel *something* when I saw you two together."

"Hey, it's okay," he replied, lifting my chin to meet my eyes. "I have to admit that I was a bit harsh with you that day." He stroked the back of my hand with his fingers. "I wished I could've told you from the start that she's my sister, but I couldn't. Zara wanted to do things her way and on her time, and I had to respect that. I couldn't start revealing that because it was convenient for me. And I couldn't tell her how I felt about you either because I knew it would be an issue for her since you were with Nathan. That's why she was so angry with me when she caught *our little exchange* at the cottage. I'd been denying my feelings for you since your birthday, so I had to deal with that too."

"I'm sorry. I'm sure it must've sucked for you," I told him. "And Zara hates me, right? I mean, I probably would if I were in her position."

"She doesn't. Zara's been through a lot. I've talked to her, and she's mostly glad that the truth is finally out," he said, kissing the back of my hand.

"We'll have to wait and see what she has to say about me rejecting Nathan and coming here after you," I said with a frown, "because I do care about her opinion. She's your sister."

"If she cares about me—which she does—she'll be glad to know we're happy."

He was right. If we were both happy, Zara shouldn't have a problem with that. I just didn't want things to be awkward, but I couldn't control everything. I needed to relax and stop being so hard on myself. "Has it been weird for your brothers? I haven't talked to any of them about this."

"I guess they're still dealing with the shock, but they love her. They always have, and she's been doing better now, knowing how everything turned out fine after letting everyone know."

There was a knock on the door, and a server walked in, rolling a cart with our meal. The delicious smell of exotic spices being carted in invaded the room.

"Good evening, Mr. Sjöberg," the tall man said with a nod.

"Thank you, Johnny." William grinned. "This is Billie Murphy."

"Nice to meet you, Johnny," I said, offering my hand to him.

"The pleasure's all mine, Miss Murphy. Welcome to Ellerman House," he replied with a firm handshake.

Johnny explained what everything was as he placed the plates on our table and left promptly after that, promising to bring dessert up in a while.

"You'll love the South African strawberries that I ordered for dessert," William said, serving a spoonful of Cape Malay chicken curry on my plate. I widened my eyes at him, and he laughed. "I'm just messing with you. I told them *no* strawberries on our dessert."

"You're *obsessed* with strawberries," I said, trying the curry. *Mmm.* It was heavenly.

"No. I'm obsessed with the fact that *you* don't like them. But I have a feeling I might be able to get you to like strawberries someday. Just give me a chance to figure something out for you."

"I'm open to it," I said, putting my fork down and taking a sip of my wine. William chuckled. "What?"

"Nothing. I just remembered how hard it was for me not to laugh whenever Zara called you sis." William snort-laughed as he served more food on my plate. "Because the odds of her ending up being your sister-in-law one way or the other were high. And it was so funny to me that you both were clueless about that little fact."

I shook my head at him as I chewed on my food.

"Deep down, I've always wished for us to end up together," he tossed in, leaning in to kiss my cheek. "I'm glad you're here right now."

"I'm glad to be here too."

"So … you said we had a lot of things to talk about, and I'm ready to hear all about it," he said, trying the dish that Johnny explained was called *bobotie*. His eyes rolled up with pleasure, and an *mmm* sound escaped his throat as he ate.

I loved how passionate William was about food and cooking, and I had a few questions about that. I had a few questions about *a lot* of things, and I wanted to eat the world in one day, but there were other more important topics to cover.

"There are two things I want to talk to you about, actually," I said, readjusting myself on my seat. "So I'll start with the easiest one."

William replied with a nod as he dropped his fork and lifted his wineglass.

"You are having dinner with Haute Magazine's photographer of the August 2010 swimsuit edition," I said proudly, sticking my tongue out to him afterward.

"I'm aware. Joel mentioned something about it." He said with a grin, putting his wineglass down. "Congratulations!"

William wanted to know the details of how it happened, so I explained how Lily asked me to go with her and told him *everything* that happened that day. Including the details about Lily's psychopath ex-boyfriend.

"Joel wanted to go after the guy. Like literally find him and beat the shit out of him," he said with a troubled expression on his face. He seemed upset about everything that Lily had to go through with Leonard, her ex. "I know I'd want to do the same if I were him."

"I know. But the lawyers have taken care of it. I'm sure that Leonard will stop harassing Lily after this."

William looked away and licked his lips. He raised his wineglass again, took a sip, and quickly changed the subject. He asked me a ton of questions about the photo shoot, how I felt while I was doing it, and about my internship at Haute. I answered all of his questions and didn't leave anything out. I also showed him the published photographs. He seemed so proud, but confessed to having seen them already.

Then, I chuckled under my breath as I remembered how we had to name-drop William at the shoot to spark Becca's interest.

"Lily told one of Haute's employees that you and I used to date. And—I didn't deny it." I lifted my gaze to meet his and offered him a small, crooked smile. "She remembered me from Tobias's premiere, and I'm convinced that's why they gave me a chance. So thanks, I guess." I laughed.

"You're welcome." William tossed a piece of bread into his mouth and shook his head with a smile. "But I don't think that's why they did. And I'm sure they were glad they gave you the opportunity after seeing how good you were. The photographs are incredible."

"Thanks." I sipped on my wine again and said, "Please don't take this in the wrong way, but I think this wine is a new winner. It's better than the one you used to re-label as Nemorino's, which used to be my favorite until now."

"Well, it's great to hear because Nemorino's needs to be reformulated as soon as possible," William said with a laugh. "It didn't work *at all* on your birthday. It only made you sick and walk out on me that night."

"It works every time," I told him. "I just had the wrong dose." I laughed too. "But I had so much fun with you that night. And you have no idea how much our conversation out in the back helped me." I dropped my wineglass and reached out for his hand again. "You keep showing up for me every time. And it was so hard for me when the band started playing, because I wanted *so badly* to stand beside you and watch them perform and sing our hearts out together. And when you went up the stage and sang that song, I swear I almost passed out."

"You almost passed out because you had too much Nemorino's." He teased.

"I don't think so." I squeezed his hand. He took the back of my hand to his lips and kissed it.

"Let's make a toast," he said suddenly, lifting his wineglass. He stared at me, his gaze piercing right through me. And I let him right in. I raised my wineglass too and waited for him to speak. "May our worst nights be like this one."

I offered him a melancholic kind of smile, remembering our toast that day. And it couldn't have been more suited right now. I truly wished for that.

"Skål," we said in unison as I bumped my glass with his. We sipped on our wine and smiled. William placed his wineglass on the table and leaned in to kiss me. It was the sweetest and softest kiss ever. His wine-tasting tongue brushed gently against mine as he removed my wineglass from my hand to put it back on the table.

I reached out and combed his hair with my fingers while he pulled my chair closer to his. He ran a hand over my shoulder and caressed my back, drawing me in.

"I can't believe I'm kissing you right now," he whispered to my lips. "I swear that's all I'm going to do all night."

I couldn't believe it either. It was all so surreal, and a part of me feared I might be making it all up, but I wasn't.

William grabbed my waist and tugged at it. "Get over here."

I stood up and sat on his lap, running an arm around his neck. He kissed me again, and his warm hand cupped my cheek and slowly made its way down the back of my neck.

He unlocked his lips from mine and kissed my collarbones, moving further down, making my neck arch back a little. A soft moan escaped me, and William groaned against the responsive skin of my chest. He left a trail of kisses along the heart-shaped neckline of my dress.

"William ..." I said with a gasp as he did it again, slower this time. He placed his hand on my leg and scrunched up my dress as his fingers slid further up.

"I've dreamt of doing this," he said in my ear, feeling myself melt from his touch, "more times than I can even remember—*God*, you feel so good."

His movements were soft, lazy, almost exploratory, and that made me want him even more. It made me want him to let go completely, but I knew he knew what he was doing. And it was working. I was growing restless with desire. He was making me crave him so badly.

I parted my lips to speak, to tell him I wanted more, needed more. And then there was a knock on our door.

We ignored it. Instead, he kissed me.

There was a second, louder knock a few seconds later that made me tense up and shudder because what if someone came looking for me? *What if* they're *here* ...

William unlocked his lips from mine and said, "Hey, it's okay. It's probably Johnny with dessert."

Well, if it's Johnny ... "Fuck dessert," I muttered, kissing him again. William chuckled against my lips and carried on, the rhythm of his fingers intensifying around that sweet spot he so easily located.

"*Mr. Sjöberg?*" a man's voice boomed across the door. "*It's Johnny!*"

William stopped what he was doing and uttered something in Swedish under his breath—cursing for sure. He sounded frustrated and so was I.

"It's okay. Go," I said, kissing his warm, flushed cheek. "Maybe it's chocolate."

"It better be." He dropped a quick kiss on my lips, lifted me, and placed me back on my chair. He shot up from his seat with a sharp sniff, sauntering toward the door. William opened it just a tad, cleared his throat, and said, "Hey, Johnny."

Johnny asked if he could clear the table, but William refused right away. He took two different plates of dessert and told him they could clean up tomorrow. Johnny left as requested, and William walked back with the plates.

"I couldn't let him in," he said, looking down at his pants, laughing. "Look at what you do to me."

A nervous chuckle escaped my throat when I looked as he asked me too, just to confirm his statement, not that I hadn't already felt him when I sat on his lap.

William dropped the plates on the table and took the metal lids off.

"Chocolate," he said with a grin, running a finger through the frosting of one of the desserts. "Try it." He brought his finger to my mouth, and I licked it. He lifted me from my seat, and I ran a finger through the frosting too as he carried me away toward the bed. I offered my finger to him, and he took it in his mouth, his tongue brushing against it, making my body tingle all over.

"I've had more than a year to think about what I'm going to do to you, älskling," he whispered in my ear as he placed me on my feet beside the bed. He ran his hands down my arms and around my back. His fingers quickly found the invisible zipper on my dress, and pulled down on the tab. "So I hope you slept on your way here because we're going to be up for a while."

CHAPTER 49

Kindle

"YOU'VE MADE ME wait longer than anyone ever has," William said, my zipper wide open and my back bare for him. "And I *hate* waiting." His hands wandered up and down my exposed skin. He gently pulled the straps of the dress off my shoulders and down my arms. My mouth went dry, and all I could hear was the sound of our unsteady breathing.

I closed my eyes and enjoyed the feeling of his hands on me, of his breath teasing my skin. His touch was enthralling—like nothing I've felt before. We'd never touched each other so much and for this long. It was intoxicating.

"I'm shaking," he muttered, placing his hand on my cheek. He dropped a kiss on my lips and tugged my dress down until it hit the floor. "It's not like me to feel like this."

"I'm shaking too."

"God, you're perfect." William groaned a delicious sound against my neck. He then unbuttoned his shirt and said with a gruff voice, "Lie on your back for me."

I did and watched him undress.

"I thought I was the bossy one," I said with a low, breathy laugh as I took in the length of his perfect and beautiful body.

"You *are* the bossy one." William placed his lips on my knee and kissed his way up. He stopped at my hip bone and met my gaze. "But not in bed."

I didn't have a single problem with that.

He slipped my underwear down, and I let my head drop on the pillows. His fingers found me again, making me gasp. Another not entirely soft moan escaped me, and it only encouraged William even more.

He searched for my mouth with desperation, and I met him with the same impatience as if we couldn't be close enough. We wanted more. *I* wanted more. The way the strong line of his body fitted mine was perfect. Made for me in every way.

William's mouth moved to place a quick kiss on the tender skin of my neck, and then I heard him fighting with his nightstand. He finally pushed the drawer shut, and I saw him tearing a condom open.

"We don't need that," I told him as he knelt with his knees straddling my hips. He was *perfect*.

William met my gaze and widened his blue eyes at me. I pulled myself slightly up with my elbows and asked him what was wrong when I realized he'd gone silent.

"I've never had sex without a condom," he admitted.

"Never, never?" I mean, I wasn't going to complain. I just couldn't believe it.

"Never." William held the shiny black square between his fingers as he continued to aim his gaze at me, his chest heaving.

"Another first then, huh?" I said with a smile, trying to lighten the mood again. But he frowned. "William, please. Tell me what's wrong."

"Nothing I—I've told you how careful I usually am with this sort of thing. I'm not so trusting, and it's just something that I—"

"You can trust me." I tried reassuring him. But he had just

mentioned before how girls had to sign contracts just to date him. It was only natural for a guy like him to want to be *extra* careful, especially during sex. Wouldn't want any girl claiming to be pregnant with him or something—a tabloid nightmare.

He didn't have to say it for me to know it had something to do with that. And I hadn't signed a damn thing, and now I was asking him not to use a condom. It was beyond his comfort zone. I had to fix this.

"But we can use one if it'll make you feel more at ease, okay?" I didn't mind as long as I could be his and he could be mine. But I could see him struggling with his thoughts. I read it all over his face.

I reached out and touched his lower abdomen, my eyes pleading for him to say something.

"I would *never* do anything to hurt you, Billy." I called him Billy, and I don't know why I did. It just slipped out. I never had before.

"You just called me Billy." He laughed under his breath and dropped himself beside me, his hand wandering up my thighs again.

"I did," I said in a breath, leaning back and savoring his teasing touch.

"I like it, Billie," he said with a smile. I liked him calling me Billie too. It felt so intimate and special that we could call each other by the same name. He laughed a low, husky laugh in my ear and tossed the condom away. "Hey, Billie."

William made his decision and unleashed himself completely. His body curved around mine, his gaze trained on me as I finally felt him. I allowed myself to look deeply into his eyes as our exquisitely compatible bodies delighted in the rapture of the perfect closeness, recognizing ourselves and wondering why the hell it took me so long to choose him.

I'd never burned like this before, yearned for someone this way, but the realization was so terrifyingly filled with delight. So we both gave in to the fire and allowed it to kindle our souls into oblivion.

.

CHAPTER 50

Freedom

WILLIAM'S WARM LIPS against my cheek woke me up.

"Hey," he whispered, brushing a strand of hair off my face. "You were smiling in your sleep."

"Was I?" I placed my hand on his cheek and smiled at him. He was wearing his black-framed glasses again and his hair was damp. He smelled like soap and cologne. I definitely needed a shower too. "I *love* this geeky look on you." I took my arms above my head and stretched.

"I'll make sure to keep them on next time," he said with a soft laugh, pushing them up a bit. "I would have woken you up as you deserve, but I need to get going soon. It's the last days of filming, and I just want to get this over with and go back to New York."

"Well, you can wake me up any way you like, any time you want," I said, sitting up with an almost stupid smile on my face looking out the window, feeling a bit groggy. He'd woken me up a couple of times while we slept last night, and I didn't even see at what time we ended up falling asleep for good. "What time is it?"

"It's a bit past 5:00 p.m." William laughed.

"Oh, God. I think I might still be operating on Eastern Standard Time," I replied, shaking my head with a smile.

"I was hoping you might want to stay," William said. "We can fly back together. We're only five days away from wrapping."

"I—yes. I'll stay." I would miss school, and I knew they were coming to get me, but I didn't care anymore. I'd find a way. I had to stay.

William smiled the sweetest smile I'd ever seen on his face as I noticed a bunch of papers spread on his side of the bed. "Did you get any sleep at all?"

"Not really," he said with a soft, breathy laugh. "I've been going over the script. But I'm used to it. And I guess we found the magic formula to chase your nightmares away." He lifted a brow. "You slept like a baby."

I gave him a soft peck on the lips, smiled at him, and said, "I did." I couldn't have been any more drained after the last crazy twenty-four hours, so my mind had obviously shut down during sleep.

"So what's the second thing?" William asked. "I couldn't stop thinking about what you said last night. About wanting to tell me two things, but you only mentioned the Haute Magazine story."

"You're right," I said, standing up, pulling a cover with me. I looked around, trying to spot my bag, feeling self-conscious about being naked in the light of day.

"Please don't do that." William stood up, grabbed a robe he'd left on the bed, and walked toward me with one of his little smirks.

"Do—what?" I smiled nervously up at him.

"Cover yourself like that around me." William snatched the covers off my hands and tossed them back on the bed. "You don't have to. You're gorgeous." He kissed my cheeks and placed the robe around my shoulders, helping me run my arms into the sleeves. "But I guess that's the smart thing to do right now since

I need to leave soon." He chuckled as I fastened the robe's belt around my waist with a smile.

"Come." I grabbed his hand and pulled him toward the living room space, where I spotted my bag in the distance. William must've placed it there at some point while I slept.

We sat down close to each other, and I took Caleb's letter out.

"Aaron gave this to me when Caleb died. And the second thing I wanted to talk to you about is regarding the contents of this letter."

"Okay." William lowered his brows and ran an arm around my shoulders, his hand moving up and down against my robe.

"I'll try to be brief since you have to leave, but—"

"Don't rush yourself," William cut me off in a soft tone. "If I'm late, I'm late."

I took a deep breath and began to say, "Caleb, he—wrote a lot in this letter. Things that opened my eyes and made me think and confirm certain thoughts and feelings. But it was mostly very revealing and what I wanted to share with you is regarding my mother's death."

William readjusted himself in his seat and grabbed my hands, as if bracing himself for impact.

"I know why my mother died." I focused on breathing, trying to push down the gale of emotions. William's hand moved to my thigh and stroked my leg in a gentle, soothing way.

"It was all a mistake," I finally said, my words breaking as I uttered them. The tears hit me without warning as I realized William was the first person I ever talked to about this matter. More than a year ago, he was there for me when I felt like I needed someone to talk to that wasn't getting paid to listen. William cared right from the start. Even when I thought he didn't. "She wasn't meant to die. She was mistaken for someone else—a drug lord's wife. She wasn't the target. We were never—" I trailed off, unable to keep talking.

"Shit, Guille. I'm so sorry." He took me in his arms, and I found peace in them as if he'd somehow had the power to remove all the turmoil flowing through my body.

Once I felt more at ease, I explained in detail what Caleb had written in the letter regarding my mother, including my father's plans and the deal he made with the government to have them pay for my security detail. For life.

"As much as I craved for things to change, a part of me was still terrified because I didn't know I—I had doubts. But now, knowing this … I'm *free*," I said to his chest, feeling it rising with every breath he took, "just like you always said I would be."

I looked up to meet his eyes, his arms still wrapped around me, supplying me with all the sense of safety I would ever need moving forward. "I'm done living like this. Trapped. Withheld." I sighed. "It's over."

"I'll take it from here," he said, cupping my chin. His lips met mine, and he reclined me on the couch. I couldn't hold in a soft but desperate moan filled with desire as his knee parted my legs just slightly.

"Those little noises are making me want to stay," he whispered against my lips.

"Isn't that what you're doing?" I muttered with a low, pleading laugh. "Staying?"

"I'll do whatever you want me to do," he said, pulling on my robe's belt. "I meant it when I said I'm yours."

How was it that he could make me feel this way? The feeling was so achingly deep that it made me want to stop time and savor it forever.

"Billy?" I said in a breath, my neck arching back as he kissed it.

"What are you trying to do to me, Billie?" His voice was almost melodic against my skin.

"Stay." How many times I wished I could tell him that. And now I finally could.

"Yes, ma'am." William slipped my robe open and kissed my exposed skin, but the sound of a heavy knock on the door made me shoot up from the couch. William glanced at me, and something told me this time it wasn't Johnny.

I ran to the bathroom to throw some clothes on as another angrier, heavier knock that had Aaron written all over it threatened to take the door down.

"Coming!" William shouted back, anger oozing out of the single word.

"*Open the door, Mr. Sjöberg!*" It was definitely Aaron. They had probably tracked my location when I turned on my phone to talk to Alice when I arrived at the hotel. And I was expecting them to come and get me, but somehow it felt too fast like they weren't planning on allowing me to enjoy my kidnapped freedom for a second longer than the time it takes to get from New York to Cape Town.

William took his time getting the door, and I rushed out from the bathroom as soon as I was dressed, stopping mid-way as Aaron flashed his disappointment-filled glare at me. David stood beside him, and I swear I caught a slight smile drawing on his face before he switched his features back to security detail mode.

"Field trip's over, Miss Murphy," Aaron said with his firm bodyguard stance in place. I spotted a woman and two men from the hotel staff standing behind them. Their faces scrunched up with concern. I closed the distance between William and me, and I searched for his hand, weaving our fingers together. Balking.

Aaron angled his head imperceptibly, taking in the situation before him. "We have direct orders from your father to take you back right away, Miss Murphy."

I snorted and looked up at William with a half-smile, just marveling at him, at how his presence alone gave me the strength and the courage I needed to feel like I *could* change things around for myself.

That I deserved my freedom.

He smiled back a smile of a proud accomplice. We didn't need to say a word. He had my back, and I knew it. He would fight with me to the death until I was finally free.

My hand squeezed his one last time as I said, "Aaron, please inform my father that if he wants me back, he'll have to come and get me."

"Sounds about right." William laughed at my words, and that's how I knew he was the man I deep down always knew, hoped, and wished he were—perfect for me in every way. He wasn't afraid of my father, nor did he crave his approval. He'd always put *me* first.

William walked back to the living room, grabbed my bag and disappeared into the bathroom for a second. He came back, handed my bag over to me, and swapped his glasses for his sunglasses, tucking them on his shirt's collar. We were definitely leaving. I picked up my jacket from the coat rack beside the door.

"Let's go," he whispered, taking my hand and walking out of the room, shoving Aaron and David gracefully out of the way. He shut the door and pulled me toward the hallway.

"Miss Murphy!" Aaron shouted as they followed close behind us. I didn't look back. It pained me to put Aaron in this position, but it wasn't personal. I just had to make a statement.

"There's a decent shower with everything you'll need in my trailer," William casually said as if we weren't trying to be stopped from leaving together. "I tossed a fresh pair of underwear in your bag, and I'll make sure you're fed once we arrive. I've got a bunch of books in there too. You won't miss me." He laughed.

We made it to the lobby.

"Arno!" William said with a grin. "Were you able to make your magic happen?"

Arno flashed a smile back at William and said, "Always, Mr. Sjöberg." William lifted a hand in Arno's direction and caught a set of keys that Arno tossed his way.

"Thanks, man!" William replied as the entire hotel staff stared at their interaction, including a few guests that lingered in the lobby. "I promise to bring it back in one piece!"

William pushed the wooden doors open for me, and there was a red '65 Ford Mustang convertible parked in the motor lobby.

"You did say it *had* to be red, right?" William asked with a smile, taking in my reaction.

"Oh, my God! Is this—"

"Our ride? Yes." He opened the door for me, and I sat on the delicious creamy leather seat, looking around the cabin.

The promise of dusk lingered in the sky as the last bright rays of sunshine painted the clouds above in wonderful shades of blue, orange, and pink. I marveled at the sight of it.

"Miss Murphy, you can't—"

"Now, if you'll excuse us, gentleman," William cut Aaron off mid-sentence, walking around the car, throwing his Ray-Bans on, and slipping his phone into his jeans pocket. "I'm already running late, and it's take-your-girlfriend-to-work-day, so she'll be coming with me."

William sat behind the wheel, grabbed my hand, and sped off with a screech of the tires that made me let out a scream, followed by the most delicious laughter I'd allowed myself to dive into in a while.

Aaron and David made a run for the black SUV that was parked in the distance, and I wasn't sure if they were following us or not because William and I didn't mind looking back. It never felt so good to have a real taste of this extraordinarily unexpected and unbounded freedom.

C

END OF BOOK THREE

NOTE FROM THE AUTHOR

Awestruck at Dusk was the most emotional book for me to write of the first three. Dealing with Billie's grief throughout the story and trying to get her to connect with herself, her true wishes, and her ability to be honest about her feelings was a very challenging experience for me. It was also rough not being able to have Caleb there in any of the scenes. I truly missed him! At least we got to listen to him through the letter he left for Billie.

I know the ending of *Heartstruck at Dawn* was rough for all of us. But hopefully, the ending of this book will prove to be a satisfactory one for most of you. I cannot wait to share with you what comes next for Billie and Wiliam now that they were finally able to be together and openly express their love for one another. The first two characters I jotted down in a torn piece of recycling paper were Guillermina and William. *Moonstruck at Midnight* has always been about their love story. And with that being said, in the fourth and last book of the series, we'll get to experience more about their relationship through the pages and see if they can overcome the obstacles that lay ahead on their journey.

Much love,

Alejandra

ACKNOWLEDGEMENTS

First and foremost, I would like to thank my readers. It's been such an amazing experience to get to connect with you through social media and to be able to enjoy this story together. Thank you so much for the endless support. I feel like a broken record, but I cannot go without saying this every time: Thank you, thank you, thank you! It's been an honor to have been able to share Billie's story with all of you and to have such an amazing response to it. I don't take any of this for granted!

To my family: My parents, my sister, my husband, my son. Thank you all for your endless support and encouragement.

My friends, old and new, your support means the world to me. Thank you to each and every one of you who has picked up my books and invested your time in Billie's world.

Jennifer Herrington, thank you for your patience and your incredible insights, as always. David Provolo and Sulamit Elizondo: this was definitely my favorite cover. The meaning behind every little detail is beyond amazing, and I'm just in love with your work. I feel like everyone agrees on this. Pure art!

Malin Ottosson, thank you for taking the time to help out with some of the Swedish translations to make them sound natural and pristine!

Marianna Andrade, again, I couldn't have done this without you. Thank you so much for your honesty, your precious time invested in this series, and your unconditional friendship! I will forever be grateful.

My Bookstagram family! Again thank you so much for the endless support and encouragement. I promise this journey wouldn't have been the same without you. Some of you show your support by sharing, liking, or promoting my posts. Some even helped out with a few edits or tricky sentences I had last-minute issues with on the final read-through. It all is immensely appreciated. Sometimes we find love and support in the places we least expect! You guys were one of the biggest gifts and surprises this journey as an author has brought to my life.

Thank you for reading!

If you enjoyed *Awestruck at Dusk*, please consider leaving a review on Goodreads and Amazon. Reviews are of the utmost importance for authors since they help other readers decide whether to pick up the book or not. Thank you!

Link for Goodreads: https://cutt.ly/Goodreads_AAD

Link for Amazon: https://cutt.ly/AwestruckatDusk

COMING SOON ON THE MOONSTRUCK SERIES

**LOVESTRUCK
AT
SUNDOWN**

SUMMER 2022

ABOUT THE AUTHOR

Alejandra lives in Mérida, Yucatán, México with her husband and son. She's a music lover, a geek at heart, and a fan of all things romance, Christopher Nolan, Star Wars, LOTR, GOT, et cetera. You can find her on social media on Facebook & Instagram as long as her 30-minute social media app limit hasn't elapsed.

Follow her on Instagram:
@alejandra__author

CPSIA information can be obtained
at www.ICGtesting.com
Printed in the USA
LVHW110746010422
714871LV00001B/83